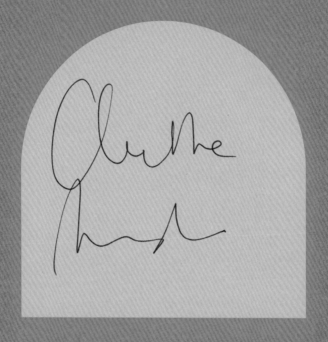

WIFE

Also by Charlotte Mendelson

Love in Idleness

Daughters of Jerusalem

When We Were Bad

Almost English

The Exhibitionist

CHARLOTTE MENDELSON

WIFE

MANTLE

First published 2024 by Mantle
an imprint of Pan Macmillan
The Smithson, 6 Briset Street, London EC1M 5NR
EU representative: Macmillan Publishers Ireland Ltd, 1st Floor,
The Liffey Trust Centre, 117–126 Sheriff Street Upper,
Dublin 1, D01 YC43
Associated companies throughout the world
www.panmacmillan.com

ISBN 978-1-5290-5281-7 HB
ISBN 978-1-5290-5282-4 TPB

Extract from *The Bay of Noon* © Shirley Hazzard, 1970. Reproduced with permission
of the Licensor through PLSclear.
Extract from *Bakkhai* © Anne Carson, 2015. *Bakkhai*, Methuen Drama, an imprint
of Bloomsbury Publishing Plc.
Extract from *My Name is Lucy Barton* © Elizabeth Strout, 2016. *My Name is Lucy Barton*,
Viking, an imprint of Penguin Random House UK.

Charlotte Mendelson is a novelist and this is a work of fiction.

1 3 5 7 9 8 6 4 2

A CIP catalogue record for this book is available from the British Library.

Typeset by Palimpsest Book Production Limited, Falkirk, Stirlingshire
Printed and bound by CPI Group (UK) Ltd, Croydon, CR0 4YY

Visit **www.panmacmillan.com** to read more about all our books
and to buy them. You will also find features, author interviews and
news of any author events, and you can sign up for e-newsletters
so that you're always first to hear about our new releases.

For Maria Rejt,
with love

'He was a true friend, hardly ever indulging the fiction that there are two sides to every question.'
Shirley Hazzard, *The Bay of Noon*

'The desire
before the desire,
the lick of beginning to know you don't know.'
Anne Carson, *Bakkhai*

'I kissed the top of her head. I thought: I did this to my child'
Elizabeth Strout, *My Name is Lucy Barton*

Prologue

June 2014, 2.47 p.m.
So now she is Lucifer.

She's on her way into the building, head down but keeping watch, when a crouching woman glances up from her bike lock and says: 'Zoe, isn't it?'

She seems surprised to have spotted Zoe out in public. She's short, wears no make-up, has been to theirs for dinner at least twice. Clasping her cycle helmet, her unthreatening bookshop tote bag, she looks kind, confidable-in; someone to whom Zoe could show her wounds. 'Where are you off to?'

Zoe checks over her shoulder, then up at the looming red brick of Cumberland House, the blankness of plate glass. She has agreed, under pressure, not to tell anyone about the appointment. But she's fairly sure that this woman works in the NHS, possibly as a social worker, so she'll be unfazed by bad situations, even ones as desperate as hers.

She takes a steadying breath of traffic fumes. 'Well. It's complicated. You might have heard? We are, very sadly, we're spl—'

'I've gathered bits, obviously,' the woman says, her wholesome face blandly non-committal; she could be about to hug Zoe or push her under a bus. 'Word gets around.'

Which can't be a good sign.

Cautiously, Zoe says: 'I don't know who you've been, well, if you've talked to . . . It has been . . . difficult.'

'I dare say.' The woman manoeuvres her bike between them, as if against the contagion of divorce. Then she hesitates.

What if she says something kind? She might; she was definitely one of the friendlier ones. Zoe's eyes are already prickling; crying would be bad but oh, a hug now, even a pat, would be s—

But the woman's face has tightened. 'God. I always thought you were lucky.'

'You mean us? Or just me?'

'I was impressed. That's all. Well.' The woman pats her cycle helmet, like punctuation. 'I should go.' Zoe steps back. 'I was shocked, if you want to know. So many terrible things you've done: so . . . destructive.'

'But—'

'I mean, you're the Devil now.'

'Sorry?'

'Like in *Paradise Lost*. Satan. You must remember,' she says, with the beadiness of the well-read. 'Your fall from . . . well, grace?'

Zoe has been counting the days, then the hours, until this afternoon, when she will be penned in a small meeting room with the three people who most wish her ill. They'll definitely arrive together, a phalanx breasting the double doors. She can imagine their sad solemn voices at reception, venom concealed under a civilized shell. Not many minutes to go, and they could be anywhere: on the way up in the lift, whispering about tactics, or already waiting in room 3/a, shaking hands, preparing the terrain by explaining her to the man they're meeting. Which would be worse?

Bumping into them down here would be worse.

Although what, realistically, could they do to her, in daylight, in a public building? She's imagined a lunge before but it couldn't happen here, could it, in this big bright Meeting Centre, clean paint and jazzy flooring, conversations in progress all around; workshops and strategy away-days but also counselling sessions, oozing little clots of hatred like theirs.

They would enjoy this: her fear. They think that she deserves it, the people she is bound to, by eggs and sperm and love gone bad.

Of the friends who've been told about today, one texted: 'Can get Valium easily, Y/N' and the other, in person, said: 'They're batshit.'

Zoe shook her head. 'But I don't think I can do it. Face them.'

'Does it help to know they think you're the baddie? I mean, I know. But maybe this could help. Shift something, like Dyno-Rod, though less stinky. Though on second thoughts . . .'

'Seriously. How am I . . . I'll need earmuffs to get through this. Blinkers. A scold's bridle. Honestly, the dread . . . even the thought of being seen by them makes me feel sick.'

'This bloke you're meeting, he is a professional? Registered with some sort of . . . body?'

'Allegedly.'

'Fine. So though you lot have a complicated set-up, this'll help. It's got to. And it's better going to an office, isn't it, than sitting through one of their fake-relaxed compulsory cuppas, God just that word, when they can lay into you like a pack of . . .'

'Wild boar.'

'Exactly. On neutral territory, with an impartial whatsit, they'll have to listen.'

Which might be true, if they sincerely wanted peace and resolution. But Zoe has seen the kind of rage which should stay hidden: a glint of bone. Last time all four of them met, the children were in earshot, yet extraordinarily awful things were said.

She holds out a hand. Why isn't she shaking?

The brutally modernized insides of Cumberland House don't help. The front desk is deserted, backed by screens with revolving logos, meaningless signs: Meridian Wellness Delivery; Unity (Pod 1); Orange Zone. She needs to ask directions, but there's only a woman hurrying angrily away from her. She checks the corridor from behind an Our Facilities Department's Values and Goals display; they may be waiting for her, planning to head her off at the pass. They'll insist on rules of engagement, then rig the duel.

Her stomach flutters miserably. Her joints are aching, as if poison has leached in.

'You've got to show willing,' their formerly mutual friend and neighbour Dawn had reminded her. 'Or whatever it's called, the thing politicians are obsessed with. Like eye-charts?'

'You've lost me.'

'Optics. So she'll look like a nutty Spiderman-dad on top

of Parliament. Which she basically is, and I would know,' said Dawn, who used to work as a children's nurse out by Gatwick. 'While you come across all sane, reasonable, open to compromise.'

'But I'm not! How can I be, when they've been . . . You're not thinking, are you, they could get full custody? Secretly? Christ.'

'No. Babe, we've gone through that. Remember what the solicitor said.'

'But she's very young herself. She might not realize.'

'You're being paranoid. Thing is,' said Dawn, 'if you have one last go at being all polite and understanding, and they see it, they'll soften.'

'Do you think?'

'You never know.'

The appointment letter said Bedford Suite 3/a but there are intermediate levels, vestibules: 'The Terrazzo'; 'BreakOut Lounge'. Anyone would find this dazzling wasps' nest confusing, particularly people with no sense of direction, who regularly dream of getting lost among multiple staircases. She's as incompetent as they say.

Passing a different booming stairwell, beside a small podium, as if for a daytime stripper, she hears voices somewhere above her, at least one female and one male. It could be them. There's a familiar sugary smell: cinema pick 'n' mix. Like a gnome, she rests her bottom on the edge of a gigantic orange plastic flowerpot containing a fake palm, and tries doing relaxing breathing, but she keeps running out of air. Her lungs are frantic. She thinks: I cannot do this.

She has written everything down. Lately she's been keeping her memory stick always on her, like a jailer's key, but, for speedy reference today, she's written notes of what to say. They're safe in her pocket. No, her bag. After an icily terrifying search, she finds them, trapped in a side-zip. Even without the torn bits they're useless; yesterday at her desk she was so worried about forgetting her calm, strong speech in the heat of the meeting that she'd reduced it to phrases, then single nouns, as if all she needed was basic revision techniques.

She stares at her list of over-compressed code words, but her mind barely moves: a mammoth heaving its rotten hooves through sucking mud. She is too tired to do this, to stand up to them.

She'd hoped there would be time to rehearse, but the minutes have collapsed in on themselves, tight as hollyhock seeds. She races up a flight of concrete steps, blocked by glass doors; there's still no one to ask. Down again, past painted-over noticeboards, ghostly drawing pins, over a disastrously loud grid of metal ventilation panels set in the cursory carpeting. It makes her teeth feel sensitive; makes her think of cattle trains.

Lucifer would do nothing by accident. They will be telling each other that she's late on purpose. They are so certain that she is a destroyer of lives, the worst kind of mother: more than careless, toxic, capable of the greatest crime, that of putting her own selfish needs before her children's. And they are right.

When Zoe said she was moving out, they claimed to be totally unprepared. How is this possible? Has nothing over the past year and a half, the fights and humiliating efforts at counselling, and her puny attempts to defend herself, convinced them that she was serious? Yet they also insist that she must have been planning this for months, even years. They tell people she hasn't thought it through, that she's leaving on a whim, or that she's doing it to turbo-charge her career, or that she's sleeping with someone: a student; Rose's saxophone teacher; the yoga instructor whose class she tried only once.

Being evil would make everything better; she wouldn't feel sick all the time. Her cuff is glazed with silver snot. More stairs, doubling back towards the middle of the building, then at last a sign for the third floor, beside a surprisingly high balcony. She looks over it, lets herself imagine. How difficult would it be to fall downstairs so that it looks accidental, but doesn't leave her merely wounded? She has to wait at least until the kids are out the far end of teenagerhood, unless the others are right, and she's ruined them already.

Last few steps. She's sweating, creased, utterly unfit to face them. She might as well give in right now, cancel tonight's plans. Her heavy Celtic Classical Association Conference 2008 bag keeps banging against her hip; during the appointment, or afterwards, they could demand to search it, find the latest batch of paperwork. Imagine their rage.

It's very strange; she can definitely smell strawberries.

Part One

Into the Woods

1

Then

December 1996

See the embryonic woman, the ridiculous adult-child, on her way to a stranger's house, already hoping for too much.

At lunch she invested in concealer, bought a yoghurt to line her stomach, collected her skirt, freshly infused with cigarette smoke, from the hopeless dry-cleaners with the ill baby. Despite trying to tamp down her hope, she was so excited that she almost rang her mother to ask about bringing wine. Instead, she took herself like a grown-up to Jayne-Anne Interflora on the corner, but nothing seemed right, too presumptuous or babyish, and she'd ended up with the worst possible option: carnations or chrysanthemums, beetroot-red, with a weird bow, nasty background leafage, reeking of wet, cheap paper. She stayed for hours at work, shutting filing-cabinet drawers and running taps as loudly as possible, but the only person around to notice was the janitor, Mr Fearn, about whom many letters had been sent, who gracefully turned with his mop like a ballroom dancer and wished her breasts a pleasurable evening.

At last, it was late enough to leave: her first Arts Faculty social gathering. She'd removed the sodden wrapping but now the flowers looked even worse, like something she'd plucked from a grave. She retied the bow around their slimy stems, wadded in green paper towels and a carrier bag. Holding them before her, she stepped out.

Everyone she passed on the narrow pavement was grinning, too: exhilarated kids, dressed-up women heading out for office Christmas drinks. Night-time makes things happen. She had been a girl in waiting. Now the second half of her life was about to begin.

Even that Athena Papadiamantis had spoken to her was a sign. Athena Papadiamantis, visiting lecturer in Numismatics from Thessaloniki, had flagrantly dyed black hair, big black glasses and a smoker's laugh: exactly the sort of person Zo had one day hoped to have as a colleague. Everybody showed off about knowing her, emphasis on the final '*a*'. When Athena turned to Zo in the tea queue and asked, her accent dense and thickety, 'Penelopé Cartwrisht, you know who this is?' Zo answered 'the Australian – um?', then blushed. Athena grinned, and that was that.

The recital was at Dr Cartwright's flat where she lived with her female . . . what word did people use? Partner? Lover. She was called Justine, apparently something in newspapers. Zo had looked them up in the phone book, even the university directory, but they weren't listed, which seemed provocative. It increased curiosity. People murmured about them, speculated.

She tugged again at her too-tight waistband. Was it possible that this skirt, long but with a modest slit at the side, could simultaneously be frumpy and signal that she was easy prey?

Almost twenty-five wasn't too old to be sex-trafficked; apparently anyone would do. And, under her plain black coat with its bobbly pocket-seams, 'like,' her mother said, 'a tramp,' she wore her new red knitted-silk V-neck top which hopefully minimized her breasts. She'd read advice on dressing for the curvaceous silhouette: no more round-necked jumpers. Her top showed not cleavage, never that, but its promise. She had double-checked that nothing was on inside-out or back to front; not because she was worthy of admiration, but to avoid generating disgust. Still, self-consciousness burned, blazing her cheeks red as a yokel's.

It was well after eight already; she'd taken a long tube and a bus, consulted the driver but still had had to walk miles. Closed shops, offices, mansion-blocks; the pavements were empty. Even the terraces were so different from home: sour brick iced by pigeons, corroded by buddleia, rotting ironwork, centuries of fumes and private grief. If she couldn't find the bus-stop home, where would she sleep? According to her father's old *A–Z*, the address was on a cursory road, barely a lane off a mews; she pictured friendly jockeys, steaming straw. Stag Street W6, although technically Hammersmith, looked dangerously close to the Uxbridge Road, where her father had specifically said never to go. Since moving to London, she'd heard that prostitutes solicited there in daylight, people writhed about having overdoses. She peeped through the window of Cutz' Ladies Hair, ghostly as a salon in Pompeii; a travel agency; Staub Invisible Mending. A stationary car ticked quietly outside Cristal Grill and Buffet; she memorized the number plate. She passed a series of unconvincing hotels, the Great London, the Gaelic, the Lord Albercorn, whose suspiciously similar lavish curtains and desperate balcony-conifers made them look as if they belonged to the same criminal family. Her shoes were so loud. Nowhere was safe after dark, but this was an invitation to attack.

Then again, Dr Cartwright must have standards. She was a sophisticated woman.

Athena had said, 'Penelope looks forward to seeing you.' This was probably a translation issue, although Athena's English was perfect, under the accent, and the fags. She'd said something about music, too; what if Zo was expected to pull out a fiddle, or sing? When she planned her outfit, she'd imagined sitting in a row of golden chairs, a chill Rococo concert hall, as if Dr Cartwright would have one of those tucked away behind the bathroom. Might this be the beginning of a period of musical appreciation, a concert-going Zo?

It was embarrassing, how much she was pinning on this evening; she'd hate herself afterwards, for the hope. But the loneliness was shameful, too. Sometimes, trying to eat her sandwich and banana more slowly, or carrying on regardless while her seminar students yawned and bickered, Zo would imagine a new life in one of the old-fashioned greasy spoons on Liverpool Road, dazzling the regulars with her way with pesto. But then she wouldn't be able to afford her own private room at the top of the house of Mrs Lewis, with politely shared bath and light kitchen use (no parties). She'd have to move home.

Last night, lying in her solitary fug, angrily squeezing the fat on her hips and thighs, she'd reminded herself that at least, in London, she could go to the National Gallery or the supermarkets of Chinatown whenever she wanted. It was possible to lean out of her bedroom window and glimpse Islington fire station, brave men extinguishing imaginary flames; in the other direction was H.M.P. Holloway. She was, as her mother often reminded her, so much luckier than her sister and brother, stuck in Oxfordshire; 'they would,' she'd tell her, 'kill to be there. Kill.'

Zo tried to feel it. She had a Masters and three fifths of a doctorate behind her, a promising career ahead, relatively. But her friends were gone to Lampeter and Naples; her family were almost sixty miles up the M40 in Headington, called by her mother 'the sticks of the sticks', which didn't even make sense. On Saturday mornings she thought up subjects to chat about with the newsagent lady, who sold individual cigarettes to children but called her Darling. The friendly Brazilians who ran the florists might one day invite her home for lunch. She cooked herself time-consuming dinners for two from the recipes in the *Evening Standard*, inexpertly boned grilled sardines, Madras prawn curry, and ate the lot, while writing out party-food menus on file-paper, laboriously hole-reinforced. Hoping for conversation, for the moment a lifelong romance would begin, she sat on Regent's Park benches with Elizabeth Barrett Browning; once, absolutely flagrant, with a novel about growing up as a gay poet in Ohio. No one took the hint. She tried to seem approachable at faculty gatherings. Yet nobody suggested lunch, let alone an evening. She smiled too hard on the stairs. She searched for bargains in unsavoury remainder-bookshops, tried to learn the streets of London, as if a cab driver might lean out of his window and ask the way to Trafalgar Square. She didn't dare invite anyone herself, to anything.

Her mother always said that, after twenty, shyness was an affectation. Tricia prided herself on her sparkling way at parties, in the days when going to them was still an option. Even now, Zo could imagine her face if she saw her daughter's ill-judged outfit. It was hard for a woman as beautiful as Tricia to have produced a child like her.

She had expected an entire Georgian house, or possibly a converted loft with glass bricks and open-plan toilets, but the map led her down a wind-blown alley towards what looked like an extinct shop: big blank-faced windows on the ground floor, a garage door of painted vertical planks. The traffic on Hammersmith Road, sirens and motorbikes, an amplified version of the perpetual London growl, was so loud it was almost a texture. Surely Dr Cartwright wouldn't live here?

Overhead, a sign swung heavily from a bracket, but there was no pub in sight. Despite the traffic, she could hear conversation, laughter. The possibilities for sophisticated adult living realigned themselves; so this was a place one might want to be. There were only two bells, labelled *Dr Cartwright/ [illegible]* and *Balder R.* Imagine being Balder R, downstairs from Dr Penelope Cartwright, meeting her on the step as you collected the post. She probably wore a kimono. Someone had said she always dressed as if she were off to a wedding, all those heels and pashminas. That was how Zo imagined her most often, laughing with her stylish friends on a beach in Melbourne or Tasmania, catching the bridal bouquet.

She forced herself to press the bell. Should she have trimmed her fringe? Same with lip balm; she'd bought a tinted one but now it seemed presumptuous. She must have mixed up the days, or they'd decided to disinvite her and were pressing their faces to the glass, gulping with mirth. But she made herself ring a second time, was nervously plucking her daring green bag strap from between her breasts when she heard sharp footsteps approaching the door. It would be Dr Papadiamantis, she thought, or a stranger. To have turned up, expecting to be welcome, was excruciating.

But it was Dr Cartwright, in the flesh. 'Yes?'

The first time Zo had laid eyes on the allegedly lesbian Dr Penelope Cartwright, earlier that term, she'd been disappointed. The only gay women she knew, all three of whom she'd slept with, were much more obvious. Dr Cartwright was always tap-tapping down the corridor or washing her hands in the Ladies, checking her reflection, removing her glasses to wipe away a mascara smudge. Her hair was somewhere between curly and wavy, between light and dark blonde, always up on top of her head in big-toothed clips or a chopstick but barely contained, fronds cascading over one blueish eye or over her collar. She wore more perfume and audible jewellery than Zo had owned in her life; knitted dresses; sleeveless blouses, short skirts. She seemed too womanly, too glamorous to fancy. Yet the fact that she was a lesbian, but dressed like that, made her impossible not to look at.

And never close up. Until now.

Coolly, Dr Cartwright gazed at her. 'You look very . . . flushed.'

'Thank you,' Zo said.

She followed Dr Cartwright up to the first floor's landing: high brown boots, a long silk-looking dress and belted waist, deep blue with lighter sprigs. Her thick fair hair, striped with the colours of sun and hay and sand, was mostly up but, as ever, prettily bursting out of its clips, the golden back of her neck revealed. Tendrils, no other word for them, had broken free, perfect loops like a handwriting exercise. One clung to where a golden chain, two, ducked beneath her collar.

Dr Papadiamantis, Athena, was crossing the hallway when they entered the flat.

'At last she comes,' she said, giving Dr Cartwright a hard-to-read smile.

'It's very nice of you to inv—' Zo began.

'Very,' agreed Dr Cartwright. She was older than Zo, but might know young people to introduce her to. That was the reason Zo had come: to meet people her own age.

With a fingertip on Zo's shoulder, she steered her into a bedroom: candles, multiple pistachio-coloured hotelly cushions and a wall-sized framed poster for an old film, *INCREDIBLE MAN-EATING WOMEN!* The air was very warm and scented with flowers. A high wide bed like a set in an opera was already piled with luxurious-looking coats.

Even without those heels, Dr Cartwright was much taller. Zo could have tipped her head back and rested it against her breastbone. 'Now, you'd better meet Justine.'

Zo frowned, looked behind her. 'Sorry, wher—?'

'She's in the kitchen. Did you think she was camouflaged? Hiding under the duvet? Also, why are you so late?'

'I got lost. Twice. Sorry. I'm not great at navigating, be—'

'Well, you made it,' and Zo noticed for the first time how Australian Dr Cartwright sounded, the unEnglish warmth of her skin. The freckles over her nose-bridge and cheekbones were too perfectly placed, like dots of kohl for a school play; usually her glasses concealed them. Zo held out the flowers, began to explain her poor choice, but Dr Cartwright didn't react, not even a smirk, as she glanced down at them. 'I should have brought w—'

'You shouldn't have. Dump your coat there.' She was pointing to a scalloped pale-pink velvet armchair. 'So you'll be able to find it, eventually.'

'Oh, but I won't stay very long,' Zo began to explain, as planned, but Dr Cartwright was already kissing a group of arrivals. Zo fidgeted nearby. She guided her to a quite ordinary galley kitchen, pans on pale-painted shelves, tiles in need of a wash, where a woman waited before a tray containing several whole fish, grasping a carving knife as if expecting to be attacked.

'Here she is,' said Dr Cartwright, to one of them.

She, the famous Justine, looked like the shoulderpaddy women sketched on eighties dress-patterns: Butterick, Very Easy Vogue. 'I shouldn't have to make my own but, well, there it is,' Zo's mother would say, which meant she was still despairing of Headington boutiques, Headington style, Headington wives. 'You know I don't like to complain.' She'd buy three or four at a time, spend hours selecting fabric, then never even open the packets.

Justine's face was long, like a handsome bony horse, her toothpaste-coloured jacket oddly formal, more coolly Anglo-Saxon than the tanned flashing heat of Dr Cartwright. 'Hello,' said Zo, in her shameful clothes. 'Thank you so much for . . . for . . .'

Justine, still gripping the knife, looked from Zo to Dr Cartwright, shrugged, and Dr Cartwright brought Zo, like a lambkin, into the crowd.

An hour, then another. Lots of red wine, small bowls of seaweed-speckled Japanese rice-crackers. Everyone was friendly, as if it was perfectly reasonable for a very junior PhD student to move among people of whom she'd heard, who'd written books she'd read, or at least had thought of reading. There were a few charming men but most of the guests were women, tanned and tall and better-formed than ordinary academics, and some of them were obviously together. Zo couldn't stop smiling. It was impossible not to stare. At last, one of the well-groomed men helped Justine bring in a plate of fish, now slashed open and baked with ginger and soy sauce, a big salad, cheese, cut-up mango and pineapple and even passion-fruit. She hurried out again; he followed, murmuring in her ear.

'Is she OK?' Zo asked her neighbour.

The woman lifted her glass. Her silver rings flashed like knuckle-dusters in the lamplight. She frowned at Zo. 'Why shouldn't she be?'

Something shameful, a blazing molecule of vanity, was extinguished. 'I don't know. She seemed . . . bothered.'

'She's used to it,' said the woman.

Justine did exude a certain tension; she lacked Dr Cartwright's sun-kissed gloss. If she hates me, Zo told herself maturely, it's not as if I'll ever need to see her again.

No one else seemed hungry, although they were very interested in the wine. It would have been ungrateful to neglect all that waiting seabass. The salad was surprising, spicy and limey, mainly rice with bits of peppers and green beans and peanuts and coriander; Zo, who'd read that rice salads were naff, made a mental note. She took second helpings, couldn't leave the mango alone. Whenever she wasn't sidling up to the food table, people were asking her interested humorous questions, as if they were receiving instructions into an ear-piece. Where were her flowers? Someone tried to open the window and Dr Cartwright called over, 'You'll never manage it, these crappy Early Victorian sashes,' and Zo tried not to look impressed.

'Presumably "Zoe"; is that with an umlaut, or as in *Franny and*?' quite a fierce woman asked and, when Zo said 'neither', the woman looked displeased. Zo began to explain but the woman hushed her. 'No, you see, it's quite funny, my mum and d—' Zo continued, and only then noticed that one of the other tall blonde women was standing alone in the centre of the room, holding a flute; that everybody else had stopped talking.

Somehow Zo alone hadn't remembered that this was the point of the evening's plans: a musical recital, provided by

Dorcas Kindersley, one of Dr Cartwright's Queensland Uni friends who was now an accomplished soloist with the Swedish National Orchestra. Dr Cartwright gave a speech, thanking ('thinking') Dorcas for honouring them with a performance; a modest pile of her CDs sat on a shelf near the kitchen, featuring her, a wind-blown Valkyrie in a gossamer shawl, standing on river-rocks, and people bought them for cash on their way out. Zo had to write a cheque.

It had seemed the least she could do. In her ignorance, she hadn't positioned herself where she could gaze upon Dr Cartwright or Justine or even Athena, so she had been right in the eyeline of Dorcas Kindersley herself. The flute had always seemed a particularly sappy instrument: the earnest waving-around of the silver pipe, the shape made by the mouths of the players, sorry, 'flautists'. The other guests' reverential stillness, combined with Dorcas Kindersley's bobbing and swaying, as if giving an energetic blow-job, made solemnity difficult; Zo had to bite the inside of her cheek, stare fixedly at the rug until her eyes watered. Surreptitiously, people changed positions on the chairs and sofa. The music, possibly Mozart or Elgar or Beethoven or Brahms, Zo decided, went on; polite clapping, then even more. Her leg ached, fizzed, went completely dead beneath her; when the recital finally ended and everyone jumped up for wine, she couldn't feel the floor and staggered, as if she were drunk, which Dr Cartwright definitely saw.

But, eventually, on a relaxing tide of alcohol and general flirtation, Zo almost forgot, and began to enjoy herself. She ended up kneeling, like a bride, beside Dr Cartwright, sharing grapes with her and a much more heavily freckled anthropologist. She watched them talk; the jawlines of older women, their slim hands. Zo's were unmoisturized, picked and punished: the hands of a child.

Time for some water. She headed for the little toilet, where rows of perfume bottles were arranged beside a sparkling illuminated mirror, as if in a shop. She pressed her nose against the glass, scrubbed at the oily smudge with her cuff. Nobody could ever know her vain hope that she'd been singled out for something, someone. What were the chances that anyone here might find her attractive? For once, researching hadn't helped. Since arriving in London she'd ordered two American studies books from academic bookshops, but they didn't seem to cover these sorts of women; there were no obvious shipping heiresses here, no breeches. She'd bought *Time Out* for the Gay and Lesbian column, memorizing venues like holy sites; bravely gone to see one subtitled comic Catalan film on Shaftsbury Avenue; owned a k.d. lang CD. She'd deduced that, in the modern world, attractive lesbians were butch (pinstripe suits). But who did they fancy? Not woman-shaped tomboys like her, terrible at being girls, un-interested in the Premier League. So, was the only alternative PE teachers like at school: practical hair, pastel tracksuits, utter sexlessness? Also, surely two feminine women couldn't be together, yet here was golden-maned Dr Cartwright, femme, and Justine, femme: more like straight women, the kind Zo's mother approved of.

It was only later, on the top deck of the bus home, frowning into flats above chip shops as she brooded on the errors of her ways, that she put her hand in her coat pocket. The euphoria was passing; she was understanding quite how repulsively gauche and earnest she must have seemed, a monster of ego, a glutton. What a fool to have imagined this could be the beginning of a life.

Groping about for distraction, a forgotten cough sweet, she touched something. There, among the tube tickets and interesting leaves, was a note.

2

Now

The flat is bright and sunny, on what Zoe hopes will be the worst day of her life.

At least she's in the living room. Each evening, when she says goodnight, there are dark comments, threats, pleading, but Zoe has stood firm. The sofa-bed is better than trying to fall asleep in the marital bedroom after hours of being ranted at, then waking up to more.

When Zoe decided to move out of their room, she asked if they could blame Penny's late-night television habit.

'How could you even suggest that? I will not lie to my children. They're already traumatized; they don't need deceit as well.'

They didn't need the bald truth either, but Penny was intransigent. She still insisted that it was temporary and Zoe, still weak, let her. She knows full well what's happening later today, but acts as if it's either impossible, or preventable. Any minute, she'll come and make tea, and start crying. She will not rein herself in. She says it's natural to express her emotions, as loudly as she wants.

Matilda has been bunking off in earnest, is edging ever

closer to another suspension, and says she doesn't care. Rose, when she should be at fencing practice, hangs about in the kitchen like a watchful parent, doing wrist-strengthening exercises and working on her Art portfolio, or runs laps around the skateboard-park where a Spanish exchange student was almost raped last year. She's too pale, too assiduous. Apparently, Zoe is the reason.

If only, oh if only Rose would come too. But she won't, even if she somehow wanted to, because then Penny will be left with nothing.

THEN

December 1996
It was a tightly folded square of thick creamy paper, one edge fibrous as if something else had been torn away. Zo opened it up like a fortune.

'You'll be missed.'

With that, her powers of concentration, the secret of her success, evaporated. She began to roam the ply-panelled passages, climbed the tiled stairwells of the Arts Faculty on invented missions, hoping to be bumped into. She bought another skirt, practised applying her new colourless mascara for both length and separation, forced down espressos in the coffee shop opposite where she'd once noticed Dr Cartwright drinking a Coke. She reread the prospectus booklet for the English department, with its bald two-liner about Dr P. V. Cartwright PhD (Queensland), until she could visualize its font with closed eyes.

Missed by whom and precisely how? Did the note mean 'You are young and succulent but I am another's', or 'You were quite fun, as a puppy is fun'? Dr Cartwright was the only person who could have left it, but why would she? Had it been meant for someone else?

Then her home phone rang.

Dr Cartwright happened to have a spare ticket to a gender-reversed retelling of *Antigone* being staged in a scrap-yard off Fulham Broadway, with spears and helmets rusting in great heaps. Zo was wedged between Dr Cartwright and her friend, tall speckled Inge, who had represented Australia for Women's Middleweight Judo in the Commonwealth Games and had problems with her knees, so needed to sit at the end of their little pew. There was no interval. Zo tried to look transfixed by the actors, but Dr Cartwright's every inhalation and exhalation seemed distractingly significant, full of clues.

Afterwards, Dr Cartwright suggested that she and Inge take her for a drink. Zo was already far gone. She asked for a whisky mac, which she remembered from university, and they laughed at her, then ordered a bottle of Australian Merlot. She looked at Dr Cartwright's exposed wrist, the hemispheres of kneecap under her silky pleated skirt, and managed not to say: you are beautiful outside and in.

Quite soon after Inge left, Dr Cartwright touched her hand.

*

Now it all emerged; poor, poor Dr Cartwright. Her life was less perfect than it appeared. There had been youthful sorrow, lightly alluded to. Her colleagues couldn't cope, she explained, with a woman like her, openly gay, clever, attractive – she actually said this. And, saddest of all, Justine, 'my girlfriend', was quite an angry person.

'But she loves you, surely,' said Zo, owl-eyed, two huge glasses of red in. 'I mean, you're happy? Oh no. What . . . she's faithful to you, at least? Sorry, sorry, I shouldn't have . . .'

'Well, you're very frank. No, it's refreshing. Well, who knows,' admitted Dr Cartwright, looking down at her bracelet, so that Zo could see, at her crown, a touching glimpse of scalp. What was an Australian childhood: sun-block and sun-hats, flying doctors, radio lessons? Might she have owned one of those tame kangaroos? How did a woman like this become?

Dr Cartwright lifted her head. Weren't most people's irises simply one colour, brown, or blue? These seemed indeterminate unless she was looking straight at Zo, grey-blue, blue-grey, with a paler inner circle which was almost green. It was difficult not to keep shifting, trying to hold her gaze. Blue, thought Zo. No, hang on . . .

'It's not been easy,' Dr Cartwright confessed.

'That's awful. Cheating: I can't believe it. That people would actually do such a thing. How could she, to you?'

'Oh, I know.'

With perhaps not the most discreet of questions, Zo discovered that Dr Cartwright's life had first become difficult, domestically, a couple of years ago.

'Which is about when I arrived,' observed Zo.

'I promise you it's unconnected. But I would say that, wouldn't I?' Her smile was distracting. Eventually, she admitted that she and Justine lived more as flatmates than as lovers. She didn't want to engage with the misogynistic trope of My Mad Ex, let alone the deranged-lesbian conceit but, well . . . very sadly, nothing could be done to make Justine happy. Yet she was determined, despite provocation, to do the right thing.

'That's good,' Zo agreed. 'Honourableness is important. You must be such a decent person, to . . .'

'No, no,' Dr Cartwright waved her hand. 'But the truth is she does depend on me, not least financially.'

'Wow, she doesn't even have a job?'

'She left it, unwisely. It was sub-editing, which she hated, of course. And she always found offices difficult, which didn't help.'

Right there, in the oxygen of Dr Cartwright's smile, Zo had a revelation. She had been fearing that academia was not for her; that she was neither an adequately brilliant mind, nor a charismatic enough tutor, nor sufficiently competent at the rest of it, blundering through admin, gauche in commit-tees, blind to undercurrents. Compared to her peers, demure Paola Fry who was reputedly the girlfriend of wild-bearded old Professor Harriman, or the dourly sexy Mercedes, black bob and tie as if she had escaped from *Cabaret*, Zo was failing. What she needed, she now understood, was an experienced role model, neither dry nor dowdy, who could lead her by the hand towards her, ideally brilliant, future.

'She thought she'd like to write full-time, which is always a mistake, don't you think?'

'Definitely,' said Zo, as one who knows. 'Though she must be very clever,' she added encouragingly. 'Is she, has your, er, Justine publ—'

'She's been working on a biography of Vera Brittain, Lesbian. For years. Ever since I've known her, actually.'

'Sorry, was Vera Brittain a lesbian? I thought . . .'

'Precisely.'

'Ah. I see.'

'Yes. To tell you the truth,' offered Dr Cartwright, leaning closer, 'I'm not perfectly convinced she's started the actual . . . writing.'

Soon she was alluding to other problems: Justine's drinking, like Dr Cartwright's own father's; the suffocating depressions. Zo almost admitted she'd never met an alcoholic knowingly, that depressions weren't something she'd ever heard talked about, but her stomach was beginning to rumble so loudly that she could hear it above the noise of the pub, like a wolf under the table. Would eating the pear in her bag be crass? I need a mere sandwich, a humble nut, she thought, and accidentally giggled.

'You are a very strange child.'

'I'm not. I'm . . . so how old are you?' she asked perilously, but Dr Cartwright smiled.

'Guess.'

'I can't. You don't have to tell me, I shoul—'

'I am thirty-five.'

'Wow.'

'What "wow"?' but Dr Cartwright knew perfectly well.

Zo couldn't tear her eyes from that mouth, the deep indentation in the top lip like the press of a fingertip, the pair of dark freckles beside it. Justine, presumably, sometimes saw Dr Cartwright with her hair down.

She swallowed. 'Have you always been g-gay?'

Dr Cartwright laughed. 'Oh, always. Very. The odd man, or boy, obviously, but that's more . . . light relief.'

'Oh,' said Zo, trying not to goggle.

'My first female lover,' Dr Cartwright went on, 'was, well . . .'

'Justine?'

'Are you mad? No, it was my netball teacher, Suu.'

'No.'

'You bet. Co-founder of the seminal Murrumbidgee feminist 'zine *OFF OUR TITS*. A Kiwi. Although she is, genetically, German.'

'My God,' said Zo.

'Loads of Germans in New Zealand; they love that fifties vibe. Not that she often admits to b—'

'No, I mean, wasn't that, the age gap, illegal?'

'Maybe technically. But no. Full consent. Full.'

'Wow. Wow. What . . . was she like?'

'Sickeningly old-school. Very into the sisterhood, all the amazing Womyn, with a "y". You must know . . . ah, you innocent. Seriously, Merril Mushroom and bell hooks and that lot. No?'

'I . . . think I've heard of them.'

'Interesting,' said Dr Cartwright, nodding slowly, still smiling, and Zo's legs jiggled with excitement: an antenna, a tail twitching autonomously. 'I hated all that stuff,' she added. 'Repelled me utterly, their tedious seventies earnestness. Semiotic texts, grim novels where, of course, they end up slitting their wrists because why should lezzies have happy endings? Bet you've never read anything where we're not either tweedy or titillating; it just doesn't exist. As for the Ladies of Llangolleoclloghlan, bloody John; honestly, it's embarrassing.'

Zo reached under the table for her bag, nudged Audre Lorde under her scarf. She was casting around for an intelligent question about Christina Stead, the subject of Dr Cartwright's book, when Dr Cartwright said: 'So, is your mother on side?'

'My . . . Christ. No. Ugh. My God, she doesn't even . . . she's the opposite of a lesbian.'

'I didn't mean *is* she one, although you'd be surprised . . .' Dr Cartwright held her gaze. 'And you?'

'Sorry?'

'What about you?'

Zo's mouth dropped open. 'How, how do you know about me?'

'Darling, it's shining out of you.'

Later, she'd say it was like hitting a piñata; one little tap and out it all fell. For years to come, Zo would squirm at the thought of her revelations: about the kind but agèd sociologist Ali Bridge, closeted at work without realizing the popped-collar shirts were a giveaway; then the freelance illustrator she met at her sole attempt at going to a bar, hip-bones like a trouser-press; the one-night stand with a fellow twenty-two-year-old who worked at British Telecom, but only in order to fund her dream of running a women's hockey club in Stratford-upon-Avon.

'Loads in common, then.'

'Exactly.'

'And that's it?'

'That . . . is it. You?'

Dr Cartwright ignored this, was much more interested in Ali Bridge: why exactly hadn't Zo loved her? Was she attractive? If she'd worn make-up, which brands? She marvelled that Zo didn't know.

'So you do have to be one or the other?'

'Definitely. Always in a couple, there's . . .' and she trailed off, smiling. 'Never mind.'

'Have you ever . . . I read a saying, "Butch in the sheets, femme on the streets"; is that true, or an ideal, or n—'

'Oh, sweetie,' said Dr Cartwright. 'You have a lot to learn. And your ponytail's gone wonky. God, I wish my hair was straight like that. Mine's impossible.' Zo thought of what her mother would say, hurriedly tightened her hair-band, then hid her grotesquely nibbled hands. 'So, tell me, did this Ali teach you everything you know?'

'Well. I'm more . . . self-taught.'

Dr Cartwright laughed. 'Fair's fair. You have to tell me, though. Exactly how ancient was she?

'Then? Or now? Er, she'd be . . . wasn't Suu even, I mean, much, much older than you?'

'Couple of decades, I suppose, but she looked more.

Sun-damage,' and she shrugged. 'So . . . you do have to confess. Twelve years? Fifteen?'

Zo, counting on her fingers as if for the first time, looked up, grinning. 'OK. Twenty-six years. I know.'

'And what did your, well, friends think?'

'They never met her. Can you imagine how that would . . . I mean, they were all straight. Still are, in fact. I never meet lesbians. Whereas you, at your party . . . you have a ready-made batch.'

'Oh, you poor starved child,' said Dr Cartwright. 'You have no idea. Well, maybe your world is going to open up.'

By the time they left, it was night; frost on the pavements like diamonds, an areola of haze around each streetlight. 'Call me Penny. Dr Cartwright sounds like a farrier. I certainly will not call you Zo.'

They stopped by a bollard on one of those cobbled lanes where, if one squints, the lamps produce magic, and one becomes a Victorian, up to no good. Obviously, she explained this to Dr Cartwright, who laughed, then kissed her. And so she fell.

3

Now

So this is the plan. The minute the kids have left, allegedly for school (Rose in good time with all her clean sports kit, her cuticles raw; Matilda messing about, late, textbooks and Zip card forgotten), Penny is off to stay with friends ('of course I'm not bloody teaching, what do you expect? Sally and Erica know I shouldn't be alone. They're desperately worried for me') and Zoe will frantically pack up as much of their life as she can, before rushing into work for the second-year seminar group. After period eight, while Penny and Zoe are at the mediator's, the kids will go together to Marylebone station to catch the train from which Zoe's mum and dad will collect them. By tomorrow afternoon, when, fed and rested and, with luck, indulged, the kids return from Headington, Zoe will have moved into Goldhawk Road, and the next stage of their lives will begin.

That is the plan.

'Obviously,' Zoe's mother, Tricia, likes to say, 'what you need is better therapy.'

When she still lived for shopping ('well, window-shopping.

I can't afford much, thanks to you know who'), Tricia was persuaded by a friend to pop into Headington Citizens Advice. She never became an Adviser; 'I'm not talking to strangers!' and there is some doubt that she turned up for the induction. Yet it convinced her that she should have been a therapist, probably still could be.

She kept demanding, via Zoe's father, Clive, the credentials of everyone Zoe and Penny saw. 'Don't like the sound of that one,' she'd say in the background. 'Though I wish we'd had support like that when we were newlyweds,' as if Penny and Zoe were still skipping about in the golden uplands. 'Tell the girls that marriages take work. And I should know.'

Tricia thinks she's being supportive, has wept about the situation to Zoe's sister, cousins, her favoured beauty professionals, although not anywhere near Zoe. Her worry is mainly how this will affect 'my grandchild', by which she means Rose. Rose, she always says, takes after her, looks-wise.

'You will support Rose and Matty, both of them, won't you?' asked Zoe, when she first told them what was happening. 'They'll need you. And me . . . me too.'

'Don't be silly,' said Tricia. 'Haven't I always? That's what mothers do.'

Now Zoe and Penny move around the kitchen, filling then forgetting the kettle, pretending to recheck their bags. Usually, Penny will have begun a fresh argument, or resurrected one from the night before. But, strangely, not this morning.

When the kids were little, they had this kitchen painted an accidentally bold blue. Penny called it 'frozen kingfisher', which led to years of bad family jokes about animals in peril; it made Zoe think of too-minty toothpaste, the feeling of air on sensitive teeth. Now she touches a stray bristle from the decorator's brush, the claw-marks scraped by the arm of Matty's chair, through the paint to plaster, dust beneath.

Matilda reaches behind her for her denim jacket with SCREW THE PATRIARCHS painted on it, as if she's a runaway from an Orthodox seminary.

'Right. Tilda.' Penny stands. 'Come on. I'm driving you in.'

Matty's eyes widen; she's biting her lip. Earlier this year, Penny wept audibly right through Matty's school talent show, harangued Zoe afterwards in the dark playground, in front of Year Eight and all their parents. 'Why shouldn't they know what I'm going through?' she demanded afterwards, on the bus home, the kids wisely sitting upstairs. 'What *we* are? Are you imagining that anyone will still speak to you, when they hear what you've done to me?'

'Doesn't Dad need the car?' Matty asks now, sliding a glance towards Zoe. 'For something?'

'Don't, don't you want me near you? Is that it?' Penny's voice is breaking. She has told Matty, several times, that she will not allow Zoe to take her away, to deny Penny the right to bring her up. 'But I need to.'

'I don't . . . I'm really OK with the bus,' Matilda says, flushing, and Zoe could blush for her. She's been trying to bend one of their old forks into a useful hook; once, long ago, Zoe would have helped her, and Penny would have been annoyed but only barely, and they'd have put it up at an angle in the hall. Matty looks so young in her red school sweatshirt: freshly hatched, as if dotted with bits of yolk and eggshell. Usually, on a normal day, they'd be in a vortex of lost Geography forms and calculators and unnourishing cereal, dirty socks, meter-readings, whirling like a cartoon punch-up, but everyone is too subdued. 'Thanks though,' she adds.

Penny thumps her cup down in the sink, bolts from the kitchen. They can hear her sobbing through the toilet door.

'Super,' says Rose, grabbing her fencing-case, her art coursework portfolio and calculator. This was Zoe's last chance to talk to her about today, to try to find a way to ask if she wants to come with her and Matty, and she's missed it. Be brave, she instructs herself, but what if she is about to lose her girl?

'Look after yourself,' she calls weedily, which Penny hates. She and the others say Zoe is neurotic about their daughters, that it's perfectly safe to walk around west London in the dark; that one can be repeatedly groped as a teenager and turn out OK. If Rose were attacked, they agree, she could defend herself with a swift parry. And Matty would be so outraged and scathing that her attackers would apologize.

Zoe is digging her nails into her palms to force the tears down, but they're gnawed too short. Then Matty murmurs: 'Can you pretend you've got to bus with me?'

Zoe allows their eyes to meet. Even brave Matty would never usually have dared express a preference aloud, at least until last year, and Zoe always hushes her, to avoid enraging Penny even more. But, this morning, it's as if they're stepping over a barrier towards something holy, or unholy. Touch it, her daughter is willing her. Zoe reaches out a hand.

Then

December 1996
Zo couldn't help it. She had to write her a letter.

The plight of Dr Cartwright (Penny), her courage in standing by Justine when their relationship had died, moved Zo almost to tears, over and over again. She had always known that love was a form of chivalry, putting somebody before oneself: like her father, making her mother's lunches, the tray, the napkin-ring. They had a good marriage, everyone agreed. And Zo had always thought it would suit her, throwing capes over puddles. What could be sexier than being a Thracian serving-boy, meeting every need of one's older, definitely more commanding, master?

Dr Cartwright, Penny, 'P', wrote back, almost instantly. When Zo read her postcard at work, sitting on the staircase for privacy, the lino seemed to rise up beneath her. Aha, she thought: a swoon.

Even in the first days, then weeks, sadness glinted through the euphoria. Penny wanted nothing more than to keep meeting and kissing, said the most incredible things about passionate fidelity, certainty, but explained that carrying on in secret wasn't fair on Justine. Being fair, moral even, mattered intensely ('intinsly') to her. 'When something wonderful happens,' she'd explained, her voice a burr of promise in Zo's ear, 'when you meet someone truly important to you . . . oh, little one, I heard you gasp.'

'Might have.'

'You see, we must start as we mean to go on. Clarity. Firm foundations. I do know how these things work.'

'I completely understand,' Zo said and, in the absence of comparisons, or people in whom to confide, it was a relief to be told what was right.

Penny couldn't get over Zo's first letter, the alacrity, the disinhibition, but Zo could not stop. Writing was a remedy for a longing so sharp it seemed to flood her lungs. She wrote pledges of lifelong devotion, comparisons to famous beauties, confessions of past troubles and future fears (although not the greatest; even she knew to wait for that).

'You plighted your troth,' Penny would say. 'Premature . . . plightaculation. But restraint is not your strong point, my sweet. Luckily.'

So that was another thing to work on: a weakness to be scrubbed out, like the bone structure which, Penny assured her, would slowly emerge from her sweet young cheeks. 'You'll get more and more lovely,' Penny promised her, and it was mind-bending, to imagine that this, with Penny's guidance, could be within her reach.

She signed the second letter 'Zoe'.

At the start, the need for secrecy was always with them. Zo, now Zoe, wasn't Penny's student, or even her underling; oh that was a word they enjoyed, pressed together against the red oaks of Ravenscourt Park, the shiver of cold hands against heated skin. It was generally known that Penny lived with Justine and, said Penny, 'it wouldn't look good. They wouldn't understand.'

'Why not? People do . . . fall for people, don't they?' asked Zoe, who couldn't yet voice in person what she had committed to Basildon Bond writing-paper and ink. Even postally, Penny hadn't said it back. Yet she wasn't trying all that hard to hide whatever it was that was happening to them; some of the other staff seemed to have an idea. She sent Zoe filthy letters as if from long-dead archaeologists to the shared fax machine at work, where they were sometimes retrieved by her senior colleagues and placed, neatly folded, in the TEMP. LECT. pigeonhole. But no one said a thing. Maybe they were looking at her differently but Zoe was well past caring, wrapped in a penumbra, a Ready Brek glow, of being wantable.

Everybody knew that Penny was gay. When she first came to London and went on marches or to lesbian bars, nobody believed her, with those painted nails, all that hair. 'They'd never met one who looked so straight. Nobody had. I was physically stopped from going into the basement at New Earth . . . oh dear lord, don't tell me you haven't been there either. Time you went. I'll introduce you to the ladies. They'll mob us. I've been going there for years. And it'll help you clamber out of that closet,' she'd add, even though Zoe wasn't exactly in it. It was simply that telling people about one's . . . inclinations, without a specific person to attach them to, was awkward. 'Although,' Penny pointed out, 'admit it, the signs were there.'

Penny had shown her photographs: white-blonde toddlers camping beside the Cudgegong River; mid-pass in the Grand Final of the West Central West Netball League Tournament, '78; god-like teenage surfers, unselfconscious in zinc sunblock and neoprene. In return, Zoe handed over evidence of her own unfortunate youth: anxiously squinting away from the camera on a difficult family holiday to Tricia's sister in Northamptonshire; fiddling with her stamp collection or inky from Calligraphy Club. 'My sweet girl. It actually hurts, that you look so sad. And so deeply proto-Lesbian. Look at those heartbreaking cross-bar specs, like an infant publican. Oh my God, are those binoculars? And so, so many teeth. Where does one even get such a hairstyle? You look like a little Maoist; poor girl, why didn't Mother Trish sort you out?'

'She sort of . . . gave up. Quite quickly. I mean, she was beautiful, whereas I was horrific, obviously. You can see. Like a – a quiche in a wig.'

'Well, you're safe from terrible tomboy cuts now,' and Zoe, who had secretly loved the feeling of a shaver at the nape of her neck, kept quiet. 'What about when you were a teenager? Couldn't your friends help, crimpers or lippie or something? You did have sleepovers, didn't you?'

'Not much.'

'Christ. Poor you. Mine were hours and hours away and we still spent as much of our lives as possible in each other's bedrooms, practising eye-liner. We were sure every male teacher was problematically obsessed with us. I'm not even joking. Sitting in the staff room deciding which of us to marry; me first, obviously. I know, nutcase.'

Zoe thought of her unkissed school self, a heifer among deer: utterly innocent yet brimming with desire, desperate to be wanted. All that mattered was what boys liked, any boys, and it definitely wasn't Zoe Hannah Stamper, a lonely heart waiting to be filled.

'But, honestly,' asked Penny, 'not even a tiny crush on a woman? You only ever fancied boys?'

'Definitely. Loads of them. Amazingly heterosexual, in retrospect. Retrosext.'

'No.'

'No. But totally unable to flirt, or, you know, wear unhideous clothes. Do girlhood. You can't imagine it, the agonies of not knowing how to . . . be.'

'Well,' said Penny, pulling her closer. 'You'll know now. Aren't you a lucky girl?'

Penny had had boyfriends in Queensland, Sydney, even Mudgee, but the minute she'd arrived in London she'd joined the University Gay and Lesbian Society and that was that. Now she was an Honorary Member, which meant, she said, 'giving my Erotic Outback speech once a year and being mobbed by all these baby lesbians. Luckily for you, they're very boring. Young people always are. Except you, my brainy little specimen.'

Zoe, still young, couldn't stop thinking about this. Wouldn't Penny be happier with someone her equal? Whenever she went out with Justine, or anyone else, Zoe expected her to realize what she was missing. With perspective, she would surely see that Zoe wasn't up to much.

They'd walk to South Kensington and Penny would get

off with her in full view of the tourists, or over a restaurant table, or at Zoe's friends' parties, while everyone tried to look nonchalant. On the twenty-ninth day of their relationship, she took Zoe to her married friends' immense basement flat, underneath a restaurant in Notting Hill. Jen and Bill's was the most alarming home that Zoe had ever seen: drifts of Lego and flip-flops and Shreddies and felt-tips and fermenting cherry tomatoes and scissors and cat hair and clay and doll torsos and replica Viking long ships and icing and Christmas baubles and plastic walking-casts and partial apples and ping pong balls and matches and teabags, crunching underfoot like snow. There were already five empty bottles on the table. They ate posh tinned food from Bill and Jen's Languedoc holiday, sardines and peas and cassoulet. It tasted like canteen lunches. Everyone discussed their ailments, as if they were already middle-aged: sciatica, tachycardia. Jen and her friends had Brutalist fringes and art-school blusher; apparently Jen, currently a nutritionist, often kissed women but wasn't interested in sleeping with them, and Bill, pouchy clowning Welsh Bill, encouraged it.

'Have you kissed her?'

'A bit, obviously,' said Penny. 'Though only in a hetty way.'

To console Bill, Zoe smiled at all his witticisms. When Penny referred to the fact that Jen ('Jin') was almost forty, all the women turned to assess her. They started discussing who of their gang was totally grey, who was stuck in the eighties. Everyone admired Penny's incredible hair, the weight and wave and fairness, how it looked as if it smelt of sunlight and the contrast with her tannedness despite, she pointed out, the vile English weather. 'Bloody impossible keeping my colour going,' she said, 'unless I go back to Oz every winter. Which, obviously, I can't and won't,' and Zoe tried to look as if she understood. 'You back at Christmas?' she asked Jen, and then they started rediscussing what everyone they knew was doing, who'd married whom. Zoe looked at her own scattered social life, and worried.

'Are all your friends Australian?' she'd asked her, and Penny had looked annoyed. 'My friends,' she said, 'are very cosmopolitan.'

Never before had she been with Penny among so many people. It usually turned Penny on that Zoe would pull away out of shyness when people could see them; she'd whisper filthy plans for her into Zoe's ear, watch her writhe. And, afterwards, in private, she'd torment her, call her her little virgin, her sexy slut, with predictable results.

Hair-washing, she announced during pudding, was the only way to get one's nails really clean.

'You're embarrassing the child,' said Bill.

Later, in the living room, Penny slipped lychees, unpeeled, inside her. They were definitely alone; the others were in the kitchen, with the door shut. But at the beginning, when Penny put her hand inside Zoe's tights, this was not the case.

That night, and whenever they met, Penny and Bill talked about sex as much as possible. She would say, 'he admires me, it's totally normal,' but Zoe couldn't imagine being flirted with like that, by a heterosexual man, let alone wanting him to.

But Penny adored it. She'd give anyone, even strangers at

parties, far more detail than Zoe wished she would about their first kiss, their first fuck, how frantically Zoe had fancied her from the very beginning. If Zoe objected, Penny was nonplussed: was Zoe secretly puritanical? A prude?

Clearly, she needed educating. Penny took her to a famous lingerie slash feminist erotic shop in Belgravia where, in the silk-swagged changing room, they felt each other up. 'Why,' asked Penny loudly, 'would anyone want a vibrator?' The bosomy salesgirls smiled. As they left to meet Penny's friends for dinner ('we'll order, Brits don't understand Asian'), Zoe peeped behind a curtain at the back of the shop and found a drying-rack of dildos, dildi: molten rainbow silicone setting in their moulds. 'Imagine needing one of those,' Penny said.

Penny's friends were already quite drunk, sloppy kisses too near to Zoe's mouth. One, Nikki, seemed friendlier than the others, didn't comment on Zoe's youth or being from Oxford, or imply that she was lucky to be included, like a poor relative. Are you fanciable, Zoe wondered, when Nikki linked arms with her; might you even fancy me?

Afterwards they had their worst ever row. Nikki was one of Penny's closest friends; why was Zoe pretending she hadn't been trying to flirt? And how could she possibly mind that Penny had told everyone what they'd bought?

Zoe had been so embarrassed that she'd hidden in the toilets, her lungs hurting as if with grief but really, she knew perfectly well, with shame, because she was too uptight. When she came out, Penny was demonstrating what was in the bag, saying that she'd made Zoe promise to keep the items at her flat, until they could be properly employed.

The great thing, the goal, was nudity. Zoe could hardly work, she wanted it so badly. Sometimes Penny would refuse to communicate all day; by the time they met, Zoe would be melting with need. The moment they had their hands on each other they'd snog fervidly in semi-public: department-store toilets, the stacks, once backstage after a lecture given by Penny's former supervisor. 'What if people see?' said Zoe, and Penny said: 'Who cares?' Or, occasionally, on the bedspread of Inge, who was in Perth; not complete sex, because Penny was trying still to be faithful, 'though,' she'd say, 'given the absence of penises, who's to say where fucking begins and heavy petting ends?'

Zoe was pretty sure that this did count as sex, although what did she know? But always, before more could happen, Penny would be dressing, sexily hailing a black cab, rushing home to mollify unreasonable, jealous, impossible Justine.

It was like drunkenness, trying to contain so much feeling. With Ali, the Old Girlfriend, Zoe had struggled with certain aspects: her *Hawaii-Five-O* pushed-up shirt-sleeves, all that folk-singer silver-and-turquoise jewellery. The hat. She'd tried to find the British Telecom hockey player's wash 'n' go haircut and warm-up gear alluring, and failed. Whereas with Penny, under Penny, Zoe would look at her slender wrist, or the soft stretch of her under-arm, and wonder if one could pass out with desire.

She hung around the English faculty library, shunning what Penny said was cynical populist crap by her rivals, bouffant old Ginny Buffery, Euan 'Always' Wright, simply to be near

Penny's own book. One day, her love-pangs unendurable because Penny had vetoed contact until the following Tuesday, she eased it off the shelf and discovered that no one had borrowed it in eight months. She took it out herself, then had to hide it under her packed lunch because Penny dropped by in leather trousers, biker-tight, distracting Zoe's colleagues. She was, Zoe had discovered, easily knocked off-kilter, more sensitive to perceived slights than others could guess. One had to be careful; more careful than Zoe was good at.

But the self-editing was worth it, for all the perfect and wonderful times. Penny's daring was thrilling. Other people's rules did not apply to her; they were inconveniences, easy to ignore. She'd send Zoe to the front of a queue, instruct her to book a table in the name of Aubergine Stamper. Zoe, Aubergine, would do anything to make her laugh.

But she couldn't get used to not caring about what strangers thought.

'I'll soon train you up,' said Penny. All the Brits, she said, were uptight, but Zoe took it too far. How could she, although such a fan of sex, still be shy about the toilet and changing rooms? She couldn't believe that Zoe had never owned a bikini, or shown her unfirm flesh to anyone she wasn't in bed with: barely even then. 'What a waste of that young body. My friends and I are always flashing each other, talking about everything: shit, sex, periods. I wish you could.'

It was so easy to ruin the little time they had with thoughtlessness, insults, a wound to Penny's pride. Zoe's joints would ache; it felt unendurable, not knowing what she'd done wrong. They'd make up after three days, four, five, whenever Penny would be in touch again, turn up at the Classics Faculty with flowers or ring in the middle of a grey day of self-castigation with instructions to meet in Notting Hill or Soho, by which point Zoe was a mess of need and fear. The sense of being set constant tests was bracing and, if the test seemed unpassable, that only increased the tenterhooks, the thrill.

She'd begun to miss Penny's world when she wasn't in it. It was so much more exciting than her own: a soap opera of estrangements and affairs and aspiration, terrible rows, ostracisms, and Zoe gobbled up the details.

'Hardly surprising,' Penny pointed out. 'All that arguing: fiery continentals.'

'How do you mean? I thought you were, you know. Irish, or Scottish?'

'Me?'

'But . . .' Penny had mentioned English prejudice against Australians' origins, which was heartbreaking, if you thought about it. Zoe would imagine one of Penny's forebears cruelly transported to Van Diemen's Land after the theft of a stale loaf, and tears would spring to her eyes. But it now seemed this was wrong and insulting. Look at her skin colour, her shoulders, demanded Penny. Couldn't Zoe tell she was more Italian or Spanish, even Greek?

She was right; she did look Olympian. Sometimes she called Zoe 'tiny one', 'my little Joey' and Zoe, who had previously been proud of her strength, couldn't hear it often enough, imagining herself small, in need of protection.

When she tried to extract more detail, Penny clammed up. She rarely talked about her parents, much preferred her step-father in Port Moronga, her 'whole tribe' of athletic step-cousins with names like Kyle. Zoe ached to think of her hidden sorrow, her poor, practically orphaned heart. Penny confided that she despised her mother, 'not much of one, at least to me,' but many months passed before she trusted Zoe enough to reveal the details of that particular tragedy: pills, miscarriages, a brief absconding to Narromine with a sales rep for cattle medication. The pain still wracked her; Zoe held her, promised to keep her safe. It was an honour to have been confessed to; frightening, too, to have this insight into Penny's fragility. She, too, might snap.

Penny's violent half-brothers, whom Penny called The Fools, 'try to take everything from me. I wish I'd had your childhood,' she'd tell Zoe, whose parents were still alive, still married, who had harmless and home-loving siblings. 'Your only problem was having to bring little Benjy and Clairey along too, if you popped off to the Ashmolean.'

'It wasn't exactly . . . I mean, we didn't go. That's the point, Mum st—'

'My poor little culturally rich girl. I'd have killed to have a book within three hundred kilometres. No wonder you're such a genius. So when,' she kept asking, 'do I get to meet the Stampers? What are you hiding? You realize they'll be thrilled with me, don't you?'

The longer Zoe stalled, the worse it became. She had told her she was from 'near Oxford' but, spiritually, Headington was more like Buckinghamshire: hair salons and Rotary-club-sponsored flower-beds, resentment, inertia. The bakery sold jam splits, which one could buy at lunch break; why would anybody ever leave? Even the scariest girls, hell-bent on Bacardi, or Snakebite's sophisticated sibling, Diesel, rarely went Up Oxford mid-week. On Saturday mornings, Zoe would accompany her mother into the city centre, then run, weaving through the tourists, gross, ridiculous, to Blackwell's for ten frenzied minutes. Then back, panting, to face whatever had upset her mother. Clenching the parking ticket between her teeth, Tricia would speed down the ramps out of the multi-storey; in absolute silence they'd arrive home via what she called the Ironically Named London Road, and the weekends never recovered.

Penny had no idea. She grew up on a sheep farm, near Mudgee, New South Wales: shimmering mountains, basalt and rainforest and pink granite. It was impossible to imagine exposing Zoe's parents. They had a small paved front yard with, depending on her mother's latest fixation, a lonely hydrangea or single yellow rose, always struggling, for which Zoe's father would be blamed.

'He's useless,' she'd say, in front of him. Once, Zoe came home after midnight and her six-foot-four father was out there in a head-torch, bleeding lightly from a secateur incident while he tried to prune a California lilac. 'I just,' he explained as Zoe applied plasters, 'want her to be happy.'

One evening, Penny took Zoe for dinner with a big-in-the-eighties film journalist: 'I'm going to show you off.' They passed a semi very like the Stampers': stained pebbledash and a row of concrete starburst-patterned decorative bricks. Zoe must have broken stride, because Penny, who'd been commenting on every front porch and driveway bird-bath, dressing-table mirrors pushed up against the double glazing, said: 'Look at that one. My God, I'd rather die.'

Zoe went quiet. At last, as they were climbing the oozing tarmac-coated steps to the front door, she forced herself to say: 'I know I'm being annoying about not taking you home. But I do need you to meet my dad, at least. Before he . . . well, dies.'

'Oh no. Is he ill?'

'Not yet.'

The next morning, Zoe took a train to Headington to bring her parents the joyous news: she was in love.

4

Now

There are unreliable narrators in real life, not only in fiction. It is amazing how few people realize this.

'Am I vile?' Zoe texted her friend Dawn last night.

'Not,' said Dawn. Which would have to do.

But what if Zoe is as delusional as Penny? So many of their acquaintances believe the version Penny's told them; she is very convincing. She even convinced Zoe.

Now she is categorically refusing to leave the flat. Everyone, she keeps saying, is appalled, sickened by Zoe's nastiness. 'You're not getting rid of me,' she announces, 'until you admit precisely where you'll be staying. And who else knows about this, this crime? Don't pretend you don't realize it is a criminal act, what you're insisting on doing, to us all.' She's beside herself, tearful, raging. Zoe feels like a prisoner being brought to court, police holding back crowds who have been waiting in the rain to hammer on the van. 'How will I explain this? You are tearing our children apart. You have to tell me where you're taking my baby girl, my own child. It's technically kidnapping, you do accept that?'

And clearly there is something wrong with Zoe, to have

such naivety, such tunnel vision. Only a fool would assume that hatred like Penny's has limits. How could Zoe have imagined that, because of the happiness she and Penny definitely have had, lots of it, all the good things about her, her intelligence, her common sense, Penny would come to accept the situation?

And what if she doesn't; if she refuses to leave? Today's timetable is so tight; there's no leeway.

Dawn will be here any minute. She needs to be warned.

Dawn is the only person who knows everything, almost. It was she who registered at the letting agents, using her own email address, in case Penny can access Zoe's inbox via the university intranet.

'I don't think she could.'

'Bless,' said Dawn.

Dawn, thrice married, had a bad childhood. She can handle almost everything; if not, she looks it up on forums. Even when Dawn was merely a friendly neighbour, Zoe had identified her as the person who'd hide them if needed; although, given the size of her flat, they'd be sharing with the foot-spa and true-crime collection and overflow clothes rail. When the kids were little, and they all loved each other, Dawn was the sole outsider authorized to collect them unannounced from primary school. 'Nobody else, ever,' Zoe would say, perhaps a little too often. 'No one's . . . dad, or a nice neighbour. Even if they say, you know, Mummy's ill, or Mama told me to, or w—'

'But Dawn's OK?'

'Always. You can trust Dawn.'

It was Dawn to whom Zoe first hinted about the troubles; who, more recently, said: 'tell me what you need me to do.' She went with Zoe to view the basement with a windowless second bedroom; the pretty maisonette above the swingers' spa; the artist's studio with the mildewed carpet; the new-build right on the canal ('I'm not letting my Matty catch that duck-shit disease'). And now, thanks to her brainwave, Zoe and Matilda, but definitely not Rose – don't think about it, don't torment yourself – are moving into the converted attic of Ozman, Dawn's second ex-father-in-law, on Goldhawk Road, right by the railway bridge and conveniently close to Tesco. Well, above it.

Absolutely not Rose.

Otherwise, it's perfect, particularly because for months a bed in someone's spare room seemed to be all they could manage, money-wise. Thanks to a small issue of non-compliance with building regs, it's cheap, and self-contained; she's lucky, although he keeps threatening to Airbnb it. Part-furnished, with a kitchenette; imagine not being followed from oven to fridge by Penny in her silk dressing-gown, berating. They'll still be close to Stag Street; a seventeen-minute speed-walk. And it's busable from the girls' schools, even Rose's, in the unlikely . . . never mind.

Zoe and Rose have not talked about What Happens Next. Zoe is too terrified of losing her to ask. She wants to live with her, as she wants limbs, or air. But it would kill Penny; no one can doubt that. And what if Rose doesn't want to come? She loves Penny, and Penny gave birth to her; it's arrogant to imagine she might want to be with Zoe more than with Penny.

Anyway, Penny has made it clear that spending even a single night in Zoe's new flat would be an unbearable betrayal.

Then again, Rose is such a people pleaser; she might feel obliged to come if Zoe asked. Although, if she wants to see both mothers often but, at least tonight, come with Zoe, she'll probably feel she can't because she'll know it has to be perfectly symmetrical. And Matty has made it clear that, as she's getting on so badly with Penny, she wants to be mainly with Zoe. Oh, Christ. Also, wouldn't asking Rose to choose be evidence of exactly the cruelty of which Penny accuses Zoe?

Zoe has not actually said to Rose 'please come'. Coward that she is, she's putting the onus on Rose.

There are no cheery moving-day checklists for when only half a family is leaving.

No one explains how to walk out on somebody who is ceaselessly present, who knows how you think and does not believe that you're going; who has forbidden you to go. In films, when ordinary people flee drug cartels or shadowy government departments, they instinctively know how to go off-grid, drive evasively, harvest condensation with a sou'wester and a conical flask. But even the basics of moving are sloshing around her skull like dirty water: mail direction, the rabbit's extortionate arthritis-drops, mixed-up laptop chargers, joint-account cards. There's surely too much for even a normally efficient person, and Zoe's already flustered by the thought of a new commute, let alone sorting out fixed tariffs, running a home by herself.

Penny has told everyone who will listen, which is most people, about the many other reasons Zoe is unfit to mother anyone, least of all alone. It's as if she's going through a spread sheet, ticking off recruits. She rang Zoe's aunt Lorna; wrote in fountain pen to Professor Hilary Mint; turned up at Dawn's where she was captured on CCTV by the security doorbell, insisting that she stop taking sides. She sent an emotional email to Zoe's parents, cc'd to her own solicitor, referring not only to their years of family intimacy, comforting Tricia when Clive had his knee op, Headington weekends, but also to 'the tax man', who might be interested in the source of Zoe's future rent money. As Penny knows perfectly well, because Zoe unhesitatingly told her, Clive is sometimes paid under-the-counter for archiving the manuscript collection of a rich and peculiar music producer with a Tudorbethan mansion outside Wantage.

Then Penny deployed her old friend Jo, much-mocked for her doormatty parenting style, her husband-surrendering and adult son-placating, her exercise-crazes: kettle-balls, spin. Jo lives in York, in a noisy small house. When she rang, Zoe, naively assuming that she was offering support, took Jo's questions at face value. Yet Jo kept probing about why Zoe would destroy a wonderful woman, tear apart a happy family home.

'It's much less straightforward,' Zoe tried to explain, but nothing seemed to penetrate; she had to lay it on thicker, make Jo understand. 'You know Penny, she honestly believes she shouldn't have to contain herself, that it's uptight *not* to sob and shout right outside the kids' rooms if that's what she . . .

needs. She told me, in front of Matilda, that I mustn't let Matty pack in her presence, because it was too upsetting for her. For Penny. So the secr—'

'She's very sensitive, under the surface,' countered Jo. 'After what happened with her parents, you have to cut her some slack. I'm sure she does for you. Look, you can tell me: why would you spontaneously decide . . . I mean, you were so good together. When we all went away, we used to hear you nattering and giggling in bed together at one, two a.m. It was lovely.'

'It was. Don't, I know. But this has been brewing for . . . It's been wrong for years, and getting wronger, and she's so sure it's my fault, and nothing seems to . . . OK. Did you know Phil, Philly? Rush? One of my best friends, we wrote . . . we worked together. But we used to be friends, all three of us. Anyway, we met, recently.'

'Does Penny know this?'

'No! God, please don't tell her. Anyway, Phil mentioned this holiday in Spain we all had together. A few years ago. I was meant to go to Texas to give a thing, not even important, or prestigious, at all, but Penny was completely furious. Thought I was intruding on her terrain, because it touched on women's writing, though about two millennia before and the opposite side of the world. Anyway, Phil said, in Spain Penny was obsessed. At night – I don't even remember it – apparently, she wanted to stay up late, complaining about me.'

'Well, maybe she was upset,' said Jo reasonably. 'I still don't see why you would want to leave. Are you not in love with her?'

Penny has asked this, often, as if the truth were something one could say to a person's face. With Jo, it was like narrating soup; Zoe could not grasp at the facts which would convince her. Never such love, and now there was nothing; could normal life, disappointment, really lead to that?

Of course not. It takes a breaking of trust, a fissure opening to let the salt water in, eating away at what seemed solid and true as stone. And Penny won't have wanted Jo, her old stalwart, to know what caused that first rupture. If Zoe explained, Jo would understand everything better, but then Penny would be more isolated, and that would make her madder.

That is what Zoe told herself. Or was it simply because Penny had insisted on silence?

'Besides,' Jo added, 'if Pen really has been unreasonable, why would the kids' dad be on her side?'

'Because she's so persuasive! Incredibly so; you know how articulate she is, how charming. She's got him believing that this, our split, will affect his time with the kids. Which, because he's more rigid than you can imagine about it, even now the kids are older, means I'm the enemy. Not both of us, the mums, which we secretly always were, I think, but only me.'

'Not really?'

'Yes, really! Did you hear that Rose tried to have a spontaneous half-term sleepover at a friend's, which she hardly ever does, she's so domestic, and he wheeled his electric bike into the friend's mum's kitchen and refused to leave, for hours, until he'd forced Rose to go home with him. Can you imagine how humiliating, for a fifteen-year-old . . . it's so stupid, because Rose loves him, both kids do, and definitely want to spend time with him. But by being so, I don't know, authoritarian, he's . . . Oh, and Penny says I'm also doing all this to get Matty to myself.'

'Aren't you?'

'Of course not!' It was deranging; Zoe wanted to climb into the phone, give Jo proof.

Penny always said that her interrupting and over-explaining made her impossible to listen to. She tried to lower her voice. 'He and Penny want to divide up the children's time like a pie, pies, and all I've done is refused to agree to it. For the kids' sake.'

This is true. She's sure of it. Almost completely sure. But she's under siege, no time for wavering, and then Jo tells her: 'But Penny says you've completely brainwashed Matty. That's why she wants to go with you.'

'Yes, it's definitely my evil sorcery, not because Penny's been acting like a . . . OK. Look. I don't know about Rose, no, I honestly don't, I can't . . . but Matty, at least, has been really clear that she wants one main home. An unshouty one.'

'Pen promised me she's always calm with them.'

'Wow. Well, you haven't seen . . . *I* promise you she . . . OK, well, the main issue is that it's not only me who says they need some . . . what's that word? Agency. Rose took herself off to this lovely GP, years ago, since long before this mess. He's an ex-psychologist, or current, and thinks the whole situation's so mad he gave her a standing appointment, every single week. And also she goes to an actual teenage outreach place in Barons Court, a sort of drop-in. Did you know that? She's meant to be this good trouble-free girl, winning tournaments, but that's not strictly true.'

'What can they talk about? She's always seemed such a cheerf—'

'That's the point! It's because she thinks she has to hide it; she's specifically said so. Christ, is that what Penny's claiming, still: that Rose is fine? Rose hates it when Penny goes off on one, always has, it makes her frantic. She tries to soothe her.'

'Hmm.'

'OK, well. Matty, you know how she mucks about, makes everyone laugh? Penny says it's to please *me*, but she enjoys it too, thinks it's funny, the naughtier Matty gets, tells her I'm much too strict. But on some weird level I've started to think that Matty's scared by it, that she can cause chaos and it's overlooked. She's not an idiot. Did you hear how bad it got?'

'I know school gave her detenti—'

'God, that's the least of it. Has Penny really not told you? She's quite proud of . . . OK, well. Things got serious, the Safer Schools officer wanting to escalate it, as in legally, which apparently is entirely my fault, and then when Matty finally got to see CAMHS, which yes, I wanted, to the others' outrage, but she was getting to the point where—'

'CAMHS?'

'Child and Adolescent Mental He—'

'Oh, yes,' Jo cuts in, as if Zoe's offering to show her a suppurating boil. 'Well, I doubt very much . . .'

'And *they*, eventually, understood parts of it, which was . . . unprecedented. But Matty so clearly knew what she needed, so they asked her directly, did she want to see her other parents? And Matty incredibly courageously said, "Yes, I really do, but from one place, not be passed around like a kitten". Those words. And CAMHS wrote us an official letter about it, earlier this year, all her issues, all the trouble she's been in, saying that it was essential that her needs and wishes were respected. And the others ignored it!'

'Well, I'm sure th—'

Even now, when explaining was clearly pointless, she kept hoping that a grain of sense might stick to Jo, be passed to Penny. 'The thing is . . . we've always given them no choice but to go along with our, the parents', division of time. Because at first it had to be that way. We thought that structure, consistency, mattered above all. But once they got older, we should have been open to adapting the schedule, if they needed . . .'

'It has to be fair. You can't j—'

'But how? That's the problem, it was never fair. On the kids, at least, and it hurt us, being apart from them, it was horrible. But how else were we . . . it's like we *started* from a position of divorce, forgetting that that's always shit for the kids. So now the others keep drawing up contracts, these nutty time-tables, for what they think they are entitled to. Which mean the kids having to alternate practically every night between me and Penny and him, plus extra weekend segments, so that it's fair on the grown-ups, in terms of hours. And even Matty, stubborn as she is, goes along with it at the time, because how can you say to a parent's face, "I love you but this is stupid and you're not even thinking of what we need"?'

'Well, if Matilda does agree . . .'

'No, because then she, Matilda, shows the plan to her friends or teachers who say: "hang on, they can't expect you to chop and change even more than you do already. It would be hell for you, never mind them." Although, until CAMHS, no one in the NHS, not a single professional we'd ever met, had even gently hinted that there were problems with the whole inflexible timetable thing. Or that maybe what the parents want shouldn't be the priority. So no wonder . . . all Matty wants is some understanding that what we agreed when the kids were foetuses, no, even before that, eggs, doesn't work when they're teenagers. And she's super independent, you know that; I haven't brainwashed her. No one could. It doesn't help how much they bully . . . are you still there?'

'Bully's a strong word.'

'But . . . well, when they're not screaming at me in person, they send these almighty emails, thousands and thousands of words a week.' She manages not to add that she'd counted: today's offering was longer than book VI of the *Odyssey*. 'About how the problem is actually me, because I won't communicate. Which means: I won't do what they tell me to. Sorry, I know I'm banging on, but I want you to understand.'

'Might Tilda be going along with your plans,' asks Jo, 'because she's suffering? Pen did say she's not herself.'

'Well, exactly! How could she be? Both of them hear such horrible mad accusations . . . But when I try to get bloody help for them, that's somehow proof of my own weird neurotic agenda, too. They claim I made Matty see the school counsellor, then magically convinced CAMHS to agree there was a problem, as if you can waltz into a scary NHS clinic and,

and force them to see your child. When in fact school was getting so frustrated with Matty, and I suppose worried, that *they* involved CAMHS. And thank God, seriously, because things have been much worse with her than Penny's clearly said. Look. You know Matty, she's so entirely her own little person, so uncuddly and indignant. So, if she's saying she wants to be with me primarily, for more than a third of her time, w—'

'Why does she?'

'Because she . . . she loves me.'

'She loves the others! She adores Penny. Didn't they use to watch box-sets together? And bake? They'd cuddle all the time, pretend to be a family of giraffes . . .'

'Wolves. They did. It was so sweet, I can hardly . . . Penny would take her on little outings.'

'It's natural to be jealous.'

'Me? God, I was the opposite. Relieved that Penny wouldn't feel left out. I'd push them together, do everything I could. But the last couple of years, since Matty's been rebelling, she and Penny fight constantly. Penny hates that she's not using her intelligence more, won't read Virgina Woolf, doesn't care about clothes . . . and meanwhile Matty and I still have all the stupid games and long chats we always had, and the angrier Penny gets, the more Matty wants to be with me i—'

'You're not saying,' asks Jo, shocked, 'that it's because you're her . . . you know. Surely that's never counted. Who was the . . . who gave birth to whom doesn't matter, that's the whole point.'

'Well maybe it's not totally meaningless. Who's the –

well . . .' Say it. Say it. 'The biological mother. It isn't a given that it matters, obviously, it can't be. But the problem is when it's totally denied. Anyway, the issue is that the kids *did* have phases of being closer to one of us, the mums, or missing us when they went to their dad's, but they weren't allowed to express it. Because of this weird Stalinist commune we imposed on both of them, where it was a taboo to need one parent more. The parents' bonding had to be totally equal, so how we divided up the care came before what a baby might need. Which no one outside ever dared point out. God, I wish they had.'

'But . . . but you agreed to it, the timetable. Before they were born.'

'Yes, but we didn't have a clue. And afterwards there was no space; it was un . . . unqueryable. The kids changed and we still put the parents' needs first. In all sorts of ways.' Her cowardice was too terrible to contemplate; even the thought of it made her want sleep, unconsciousness. She swallowed hard, sat up. 'And now they're bigger, why shouldn't they have a bit of independence? Let alone as there'll be three households. But when I said that it's a bit weird to expect even Rose, aged fifteen, to obey this rigid division of days and nights, everyone totally lost it.'

'Well . . .'

'It's true. I know I sound like I'm over-egging it, but I want you to understand. Has – has Penny told you she's hinted they might all . . . it's too awful to think about. All move to Australia? With the other adults too? She says they're "keen".'

Jo sighed. 'Anyway,' she said brightly. She was pulling up the drawbridge. 'Marriage can be complicated. And tiring! But, speaking as the child of a broken home, I'd do anything to protect my own kids' happiness. Is it really the end of the road? She adores you, she's always said so,' and stupid Zoe's stupid heart swelled at this too-late proof of love.

'The main thing,' Jo added, 'is thank God you're not taking Rose.'

There are three beds in the flat. Dawn has seen them: also a big shiny dining table and eight chairs, a microwave, definitely a toaster. No, a kettle. A Turkish satellite dish but probably no broadband, possibly no washing machine, definitely no garden for lazy Todly, who, with his late sister-wife Basil, Matilda had laboriously trained to be an outdoor rabbit. Ozman doesn't do emails. But Zoe can have Dawn's old telly and dead mother's plates; it'll be fine.

Dawn has been scrounging boxes from the offy and storing them in her Nissan Cube, which she's been parking round the corner on Terbridge Road. She's told work she has a dentist's appointment this morning. 'Worried she's not leaving,' Zoe starts texting, but Penny looks as if she might snatch the phone.

Even when they were all friends, Penny often accused Dawn of preferring Zoe. If Zoe and Dawn spontaneously had coffee, Penny reacted as if it was infidelity. Penny must never find out how much Dawn's helped her. 'I do not need that mentalist back on my doorstep, letting rip,' says Dawn.

Dawn knows how little Penny cares about public arguments, her view that it's her right to emote in front of anyone.

Letting off steam is fine and normal. In fact, the damaging bit was that Zoe tried to make her stop. 'You're lucky I care enough to stand up to you. Not everyone would. And to resist the sulking, Jesus.'

'I'm sorry. It's the bouncing back from arguments, you know I'm rubbish at it,' Zoe would say. 'It's hard.'

'Just because your parents never fight, you think it's a disaster. You'd better accept that this is what grown-up relationships look like.'

Soon Dawn will arrive with the boxes, but Penny is still here. 'I simply don't understand,' she's saying, 'none of us do, how you could throw this away. When we've had so much happiness. You'll never be loved like this again. You do realize that?'

THEN

February 1997

'I cannot believe,' said Penny, 'that your mum turned out to be my first real homophobe.'

It had been six weeks since Zoe had visited her parents; she'd even written a letter. Tricia was still refusing even to come to the phone. Zoe's father, saying goodbye on the doorstep, had said: 'You shouldn't have told us. For her sake.' And when Zoe asked: 'You mean, lived a completely wrong life, to please her?' he'd nodded. 'Yes. If that's what it takes.'

Zoe couldn't lose him too. Also, what if he died before realizing how wonderful Penny was? Her behaviour about Zoe's parents simply proved it: no one else was so irreverently insightful, able to lift Zoe from her despond and take her out, for fun.

Yet Zoe worried, although she was happier than she had ever imagined someone like her could be. Penny feared that Justine might turn up at work asking questions; she couldn't bear the idea of losing the flat, or of lies being spread, damaging her professionally, or among their many shared friends: 'there's so much overlap'. But passion like hers and Zoe's was hard to contain. They were already going to English faculty events and the theatre together, rushing back to Zoe's increasingly humiliating bedsit for an hour or two. The nervous excitement in Zoe's stomach whenever they met, the uncertainty about how to be even remotely good enough, made her pity everyone else on the planet, for not being so lucky in love.

And at least Zoe's father was still talking to her, although mostly to defend Zoe's mother. When he rang unexpectedly, she decided to be saintly. She would forgive him. Even Penny might, given time.

But Clive, unusually tetchy, was phoning to say that Tricia needed to borrow their daughter's flat.

'I don't understand. Has something happened? On top of, well, me?'

'She wants space, that's all.'

'But s—'

Clive swallowed. 'She says she isn't . . . Er. Precisely, leaving, er, us. Me.'

'God, Dad. I'm sure she isn't,' said Zoe, as if she couldn't hear the slow collapse of hierarchies, the rock of ages pulverized to dust. 'She needs you.'

'Hmm. Well, I'd be grateful.'

'Are you sure there's nothing else wrong? You're not ill, or . . . I still don't get it. But OK. So what are we talking? A whole week? More?'

'You'll find somewhere to stay,' he said doubtfully. 'But give me the address. And an extra key, in case there's a . . . problem. And let me know you're safe. I love you, love.'

The cheek, the gall . . . the opportunity. Later, Penny would say thank God for Zoe's mother, who'd pushed Zoe into her arms. Because, that evening, when Zoe was telling Penny, wondering which of her friends to stay with and how much rent to offer, she put down her wine-glass, took Zoe's hand.

'Actually. There's something I need to tell you.'

'What?' asked Zoe, although she could already guess: the worst.

'She knows.'

'What? Who? Mum?'

'Justine, you plonker.'

'Jesus.' Zoe thought about Justine almost as much as Penny; what she must tell their friends; how she had shrugged in the kitchen the night they met, with her slashed fish and that big kitchen knife. 'How?'

'No, it's good. I mean it, scary, but good. Wonderful, in fact. It was Call Minder. Come on, those electric beeps when someone else is waiting to get through on the phone. No?

Well, it seems that there were times at work, when she was trying to get through and I must have been on the phone to you. Apparently, I was ignoring the beeping. So she guessed that I was having an affair.'

As it turned out, Justine was quite unstable. Zoe kept expecting her to turn up at work, sharpening her carving knife. For a week, ten days, she barely heard from Penny. She couldn't remember what the point of life pre-Penny had been; besides, she'd seen their glorious future. How could she lose that?

Then Penny left her a note: '*Must meet at 12. P.*'

Zoe was meant to be seeing Professor Hilary Mint, her friend and mentor, to compare the Lemnian women of Apollonius Rhodius, the *Thebiad* and Valerius Flaccus; she'd been understandably excited. Hilary Mint knew how wildly happy Zoe was: no one could miss it. But Zoe had managed not to reveal Penny's name or department; not even her sex; Hilary, appalled, would be hard to bear.

Zoe had imagined bringing Penny to dinner in the Mints' covetable kitchen. What an idiot.

Were it not for Hilary Mint, Zoe would be spending her life on trains to Sheffield or Warwick, scrounging what scraps of teaching she could muster. But the fairly world-famous Prof. Mint, deciding her sixth book would be an Encyclopaedia of Classical Women, had invited Zoe, out of the blue, to help with a grant application, and so had saved her. Now Zoe was an official AHRC-funded research assistant, with part of a desk and a photocopier code.

Professor Mint would be waiting. In almost any circumstance, Zoe would fight or steal for her, would follow her anywhere, as a confused duckling waddles after a hen or a swan.

Yet Penny needed to see Zoe, if only to tell her it was over. Hilary Mint was a woman of the world, mother of four men and wife of one. She'd understand. Zoe shoved an incoherent excuse in her pigeonhole and ran to the English Faculty.

Penny gestured to close her office door. If Zoe could have split up with herself, she would have, thrown herself under the horses' hooves to end the uncertainty. But then Penny stood. She was smiling.

'She says she can accept it.'

'Sorry, what? I mean who?'

'Justine, you wally. She's obviously devastated, but she is being very adult, and says it's better than the alternative.'

'I'm lost. What alternative? Us breaking up? What can she accept?'

Penny touched Zoe's flat hair. Her lips, fuller than Zoe's, her hand, more elegant than Zoe's pink paw; all this, and the end of loneliness. Why would Justine give them up?

'You,' she said. 'My darling. I'm so excited, I couldn't wait.'

Would Zoe be snuggling between them in their bed: a delighted succubus? She was about to ask about practicalities when Penny added: 'She'll be fine in the spare room. Half her stuff's there anyway. I've said you're arriving on Saturday, first thing.'

5

Now

Penny is pretending that last night didn't happen.

It had been after midnight. The kids were upstairs in their rooms, busy chatting to paedophiles or having nightmares. Zoe was still trying to finish her secret packing-list: at least one of the annual primary school Polaroids at the London Aquarium; her grandfather's shoe-cleaning box; kitchen scales + weights. She kept crossing out things she really wanted; anything to avoid more fighting.

Dawn says it is pointless trying not to enrage Penny, not to poke the bear. 'You might as well give up. That bear's reversing onto everything she can find. Take whatever you can lift.'

But Dawn, as she says herself, is a fighter, not a lover. Besides, Penny has been absolutely clear, repeatedly and in many formats, including an actual letter on the kitchen table, that Zoe had to leave everything, or risk legal Armageddon. All week she'd been coming up with new, better, arrangements: proposing that Zoe and Matilda move in with Dawn, or with one of the old ladies in the next-door council-block, who mostly assume Penny and Zoe are sisters. Why else would women live together, unless lonely, peculiar, poor? Penny says they'd been asking if Zoe has got married or moved abroad. 'Wait till I tell them what you've done. They'll be devastated. You'd convinced them you were a decent person, but it was a lie, wasn't it.'

Then she suggested that they get the man in the basement of the block evicted. 'We'll take it in turns to live there with the kids. Like Bob Geldof. Why wouldn't Tilda prefer that?'

Because, Zoe wanted to explain, you've been being frothingly insane, but how could she say it? Instead she fudged and hedged and evaded, and Penny said she was obviously hiding something and was it a lover?

So: a quarter past midnight, half past. Zoe, dead on her feet, was in front of the plate-cupboard, trying to make a decision about bringing Rose's *Ammonites are People Too* latte mug. Then Penny came back in. She was holding the envelope in which their civil partnership documents, a pinch of browned rose-petals and an angel-hair tangle of party-streamer had been filed, between the Parental Responsibility Agreements and drafts II, III, V, V/i and VI of the co-parenting document. The envelope, sunshine-yellow, had been torn open, perhaps freshly; she tipped its contents solemnly onto the floor and Zoe was too exhausted to laugh.

'You will ruin their lives,' Penny prophesied. 'You must know that. Even if Matty goes with you, she'll hate you soon enough.' She sat at the kitchen table, began threatening court orders, expert witnesses, Child Protection, the wailing gaining ground. 'At least,' she said, 'there's no question of Rose leaving me. You'd better not have told her there's a bed for her. I'm warning you, don't you dare. And it's not as if you have rights. Parental Responsibility means nothing to a good judge.'

Even Zoe knew not to disagree. Instead, she began again to re-explain, to reason, as their chances of sleep receded. She was beginning to feel crazed; when at last she tried to go and brush her teeth, Penny ran over to the doorway and started to bang the side of her own head against the wall.

'What are you doing?'

Between bangs, Penny was screaming. 'I hate you, I hate you, I cannot be alone, I can't br—'

'Stop that!' Could she draw blood? 'Fuck. Stop it.' She grabbed Penny's shoulders, pulled her away; Penny was moaning, but she couldn't have given herself brain damage, could she? Without parting all that hair it was impossible to see bruising. Zoe thought: she is mad. In her least aggravating voice she said: 'Shh, shh. I know you're upset, I'm so sorry, sorry. But the kids mustn't, we need to protect them, we nee—'

'In the name of God,' yelled Penny, and a fleck of spit landed on Zoe's eyeball. 'Is that all you care about? What about me?'

THEN

Spring 1997

Everybody wants a wife.

'You are so lucky,' old friends and new acquaintances would say, looking wistful. 'Must be so much easier, being with a woman. God, I wish I was a lesbian. I might give it a go.'

According to Penny, they weren't talking about sex. If they ever actually got down, as it were, to it, in real life, hardly any of them would fancy women. What they envied was the absence of all that gendery crap about who does what.

And this, it turned out, wasn't straightforward. Sadly for domestic peace, Zoe was a slapdash bed-maker, a desultory folder of washing; she couldn't force herself to care enough about how things looked. This, Penny pointed out, was completely unfair. They split the bills but not the rent, not yet. It was embarrassing never having hired a locksmith before, or having dealt with drainage; she tried to share the burden, ineptly. And she cooked, which didn't count because she loved it, and Penny could happily live on tinned soup, white grapes, microwaveable moussaka, but at least it was something Zoe could offer, which delighted and impressed Penny. Who, if she ever gave up on cold hostile fun-hating England, as she occasionally threatened, would surely miss all this home-made food. Zoe bought a book of easy Australian baking, tried to impress with her dicing skills.

It was, Penny told people, hilarious that Zoe had turned up with a trousseau: country music CDs at which Penny would dramatically pretend to fall asleep; mismatched knives; miles of paperbacks; a teapot; a shoeboxful of very ordinary fossils. Together they cleared space on most of the bookshelves, a low drawer in Penny's bedroom. She was given clattery hangers and a wicker basket for under the bathroom sink, in which something jasmine-scented had spilt and soaked in, and it didn't matter that there was vaguely heart-shaped sea-glass with *P 4 J* scratched on it sitting on the window frame, or that she was using Justine's fresh-breath toothpaste. The bathroom was unnerving; the only lock was a wire loop, a little finger weakly curled round the door-frame. Penny said she was absurd, to worry about bumping into Justine at night.

And it was worth it, to be able to go to bed with Penelope Cartwright and wake up beside her. She could kiss her almost whenever she liked, unless she'd had dark chocolate, which Penny detested, or they were with other people and Penny thought she was being needy.

The greatest joy was evenings when it was only them, but Penny wasn't going to see her friends less, no way. 'They'll get used to you. They're being protective. And jealous, probably. Look at their relationships.' In bed she'd talk her through their backstories: who threw things at their ex; who once put their hand on Penny's breast when dancing; who thought they were femme, although none of them was as femmey as Penny. Zoe admitted that she'd once dreamt of owning a bicycle, a racer, with a slim boy-saddle, on which to ride like a lithe young man. She raised, cautiously, the possibility that women in shirts, slim trousers, could occasionally be sexy, too.

No way, said Penny. Fancying women in trouser-suits was unfeminist: even Linda Evangelista. She said the sexiest woman she'd ever met was her extremely feminine ex-girlfriend, Leonara ('two As') James, a famous musical-theatre star, who had lived in Penny's flat for four exhilarating years of mind-games and erotic disappointment.

'But it was definitely a relationship? I mean, wow, so she is genuinely gay-ish, despite all the husbands?'

'She said she adored me.'

'Of course she did. But . . . sex?'

'I am not going to betray her confidence,' Penny said sternly.

'Sorry. So, this . . . thing with Leonara, it was pre-Justine?'

'Of course, you loon. Long before: Leonara was born in 1941. Are you completely sure you haven't heard of her? Anyway, I don't exactly make a habit of this.'

'Of what?'

'You know,' said Penny, kissing Zoe's ear until she shivered.

After many weeks of preparation, Penny introduced Zoe to Leonara in a jangly businessmen's bar in Covent Garden. She looked celluloid, with long clacky nails, tonged hair piled up like a Hollywood Princess Anne and a waist cinched with a belt half a foot wide, as if holding in her intestines. Zoe didn't realize, Penny explained on the tube home, how lucky she was to have met Penny at very nearly twenty-five: to have been spared the hell of dating, wading through all those pissed old lesbos and babydykes, the curious straight girls, for herself.

'Are there really no sane other attractive ones?'

'Honestly not. You have to trust me. It's weird, though,' she added, turning her lovely sea-glass eyes on Zoe, 'that you don't actively enjoy being the youngest. I used to adore it, swanning around with Leonara, even old Suu and her hippy friends; the nubile maiden, being gorgeous.'

And where was Justine? Still officially in the spare room; Penny wouldn't discuss it, even when they found a rinsed glass, a folded note ('*P.*') beside the still-warm kettle, a breath of shampoo in the hallway. Was she really unhinged? Maddened with jealousy? If Zoe asked why she never seemed to be here, Penny would claim that Zoe was becoming fixated. Eventually, Zoe asked a different question. 'So, whose flat was this originally? Before it was yours together?'

'Justine's brother's. The biscuit prince. We – I – still rent it, from their mother.'

'Wow,' said Zoe, not understanding at all. 'Sorry, biscuits?'

'It was a bargain,' Penny went on. 'Nobody wanted to live around here. They were such snobs about the area, plus it being an ex-shop. But hello, it's in bloody Zone Two. Just up the road from High Street Ken. Sorry, Dubbo.'

'Who's Dubbo?'

'It's near Mudgee. Well, hour and a half. And we weren't even in Dubbo, to be absolutely honest. Bumfuck nowhere. Those hicks didn't know what had hit them, when I was born.'

It was a privilege, to have left the white plastic furniture in Holloway for this warm elegant nest, everything chosen, all antique, or at least old. The floor-length curtains, ancient ceramic ornaments and fireplace tiles, footstools embroidered with improbable castles, belonged to a world she'd barely dared to imagine. It was easy to visualize them in Hilary Mint's professorial house, although perhaps not all at once. The walls, painted dark green and terracotta, were thickly hung with bosky landscapes, noble profiles. Zoe had imagined them as the trappings of Penny's childhood; months passed before she realized she'd hardly have shipped them over from

Australia. They must be Justine's. When she told Penny this (she told her everything), Penny laughed at how little she'd thought it through.

Sometimes, despite the backdrop of Penny's music, the soaring scores of her favourite films or Serge and Charlotte Gainsbourg together on their big white bed, she heard thumps from the rooms downstairs, voices fuzzily disagreeing. They were in the bath together when she asked: 'So who does live in the other flat? Underneath us.'

'Robin.'

'Who's Robin?

'Oh, my little fool,' said Penny fondly. 'My child-bride; what a silly you are. You can't not know, surely? The brother. Justine's brother. The biscuit prince. Where on earth did you think she had gone?'

Now

9.34 a.m.

Penny is raging around the living room, reading the acknowledgements in *Dark Love: Ritual, Nourishment, Nurture in Fragmentary Greek Tragedy*. 'You can take this one to your love-nest. And this. Or home to Mummy Trish. I don't even care anymore.' When Zoe tries to convince her that there isn't a love-nest, Penny tells her: 'No one I've spoken to believes you.'

Zoe risks a text from the toilet: *Trying to get her out of flat.* Dawn, for all her kindness, has a short fuse.

When Zoe was quite young, her mother had to go to hospital for some sort of arthritis in her neck. One night she had been crying in her bedroom, while Zoe crouched in the hall wondering what to shout through the keyhole. The next morning Tricia wasn't there, or for weeks of breakfasts and dinners and weekends. Could it have been longer than a month? Her father's mother came to help with the babies, all the way from Wembley, and waited for Zoe inside the school gates every afternoon in a pleated olive-green hat, emitting wafts of the stultifying breath of the Old Country, perfume and garlic and fear. She would wait while Zoe ate a squashed cheese sandwich and two squares of Bournville cooking chocolate, then refold the silver foil into her worn Harrods shopper and take her to buy stamps for Zoe's get-well-soon poems. These were not mentioned when, at long last, needing quiet, her mother came home. Zoe's grandmother was sent back on the Oxford coach to Wembley with her blue cardboard suitcase, before breakfast. Everything that Zoe did set her mother's teeth on edge, even more than before.

Penny has theories. Once, during a very long weekend when they were staying, with the kids, in Tredgar Avenue, she told Zoe she was taking her on a Magical Mystery Tour which culminated, blindfolded, at the gates of the Warneford Hospital, which people who live in Headington don't talk about.

'Your mother,' said Zoe's father yesterday when he phoned her at work, 'thinks you're making a big mistake, sneaking off like this. You've always claimed to be married, she says.'

'You've told me. And, Dad, it's civil partnered, y—'

'I know, I was there, and we went beachcombing on the foreshore and I lost my Croc in the shingle. Remember? Anyway, Penny's spoken to her, and she's devastated. Your mother, I mean. Maybe give her a ring. Thank her for trying to broker peace. It would mean so much.'

When the kids arrive at Haddenham station, will Tricia even be out of bed? How long will they have to wait on the turning, the air sickly with hawthorn blossom as they watch other cars drive away? Either that or she'll be there early, will already be complaining about wasting her time.

Right now Zoe has to lure Penny away from the window before Dawn arrives with her piles of boxes, rings the bell and sweeps in like Aphrodite on a wave of fag smoke and fabric softener. Penny is strong, and women do sometimes manage to lift buses off prams, tractor axles from the crushed limbs of their menfolk. They can steel themselves to super-human feats.

Last night, Zoe did eventually persuade Penny that it was time to sleep. A few minutes later, she'd been struggling with the sofa-bed when there was a soft knock on the living-room door. What if it were Matty, even Rose? Penny's ear is always cocked for betrayal. The last thing the children need is for her to catch them whispering with Zoe: traitors with one foot in the rowing-boat, fleeing from, or to, safety. The knock came again. Then the door swung open.

There stood Penny, in her silk pyjamas. She smiled at Zoe, closed the door.

Was it possible that she was armed?

'Hi.' She smiled, wryly. 'I'm not going to ask if I can come in.' Zoe reorganized the sofa-bed cushions, not taking her eyes off her. 'So. Sorry about earlier,' she said carelessly, fiddling with Rose's Under-Twelves Women's Sabre trophy. Only a couple of hours before, Zoe had been trying to stop her caving her own temple in. 'Got a bit . . . overemotional.'

Her toenails, unprecedentedly, were unpainted. She caught Zoe looking and grinned, almost like normal. Zoe thought: how do I make her leave?

'Don't speak,' said Penny. 'Let's not talk. Talking ruins everything' and, removing her pyjama bottoms, she climbed up beside her into the sofa-bed.

6

Then

Summer 1997

Penny kept threatening to confront Zoe's mother. Every time her father rang, she pretended to grab the phone, for Zoe's sake.

'Just wondering how things, you know,' Clive would say, never asking for details, not even Penny's name, 'are.' He deserved to be uncomfortable. He was the one, Penny pointed out, who was married to Zoe's mother.

But it was unfair on Penny. 'Is she going to ring me herself, ever again?' Zoe would say, and her father would sigh into the mouthpiece, and ask her what she was reading, or tell her an anecdote from work, a famous poet found asleep in Slavonic Languages, and Zoe's crime could be, if not forgotten, then filed away.

'When I do have my chat with Tricia, Tiny Trish,' Penny said, 'I'm not going to mention that you've moved in. Don't you dare, either. People, specially if they know about Justine, will assume it's a sexual thing, a ménage à trois. I despise how, when people think of lesbians, we're either sexless dog-breeders, or titillating. Don't you hate it?'

'Yes,' said Zoe.

Sometimes she'd accidentally imagine Justine bursting in on them: what she might do, for better or worse. Zoe was trying not to find it unsettling that Justine had officially moved into her brother's flat downstairs. Then Penny explained that the Balders, senior, had bought the building as a wreck, had done it up and split it and let their two lucky children live in it, rent free. So why should Justine, who was quite fragile and very loyal, rent somewhere on the other side of London, far from the two people who knew her better than anyone in the world? She loved the area, loved Robin. 'You and I,' she'd murmur, kissing Zoe's neck until she dissolved, 'don't need to bother about pruney old Justine. We're together now.'

Justine's bedroom wasn't even below theirs. But the thought that she might hear them kept putting Penny off, or it was that Zoe had annoyed her, or the day had been depressing. Zoe needed clues. Penny wouldn't say how her sex-life had been with Justine, but it was probably perfect. Or with any of her previous girlfriends, of whom there were loads, so she must like it, in principle. Stress apparently could affect female libido; Zoe read this in one of Penny's books. Zoe was apparently much more tiring, more unattractively frisky, than anyone had told her before.

She was also disappointingly squeamish, at least compared to Penny's exes. There was a bronze of Leonara James's vulva in a Santa Fe gallery; apparently Penny's seventeenth-century tutor Lisa, still a friend, had been a big fan of threesomes. The German ex, Karolina, who had a husband and kids these days, was always begging Penny to stay, bedroom permutation unspecified. She was as proud of her own conquests as any hunter but, because she loved her so much, she found the subject of Zoe's few exes upsetting. Twice now, when she had panicked about her age, Zoe had tried to reassure her by explaining that Ali, who'd been so much older, was sexy too, in her quiet way, but it misfired.

She became insecure so easily, needlessly. 'At least she wasn't beautiful. Am I better-looking than, say, your mum?' she'd ask. 'Not that I remind you of her. Or do I? Uhoh, poor confused Zoe has a crush on Mum. No, it's funny.'

The previous month, Tricia and Clive had planned to come to London to see an old friend from their youth; 'terribly ill,' Tricia reported. 'Looks dreadful.' Then Radio Oxford mentioned rugby fans marauding through Twickenham, and the visit was postponed. Every time the urge welled up to bring Penny to Headington, Zoe remembered new obstacles. The front door was still wood-effect plastic, cleaned once a week, by Clive. The moment you were inside you had to remove your shoes and put on stolen aeroplane slippers, watched by Tricia, arms crossed, if she was up. And one room would always be enduring refurbishment: new beige carpet, fitted units, chair-covers.

'Why should I have to be ashamed?' she'd demand. 'Now my London friends can visit,' as if faded soft furnishings was all that was keeping them away.

They wouldn't be able to sit in the kitchen. There was always a fuss about having enough of the right-sized plates, or disturbance to the sacred order of the countertop: corn oil and lo-sodium salt in their own little dish; teapot-shaped teabag-saucer; unopened gift flask of balsamic vinegar; empty chrome fruit-bowl; pine mug-tree. Zoe imagined Penny's gaze upon the *London Landmarks By Night* calendar, pretending to admire the napkin rings, through which individual paper towels were slotted every morning, and knew she was not strong enough.

Taking them all out might be better, if Tricia could be persuaded to come, and stay to the end. Plus, there was the awkward question of money. Zoe's father would want to pay, but so would Penny. She seemed to have lots; Justine's mother, the biscuit heiress, charged her under market rent for Stag Street because, she explained, she still loved her.

'Who loves who . . . m?'

'Carolyn Balder loves me, obviously. Also, remember my other little flat.' As further proof that they'd be together for ever, Penny had confided something only a few of her close friends knew: she still owned a studio flat in Earl's Court from when she was first in London. 'While my mates were off getting pissed with backpackers in Chile, I was applying for a mortgage on a buy-to-let. Justine's mum doesn't know I have somewhere else, though, so shhh.'

Zoe's mum and dad would be embarrassingly impressed. Also, Zoe dreaded her father's game generosity. He'd be worrying about ordering extra new potatoes; her mother would scowl at every waiterly hesitation, or show off about having worked, fleetingly, in a Danish restaurant in Hampstead in the sixties. 'I was front of house, naturally.'

Zoe's parents met in a dance-hall. Tricia, dangerously pretty, barely five foot two and already illicitly engaged 'to a

Portuguese', was living at home, dreaming of a place at art college, shop-dressing or fabric design. But her father forbade it. His other daughter Lorna, Tricia's almost-as-pretty twin, freshly married, was already going around saying she should have pushed her new husband out of the train window on the evening of their honeymoon. What the famously lovely Tricia required, her father decided, was to be steadied.

So she was passed directly from his care to that of Zo's future father, a gentle Old Norse translator and antiquarian book semi-expert who, decades later, still couldn't believe his luck.

It was impossible to visualize Penny in a Headington restaurant: the Shotover, with its Signature Asian-style Chicken Risotto; Tolkien's Bar and Grill.

'If you're thinking,' Penny kept saying, 'that I'd be insensitive to their – their limitations, that's not fair. I'm excited. Anyway, they're probably nervous about meeting me. I'll be gentle with them, don't you worry. Sally's dad still invites me out to lunch. And won't your mum be relieved that, if you did have to ditch the ways of men for sexy older women, it wasn't for a great big diesel dyke? I bet that's her main problem, imagining you going at it with a plumber called Bernie. I won't frighten the horses; you've told her that?'

'I tried. She might be a bit funny about you, b—'

'Christ, not another stuck-up Brit assuming Australians are criminals. That's outrageous, some of us are soph—'

'God no. Not that. I meant, she's used to being the beautiful one.'

Penny smiled, took Zoe's hand, turned it over to inspect

the state of her gnawed thumb-sides. 'Hmm. I suppose she was a looker, wasn't she, Tricia? I've seen those photographs: sunnies, wedge espadrilles, all trim and pretty, barely up to your poor dad's chest. He had taste.'

'You can discuss foundation-sheerness-enhancer-serumizing-essence,' offered Zoe. 'Gorgeousness might bond you. Like species recognition. She does hate it, that I don't know how to Make an Effort.'

'You really don't, do you? God, the outfit you were wearing when I got you. Didn't you say she's obsessed with Dickens and Jones? I could bring her an item from there, even one of their carriers; that'll win her round. She'd better buck up her ideas, start being nicer to you. If she makes a single comment about your sacred brother, I'll smite her,' and Zoe glowed; she had an ally, a defender.

7

Now

Don't worry, says Dawn's text, *moved car now smking fag round Corner TIL YOU oops til you ring.*

Not offering to make Penny tea, or saying 'Are you OK?', not softening the blow, feels unnatural: seventeen and a half years of tenderness turned off like a tap. She has to leave, she wants to.

But Penny has stopped ranting.

'Don't you cave,' Dawn has warned her. She understands that, every time Penny is sweet, it's impossible to remember the fights, the compounded sadness which made Zoe think she needed to go. And hasn't she always, since she was a teenager, wanted a lifetime love? Penny knows so much; if she says they could still save something, mightn't she be right? There's been so much happiness; this flat was full of it.

She opens her mouth.

And at that moment, as if in a dream, Penny's phone begins to ring. She takes it into the bedroom, shuts the door, and Zoe is lost in another time, when there was nothing but pain: Rose a tiny child, Matty not even conceived, and Penny murmuring, behind closed doors.

*

It's over quickly. Penny rushes down the hall, pulling her smart new teal shawl-necked jacket from the hallway hook.. She buttons it, one, two, three, straightens the lapel, smoothes her scarf. 'They've arrived early. My friends care about me; they're so worried that they're collecting me right now. I'll see you at three, you have the address. I sent it to you; everyone knows that you're not reliable. And they all say it is disgusting, what you're doing to me. Well, I hope you're happy. Anyway, the second you realize you can't manage, you'll be back.'

Zoe is nodding, as if handing a mugger her purse, promising not to call 999. Last night, in the sofa-bed, she did try to be gentle, or at least unprovoking. She kept saying: 'I am sorry.' But Penny wouldn't go. Her breasts pressed against Zoe: nothing to do with love, or sex, but the flesh of a stranger. She talked and talked, the romantic weekends away together, family mealtimes, laughing with the kids on pedaloes and in local museums, until Zoe pretended to have a headache, then to be feeling sick. Penny was kind. She made a fuss about basins and Pepto-Bismol, fetched a damp cloth, reminded Zoe that she'd never find another love like this, that she had promised that this was forever, had given no warning, and then they were back to the threats of catastrophe, the insistence that everything Matilda thought she wanted was because of manipulation, or bribery, or . . .

But Penny's friends are waiting. At last, the flat door slams, rattling the bottles in the fridge; Zoe runs to the window, but the angle is wrong to see if she's gone left, up to Galton Gardens, or towards the little park, and Dawn.

Then

Summer 1997

Penny said it was completely normal, how often her exes came to stay.

She scorned them all, too self-obsessed, too vain, yet she kept in touch, to annoy them with her triumphs. Most of all, she despised the famous Suu, her first. Suu visited for a very long weekend in July. She was skinny, spry, bangled, in a khaki linen singlet and wide orange trousers gathered at the ankle, like, said Penny, hot air balloons. Her upper arms were profoundly tanned. Penny, who had taken extra care to arrange the flat, and herself, and Zoe, kept smirking at Suu's *Still I Rise* tattoo, Suu's dragged-down over-pierced earlobes. There was an edge to every sentence. She crossed and recrossed her legs in their ten deniers, dangling a suede high heel from her toe.

'Didn't you have bigger boobs,' she asked, 'before you went vegan?'

'Yis,' said Suu.

Zoe whispered, 'You can't j—'

Penny only shrugged. 'It's fine. We can say anything to each other. And stop interrupting me, it's incredibly rude.'

They sat up late all three nights, discussing other people. Zoe stayed awake as long as she could; usually Penny was sad if she went to bed before her but, this time, she barely noticed. At breakfast, Suu seemed to know everything about Zoe, her parents, her loss of virginity. Zoe looked to Penny for reassurance that some things were still undisclosed, but Penny's expression said: You're on your own.

On their last morning they all went out for breakfast with two of Penny's closest friends, Nicky-and-Steph, who had copied her by moving from Mudgee and set up their own cafe on Cromwell Road, Coast Coffee, where Penny and the Australian gang met for brunch most weekends. Nicky laughed at Zoe's accent and called her a 'dark-eyed exotic'; everything Steph said sounded like a telling-off. Zoe felt undercooked, unready. Hot and awkward in a wool dress Penny had convinced her to buy and a pair of falling-down hold-ups, she nudged Penny's lovely knee with her own. Penny moved her leg away.

They were in a patisserie near Turnham Green so Suu could catch the District then the Piccadilly Line to Heathrow. Nicky wore a tight fawn top which laced up over her spine, like a middle-aged wench. She definitely had a Maid Marian thing going on. She owned a floor-length waisted coat in forest hues, drank a hell of a lot, Penny said; she wasn't ageing well. Steph ('Stiff') with her long lank hair, long unsmiling face, was in her usual unflattering work suit; she looked as if gravity had oppressed her. Smiling Nicky, in full-charm mode, tugged her cuff-frills down. She was wearing the ring she'd apparently bought herself when she proposed to Steph; Steph kept turning her own hand, looking at her smaller version, as if she was trying to get the idea into her head. She was virtually mute. Was she depressed? Apparently, if they ever could get married, they'd invent a fusion name. Penny always said she seemed semi-captive, called Steph a prisoner in dykeland, guessed she felt guilty about the man she'd been engaged to, before Nicky came along.

'Soooo,' said Suu. She had an adult son, Spike, father undisclosed, who was teaching his dog to surf. 'C'mon. You girlies. When are you going to start making babies?'

Zoe stared. Time slowed. The table was scattered with curled croissant-feathers; she blotted one up with her fingertip, touched it to her tongue.

'Any minute now,' Penny said.

'Hang on,' Zoe whispered. Had Penny been telling other people? Zoe hadn't said a word, not a breath of it, to anyone. 'Sweetheart, please, let's n—'

'Don't be precious. We have a very frink relationship,' Suu informed her. 'Full disclosure. Transpirincy. There's nothing Pinny doesn't feel she can tell me.'

'But we were going to decide,' explained Zoe, glancing at Penny. 'Just us, weren't we?'

Penny sighed; it was a corkscrew, twisting fear into Zoe's chest. Was it this, her cowardice and caution, which would make Penny lose interest in her? There was so much about Zoe which exasperated her; even in their first little spats, she did not pull her punches. Her brothers, full and half, were bullies; she'd had to fight to win. Zoe needed to get used to it.

'Can this,' Penny said wearily, 'not now be one of your . . . things?'

On their second proper date, whispering on a park bench about how intensely they'd fallen, hard and wild and permanent, Penny had told Zoe that 'whatever happened', she needed kids. Luckily Zoe was already completely and totally besotted, so it was fine. And hadn't she always wanted children herself, unquestionably? Although admittedly she'd expected a husband too.

But wanting to have a family, together, had to remain completely secret, for now. People wouldn't understand how serious they were about each other so swiftly; they couldn't, Penny explained. It was rare to have found one's person, the love of one's life: to be so sure.

Even now that Zoe had moved in, their discussions had to be private. They needed to work out the practicalities between themselves, before letting other people weigh in with their assumptions. At night, in their duvet bower, they'd listen to the last punters leaving the lap-dancing club round the corner, under whose awning Zoe refused to walk on principle, and the always-empty Italian rattling down its money-laundering shutters for the night, and whisper plans, like words of love. Penny was so desperate to progress that she'd saved a doll's house for a future child, kept Sudocrem in her medicine kit, had already bought a Baby's First Year photo album. She was a pioneer; none of her late thirties, early forties friends had done this. The even older lot, the Gateways generation, were hard-drinking thesps in Housing Association flats, sleeping with each other's exes, or running Sober Yoga retreats in the Welsh borders. The only ones with kids had either been married to men long before, or suddenly claimed to have turned straight, although everyone knew it was because they didn't dare have children with another woman. You could always tell their hearts weren't in it.

Penny did confess that, before she and Zoe had met, she'd been so broody she'd considered a one-night stand with some man at a club. Which obviously, now, she wouldn't do. Unless Zoe was fine with it. But wasn't it enormously unfair that they couldn't make an omelette from their eggs; that a baby wouldn't manifest by sheer force of their love? 'I'd do anything to have a half-you. Imagine our genes, mingling. Your eyes, my hair. Or the other way around?'

Then she said how perfect it would be if their babies had the same father. 'Basically siblings. And you love your sweet giant daddy. Maybe it's wrong to deny our kids a lovely dad like that. If we can find one.'

'But I thought we wanted to be a little family? Just us?'

'We'd still be. The dad would have to be completely separate. But at least they'd know his name, maybe meet him once or twice; that's miles better than some anonymous faceless donor. You get that, surely?'

'What about someone . . . semi-detached? So they'd see him, say, a few times a year, but it could still mainly be us?'

'No way. Imagine knowing your dad didn't care enough to be more involved. "Oh yes, Daddy lives in Seattle, he doesn't mind hardly ever meeting you." Anyway, what if he started getting ideas, thinking he could come over all the time? You don't want him hanging around at ours, do you? Cluttering up the love-nest?' and she kissed her, and Zoe agreed.

When Zoe worried that her career was just beginning, Penny explained that hers was on the up, more demanding than ever, and she wasn't going to sacrifice being a mother to ambition, so why should Zoe have to? There was no right

time to have babies; everyone said so. Penny knew loads of
mothers at work, straight ones, and they all said it was the
best, the most worthwhile, thing they'd ever done. 'Imagine
us, a family. I can't think of anything I want more than babies
with you,' and Zoe thought of twin conkers in a shell.
'Anyway, we'd make him do his share. He'd better. Because
we're the mothers. Whatever he might think, whatever we
let him believe, we're in charge.'

Now

10.03 a.m.
Dawn is standing on the corner of Stag Street, alone. The
balm, the peace of seeing someone who wishes you well.

'Yeah, I know I'm meant to be giving up,' she observes,
stamping out a fag-end, patting her back pocket for her
hand-cream. 'But needs thingy when the devil whatever. Want
one?' she offers. 'Emergency?'

'Too jumpy. And sleepy.'

'Just stress. Like a baby monkey. She's got a nerve,' Dawn
says, pointing her chin towards the flat, 'loitering like that
when she knows you need to be packing.'

'Weird how knackered it makes me. I could curl up right
here, on the pavement. Apparently, you used to be allowed
proper sleeps in Senate House, you know, the university
library, but someone died. Now they wake you after forty

minutes, in case. I realize I've asked you this before, but is it strange that I keep thinking I must have made all this up? If it really was so bad, why didn't I notice sooner? That's what she says.'

'Course she does. Always was a bully. Remember? Even though she'd make it into a joke, or say it was for your own good, or the kids'. Like that time she was set on going camping with those nasty old friends, and you'd had flu, were still feeble, but she wouldn't let you stay in a B & B. Said Rose would be disappointed. Not that Rosie gave a toss. It was about what Madam wanted. Always. The control.'

'I suppose . . . Yes, you're right, I hadn't thought . . .'

'Yeah. Loads of things I'd have worried about if she'd been a bloke. Then I'd think, leave it, Dawn, maybe it's norm— Oh, shitting mother of God.'

Zoe follows her gaze to the second set of traffic lights on Brookville Gardens, where Penny, shoving her phone into her 8 per cent cashmere jacket pocket, is crossing back over the road, heading in their direction.

Zoe gapes; Dawn's eyes widen. Her stomach grips; this is the final hurdle, at which she falls. Penny can't have noticed them, or she'd be shouting. For a moment, maybe an hour, Zoe and Dawn stare at each other, until Dawn grabs her arm, pushes her further into the shadows.

8

Then

Summer 1997

The problem was that Penny hated gay men. For starters, she claimed, so many of them were misogynists; also, she refused to have her future baby be embarrassed in the playground. 'We're not going to be like that couple in the documentary, all cosy in Manchester with their camp Best Male Friend, matching buzz-cuts.'

But straight men weren't going to work either. She was friends with quite a few of those, all married to disappointingly boring women, or gay without knowing it: 'hadn't you spotted how many of the wives are beards? Some women will settle for anyone.' They had lunch with one couple in Clapham, but the wife had always been jealous about Penny; wives often were. Besides, straight couples were dangerous. Didn't Zoe realize that a wife could claim custody, if her husband had kids with lesbians? It did happen.

Zoe looked again through her address book. What about gentle William from HR, or clever Huw the trainee tapestry conservationist, whom she'd met on a library tour? For the sake of sperm, she agreed to ask them if they wanted babies: a baby with Penny, initially.

They said no.

Penny wasn't surprised. 'Men your age are basically foetuses. Your William's way too sure of himself for somebody so short. We can do better. And why did Huwww keep talking about "making art"? He basically does sewing; it's hardly the *Mona Lisa*. They should feel honoured we asked. Sod them. Well, not literally.'

She ordered a wonkily photocopied how-to guide from the San Francisco Free Woman 2 Woman's Collective, which, along with hand-drawn illustrations of healthful herbs, explained that insemination could be a very easy and completely organic process: no need for scans or dry ice or fertility drugs which gave you cancer, everyone knew that. She kept hearing of newly pregnant acquaintances, colleagues starting on IVF, and would be devastated. It was so easy for the hetties; why should she be deprived because she and Zoe were a couple?

'It's OK,' Zoe would say, smoothing the fair curls at her temples, kissing her narrow, neat nose, her absurdly perfect cupid's bow. A couple, she'd think. 'We'll have babies, definitely. Whatever it takes to make you happy.'

'You know that this matters more than anything.'

'Oh. Well. Yes, I do.' And, if she worried, she knew better than to admit it, give Penny any reason to doubt that she was the one to do this with. Only a truly selfish person could put their own needs before those of the person they loved; Penny made her want to perform feats of self-sacrifice and gallantry. And wasn't a shared happiness what she most wanted, a future she could rely on, unless she messed it up?

*

Thom, yes, Pershore was Penny's first male English friend; she'd been, she often explained, basically adopted by the Pershores, would have married his divorced dad if he'd been interested, even his boring sister who bred, no word of a lie, Great Danes. But in hindsight she could see that was naivety. Thom had not kept his looks, was one of those men who claimed to be straight but, well . . .

On a date in an exciting multi-level Notting Hill pan-Asian restaurant, with elaborate bland dim sum and women selling cigarettes, Penny, after her second Mai Tai, said lightly: 'in fact, he and I have been discussing how it might work.'

'Not seriously? I thought . . . didn't you say we weren't letting other people chime in, till we'd decided how to do it ourselves?'

'I mean,' said Penny, 'work with him.'

They had to pay quickly and continue the row outside, by the famous minicab stand run by the man in the bucket-hat. Penny, through tears, demanded to know how anyone could object to a lifelong friendship bearing fruit. If Zoe really cared, if she was the girl, woman, Penny had believed, oughtn't she to want whatever Penny wanted?

Zoe was in not the slightest doubt about having children. If, she reasoned with herself, they came a little sooner than she'd imagined, how could that matter?

So a plan was made.

Penny arranged for Zoe and Thom to meet in the Old Crown on Ceylon Street. The Old Crown haunted Penny's previous life: it was the place she'd met half her friends, celebrated her thirtieth, cleverly choreographed an encounter with her long-time crush, Leonara James, by chatting up her husband. It was where she'd first laid eyes on Justine.

This was one of the subjects Zoe hoped to raise with Thom Pershore, if they became friends: how might Justine feel if he, Penny and Zoe had a baby together? Zoe had been officially Penny's girlfriend for months; it was already August, almost the nine-month anniversary of the famous flute recital when they met. Also of when Zoe first encountered Justine. Her quiet was inexplicable, and very noisy. Was she plotting, cold with fury? Why would anyone give up Penny so easily, or allow herself to be given up?

Although, technically, there were still plenty of reasons for Penny and Justine to stay in touch. They'd been united by possessions: too-low nursing-chairs; a mahogany bed-frame like a twin coffin; an extensively-framed oil of an old hedgehoggy lady in a bonnet. Every time another fragile teacup or murky semi-aqueous landscape disappeared, Zoe would suspect Justine, and her overprotective brother, Robin Balder. 'Thom,' Penny said, 'never liked the Balders,' and Zoe's hopes rose.

Thom Pershore, possible father of their children, was easily recognizable. The poor man must have looked perfectly fine once; there were still photos of him on the fridge, beside Penny looking lovely by a river in plunging emerald taffeta. But now his hair had more height than depth, and he was wearing tinted glasses, like a suspect.

Penny had reminded her not to let him dodge the subject of babies. 'He's such an odd bloke, you'll need to winkle it out of him. Don't wuss out on me.' Only that morning she'd confessed that she'd bought Zoe a ring, genre unspecified, but hadn't felt she could hand it over because their future wasn't as secure as she hoped.

'What do you mean?' asked Zoe, feeling her heart tear.

'I just,' said Penny, 'want to be sure of you.'

Zoe would do it. If there were no actual flames to extinguish, no dragon to spear, she could still be a knight errant, bold for her waiting princess. This nervousness was simply because she was gauche, unsexily earnest. She definitely wanted Thom Pershore to agree.

He looked her up and down. 'Aha, our little Oxonian.'

Zoe stood at the bar on one leg, trying to appear experienced. She ordered herself a glass of red and he gestured at the barman to make it a bottle, kept topping her up. When she tried to clarify how far, in all respects, she had grown up from the university, he leaned back, smiled, tried to catch her out. 'But you did go there? But your father is connected to the Press, is he not? He is Gown?' He knew far more about the University, sic, than she did, although he hadn't bothered to go himself. 'Unlike my wife's brother, who went to the right kind of school. Of course if I had b—'

'Oh,' Zoe interrupted. 'Are you . . . married? To a-a woman?'

'Ha. Why? Didn't Penny say?'

'Maybe. Yes, I'm sure she did, yes. So. Actually, I wondered, h-how are you feeling, about, you know, being, having . . . with Penny and, um, me. Children?'

'Well.' He raised his eyebrows encouragingly at the barman. 'The interesting point is how would it . . . occur.'

'What do you mean, as in raising them? It?' If she came home without a definite commitment, would Penny even let her in? 'I know she'd absolutely love to do it, have a baby, with you. She's so excited that it'd be part of your fam—'

'No, no,' he said, smirking. 'The . . . act itself.'

Zoe prickled the remains of her fingernails into her palms, then her clumpy shoe-heel against her ankle, until the pain forced her to say: 'I don't think that was . . . what Penny had in mind.'

In her own mind was a picture, for some reason in fuzzy black and white like a tabloid shot, of Thom Pershore prone on her beloved. No, she thought. But she was not absolutely certain that Penny would feel the same.

9

Now

The boxes smell of family celebrations: apple juice, sharing bags of onion-bhaji flavoured potato snacks, iced party rings. Dawn has brought an optimistic number, is convinced that Zoe is underpacking.

'If it was a present, it's rightfully yours. Remembered duvet covers? The good kitchen scissors, they're not cheap. Did you give away your seed-packets? Gutting about your window-boxes,' she says kindly. Zoe presses her forehead to the window, gazes down at the yard, the stunted currant from the pound shop and lemon-pip saplings; spindly sage and sluggy kale and pale salad, wild-strawberry runners dangling like unkempt bikini-lines from recycling boxes, each carefully lined, to prevent chemical leaching, with equally toxic but vaguely food-related polythene bags. They are filled with compost carried, sack by sack on her shoulder like a porter, from the hardware shop on Edith Road. She has spent, increasingly, every possible moment out here, on what Penny calls her old-man hobby.

'You're sure there's nowhere to squish them, at the new place?'

'No chance,' says Dawn.

She became obsessed with medicinal herbs because of Rose's eczema, and the plant-lust has stuck. The love she lavished on every feeble seedling riled Penny; she couldn't believe the effort Zoe put into aerating the thyme with gravel lifted, pinch by pinch, from the paths of Brook Green, or the Polish Spirit clematis, in honour of her father, its roots insufficiently protected by three cobblestones stolen from outside the police station. And the unwell bay tree, and the tomato plant she'd found, bravely self-sown in a paving-crack by the Lyric. Penny referred to the yard as 'your boyfriend'.

To compensate for the growing-mania, seedlings raised on the bathroom window, pots ever encroaching, Zoe had bought her a beautiful bench, for the sunniest spot; the next year, a barbecue, with accessories. But every February she kept sowing seeds; until this year.

Penny noticed. Now the plants are her hostages.

'Not even my Greek widow geraniums?'

'Why'd you call them that?' asks Dawn.

'She calls them that. Bet you she never waters them. Or strangles them individually: little garrottes.'

'Forget it. What about the bike?'

'It's . . . she bought it for my birthday. And presents are, you know. Sensitive. Most of my stuff is from her, let's be honest. But sod it. It's heavy, an—'

'Why'd she have to choose one like a penny farthing? Christ's sake. Yep, you're leaving it. All right. The massive water-jug's definitely yours.'

'But it lives on the dresser, and she's said I can't take things whi—'

'The food processor, she never even cooks.'

'She'll say Rose'll need it.'

'Fine, fine. Leave it, for now. That stool, next to your bed? Tell me why you're not bringing one of her two sofas, again, or the armchair? You know what? Screw this shit, take the lot. You look ready to pass out.'

It's like when the kids were tiny, able to fall asleep mid-spoonful, and Zoe would want to do the same, anywhere flat enough: under plane-seats, on the kitchen floor. She longs for that blankness again, but a more dangerous kind: at the wheel, in the bath, under a lead-poisoned eiderdown. Her flesh feels insufficient, her marrow exposed. How had she imagined she could manage this? She might as well have decided to swim the Channel. She tries to explain that Penny will lose it about the kids' fridge-photos, or anything at all of Rose's; will treat taking one of the rugs like a declaration of war.

'How will she stop you? Force?'

But Dawn doesn't understand how exhausting it will be, fighting back. So instead, Zoe fills the boxes with pathetic items which might not be missed: half-full boxes of tampons; her old diaries; her father's clothes brush, as if he's already dead; Rose's MY FREINDS Reception-class scrapbook and her Isle of Wight Donkey Sanctuary 'I fell off my Pony!' badge; Matilda's signed copy of *Dorothy Hazelnut, Supermouse*, not read aloud for years but whose loathsome phrases still pop into her mind like Homeric epithets.

Dawn says: 'Tell me you're not bringing straw.'

'I've got to. Once they're Senior Rabbits, over six, they

need warmer bedding hay. Poor Todly. He's so ancient now; even with the ramp and the little rug he can't stagger up.'

'Feral, isn't he? Or was that the other one? The biter?'

'Don't. He had very specific needs. I know.'

'Why've you gone and left his biscuits behind, then? Don't tell me she's after joint custody of the shitting machine?'

'Yup. Apparently, she has to have a supply of the special food, for when Matty drags him back here, every third night.'

'Jesus. She's not still banging on about that? Poor wee Matty, it's sickening. No wonder she's avoiding her, with the madness and shouting, the horrible things she says. Then expects you all to snuggle up again like nothing's happened; that's a red flag, remember? On my forums. Plus, the way she treats you, like she's . . .'

'Don't,' Zoe says.

Dawn wants to help pack, or at least bleach, but there's no time to explain exactly which nostalgic DVDs to bring, which *Simpsons* flannel might comfort Mattie without being too missed by Rose. Rose, Dawn thinks, might come to Goldhawk Road soon, for a bit, or a night, but if she doesn't, it's not a disaster, not yet. She claims that, if Penny tries to stop Rose visiting, she, Dawn, will personally make sure it happens.

'I'm still pissed off about the sodding rabbit-biscuit container,' Dawn announces. 'Tell her to buy another. Way she's behaving, it's the least she can do. You could sue her, you know, for what she's saying to people,' and they exchange a look which says: money.

Penny tells everyone that Zoe is a thief, while still entirely refusing to discuss what they should do about the flat. She claimed her (old, posh, lesbian) solicitor was instructing her not to; Zoe's solicitor (newly qualified, engaged to a man) said 'bollocks to that', then apologized. It was, she explained, irrelevant if Penny had paid more for the Stag Street flat, when they finally bought it after Rose was born; contractually, it was equally theirs. Also, they are legally civil partnered. It must be shared.

All of this appals Dawn. She's witnessed many divorces, insists Zoe should push for more, take half of everything: the furniture, the rent from Penny's secret studio flat, her Australian savings and ISAs and bonds. 'All that mad stuff about having known Robin first, maintaining joint parts, my arse. She's always been a blagger. And secretly loaded. That estate agent she had round is a total shyster, oh how convenient, that your lovely flat's suddenly worth much less. And it'll only increase.'

Zoe's trying to stuff cookery books into a Bag for Life; Dawn rolls her eyes at a guide to European seaweed. Penny gave it to her with a loving inscription; leaving it will enrage her. Also, one day it might be all that stands between the children and malnutrition. When she starts to explain this, dithers about tearing out the page, Dawn simply says 'hush now', and hands her a tissue.

'By the way,' she adds, 'when you asked, the other day, if you should have got out earlier, years ago? Well, yes, signs were there, red flags flapping away all over the shop but, even when I got to know you, you were still quite good together, weren't you, babe? And with this type, there can be a sudden escalation.'

'Really?'

'Definitely. She was bad before, not exactly stable, but . . .'

'God. Wasn't she?'

'Oh my lovely, not really. Bit barking. But she was a laugh, and you had loads in common, and she functioned OK, with you soothing and protecting her, and telling her she was great.'

'I was the crutch.'

'You were.'

'I'm an idiot.'

'Well. No. You loved her. That's all,' says Dawn. 'Even though these days she dresses like a Tory, with her clacky heels and crocodile handbags and . . . OK, ostrich, whatever, but it's true. Problem is, someone like that, they rely on their partner or kid or whatever to prop them up. And when they have enough . . . kaboom.'

From her swim-bag she pulls a triple-pack of sandwiches ('Cheesy Feast from Marks's, keep your strength up'), slices a pre-refrigerated Snickers, takes off her Sellotape bangle and pats Zoe's head. 'There's a bag of sugarsnaps in there too. I know you like your vitamins. Sure you can finish the boxes in time?'

'Have to.'

'Don't let Des down.' Another of Dawn's network of exes and favours, Des, a local builder, is bringing 'the lads' round tonight to help move Zoe, Matilda, Todly and their boxes to the new flat, for beer money. Ladycabs won't take pets and Todly is Matilda's; Penny's never liked rabbits. Still, she's wept publicly about being parted from Todly, in front of Matilda, often. 'You-know-who'd better not be here when they turn up.'

'What if,' asks Zoe, 'I don't manage to go?'

'Course you will,' Dawn says, and Zoe, pulling herself together once again, explains that there's no chance of Penny bumping into the movers because, after the mediation, she's off to stay in Battersea. 'Thank God. Her friend's ex is visiting, apparently, but that's OK because "she's been very kind".'

'Can you imagine? Those witches. It'll be OK.'

But Dawn has said this for years, whenever there's been the sort of row that salts the earth, leaving Zoe flayed, all her faults exposed. When Penny, in front of half the neighbours at the Sacred Heart summer fête, said Zoe was essentially a child abuser because she'd told off Rose for coming home late; the night Zoe ended up sleeping at a Travelodge; the argument when Penny told the kids that Zoe was an unfit parent; each time, Dawn promised that it would all come right in the end.

On an autumn night a year and a half ago, Zoe confessed that there was a piece of the jigsaw she had failed to mention, from when she was first pregnant. Penny had made her swear never to tell anyone, including Dawn specifically. But it seemed important.

Tell me, she asked Dawn. Am I overreacting?

Dawn hasn't spoken to Penny since.

'You'll get through it,' she promises now, hand on the door, but she doesn't sound convinced. 'This mediator, he's got to make the others see it's not right, Matty waking up somewhere different every morning. And I know you're dreading it, but

Mediation isn't going to be as bad as Family Therapy. I swear. Why, what's the worst they can do?'

THEN

September 1997

Penny was outraged: Thom Pershore's nerve, to assume that she would ever have sex with him.

But she'd been counting on him. For a whole week, she was too devastated to teach. Zoe tried to comfort her but someone was always passing with a buggy, and she would start up again: 'I've never been pregnant. We don't even know if I can. This whole year that we've been together, my fertility's been plummeting. Everyone knows thirty-five is the turning-point. You've read that book. Maybe I should have shagged a man.'

One night Zoe, in desperation, suggested that Penny have sex with Thom Pershore after all.

'No,' said Penny. 'I wouldn't do that to you. Besides, even if I could grin and bear it, what kind of a father would that make him?'

Then, on the very day of her thirty-sixth birthday, a miracle took place.

The celebratory dinner had happened the previous evening: sixteen people in and outside Antipodea on King Street, rare steaks and Merlot in a mild September drizzle. Thom

Pershore was there ('I still love him,' Penny said reprovingly). Also present were various friends of Penny's, fellow émigrés from Sydney, Jo'burg, Auckland, whom Zoe only knew by repute, like celebrities: someone called Norma who married men but only slept with women, compulsively: 'a kind of Lesbithario. Aren't you glad I'm not like that?'; a rude geologist in a hat; Bridget and Chrissie, about whom Zoe had already heard so much. Penny was obsessed with why Scottish Chrissie, pale skinned, pale eyed, lovely to look upon, was still with 'Sister' Bridget, ex-nun and very senior clinical psychologist, in charge of Youth for South-East England: almost fifty, short-haired, stout. She and Chrissie had been together too long; Sister Bridget was the only person who didn't realize it.

Chrissie, famously, was bisexual. Penny always said bisexuality wasn't a real thing; that they were only doing it for attention or, in the case of Zoe's previous love of boys, mere ignorance of her true nature. But somehow Chrissie's made her more fascinating. She was an actor but wouldn't go to auditions, simply stayed inside their perfect Chiswick house practising calligraphy, expecting to be discovered before she was forty. 'Better hurry up,' Penny said. She thought that Chrissie, who usually wore wide-legged stiff linen trousers and smockish tops, was willing herself to be Japanese. She definitely looked like an actor. Everyone agreed that one day it would happen.

Penny was determined to shed the boring partners. They lost Sister Bridget and, accidentally, also Chrissie, with some fancy footwork off Brook Walk, where the pavement smelt of piss and old flowers. Bill and Jen persuaded Jen's daughter, Marnie, sixteen and very wild, to head home to their mad flat and relieve the babysitter, so they could go back with the others to Stag Street. They drank more, turned Celine Dion up even louder. Penny was always happier when her friends were around her, less tense. Very late, somebody called Beth arrived. After she had embraced and stroked everyone and left perfume on their clothes, told Penny she was a beauty and Zoe that she was a very odd child and opened a bottle of duty-free vodka from Jersey airport, she flopped on the sofa and, holding Penny's hand, began to describe a Conservative MP's wife she had had near Plymouth. If one saw Beth in passing, one would assume that she was a Conservative wife too, with those excellent legs, the collarless blouse with pearly buttons and pin tucks over the bosom.

As she grew drunker, her lids fluttering, her affection mounting, Zoe shrank back. It wasn't that she was sober herself, but she'd never seen either of her parents even tipsy. Older people, proper adults, ought to keep it together, she thought, tearing off more baguette to soak up the wine.

Beth was an illustrator; later, she told Zoe she had an interesting face. 'And you're lucky. Your nose isn't even that huge.'

Penny said that no sophisticated person could mind Beth's demonstrativeness. About the nose, she was simply trying to be sweet. And, yes, she did go on about Zoe's bloody youthfulness, but everyone else said Zoe seemed as if she was the older one.

'True. Given you're . . . you've lived longer than me,'

amended Zoe, for safety, 'it's amazing how young you look.'
She heaved herself out of the sofa's sag, pulled at her top.
Penny loved polo necks, tried to push Zoe into joining her;
Zoe resisted, as if this would give her dignity, but today she'd
agreed, and now she was perilously hot.

Later still, Bill, the token straight man, removed his T-shirt,
revealing a pale hairy belly. He and Penny did fake-snogging
and Jen joined in. There was dancing; Zoe joggled briefly
from foot to foot, mouthing the words, but Penny and Beth
kept trying to drag her up from the sofa to slow-dance with
them, pretending to smooch. She was entirely unable. Bill
came out of Penny and Zoe's bedroom topless, a black lacy
bra barely clinging on around his wide back. 'How do you
do them up?' he asked.

They explained he must be a 42 chest, minimum, whereas
– and how did they all know this? – Penny was 34D. Then
Jen took off her shirt, and Beth unveiled her own bra, over
which her small round breasts brimmed.

'Come on,' Penny said. 'Woman up,' but Zoe, trying hard
not to look at Beth, couldn't join in. She'd dropped a prawn
on her top; her German tights, bought at Penny's suggestion,
good quality but in a strange shade of rust, were too low at
the crotch and uncomfortably tight at her waist. Penny hated
it when she was prim and worky, had insisted that she release
her boring ponytail. She even claimed, surprisingly, that Zoe
had a waist. It should be flattering, when Penny said admiring
things about her body, the breasts which men and boys
noticed, or probably did, although Zoe always averted her
eyes to spare them all the embarrassment. Now, starting to

unbutton her own silk blouse, Penny pressed up against her in a winey lipstick kiss and said: 'Please? For me?'

Zoe saw how Penny loved them, these carousers piling in, practically groping each other, dancing so close they were touched with each other's sweat, and she understood that her own world had to be quickly shed, or she would never enter this one. She wanted Penny to want her. This was the price. Biting her lip, she unveiled her plump white terrible body.

10

Now

11.15 a.m.

There is a moment, before she leaves, the flat so quiet, when Zoe dares to think she might be getting away with it. There's no time to gaze about, poetically remembering; besides, arguments, old and fresh, have stained every Georgia O'Keefe postcard, the Ponies of the World dishcloth, a china cockatoo from their first Australian trip together, the children's violent crafts. But there is, too, no Penny.

For now. It's like a tic, this jumping at noises, glancing up at the door or over at the block opposite, as if she'd recognize the red laser-dot which means, in films, annihilation. The other way, if she looks out of the kitchen window or Matilda's ransacked-looking room at the back (Rose's too, but she can't face the display of fencing-tournament medals and certificates, the polished gem-stones, all sitting there as if nothing will change) it's the usual bins and England flags of Perry Place; no sign of neighbours with telescopes. Penny really has gone, and left her to it. They'll meet this afternoon and then, conceivably, Zoe will be free.

Then

September 1997

The next morning, the sunlight hurt, though less than Zoe pretended, and she and Penny had a miserable and fruitless row at Penny's birthday breakfast, pain au chocolats and hand-squeezed orange juice, because she had embarrassed Penny with all her protests about undressing.

'Although,' Penny said, 'you clearly were fine, in fact. Loving it, all that prancing about. Thom sent me his photos. You looked quite sexy.'

'The ph— oh.' Zoe had forgotten about the camera. She'd been busy trying not to remember how, very late, Penny insisted they have a bath together, receiving visitors while Zoe lumberingly crouched in the shallows and implored them not to turn on the light.

But Penny wanted her to look at the photos with her and so, to make up, she endured, squinting, as if lowered eyelashes would blot out the sight of her grossness, this shy pallid whale: even worse than she had imagined.

Penny came back from a long lunch with Beth and Inge slightly mollified, so Zoe managed to pretend she'd recovered, too. She gave her more presents: Penny's favourite crisps, Samboys, which she'd tracked down in Putney and meant to save for their first Christmas stocking, although Penny still hadn't said if she was going to Sydney in December; an almost-first edition of her favourite childhood book, *Snugglepot and Cuddlepie*. And a secondary bunch of flowers, in their bedroom. Penny was always so generous, bracelets and roses and eye-shadow, better shampoo, frilly blouses; Zoe had to raise her game. Also, there was a risk that, in person, Penny would guess she was still upset, leading to another row, accusations of being joyless. For Penny, everything should be fun; it wasn't her fault if Zoe chose to be insulted. Also, she was miserable that they had to go out somewhere rubbish, on her actual birthday evening: an unpostponable dinner with an old colleague. 'Sociolinguistics, snore. But her husband's hilarious. He and I used to have amazing dinners.'

They took a black cab to make it special. Penny made the driver stop so Zoe could buy their host lilies, but Zoe panicked, bought a weird posy of dahlias and ornamental brassicas instead. 'My poor love,' said Penny. 'You're not fit to be let out alone,' and it was true. Zoe, happy again, kissed her.

At dinner was Robin Balder.

Despite living at Stag Street, Zoe had rarely caught sight of him. Penny had warned her to give him and Justine a wide berth. 'Trust me. He's ripplingly repressed: that kind of aggressive pleasantness corporate bosses lap up. Makes about triple what I earn, doing the dirty work at that ridiculous men's magazine, never actually writing. Have we discussed the, quote, gathering he had at a bar in the City? Me, and loads of rock-climbers, literally crampon experts, on about their bucket-list bungee jumps and moisture-wicking running shorts. Though I did meet one colleague who saw through him. A woman, obviously. Said old Robin's a genius at meet-ings, making people agree to things without them noticing. No wonder he's endlessly being promoted. Imagine that being your special skill: Management. Though Justine adores him – too much, if you ask me. Did I tell you she used to call him the Black Prince?'

When their host introduced Zoe, Robin gave a perfectly convincing smile of welcome, and kept up the pleasantness all night. He was tall, solid, fair hair with a boyish skimpy fringe, wearing a Nehru-collared man-blouse in rough orange silk. 'The kind of garment your husband would wear in the shtetl,' Penny said later. 'Though in hessian.'

Extraordinary, that Justine's brother was simply sitting in front of them like a smug monk, being beheld. Zoe half expected Justine herself to be lurking in their hosts' kitchen, angrily filleting fish, even though Penny insisted that she was OK, considering. Justine only wanted her to be happy.

Everyone but Zoe was ostentatiously omnivorous, and at least a decade older; Robin was forty. There was much exclaiming about her youth, which she had to try to cut off before Penny was offended. She meant to keep quiet, to watch and learn, but relief at Penny's improved mood made her boisterous, over-relaxed. Robin, in his lightly posh-boy voice, kept trying to take charge, decide who sat where, educating their hostess on the difference between rock and sea-salt. Penny and Zoe caught each other's eye. No one mentioned that Penny used to be with Robin's sister; the humming cord connecting them seemed visible to no one but, humiliatingly, Zoe.

Robin was frank, or seemingly so, about his managerial 'winging it'; his amateur jazz-piano playing; his mother's considerable income from a successful Hampshire biscuit factory. He had an ex-wife ('troubled, I fear,') and a daughter fairly close by; when Zoe glanced at Penny, Penny shook her head, mouthed 'weird', and Zoe accidentally gave a little snort.

So, she asked Penny later, did that mean Penny had met her?

'In passing. He's the type who always pretends he's very kind to the wife, that he married her for charitable reasons because she's nuts, or drunk, probably both, but he's shoved her over in Bow, or is it Deptford, somewhere Ripperish anyway, in a tower block. Apparently, the daughter's troubled. But he's always been the golden boy, the Black Prince, so everything's forgiven.'

When he mentioned that his mother and father were 'pretty liberal', Zoe sat up, an excited hound.

'Seriously? So they didn't mind about, well, your sister?' Everyone else was bored of coming-out stories, but there was so much Zoe needed to ask. Had his parents been easier on him for being divorced than on Justine for lesbianness? Did it make it worse for them, or better, that Justine was pretty; the last person you'd imagine becoming gay?

Someone coughed. 'You can't say that!'

But Zoe and Penny often talked about this very issue. Practically all other lesbians really did wear what Zoe's mother claimed, pointing them out if ever one appeared on television: dungarees; rainbow glasses with dangly earrings, the very opposite of attractiveness. It was truly astonishing that a woman who looked like Penny could fancy other women. Zoe simply couldn't get over it.

'They've always been very kind,' said Robin, gleaming with conceit. Zoe, lost in the mystery of Penny, Penny and Justine, hauled her interest away from his sister and tried to care. 'It probably helped that I'd given them a grandchild: Natalie. My daughter.'

'Oh ah,' Zoe mumbled, as if she and Penny hadn't stayed up late discussing this very fact, and Penny shot a look which said: See? Black Prince.

It was when they moved into the big lamp-lit living room for lemon possets that he crossed his leg, revealing inches of bald shin, and added: 'Of course, I'd hoped for further children. Always meant to have three, at least. Luckily there's still plenty of time.'

11

Now

Dawn is right. Mediation really can't be as bad as Family Therapy.

Last year, Matilda was brought home during lunchbreak by a furious supermarket security-guard, who said he was sick of her bunking off school and hanging round his store, defacing the community notice board and trying to trick the toy vending machines. As a result, Gerard the school counsellor referred them all to a Family Therapy pilot scheme.

Robin convened a crisis meeting in Starbucks. He arrived with Justine, who obviously, he explained, needed to be present; 'the children live with us both'.

Everyone was still kissing everyone else hello, although Zoe had already raised the idea of separating. It was obvious, apparently, that Matilda, still a child, was going off the rails because of Zoe's unhealthy parenting: smothering her, trying to turn her into a replica of her tricky self. This was the proof. Perhaps Family Therapy would force her to see sense. Zoe agreed to try it, although it seemed shameful how much help they'd already had, so many counsellors unwisely trusted to fix them.

'One good thing,' said Penny, 'is we won't have to wait long. They'll be desperate to get their hands on a set-up like ours. Three lesbians and a straighty.'

'No question,' Robin agreed. 'Box-ticking, diversity.'

Penny frowned. 'Ridiculous, given that we're not exactly diverse. I mean, look at us. But good, great, if it means we jump the queue.'

Maybe Penny was right, and Matilda had picked up on the reek of betrayal. 'No wonder she's out of control,' Penny said. 'We all know you've groomed her, her whole life.'

Apparently, turning Matty into a little clone had always been Zoe's plan. The greaves and arrow-heads they'd made together, the divine powers they gave her axolotls, even her frog collection, were all youthful attempts to suck up to Zoe. As Matty advanced through primary school, she still wanted Zoe at bedtime, perching on the rockery of matted panda cubs and raccoons, promising her that leprosy was rare, and she couldn't suddenly forget how to breathe. Sometimes Zoe would close her eyes, just for a second, and fall asleep, wake to find Matty still chattering about wingèd foals, while downstairs Penny would be in a fury.

'Don't you think I might want time with her? Or an evening with my wife?'

Zoe and Matty grew better at rigging up diversion signs, covering their tracks; Zoe would claim that she couldn't stand another story about magic saddles, or that she dreaded taking her out to Teddington for wildly anticipated pony rides, and Matty would pretend she loved quite scary books, swimming, jigsaws, like Penny. But Penny always noticed.

Every hesitation proved that Zoe was making Matty in her image, as if, were she left to develop normally, she might have become the sort of girl Penny once was.

Although, confusingly, now that Rose was struggling, that was Zoe's fault, too.

'At least a professional will get sense into you. Nobody understands how you can claim you love them, when you're abandoning me, and poor, poor Rose, and ripping her sister away from her.'

The wait for Family Therapy was, as Penny predicted, short. At the bottom of the appointment letter to Penny and Zoe, it said 'cc. Robin and Justine Balder.'

'Maybe the therapists think they're married?' asked Zoe.

Penny was not amused. 'And before you make a fuss,' she told her, 'of course Justine's coming. Just because you have a-a thing about her . . . she's as much their parent as bloody Robin, that's for sure. Did most of the childcare. He's luckier than he realizes, as usual.'

Zoe tried not to sound as if she was pleading. 'But won't they, the Unit, think it's weird? She's their – you know, aunt. Maybe it's better if we can talk a—'

'At least she's related to both of them, Robin would say. If we're going to raise genetics, what's to stop him challenging *our* rights? Jesus, you'd better not start that.'

They were sent to a mostly empty Victorian maternity hospital near the river, beside a chemist's specializing in weight loss. It was led by Nadia, a lead care-team co-ordinator, who claimed to have had 'training' and who . . . paused thoughtfully at . . .

irregular points in each . . . sentence, plus Lennie, who dressed wholly in brown – suit, shirt, tie, socks, shoes – but there were also Riccarda and Zofiya and Tariq and Sorrel, who emerged in various combinations for Reflecting, from an anteroom separated by, confusingly, reflective one-way glass.

In pairs the therapists, qualified and student, would enter the main room as if onto a stage, to sit on whatever folding chairs and foot-stools they had scrounged from other areas and discuss, in a carefully positive way, what they had thought, noticed, were curious about, during the previous forty minutes of uncontained raging and accusations and claims about Zoe's mental health, as Matilda's parents, including Justine, sat there listening, fiddling with their water cups, keeping watch for anything which could possibly count as a vote for, or against, them.

This wasn't even the worst, or the stupidest, part.

By the end of the fourth session, Nadia had begun to look pained, despite her formal expressions of gratitude for coming, for Sharing, and her unrecognizably optimistic summary of their previous conversations. She had instituted the holding of a particoloured juggling ball by whoever was speaking, to prevent interruptions, but this meant that no venomous claim, no waste of time, could be stopped before it had run its course. Penny sobbed, face pressed in her hands; ranted about Zoe's destructiveness; scribbled notes like a furious court recorder. What possible reason did Zoe have, *think* she had, to put a car-bomb under their extremely good, in the circum-stances, relationship? Was she hooked on her hay fever medication? Hoping for financial gain? Under the influence of their GP? Was she trying to keep Matilda all to herself, to punish Penny for some unknown crime? Her friends thought that she was a saint to put up with Zoe.

Everything Robin said was praised by Nadia. Once, nauseatingly, he complimented her natty red blazer. She couldn't, in fairness, be blamed for not knowing about his furious group emails, that very morning's deposit threatening Zoe with social services, again, unless she both a) abided by the agreed division of the children's time and b) explained her hysterical and disgusting behaviour 'in a civilized setting'. In person, he could pass as moderate. He gave long reasonable-sounding speeches about the importance of close communication within 'the family', explained about trying to exemplify a new, more open, fatherhood paradigm.

'I think we can all agree,' agreed Nadia, 'that being . . . a role model, or an ally,' and she nodded meaningfully at Robin, 'for the gay community is important . . . work.'

Robin looked deeply moved. 'Thank you. *Thank you*,' he murmured. 'But . . . well, let's just say I've suffered much loss, and this, this betrayal, is worse than anything I've ever experienced. Like a-a terminal diagnosis.'

While he gathered himself, Penny squeezing his arm, Nadia passing him the two-ply tissues, Justine explained calmly that she'd entered into this arrangement believing that they were creating something great, but otherwise was more than willing to defer to Robin. Zoe waited for Nadia, or Lennie, to ask what the kids wanted, even to question how well their set-up had worked until now. Robin implied, as always, that the kids were at his half the time; Zoe bit her lip. As the clock ground towards the hour, he praised himself for how relaxed he'd been as a father, claiming he'd have been delighted for the kids to phone the mums on his weekends, and Penny, Judas, nodded.

'But . . . but,' Zoe began, 'that's not true. They were really happy with him, definitely, loved the trips, the, the barbecues, but never ever seeing us when they were with him was hard. Having two households from the start, with tensions. I know it was.'

'Ha!' said Penny. 'She throws out these accusations, without a grain of fact. No one understands why she's hell bent on this oppressive—'

'But it is true.'

'No it's not,' said Justine.

And Nadia said, with relief: 'Well. We . . . are very sadly out of time. For our . . . next session, we will try something different. Yes? I'd like to invite your children to join . . . us.'

Is this, Zoe texted Dawn later, *what fam therp is meant to be like? Feel like trapped in room w 3 dominating husbs + 'the team' are dlighted to have them there.*

In right sitch is v helpful but Unfort, Dawn texted back, *in wrong hands it can = pile o shite.*

'Well, I'm not coming,' said Rose, standing nervously on her tiptoes, when they asked her. When she was a little girl, she'd be sick with fear before speaking in public, even Show and Tell; Penny said it was Zoe's fault, for fussing over her.

'I will,' declared Matilda.

Penny, staring at Zoe, said: 'Good girl. As long as you can talk without constraint, or control, not try to please . . . somebody. You can say anything at all, and we won't be upset.'

Over the past year, every time Zoe yielded to the pressure from Penny and Robin to discuss a timetable 'acceptable to all parents' for where their children would stay nightly, they'd maintain that Matty and Rose couldn't possibly know their own minds. Matilda least of all: poor child, how grotesquely Zoe must have manipulated her if she could even suggest she preferred to be with her, primarily. It would be overturning a lifetime of fair division of time; why would their children want that?

But this session, the fifth, had to be different. They would all hear Matty's wishes, from her lips. What a relief: afterwards, surely the other parents would have to accept what she was saying. Nadia was a trained mental health practitioner; she'd make them listen.

'Though,' Zoe told Dawn, 'I can't begin to say how much I dread it. For Matty and, frankly, me. It's amazing, the stuff Nadia lets the others come out with. She must see that I'm shaking? Surely, if I were a straight woman, with an enraged husband who behaved like that, twisting everything, calling me grotesque and monstrous, let alone three of them, she wouldn't tell me I had to sit in a confined space every week and be yelled at?'

'You'd be surprised,' said Dawn.

'But I can hardly speak; as in, hardly get a chance, but also my voice wobbles. Even The Team must notice.'

'It's abuse,' Dawn had told her. 'Pure and simple. Though I reckon that, when it comes to the gays, professionals are even blinder than usual. Being all PC is fine, "community" this and that, but it's stupid to think that gayness, whatever, makes people any more decent, better parents or partners, than straights. But in the NHS you can't say so; I reckon they were too terrified, or impressed, even to think of the kids' attachment, ever to say "stop wanging on about *your* bonding, *your* rights; what do the kids need?" Plus, you go and say stuff like "confined space", all wear nice clothes, are polite to the staff, and they think: "Well, they're middle-class so it can't be that bad."'

Back at Family Therapy, Lennie, stepping theatrically aside as they filed past, led them into an unfamiliar room, as if bringing a child required different conditions. Against the wall stood a pink-and-white plastic stable filled with scribbled-on wooden doll-furniture. On a foot-high table, coloured pencils lay in a brown-paper-wrapped shoebox, as though dropped out of the past. A leak from the heating unit dripped onto a sponge in a bowl like a pathologist's specimen: thk, thk, ching. Matty tried to sit beside Zoe.

'I hope you noticed that,' Penny told Nadia, leading Matilda towards the furthest chair. 'She's completely under her spell.'

Robin had brought all the versions of the timetables, a crazed disciple waving the gospel. 'You see,' he explained reasonably, but with an audible tremble of rage, 'we have tried to draft something fair to all. It's appalling she wrote "biological"; that's a word we never use.'

'Absolutely not,' agreed Justine. 'We have never given anyone's wishes precedence. The idea that she should take Matilda, when the very idea of biological preference is, is . . .' Her face puckered with disgust. 'Beyond anathema.'

'There's nothing beyond anathema,' noted Robin. 'Is there.'

Zoe couldn't leave it. She said: 'I wrote that as shorthand! All the initials, the "Rs", were getting mixed up! You know that. Penny was getting so, so distressed about the idea of Rose not staying with her, so we were trying to work out a way for some kind of realistic . . . a way to take into acc—'

'No,' stated Robin: judge and juror. 'No parent should be denied the right to see their children, just because one of their number h—'

'Has decided unilaterally to stamp on everything we have built together,' said Penny.

'The kids love us absolutely equally,' insisted Justine.

'Absolutely,' Penny agreed.

Nadia was nodding understandingly; Lennie gazed thoughtfully at his brown shoe. Were they really going to reach the end of the sessions and not even fleetingly question how beautifully this system had worked until now, if people were honest; why parental equality always came first?

'But,' began Zoe, 'what if th—'

'If I might just clarify,' said Robin, and he spent the next vital chunk of minutes talking the team closely through the 'very reasonable' organization of their children's days and nights, plus how the recent conflict had made him feel.

Whenever Zoe tried to break in and say, 'Matty's here, shouldn't we ask her what she wants?' Nadia pointed to the juggling ball in Robin's hand. Matty started to line up coloured pencils in order of – what? Length? Sharpness? By this stage, Penny was wailing, virtually ululating, while insisting that she'd always kept a lid on her sorrow and trauma, would never cry in front of the kids. Robin was explaining, again, that Rose, 'my daughter', must not be forced to spend any time with Zoe.

'She's intensely distressed by this, isn't she, Robin?' added Penny.

'Deeply. She's always been a good student, an all-rounder, but now she's almost too conscientious. And Matilda, well, we're all aware of how her behaviour's degenerated recently, to the point where actual truancy . . . which was probably a misunderstanding, but I still b—'

Matty was craning forward in her chair, silently signalling a plea to Zoe who, even here, had to steel herself to meet her eyes, not pretend not to have noticed. At last Zoe gave a minimal nod, opened her mouth, and Penny gasped.

'See?' She pointed; everyone looked. 'See how she controls her?'

'So Rose is . . . willing to do whatever is agreed by the . . . family?' asked Nadia.

'Yes. Of course. Of course she is.'

At eighteen minutes to, Nadia said, 'It's . . . important we make space . . . for Reflection. But first I'd like . . . to ask . . . Matilda if—'

'She can't talk in front of her,' said Penny. 'Not freely. If you knew the brainwashing, th—'

'I can,' said Matty.

Nadia, slowly, instructed the parents to follow Tariq, and a new woman with a sarcastic smile, into the anteroom. Crammed together, eyes inches from the glass, they observed Matty being asked by Lennie and Sorrel about her feelings. She was wearing, as usual, shorts; Zoe focused on her impressively bruised – leukaemia? – knees as she insisted she knew exactly what she wanted, and all she needed was to be listened to.

'I can't bear it,' said Penny, beginning to cry again in coughing gasps.

Tariq knocked on the glass to signal that they wanted to come back in. The adults were asked for their feelings about Matilda's comments, but Matty herself was told not to add anything, like a child actor relegated to her trailer. Robin's foot jiggled.

'You love all your . . . family very much, don't you,' noted Nadia.

'Obviously,' Matty said, but politely, like a child being asked a simple historical fact. 'They're my parents, and Justine. I really love them. But I don't get why what I want isn't taken seriously. I know my own mind; I'm not a baby in a pram, to send wherever. However much I want to see them,' she explained steadily to Nadia, 'I can't share myself out equally if there are only seven days in a week. I mean, we never could, but now it definitely isn't possible. Maths.'

'Ohhhh,' wailed Penny.

'Twelve,' she added quickly, 'is old enough to know my mind. Not to be sliced up into thirds like a-a bagel,' and she shot a look at Zoe, who suppressed a smile. 'It's not like I've ever refused to go to Dad's, I love him, spending time there. Course I do. But if there are going to be three separate households I can't . . .' She glanced at Zoe. 'I want to spend time with them all, but it's not possible to have three equal homes. It's just not. And so somewhere has to be my base, which I want to be with Mum, Zoe, and then I can see everyone, but it's not realistic like this. Or fair. On me. Or Rose even. It's not what we want.'

The room hesitated. Then Robin began: 'As a matter of fact, our family is actu—'

'It's excellent, really . . . positive,' said Nadia, 'that this . . . *family*, thank you, Robin, beautiful, has built such . . . a safe space for the children. Where all can have their needs . . . met.'

'But surely the kids' happiness is important, more so than ours?' said Zoe quickly. 'We're all desperate for bonding, closeness with them, but it's not up to the kids to provide . . . Matty is really responsible, everyone knows that. She will spend time with us all, look, she's nodding, if, if people can be – be calm, and a bit less rigid . . .'

'Did you spot,' Penny was saying to Nadia, 'how poor Matilda has to glance at her for reassurance? She doesn't even know what she wants.'

'No, I do,' said Matilda, but by that point Tariq and Lennie were coming back in for Reflection, and after they had discussed how they felt about what they had observed, their time was up.

12

Autumn 1997

Everything had to happen quickly, for Penny's ovaries' sake.

Never mind that they sort of hated Robin Balder, his rock-solid self-satisfaction, the preciousness about his public image. And yes, he dominated his sister. But Penny's fertility window was closing; anyway, she was excellent at handling men.

Penny wasn't worried. She held all the cards. He was desperate to have more babies, and could hardly do that alone. 'Did you notice how he casually mentioned he "might" get a surrogate . . . hello, it's not legal in this country, you idiot.'

The first step, she explained, would have to be HIV tests. Not for them: 'I know you're practically a virgin, and I'm fine.' But he was bound to have several women on the go. Justine believed he was still looking for someone worthy of him, but she was very trusting.

'Tell me again,' asked Zoe, 'why you didn't do this when you were with Justine? Getting pregnant by your girlfriend's brother; people do do that. Remember we heard about Gil—'

But Penny would only say that Justine would never commit to having children, or that Robin had still been with his daughter's mother, hadn't wanted kids until the last couple of years. 'Clock ticking. Even applies to men, apparently.'

In her fearful moments, Zoe clutched a version of this to herself. Penny had loved elegant experienced Justine, but she only wanted to produce a family with Zoe. Besides, Justine was now with Jayne Shaunessy, who worked in finance ('though at least it's for the BBC'), who wore synthetic suiting, sailed. Jayne was, Penny said, a practical choice, like a freezer. They never went out as a four; if anything, Justine and Penny seemed to spend more evenings together, laughing about Jayne's nautical friends. Sometimes Zoe would try to think of reasons for Penny not to meet Justine, which Penny saw right through; she said it was insulting, but the fear that there was unfinished business would not go away.

And now they had to have pretend-relaxed dinners with Robin as well, even endured an unfunny panto directed by his colleague, then cocktails with his current girlfriend, Very Young Aisling, on Chiswick High Road. Penny tried to make Zoe sway with her between the tables, ended up sexy-dancing with Aisling with her skirt tucked into her waistband.

'How long have you been going out?' Zoe asked Aisling directly. Robin had been noticeably vague. Penny had said it was clearly a fling, but it turned out that Robin and Very Young Aisling were longer-standing than even Zoe and Penny. Zoe tried to establish what Aisling felt about the reason they were all meeting; Aisling looked delighted, but Robin said: 'enough of that'.

Afterwards Penny led Zoe round the corner to a dimly lit bar, and put her hand inside her bra. 'Justine and I were over even before we began,' she said, which seemed, through the raspberry daiquiris, very wise.

The only time they weren't discussing the Black Prince was when they were with him. It turned out that Penny knew the Balders well, from when she was first with Justine. She had been away with them in five countries, if you count Scotland. Zoe learned all about Robin and Justine's strange crooked childhood: the well-connected cultured parents and their lovers; the uncle who'd married a Senegalese woman and was never mentioned; the minor-boarding-school travails. Even before meeting Robin, Zoe had been drawn into this rich seam in Penny's soap-opera, helping to identify the harbingers of his family's decline, the synthesis of nature and nurture which had produced their fatal flaws. She could list them: an inability to commit, self-obsession, dry skin to the point of scrofulousness, thin lips, secrecy.

Yet, now that they might be relevant, these genetic trip-wires did not put Penny off; if anything, they made Robin more compelling. She couldn't get over how he treated Aisling: the put-downs, the small controls. She'd say: 'He's keeping his options open. Wants to hang on to all of them, Aisling plus whoever he's canoodling with, and that poor ex, and his claws stuck in old Justine.'

But, when Zoe started to ask why she wasn't more worried about Aisling, custody-wise, or some unimaginable future wife, Penny insisted it was different, because she was practically family. 'They'd never hurt me,' she'd say. 'And because of the past with Justine, that'll never change. Doesn't matter if sometimes she's fed up with him, the bloody Black Prince. This way we get the best of them both; has to be good.'

She mused constantly about Balder psychology. 'His problem is he's never got over being the favourite. While the rest of us were completely overlooked and pushed aside by our own crap mothers, nothing like enough care or attention to go around. If I'd had someone like Carolyn Balder . . . she's quite sexy, by the way, under the quilted boho jackets.'

Whenever she made comments like that, Zoe pretended not to notice; sophisticated people couldn't possibly mind if their girlfriends noticed other women.

'Look around,' Penny would say. 'It's not as if west London's heaving with lipstick lesbians. Don't go all needy about it. Silly, of course there's no one else I'd want.'

But Zoe's fear was a sink-hole; nothing would fill it. She had to try harder. Being with the love of one's life was meant to be exciting, surely: a reason to strive. Without that flutter of uncertainty, what would love feel like?

In fact, she needed to make more effort generally. Privately, Penny found her unconfidence about clothes touching, would retrieve fluff from her hair and, when Zoe pulled away, embarrassed, she said 'my feral love, you scrub up well, actually. You just don't know how to, yet.'

Nevertheless, every time they met Robin, she could sense irritation. Was Penny ashamed of her? Zoe explained that dressing-up felt like drag: mutton dressed as lamb, although she was, technically, lamb. Penny took her to department stores for wrap-dresses and heels; explained, repeatedly, how to check one's profile in windows, angle the bathroom mirrors to show the back of one's hair.

But, if Zoe managed to leave the house with mascara on, unladdered tights, not actively encrusted with leaves or ink, or, worse, wore something Penny liked, such as her new grey trousers, Penny was suspicious. When Zoe dared to buy something Penny didn't approve of, like her red-and-white jacket, she teased her, lovingly, so much that wearing it became impossible. It was simpler to stick to boring clothes, in which she hated herself even more.

And, hard as she tried to avoid seeing her own reflection, her pitiful attempts at style, Zoe did know how her body looked. She had seen the photographs from Penny's birthday party, more than once. They were barely hidden in a drawer; anyone could have spotted them if they fetched their coat from the bedroom, as Zoe once had. When she couldn't resist self-torture, she'd slide them out to confirm that she was even paler and plumper than she'd remembered: a suet-dumpling, a golem.

Unfortunately, Robin enjoyed telling them about his youth. Penny would encourage him: guileless French exchanges; pubescent courtship in the Youth Orchestra of Hampshire ('YoH!'); every family dachshund's full name and age at death. 'Remind me,' Penny would say, 'who was sweet Button's mother?'

Afterwards she'd ask, 'How could we deprive our child of that?', as if 1960s seaside holidays in Andover and the Isle of Wight were part of the deal. From her fascinated questions, she seemed to have forgotten the world-famous beaches of her childhood, the rampant tropical forests of the Central West Region, tawny sandstone rocks changing colour under the hours and hours of winter, or was it summer, sun. Robin was still the Black Prince, she didn't trust him, not one bit, but she kept telling Zoe to make an effort. Her lack of friendliness was embarrassing. And she needed to be warmer with Justine, who met them all in Barnes for tea after an awkward river-walk.

Zoe talked, Penny pointed out later, without stopping.

'I was nervous.' These meetings weren't the sort of thing one could tell one's friends about, one's mother and father; at least, not Zoe's. She didn't know how to be with Robin, let alone Justine.

'Think how she felt,' Penny said mysteriously.

At their next date with Robin, for an expensive Italian set lunch off Piccadilly, balsamic glazes and vomity dry parmesan and anxious Albanian waiters, Justine was at the table when they arrived early, 'which was a bit peculiar, wasn't it?' asked Zoe. This led to an argument, which Zoe had had to apologize for comprehensively so that Penny, who had a big lecture in the morning, could sleep.

'To be fair,' Penny said dreamily, moving her foot, 'you can't be expected to see how hard I'm working in the background. It's delicate. Justine said . . . never mind.'

'What? Tell me. No, don't fall asleep, I'd rather know.'

'She said . . . not about her but Robin, that maybe he's hesitant because . . .'

'Oh God. Not me?'

'Well. It is understandable. Most people, if they could choose the perfect way, wouldn't want babies with a twenty-five-year-old. I'm sorry, but it's true. Christ, I hope he doesn't back out now. I'd be devastated.'

'God,' Zoe said, eyes open in the night, her heart quivering like a beached jellyfish. 'OK. Look, please don't worry. If he did, I'd find a way to change his mind.'

At last he invited them downstairs to his flat for dinner: Delia's chargrilled tuna, roast vegetable couscous. They marvelled at his dramatic paint-colours, Germanic school-room charts labelled Europa 1933, Togoland, *DIE WIRKUNG DER VEGETATIVEN NERVEN*; the famously awful draw-ings by, or was it of, one of his exes: tragic-looking women with hungry charcoal eyes. On the living-room wall, a fridge-sized glass case had been mounted where a television would normally be, containing a pissed-looking arctic fox, pawing irritably at a tableau of field mice and teasels. There was no sign of his daughter: not a single toy. Very Young Aisling, too, was always elsewhere whenever they started discussing how it would work; the practicalities of paternity leave and overnights, school holiday division, money. The rest of it, his woolly claims about a 'chosen family' and 'dadhood', were for analysing later, in bed: his claim to be relaxed about everything except being an absent father.

Penny saw through his fake flexibility. They would be two separate units, and he'd be the minor one; he'd better hurry up and accept that. Maybe she couldn't bear to reproduce with him, after all.

Zoe always ended up being the one to reassure her, urging her not to back out. With no babies, Penny would despair, and then she might dump Zoe. And what would Zoe have then?

Now

11.24 a.m.
Go. Leave now, while there is still time.

Why isn't she leaving?

Bin-bags of clothes are stacked in the hall like hay-bales. She's stuffed her grandmother's photo-album into a pillowcase, a handful of batteries, vitamins, plant food, charger, passports and EHIC cards, Matty's school reports stolen from the filing cabinet, a slithering wodge of baby pictures, mortgage evidence, Spanish and German dictionaries because you never know, half the Euros, a spare rabbit water-bottle. Too much to remember: Penny's raging emails have been coming thick and fast and Zoe still needs to send one back, explaining in dreary detail the transfer of joint bills to Penny's sole name, parking permit rules, what the water people said. She used to spend days comparing phone packages, proving her devotion and competence by conquering their dullest admin. It had never occurred to her that all those household bills in her name would be a problem. She was never going to be the one who left.

Matilda is a girl who needs accoutrements: souvenirs from

School Journeys to Hanwell Zoo and Arbinger Roughs; sea-horse-related goods; signed end-of-Year-Six T-shirt; signed plaster-cast; a papier-mâché Egyptian-effect urn, containing the expensive cremains of Basil, the previous rabbit, plus twice-sterilized food-bowl and ceremonial wisp of hay. And her terrarium: damn. Zoe brings it down, tries wrapping it in a dishcloth but the chipped glass lid comes off; she jams it back on at an angle. She's meant to be running a seminar on Gender and Othering in an hour and fifteen minutes, but any possession, left behind, could be the nail in the, don't think it, which pushes Matty into real delinquency or despair. London is full of lost girls. Fingertips bleeding, coffee sloshing in her guts like accidie, she is trying to pull herself together when she sees a note stuck to Todly's litter tray:

DO *NOT* TAKE THIS. DON'T DO THIS TO ME. AND TO ROSE, SHE LOVES HIM TOO. YOU ARE BREAKING MY HEART. YOU ARE A MONSTER. TILDA WOULDN'T HAVE HER BUNNY IF I HADN'T BOUGHT HIM. SHOW THIS TO HER SO SHE KNOWS THAT I LOVE HER, THAT YOU HAVE DESTROYED US ALL.

The sense of trouble gathering overwhelms her: thunderclouds with manes and hooves. She sits on the floor, shuffles over to the wall on her bottom and leans against it.

Last week they'd had one last pre-Mediation group session with Matty's school counsellor, in the corner of the library, after hours. There, among the Black History Month and

Anime displays, Gerard suggested they try Family Sculpting. Matilda, frowning, had to physically place her family members (a chair representing Rose, who had a sore throat) where she wanted them to be, 'subsequent to the family split'.

'It's not everyone,' Zoe kept trying to say. 'Only me and Penny.'

'Hush for the time now,' said Gerard, the counsellor. Eventually they were in position: Robin and Justine and Penny in a little knot, Zoe still in her chair ('you stay there,' instructed Matty. 'Don't move'), and Matty herself as near as possible to the Natural History section. Then Penny started keening, so noisily that Gerard himself led Matty to the library exit, beeped her through the doors. She was in bed when they got home later; that evening Penny insisted that the adults discuss it further, over crispy chilli beef. She told Zoe that she deserved to be in prison.

Dawn said she should be raging. But she barely knows how that feels. Penny's most unhinged accusations will not stick in her brain; she has to keep asking Dawn for reminders or she relapses into doubt. Have I been exaggerating? she wonders, looking up at the kitchen clock; isn't sh—?

Oh no. She's miscalculated; there are only forty-five minutes until the seminar.

She jumps up, trying to work out how she can manage it in time, and knocks Penny's collection of fridge-magnets into Todly's hypoallergenic litter. No point gold-panning for them with the special scooper; on her knees she picks them out by hand, breathing through her mouth like the dimmest of students. She rinses then dries each one individually, because

Penny will notice rust: Freda Kahlo's eyebrows; the Cornish pasty; Ayers Rock; creepy Schiele lovers from MoMA, liverish mauve and green.

When Penny was pregnant with Rose, and Zoe was in a mania of nesting, the thought of her catching toxoplasmosis from the creepy man-next-door's cat, Sooty, was deranging. These days, each time Penny threatens suicide, Zoe wants to protect her a little less.

13

Winter 1997

Their parenting agreement needed to be watertight; beyond that, nobody had a clue.

Penny rang up someone's paralegal girlfriend in Manchester, who explained that lesbians still didn't exist in the eyes of the law, yes, honestly, and so no co-parenting agreement they made between them, whether or not there was a known donor ('Father,' Penny corrected her. 'Sort of. Although less than he thinks he . . . OK'), would be legally binding.

'In a court of law,' Penny said when she'd hung up. 'Why do they always say that? Fucking Queen Victoria.'

Zoe opened her mouth, closed it again.

Penny found it exhilarating, making something up from scratch, potentially better than anything straight couples could invent. From separated parents, not that they knew many, they'd taken the idea of a one-third/two-thirds split of time, which meant dividing the future babies' lives so that they spent Wednesday nights and alternate weekends with Robin. Would that work? It would have to. What else were they to do?

Then Robin joined the west London Dads Alliance, who

lent him a copy of an agreement some men had drawn up in Oregon. He insisted that they use it, if only as a template.

'Shouldn't we find a group ourselves?' Zoe asked Penny.

'No chance. Hardly any lesbos want babies, you know that. Doesn't even cross their mind, or they left it too late, before the drinking and the madness set in. Which is why we're so incredibly lucky to have found each other. And the only other ones that do . . .' She meant the women they'd met at a friend's friend's colleague's lesbian-mother winter picnic ('Wicca-nic') in Wormwood Scrubs; hiking fleeces over tucked-in appliquéd Wild Birds of Vancouver Island T-shirts, labrys-earrings and thong-necklaces; all-round eyeliner; unironic mullets. 'Well, if that's who you want, don't let me stop you.'

Sometimes Penny claimed that Zoe was becoming more like Tricia. She'd started diagnosing LesbOedipal tendencies, often in bed long after Zoe begged her to stop. Then Zoe would keep accidentally thinking of Tricia's modest cleavage: what she remembered of it. The only person she could have consulted about whether that was normal was Penny, which was not possible, because she'd laugh her head off. It didn't help that Penny delighted in analysing the Stampers. Zoe had already screwed up their first meeting; she'd been so desperate for Tricia to like Penny that, when Penny unhooked her long green silk dress from its padded hanger, Zoe said (she thought diplomatically): 'maybe wear something a bit more . . . ordinary?'

Penny was too dumbfounded to be furious, at first. 'You're not seriously telling m—'

Zoe tried to backtrack, but the damage was done. 'Justine adored how I look, every single time we went out. And her parents were my *friends*. Are. I can't go on if you try to curtail—'

'I'm not telling. Just, just suggesting, asking. Oh God, sorry. I shouldn't have . . . you're right, that was horrible of me. Sorry. I just thought that, to help her be more rela—'

'Right. So you openly want me not to outshine your mother? To be a drab little nobody. That's what you want.'

For apparently unrelated reasons, to do with the persecutory campaign by Headington's parking wardens against Zoe's sister, Tricia hadn't spoken to Zoe since that visit.

Robin kept emailing the co-parenting agreement back and forth, suggesting little changes to what looked official enough already: lots of 'inasmuch' and 'now therefore in consideration', or a postscript to specify that 'a weekend' was exactly forty-eight hours, Friday evening to Sunday evening. They'd started describing the arrangement, whenever anyone asked, which they frequently did, as like an amicable divorce. It didn't feel amicable, more like a nervy ceasefire.

Yet, face to face with him and Justine, who was always there, no question, they never even slightly disagreed. They could hardly confront him about his pushiness, the hours he'd try to pare for himself, all the funny business about what exactly 'a day' meant, and the qualitative difference between weekdays and weekends. When he mentioned that Natalie, his absent daughter, was raised not to expect pocket money, had benefited from being bullied at school, Penny compressed her lips, gave her head a little shake. Neither of them spoke up. Zoe retched into his bathroom sink during their last tense discussion, like a coward might do before a righteous battle, but she wiped her mouth and went out again to face them. Penny deserved a supporter, a fellow soldier by her side in the Sacred Band: ἐρώμενος to her ἐραστής, strong and true.

But Robin had to believe they were all allies. He would darken, his voice wobbling, if anything threatened his belief that he was equal in every way to the mothers, as if the division of time were merely cosmetic. He slipped two references to 'Aunt Justine' into draft V as part of 'the Father's Household'; they carefully ignored it. Afterwards, when Zoe started to question why aunts had to be made official, Penny pointed out that he'd be a much better parent with Justine at home, holding the fort, than if he did it alone. 'What, he'd be dragging the baby off to *Men's Manly Magazine* teambuilding sweat-lodges? Climbing mountains with little Gertie jiggling in her sling?' Even though it didn't seem funny, more like an intangible trick, a sleight of hand, Zoe knew they had to accept it. Presumably, soonish, Robin would boot Justine out, and she'd be living somewhere else, ideally at the other end of the Piccadilly Line with Jayne Shaunessy, only popping in now and then.

Penny needed a baby, more than one. She had no spare eggs to waste while they fussed about the details. 'Fine, if he wants every other Christmas back in bloody Hampshire. He probably won't stick to it. And who cares about Easter? Yes, we'll give him that.'

One night, back upstairs after a tense game of Articulate, Penny admitted she was worried about the timing. 'Even if I could conceive, right now, I'd be thirty-seven when I had the first. And if you went next, we'd be trying for a third when I'm forty-one. Minimum.'

'So . . . ?'

'So we should get our skates on. Let's not wait. I want our little family. Who cares if he imagines he's in charge.'

Zoe had sworn not to discuss their exciting plan for impregnation; Penny was deathly afraid that some desperate lesbian would nab Robin for themselves. In any case, Zoe's friends were never at their best with Penny; they seemed almost nervous, whether Penny joined in or thoughtfully left them to it. Penny said she liked some of them, but: 'You've got to admit, they're all pretty conventional. You don't want to be held back from really living, just because they're not ready to go with their boyfriends for a long weekend.'

Yet a surprising number of Penny's friends seemed to know all about it. She said she was keeping her options open in case the Black Prince failed them. She even attempted to convince Zoe that they should try to conceive simultaneously. 'Double our chances. When push comes to . . . come.'

Robin kept suggesting addenda: that the Mothers' flat would be an agreed permanent base only for the first six months; that the Father should be fully involved in choosing a nursery place, should he not wish to do full-time day care. The Father was entitled to take paternity leave; it was, Robin said, ethically important.

'Ha! As if I'd let him spend all day with my baby,' said Penny. 'My God, he's obsessed with exclamation marks. Do you think it's a phallic thing?'

'But if we've put it in the agreem—'

'Only to shut him up, for the sperming,' Penny said. 'He'll never remember.'

He suggested they join him on a guided tour of the Barbican conservatory. Zoe forced herself to kiss him hello. She had to feign relaxation around him; he seemed to expect both intimacy and, Penny said, control. He smelt, as ever, potently of aftershave. Penny opened all the windows whenever he visited, breathed dramatically through her mouth but, face to face, she became adoring. When they met by the Cacti House, she cupped his skull with her hand to bring him closer, as if they had been separated by cruel fate.

Over Penny's head, he considered Zoe. She was fourteen years younger than him, not quite twenty-six. 'Ah, look,' he said, when the embrace ended, as if he had only just spotted her. 'It's the stripling.'

'Thank you for organizing this,' Penny said. 'It's my dream.'

Somehow, he forgot to repay them for his ticket. Penny kept shooting aggrieved looks at Zoe about it, then encouraging her to translate the Latin names of the arid plants.

'Don't be coy,' she said. 'It's very impressive. But for God's sake, can you not interrupt me when I'm spea—'

'Sorry,' said Zoe.

'While we're here,' Robin interjected, between *Gymnocalycium monvillei subsp. Horridispinum* and *Coleocephalocereus purpureus*, 'we will need a clause about the kids' schools. I can't have, well, some people insisting that they just go anywhere.'

They talked about their conveniently similar approaches

to nutrition, to discipline. When Robin asked if Penny could categorically guarantee she was never going to move back to Australia, Zoe, to reassure him, said 'there's definitely no way she'd consider it, would you, darling,' and left a little space for Penny to confirm.

Which Penny didn't. 'I wasn't,' she explained afterwards, 'about to give him everything he wants. Better to keep him on his toes.'

Robin admitted that he'd been on a Men's Health Therapeutic Retreat, 'not because I was depressed, obviously. It was actually very empowering.' Behind his back, Penny grinned. 'Self-growth, masculinity, drumming, that type of thing. Fairly helpful, but I didn't see the need to return.'

'Well, even a short course of therapy can be very pos—'

'No, no,' Robin said. 'We just had the one session.'

Later, as they filed past parasitic climbers, the dewy orifices of plants which ate moths, flies, each other, Robin observed: 'Isn't this like dating? Trying to decide if we'll still love each other when the kids have flown the nest. Nests.' Penny caught Zoe's eye among the monster agaves. 'I do. I love you already,' he said, but even Zoe could tell that he was lying.

That night, Penny was in tears. She said she despised him.

'Though did you notice that when he said, a-bloody-gain, "we'll be a family" and I said "no, we'll be two families", he shut up? I told you he'd have to accept eventually that we're separate units. No wandering into our flat when he fancies it, no nicking our evenings. When he says he wants a big family, another three or four kids, bet you anything he means being the patriarch, massive beard and us brewing his ale.'

'I'm worried, though. What if he thinks he can force . . .'

'You are so pessimistic. And negative. It did go well, can't you see that? I think he knows he's on to a good thing.'

'It feels fragile, that's all. If we don't like or trust him already, why are we doing this with him? Won't it get worse, once we have a baby, babies, when our only point of, of connection is what we're most vulnerable about, most sensitive? People say it's hard enough dealing with one husband, let alone a whole other couple.'

'"People"? You mean Hilary Mint, don't you. Christ, it's imp—'

'I didn't tell her anything.'

'Clearly you did.'

'Just as a, a theoretical idea. She knows we can't just autochthonously reproduce, or is that paretheno— I haven't given anything away, I promise. I wouldn't endanger us.'

Eventually, mollified by pledges and self-abnegation, Penny permitted Zoe to stroke her back until she could sleep. 'I can't believe I'm going to have babies with the Black Prince, of all people,' and Zoe could hear the conspiratorial smile in her voice. 'Even though he's much less clever than he thinks. I honestly don't know if I can stand his smarmy old spunk up my fanny.'

When she was in this mood, their future shone. Even Zoe's mum and dad would be thrilled, which was so rarely in her gift. Although it was definitely too early to tell them. 'I don't want you feeling hurt,' Penny explained. 'They're the last people who'd understand.'

Zoe wanted to say that her father would, he'd love it, if only Tricia could accept it too. Yet Tricia would be wounded if she wasn't informed until there was an actual pregnancy.

Penny said not to worry. Most people feared their daughters having unplanned babies with degenerate boyfriends, not with sophisticated gorgeous geniuses with permanent lectureships. This baby would be entirely planned. Surely not even Zoe's mother could object.

Now

11.49 a.m.
It feels as if she's galloping towards a fence so comically, disastrously, thorny and high that no one could reasonably expect her to attempt it and not founder, yet which she must, nonetheless, overcome.

According to Zoe's parents' friend Roge, the only tutor they know at 'the' university, a good don rips up his teaching notes and begins afresh every other year. When Zoe started, she resolved to be better than Roge, who claims that his female Chemistry postgrads find his power entrancing. She was going to write her seminar plan from scratch every September, both as a political act to nourish fresh young minds, and for her own betterment. Yet here she is, horribly late, unable to find her Oyster card, or her ClassFac key-fob, then crashing around her office, past caring that her seminar group will be so repelled by the same old nonsense about epithetic building blocks in oral poetry that they'll tune out; turn against her; gang up and switch to Alexander Tullough's military leadership Tuesday slot. They'll skewer her so effectively on their end-of-term Performance Appraisal 360° feedback worksheets that her contract will be terminated. But all she can think about is this afternoon's Mediation.

Her weakest Comedy third-year drops by to detail the literally head-splitting hangover which obliged him to miss last week's seminar on Festival Rites and the Divine. Her colleagues rarely take messages, pretending they're too deep in intellectual endeavour to notice phones, but her desk is spotted with cheap yellow Post-its, already losing their stick: *CALL PENNY/x 3; Pongus??? rang re: UCL plenary* [illegible]; *urgent; have you taken my schneiderbrot? is in packet, potentially past sell-by date. b.l.* She's rung Matilda's school again to explain that she's in a meeting, as is Matty's other mother, yes, honestly, probably better not to try her, and if Matty says she wants to leave early, again, she mustn't be sent home but wait for Rose to meet her and go to Marylebone station together. She's always been glad that Matilda is close by; if there was a bomb or a riot, it's walkable, at a pinch. But still so many work days have been curtailed. Today she wants, no, needs, Matty not to need her. And if only Rose wasn't quite so assiduous about keeping her phone off during the school day.

Of course the ClassFac printer requires restarting. Bum in the air, she's groping for the socket when she spots the lower half of Professor Carla Thackarray, black palazzo pants and snug ankle-boots, emerging from her office. Penny has known Carla since their youth, scrounging staplers when they were both officeless visiting lecturers at UCL; she always said she was monumentally boring. Now that Carla is Zoe's Director of Studies, Penny comes by to perch a thigh on the edge of her desk and gossip, stopping talking if Zoe walks past her open door.

'Oh!' Zoe staggers upright. Carla's already somewhat googly eyes open even wider as, her pace quickening almost to a run, she takes evasive action, zipping along the rest of the corridor and down the stairs.

Zoe sighs, crouches again and is about to take the opportunity to cover her face with her hands, perhaps moan softly, when her colleague, Barry Lassiter, known to Penny as Larry Bassiter, walks past, scented richly with beer-burps, and decides to clarify his new theory about the Gregorian calendar, leaning his hip against the printer just as it is rumbling itself towards a state of receptivity.

With a whine, all its lights go out.

'I just have to . . .' she tells him, with a gesture open to interpretation. Back into her office, the filing-cabinet lurching as she searches for last year's notes; she looks up to see that Sioned Lo, small, red-haired, intelligent but irretrievably wedded to writing her dissertation on Trees in Greek Epic, of which there are few, is standing tearfully in the doorway, beginning to explain that a perceived misapprehension in the covering letter she wrote to re-engage with a disastrous oversight in her now-retracted outline wherein she specifi—

'I'll have to stop you there,' Zoe tells her, like a completely different person.

'But . . . But if I wait until Office Hours . . . you promised you'd help whenever I needed. You said.'

'I'm so sorry,' Zoe says. 'I have a . . . thing,' and in Sioned's expression she sees years of trust and coaxing evaporate; she will demand a new supervisor before the week is out.

Zoe stands to guide her out, bangs her head on the shelf above and discovers that someone has left a cup of cold coffee on the sliding stack of ring-binders she's made into a sort of storage cubbyhole, for her secret rental paperwork and some of Penny's loonier letters. She's wiping coffee from her ear when an email arrives from Robin, letting her know that her first solo payment into Penny's account for Rose's upkeep is already late, and how does she think Rose will feel about that? Also, could she please note that the amount he and Penny will contribute to Matilda's upkeep will be 62 per cent less than Zoe has requested, because her financial issues are not their problem. Her father leaves a voicemail when she's on the phone to Rose's school, trying to convince them to send really important correspondence not only to both Stag Street flats, yes, honestly, both, but now also to Goldhawk Road. Clive, who was ringing officially to check the kids' preferred cereal and what bedtime to impose, mentions in passing that her mother thinks she may have a chest infection and perhaps now isn't the best night after all.

He could die of a heart attack because of this new stress; nevertheless, she doesn't call him back.

There are dozens of extremely urgent emails to scan about

research clusters and REF submissions; funding-shortfalls for conferences in Crete, Swansea, Münster; demands for extensive online references from failing second-years plus, for light relief, pressing questions about the home insurance payments for Stag Street and whether she's genuinely comfortable with her penis size.

When her phone rings again she knows it will be about her father. She visualizes the entire scene, blue lights, defibrillation paddles, but no, it's Linda again from Rose's school reception to report a small upset about next week's match against Our Lady, although she's giving History a little try. Though could Zoe pop in anyway, because school policy? Also, Rose is worried about some train tickets.

She checks her personal inbox, where she finds an urgent email from Antoinette Pike (Ms) at St Clement's Girls', cc'd to the other parents, requesting a meeting 'in the light of recent conversations with Dr Cartwright about child safeguarding issues for Matilda and the possibility of Parental Alienation'.

At which point Zoe closes her eyes, and thinks: OK. I can bear this. It's not as bad as it could be. What is Parental Alienation, anyway?

14

Then

January 1998

While Robin waited, Zoe and Penny inspected the jar.

He was sitting in the living room, pretending to be at one with the moment. They huddled in their little dark kitchen, familiar scuffed cream walls, Penny's Limoges tiles, trying to giggle quietly. Zoe had soaked off the sacred yellow label, washed it twice, yet an oniony whiff lingered, like an inexpungible memory of shame. Penny, leaning against the draining board beside her, kept whispering excitedly that no way should they obey Robin and swap it for the one he'd brought, add to his already inflated self-esteem. 'He only wants to show off that he makes marmalade. If my holy Vegemite jar isn't good enough for him, then tough. Stop snorting, girl,' which made it so much worse.

They were going to bombard Penny's womb: she didn't have, as she told her friends, Zoe's massive advantage of youth. And they could control the process. There was no need for hormones or hospitals, and certainly no turkey-baster, which even intelligent people loved mentioning. How had they never noticed that semen isn't produced by the pint? No, one simply walked into a chemist and bought a forty-nine-pence medicine-syringe, like one might use for a child's antibiotics. Zoe had done it, as though she was already someone's mother.

When Robin had finished, he knocked on the bedroom door as if he was room service. The experience was unexpectedly moving: receiving the small warm jar with a modest dab of wallpaper paste, or school semolina, at the bottom; closing the bedroom door; drawing up their future babies into the syringe. She squirted it into Penny, held her until the sperm had had a chance to front-crawl up to her cervix, and they told each other how happy they were, that they would be together for ever.

When they emerged, they joined Robin on Penny's amethyst jacquard cut-velvet sofa and he made them hold hands. Zoe managed not to joke about washing his.

They tried again the next day, twice. He said he was exhausted, which Zoe was amazed by. She had to remember not to say 'thank you' when he handed her the jar, because Penny was afraid that it might establish some kind of legal precedent. It smelled of overripe pears, of train-station toilets.

So far they'd managed to insist it happen in their flat. Whenever they were in his, Zoe would look enviously at the garden he shared with the man next door, possibly without his knowledge. Ivy flooded it, creeping into every corner, over bumps and rubbish and the neighbour's ground-floor window. Robin had no interest in cultivating it, liked hearing the foxes screwing; he and Penny laughed at how shocked Zoe looked. 'Will it be safe out there for a baby?' Zoe whispered to Penny.

'It looks like somewhere you'd find remains,' but Penny said, 'Christ. Not now.'

That time, Justine was hanging around too, when they did the deed. 'Ah, come on,' Penny told Zoe. 'Don't be a grandma. She's in the living room, not in bed with us. And it's her flat.'

It still seems very peculiar, Zoe wanted to say, but Penny's mouth was on hers.

One evening, Robin brought a videotape of a misty French erotic film upstairs; he thought they might like it. Penny wanted to have a look immediately. Robin seemed pleased. 'This one's pretty feminist.'

Zoe was curious too, but not in front of Robin. Surely it wasn't actual porn? Penny had heard that you could buy tapes of lesbian pornography, but who'd want to go to a seedy old-man sex-shop? Besides, they'd be excruciating, full of wild-bushed women in German saunas. She said she was too tired, mostly, even to open the books she'd shown Zoe in their early months: hand-tinted photographs, stories about imperious housemistresses and petulant convent girls, Edwardian gentlemen whipping grateful duchesses in basement dungeons.

They sat watching Robin's film in silence, like school inspectors before a disappointing science experiment. Every time Zoe fidgeted, Robin's famous skip-salvaged chrome-framed chair creaked noisily. Later, Penny said she found penises totally unerotic, and didn't Zoe too.

Later still, Penny woke her. 'I bet it's worked. I can tell these things. I'd better be up the duff. Oh God, how will I bear it if I'm not?'

Now

Since reading about Parental Alienation, her brain has frozen: the chemical result of terror. During the long seminar she feigned enthusiasm, affected interest, and the shock of the words she'd read festered, subcutaneously. The students file out; she sits there, dazed. Almost any one of the deaths she imagined in childhood – locked in a woodsman's hut, hung from the climbing ropes in the school gym, torn apart by, for some reason, bulls – would be better.

Zoe doesn't believe in the Fates: she who allots, she who spins, she who snips the thread of death, come on. Nor in a hairily paternal God; she tried hard in her youth, throwing herself into the Bible, but it didn't take. Yet lately she has been praying: let the kids be all right. Let Rose make more friends, and her coursework be displayed in the Faces/Places exhibition on the main school staircase; let Matty not be caught again near a still-lit cigarette at break. Today, hope comes hard. Almost the worst has happened; her children are not OK. But she's survived the seminar, at least not been fired. If she can get through the mediation unmolested, and Des's lads turn up for the move, as long as Matilda and Rose can endure this mess, so will she.

As she hurries towards the exit, she's half expecting to see Penny, wailing like a hired mourner outside the ClassFac doors, but Clyde at the desk would protect her. If she shouted, he would come. She's reached the ply-panelled stairs down to street-level when her phone rings yet again.

'Hi, hi, Dad, I can't actually . . .'

'You didn't ring me back.' His voice clatters down the stairwell, painfully loud.

'I'm in the midd—'

'I didn't want to worry you, but your children still haven't arrived. Well, not that I can see. I haven't rung home to check because I don't want to upset your mother, but anything could have happened. What if they've run away? You know what she thinks about all of this, and obviously we agree. We worry about them.'

Zoe leans against the wall. They're right. She could text Penny right now: I've been demented. I'm deeply sorry. Can you ever forgive me? And probably Penny couldn't, but she would take her back, she's said so, for the children's sake. They'd have to prove to the poor kids that they are united, as they'd sworn – had Zoe been lying? – at their civil partnership, only five years ago.

Zoe and her other best friend Cath had been inflating balloons in the gap between ceremony and party when Zoe, cautiously, had mentioned how weird it felt that Justine would be there, because . . . no, no, nothing concrete, not really.

Cath, despite her stressful daughters, had helped Zoe plan everything: so many guests in the Ravenscourt Institute hall, beef jungle curry and spicy fishcakes from Chakrii at Thai Time, Penny's favourite restaurant, and inexpert daiquiris; weeks of organizing; days of heaving around clinking boxes.

And Cath had said: 'So why are you getting married? Oh, sweetheart. Though who amongst us, et cetera.'

Zoe can't afford to do this, doesn't have the brain or energy to make it work. Think how relieved everyone would be. Even Matty: she's definitely said she wants to go with Zoe, but what if she feels it's the only way she can live in one home most of the time? Wouldn't she be happier sticking with her old bedroom, not some cobbled-together temporary stranger's place, spending the odd night back here with Penny ranting and blaming, squeezing her for love? As for Rose . . . Penny says she'll be ruined, by being abandoned like this. Shouldn't Zoe stay, for her sake too? And Penny would be happy. Zoe's parents would be happy.

Last year, when Zoe had first begun to hint at difficulties, Cath said: 'I didn't like to assume. But you usually give in, don't you? Like a dog, and don't get me wrong, they're better than people, but like a sweet unconfident dog that the others pick on. You always show your neck.'

So how, after almost two decades of neck-showing, can Zoe ruin everyone's lives, charge ahead with this absurd and selfish plan? Even she might be happier if she stayed; Penny has promised to change. She has. And, if Zoe ends up in a probably purely figurative puppy-training cage in the kitchen, being punished for the rest of her life, wouldn't it be worth it, if it's what the children need? Isn't that what good parents do?

'Pa,' she says to her father, best of men. 'Hang on, I did specifically tell Mum when they'd arrive. The train's at sixteen-thirty, ish, so they won't be there till after seven. I mean, five. That's hours away.'

'Ah.'

'Where are you?'

'At the station. It's no trouble.'

'Dad. Oh, Dad, you'll have to go home. I can't believe this . . . did Mum really not say?'

'Couldn't get an answer out of her, she's very stressed. So, I thought wiser to be in situ, as it were, then maybe I could take them out to a cafe, that would be a treat wouldn't it, you used to love that, then pop them back on the train. Zoe?'

THEN

January 1998

In the newsagent's on Hammersmith Bridge Road, blushing hotly, Zoe paid for both *Mother and Baby* and *Baby and You*, pushed them like contraband into her bag. The covers alone had given her new ideas about how to tend Penny, nourish the cells which might be splitting, splitting, inside her. She'd read their contents gradually, spread them over months; better not to tempt fate.

Before the day was through, she'd gorged on them both in the work toilet: an orgy of nipple-cream reviews, consumer tests of teething rattles, play-mat giveaways, first picnics, stair-gate warnings and, best of all, measurements on an ever-growing scale of fruit-size: blueberry, grape, plum.

She couldn't tend the child within, but she would feed Penny. She headed for the big soiled-cement supermarket behind the Marketgate flats, nationally costumed dollies and celluloid-coloured begonias crammed between net curtains and grimy glass. In her first term of teaching, a postgrad to whom she'd been politely friendly had invited her there to meet his mother. She'd read of obsessive stalkers; was this the beginning? The shame of her awkward excuses hadn't faded; she'd always averted her face in case the postgrad or his mother, for some reason weaving sadly at a small loom, happened to be gazing out. Now she could look up, unashamed. She was loved by Penelope Cartwright, Dr, protected for ever from failing at heterosexuality.

Tinned red salmon for fishcakes; Chinese five-spice for stir-frys from *Baby and You*: always the balancing of money and health and not irritating Penny, who bridled at any suggestion of frugality or worthiness. An avocado, minced lamb, Coke, limes, white flour, bacon. A pregnancy test.

But what if Penny found it bossy, controlling? So often Zoe was, unknowingly, and although she'd try to change, it kept happening; it was in her nature, Penny explained. Most people wouldn't stand it. Even after Penny's rage had passed, Zoe felt beyond recovery: limbs left on the side of the road, unstaunchable bleeding.

She put the box back.

On the other hand, despite seeming so sure of herself, Penny could easily feel neglected. Zoe's job was to fill her so full of adoration and care that she could begin to heal. She picked it up again, paid, not meeting the eye of the cashier, immediately knew she'd made a mistake. Better to avoid angering Penny, when their future was about to start. She left it on a wall with 'PLS. HELP SELF' engraved in biro on the tight plastic wrapper. The test cost almost ten pounds; some poor girl, not quite ready to be pregnant, would be so relieved to find it.

Beaming again, festooned with rustling carrier bags, she hurried home: a willing ox. The handles burned her palms but that didn't matter; if anything, it proved her love. Also, by lifting them backwards she could tone her triceps. Babies could be bad for sex-lives so it was important not to let herself go. Luckily no sighting of Robin since the video; a good sign. She was grinning. These days so many things gave her happiness: the geranium donated by an elderly neighbour; the first smudges of blossom, which she'd never before even noticed, by the bus stop. Cooking for Penny. Bed with Penny. She poked excitedly in a bag for the family-sized bar of chocolate she'd bought, hesitating about risking Fruit and Nut, weighing up extra sugar against nutrition. They'd argued about this; Penny claimed she was practically a fascist, with her beetroot and wholemeal bread; that Zoe had no right to keep her from instant noodles. Also, Penny had said some things about her carefulness with money. But now, thanks to her dithering, Penny would be annoyed by her lateness. In a panic she'd plumped for the obviously incorrect Orange Crisp.

Penny and Tricia agreed that she was as sickeningly indecisive as her father; that Zoe and Clive were barely fit to be allowed outside. But, like Clive, Zoe knew that she could carry anything, anyone: she was a rock, an anchor. Her heart beat hard, a thump of hope. Key into the lock, hand on door.

She could hear Penny's sobs as she stepped inside. Bags dropped, onions thumping down the stairs like little heads; hasn't she always been ready for this? Her father's school friend Peter Rath's wife had died during labour; a neighbour's daughter, when giving birth to a misdiagnosed breech baby, had been very slightly brain-damaged.

'Just like that,' Zoe's mother would say, clicking her fingers. 'Once a beautiful young woman, now a podgy simpleton. Sorry, but she is.'

Zoe had imagined so many ways to lose Penny; an obstetric catastrophe could not be one of them. 'It's OK,' she called. 'I'm here, I'm here,' as she opened the bedroom door, pushing up her sleeves, ready to find Penny in the act of haemorrhage.

But she was on the phone. 'Hang on,' she said, taking a great snotty gulp, 'the child bride's rocked up.'

'What happened?' Zoe looked for a pool of gore on the far side of the bed; something worse, tiny but perfect as a Kinder surprise, in a pillowcase shroud.

'Nothing. I'll . . . look, I'll call you back. Yes, yes. OK,' and she hung up, her face more angry than distraught. 'Absolutely sodding nothing.'

'But you thought, wasn't the tiredn—'

'I wasn't pregnant. Tiredness was . . . Christ only knows. A phantom pregnancy. Psychosomatic,' she said, and flopped back against the pillow, which sighed as if winded. 'Nothing.

Bought the test at the chemist's and got them to let me check in the loo. That mean pharmacist, Elsa, hugged me. Oh bugger. Do you think we really have to tell you know who?' and Zoe, so relieved that Penny could be cheerful, that she had not begun to withdraw from her in grief and sorrow, absolutely lost it. They laughed until Penny started crying again.

'I don't know. Oughtn't we, so he feels on the same side? Oh, love. Hang on, I'll get you a Coke. I think you're right, actually,' she called from the kitchen. 'He might be crap. Let me look after you,' but, when she went out into the hall, the flat door was open. Her stomach lurched. 'Where are you?' she called, and saw Penny walking carefully downstairs.

Afterwards, Penny said she should have known that the Black Prince would be rubbish. He didn't commiserate at all; his main interest was what Penny could have done better. Zoe ran upstairs to fetch Penelope Leach and read him and Justine the bit about Nature Taking Her Time and Robin simply nodded, as if he knew everything already, and went on about cutting out caffeine. Even when the sorrow hit, and Penny started saying that they should have tried sooner, that her eggs were wizened, Robin, even older, behaved as if, in his princely omniscience, he'd considered that too, and found himself blameless.

They went out to Thai Time, as consolation; the next evening, because she was too sad to be cooked for, they had takeaway. Between bites of pad kra pao moo she'd cry and rage and regret, or insist she was mostly fine, hadn't even known she was knocked up.

But, if despair sank her later, how would Zoe pull her out? Or if she couldn't get pregnant without IVF, which apparently gave you cancer? Zoe thought about cancer all the time; it was unbearable.

'Let's start trying, "trying", again as soon as we can. Next month. Three and a half weeks, even,' she volunteered, and Penny kissed her.

They began again the next month, then the next. One afternoon, drawn up by luck and chance into the plastic syringe, was Rose.

Part Two

Trapped

Then

Spring 1998
Since the magic happened, a single sperm cell squirted inside Penny not merely surviving but penetrating an egg and beginning, like her beautiful stomach, her heart ('by twenty-five to thirty per cent') and lungs, to grow, Zoe had reached the zenith of mortal happiness. This was the land of fairy-tale: on one side of the bed a gross and backward peasant girl; on the other, like a reflection in an enchanted pool, someone rare and strange. It seemed to Zoe that they were a pod of broad beans, and one was swelling; or cat-sisters, one producing a litter. Her own body had remained as pasty and disappointing, as breadily undefined, as ever, but Penny was spectacular. Despite not having generated the sperm it was easy to pretend, when they were alone together, that there was no Black Prince downstairs, no Justine his loyal consort, just a living, breathing organ of maternal love.

'Anyone would think,' Penny told her, at eleven weeks and one day, 'that you'd never seen a pregnant woman before. Let alone naked.'

'Sorry. I'll try to rein it in. But don't you think it's weird, that men aren't obsessed with this? Constantly writing poems about it, singing ballads at Glastonbury? I can't get over it.'

Penny was raring to start the NHS antenatal classes, to tell everyone. Zoe's nervousness, her refusal to hope for the best, caused rows; when she tried to suppress it, Penny said she could see everything Zoe was feeling, her skin transparent like a newt, was it? A sea-cucumber?

'Can't it be something sexier?'

'It's the opposite, I'm afraid,' Penny said. 'My little squid.'

So, to compensate, the little squid found Penny a course of Natural Pregnancy Council workshops in an Acton basement flat. Their teacher, who claimed to have founded the concept of woman-centred birth, was assisted by her furious almost-adult son. She held up a series of felt appliqué birthing constellations of her own design, deferred to the dads, told off one of the mums for not bringing food for sharing. Of course, they were the only female couple but that was part of the fun, said Penny. Robin had invited himself to the first session; the idea that he might be mistaken for Penny's partner was dementing, as was his reason for bowing out ('better to be sure that the teacher knows her stuff'). Penny's favourites were a pale woman and her well-groomed husband, who arrived late with Fortnum and Mason almond thins. When it was time to learn massage techniques, the teacher told Zoe, who was wearing one of Penny's skirts and feeling shy, which Penny always hated, to join the dads. During the coffee break ('seriously,' Penny asked loudly, 'instant?') the interesting couple commiserated with her, then exchanged numbers.

'I thought he was sexy,' Penny said afterwards. 'Silver fox. Did you see the size of her engagement ring?'

'She didn't seem that young,' said Zoe hopefully. 'To be having a first child. Maybe they only want one.'

'You'd like that, wouldn't you. You do realize it's actually very cruel to deny a child siblings? Even if they're monsters, like mine are?'

It wasn't that they often argued; they were too happy.

Zoe's mother was still refusing to come to the phone and Zoe's father was defending her, imploring Zoe to apologize, which made her miss him less. But, unfortunately, she couldn't quite stop wanting her mother, at least a mother, to delight in her embryonic grandchild's accumulations of taste buds and finger-joints, to take her daughter and daughter-in-law shopping for maternity tops. It might help her with the gay thing. A much-mocked ex of Penny's, Judy, living in Austin, Texas, had babies with her partner, and her mother-in-law had pushed the double buggy in front of the PFLAG float at Pride. Zoe wept at the thought. Penny wept too, but for different reasons. Zoe's parents were being unforgivably selfish. 'If anyone should be grovelling,' Penny would say, 'it's her to us. Christ, so outrageously rude; if she wasn't beautiful and middle-class, she'd be locked up by now. It's a known phenomenon. And where does Clive get off on speaking for her? Maybe I should ring him up myself.'

Zoe has never discussed her family before, hadn't realized that one could. Penny's dissections exposed more and more rot. Zoe needed to decide her priority: her new family, or her parents and siblings. Every time she tried to excuse them, Penny would refer to their inaugural meeting at the Ryecote Chilterne Country Hotel and Spa restaurant, at which Zoe's mother had worn sunglasses throughout, and directed her comments through Zoe's father. Even before they arrived, Zoe and Penny were arguing; Zoe had misdirected her at the round-about, so they were late and Penny hadn't had time to sort out her make-up. And twice now, when she'd sneezed dramatically in Tricia's presence, she had seen Zoe wince. She still couldn't get over how Zoe dressed whenever they met her family. 'Just because you choose your least-favourite jeans, that awful baggy top, all your worst clothes that you hate yourself in, admit it, doesn't mean I have to make myself invisible too.'

Zoe's friends also didn't seem to understand. They hired a car to visit Sara, from Zoe's sixth-form, now teaching GCSE Drama on the outskirts of Norwich with her tree-surgeon boyfriend and knobbly rescue greyhounds. Usually, long car journeys with Penny were a delicious treat, hours of running jokes, intense speculation about the psyches and sexual pecca-dilloes of their most distant acquaintances. This time, she had to work hard to keep Penny upbeat. Penny made an effort with Sara, and fucked Zoe with silent intensity in their little bedroom, but it was very obvious that she was bored. All the way back to London, through military forests and depressed market towns, Zoe tried to cheer her up. It was only when Penny started analysing Sara's decor, the vase of dusty champagne corks, the nautically themed bathroom and paw-print oven gloves, that her mood lifted.

'She really is a good person,' Zoe protested, failing not to laugh. They were listening to 'Ray of Light' by Madonna, whose own love life has had its ups and downs. 'I know she's not like your Londony friends. It's not her fault she's from Dabbington. Her sist—'

'Stabbington? Oh my God, that's beautiful,' said Penny. Thankfully, she'd started smiling. 'Did you notice the special named hooks for the leads? Low down, as if those repulsive droolly hounds could read, and walk themselves? And her sandals? She was so proud of them, I think she wore them to impress us, the London lot. Jesus,' she said, and Zoe glanced over again. 'I've had enough of this road.' Driving was a delicate subject. Penny was so experienced, trained in rural hill-starts and the correct way to handle a skid. Country roads made Zoe anxious. She'd learned her three-point turns and parallel parking in cul-de-sacs out near the rugby club, not in a forest where steep bends could come upon you suddenly, revealing boy racers, rapist hitch-hikers, straying Sylvan creatures.

'OK. I'll, I'll do my turn. Though what if I hit something? A wild animal?'

'Wild? Christ, nothing wild here. This shitty tame country. Back home, anything could kill you.'

Penny was very proud both of being from, and of having escaped, the countryside. She'd always shone above her cousins; had dreamt of Milan, Los Angeles, Knightsbridge, of appearing in *Elle* reclining in her Manhattan penthouse. Comparison with, and revenge upon, everyone who'd mocked her pretension, her farming brothers, the doubting teachers, was her motivating force.

'You have no idea,' said Penny, her accent sounding stronger.

'You in your little Edwardian book-world; thought the country was all dingly woods and fluffy lambkins, didn't you? Let me tell you about lambing: we're talking cheap gloves soaked with amniotic fluid. Defrosting colostrum; iodine and pin cushions, seriously, for stitching up the male lambs' nuts. And no buses to get you out of there, or trains. Begging a ride to Mudgee, then four fucking hours to the coast.'

'But I thought—'

'And that's in scorching sunlight, none of this drizzle. Dingoes and pissed derros on government handouts and nuns and dust. Everyone marrying each other's brother. No wonder I legged it the minute I could.'

She claimed that she could drive for miles with her eyes closed, doubtless would have, if Justine had been in the car instead of Zoe. She hated that Zoe didn't pull her weight, particularly if they'd been out. 'Course you can drive. It's a Renault Clio, not an oil tanker.'

'But I'm really not good. Doing several things at once, spatial awareness, logistical . . . everything.'

'Then practise.'

'But . . .' Actually, doing even two things, using two senses, felt implausible; she drove because Penny insisted. She called Zoe the human dodgem. It was only a matter of time before someone was killed.

'Then don't bloody tell me not to drink either, when we're out. I'm totally fine; I know the streets. And it's not as if we can tube it back home, can we? No, because you're too frightened.' She'd been in London ten years longer than Zoe; ten years longer of everything. 'Aren't you. I realize you were brought up to worry about stuff, because, well, you know. But the control: no one can stand it. I'll do what I like.'

Of course, Zoe was frightened; there had been an armed robbery at the newsagent, with guns. Stabbings, hit-and-runs; people were pushed onto railway tracks, raped in underpasses. 'Be careful,' her father said whenever they spoke, and he'd grown up here. 'Mum read a horrible story about muggers using Pit Bulls now; she was very upset.'

Zoe hadn't called her that for years: altogether too cosy a word for Tricia. It made Zoe's teeth squeak with irritation.

'Why don't you pick him up on it?' Penny would say, as if, simply by being bolder, the past could be undone. 'It's time you got over her. Mumsykins.'

'Don't. Please. I'm trying. She's not easy to get o—'

'You must. I'm over mine.'

Zoe's job as the passenger was to leap out at petrol stations and woman the pump, then queue for Penny's Coke, the tabloids she said she only read for balance, her expensive fashion magazines. But Penny needed extra compensation for being dragged all the way to East Anglia, for two nights of Hiccup and Jackson with their dry elbow-pads and aghast eyes, their ears soft as wizened apple-peelings. Zoe added a pack of strawberry gum, Penny's favourite; a Norfolk Broads fridge magnet; a big bag of cheese-and-onion. There were no oranges for her, nothing healthy, but Penny would tease her. She'd started telling everyone that Zoe was addicted to vegetation, needing a bushel of greenery every day like a baby elephant.

'Thanks again for coming,' Zoe told her, handing over the bag. 'I can always train by myself next time,' which somehow led to Penny feeling excluded. Zoe should have remembered that meeting old friends often caused ructions. These days she rarely socialized alone. Wasn't it a good sign about the health of their relationship, that Penny wanted so much to be together?

When, a few weeks later, Sara claimed (she'd phoned Zoe, twice), 'Penny is the lucky one, you do realize?', Zoe understood better Penny's theory about old friends: how one can suddenly outgrow them. It was hard to remember what they'd had in common, apart from all the painful subjects they had never talked about. When Sara's parents had separated, scandalizing everyone (Julie Prentis, face compressed behind her protective chemistry goggles, referred to Sara's mother as 'fallen'), they hadn't mentioned it between themselves, not once.

'Don't be a loon,' said Zoe, nervously checking that Penny was out of earshot. 'How are Jackson and Hiccup?'

'She hated them, too, didn't she?'

'No. Not at all. She, she had a horrible experience with a Corgi when she . . . what did you mean, "too"?'

Sara took a loud gulp of tea; Penny was right, she did have weird table-manners. 'Nothing. By the way, did you hear about Katie R's wedding? To Matthew, obviously, they got back together, again-again. She arrived astride, no other word for it, a pink b—'

'No, tell me what you meant, before.'

'I don't, I didn't. Forget it.'

'OK . . .' said Zoe, distracted by a sound outside. Was Penny home early from the cinema? She'd gone with Justine, again; Zoe had needed to work anyway, so it was fine.

'She's a really impressive person,' said Sara. 'I can really see that. And it's brilliant that you're all loved up, babe. You deserve it.'

'Well . . . thanks.'

'It was only, I didn't notice, really, but Dave said, it was a silly thing . . .'

'Sorry, where are we . . . Dave?'

'He said he hoped you were happy.'

'This is getting circular. I ought to go be—'

But Sara was, as Penny had pointed out, relentless, like a dog with a ball. 'That thing with the jug.'

'What?'

'You must remember?'

'I honestly don't.'

'When he offered you our spare filter jug. And you said, "I'll have to ask Penny" and he said, "but you were just telling us you'd like one" and you said, "yes but Penny will mind".'

'Right.'

'You said she thinks they're hippyish, or too chemically, or something. But it's not like . . . Zo? I haven't pissed you off, have I?'

'No,' said Zoe. 'She's honestly sw—'

'And then Penny came in and was quite, well, abrupt about you wanting to feed the hens instead of going into town with her, and you were so incredibly apologetic.'

'I'm lost,' said Zoe, but of course she remembered how hurt Penny had been, how bitterly she'd regretted upsetting her. Why couldn't Sara see that? It was sad how much she had changed.

15

Now

She can barely hear Matilda's voice. 'Explain again,' she says.

She should definitely be preparing for the mediation, yet she's strayed into the staff common room. The door swings open, like a saloon, but it's only Drs Armand Peters and Paola Fry, still discussing the travesty that is *Potsherds*, the respected Anglo-Saxon journal which has so far declined to publish their work. In the corner by the travel-kettle, Ariadne Prescott, historian of madness, is spreading a level teaspoonful of margarine onto her daily rice-cake. She once said to Zoe: 'Being a lesbian shouldn't be the most interesting thing about you, but it is.' P. P. Oglesbee, her friend, grins at her, but how can she possibly tell him where she's going? He's a large man with a kind wife and polite children. She points at the phone pressed to her ear, shrugs comically. Closing her office door with her bum, she tries to focus on what Matty is saying.

The bookshelf is listing to the right: Hippocrates *Diseases of Women 1–2*, angrily annotated in exceptionally small capital letters by an office forebear; Batch on Ovid; five copies of her first book, *Amongst Women: kinship, familial revenge and choral mirroring in Attic Tragedy*, waiting to impress passing professors;

her dad's grammar-school prize of Sir Leonard Woolley's *Ur of the Chaldees*. Sir Leonard has so much to answer for. Once she'd thought that the height of happiness would involve spotting, beneath the overgrown lavender at 61 Tredgar Avenue, one of Queen Puabi's golden lyres, even a single lapis bead. Then again, from childhood until only a few years ago, if the sky was blue and the traffic subdued, she could squint, part two thousand years, and imagine herself as a young Greek woman, really a girl, in an Ionian grove or on a Thracian mountain: unmarried, barefoot, her future still waiting.

She opens her eyes again, tries to follow Matilda, who isn't making sense.

'Hang on, who came to school? One of the, the other parents? Sweetheart, tell me again.'

She's whispering, much too close to the microphone; Zoe can hear every glutinous breath. 'I can't say exactly.'

'Is it . . . Mum?'

'No. No.'

'Justine?'

'It's Dad.'

'What? Why? Have I . . . you've asked him what he's doing there?'

Matty's voice has a whingey edge from trying not to cry. One day she may realize that Zoe is a coward, that any strength she did show was mined from the deepest love. So Zoe says: 'All right. Pass the phone over. I'll say something to him.'

'I can't. He doesn't know I've rung you. He hasn't seen me.'

Oh God, she's definitely crying. One of her classmates will clock it and everything will become worse. 'Where are you? I could . . . no, there isn't time.' Is this Zoe being weak, again; throwing her children to the lions, out of fear?

'On the stairs. He's gone to the Reception Area! Talking to Michelle, who already hates me.'

'She doesn—'

'Mum, everyone knows she does. He's been here for ages, by the statue, like he's on strike or something. Issa saw him, loads of people have. How do I make him stop? And there's a person next to him.'

'Who you don't know?'

'No.'

'Not . . .' Robin's love, sex-life, is multilayered, booby-trapped with exes. Penny is always trying to extract details. Zoe doesn't want to know; she holds on to the fact that he's not like his old friends, who adopted twins but have nude photography all over the walls, or his favourite colleague and her husband, whose daughters don't yet know they both have boyfriends. At least, she hopes he isn't.

'No! It's a suity man. With a sort of . . .' It's hard to hear above the yelps and hoots and donkey-sounds of hormonally unbalanced pubescents changing classrooms, but Matilda definitely says 'leather'.

A dazzlingly loud bell fills Zoe's ear. Then all is quiet.

'Matty?'

'I don't know what to do, I've got to get past but he's saying something about being prepared to wait ind— oh shit. Here comes the Head.'

'He's there? Hang on, is this a meeting?'

'Coming round the corner. Shaking his hand . . . wait, Dad just said the other man's his lawyer.'

What should she do? She can't go to the school: the mediation is almost upon her. She'd hoped to start yet another letter to Rose, an inarticulate splurge of 'please don't feel I'm expecting you to come with me, I'd love it if you did, I don't want to lose you but don't want to pressurize, but you might not realize, so do whatever you . . .' But it's twenty past. The plan was to be early, competent and sensible, as if then the mediator will deem her worthy of the prize.

She gathers her bag, finds her coat, tries to force an arm through the inside-out sleeve. At the beginning of this she'd hoped that Robin might be the sane, reasonable one, keep Penny steady. It's always been his main selling point: domineering but a good father. Surely this mediator will remind him of that.

Her left hand is still trapped inside. But what if he's even further into the crazedness than she's realized? Has he cooked something up with a solicitor? Penny does keep insisting that she can't leave until they've negotiated exact arrangements for her access to Matty, including holidays, and had it legally agreed in a family court. What if she's right? Might the children be better off without Zoe? She's never had, Penny often says, an instinct for mothering.

Is it possible that both children, her chicks, could be taken from her at one fell swoop?

One dog always wins, and it's never the weak one. The horror of being without them is back. 'See?' Penny would say. 'Now you get it. It would kill me.' Zoe's vision darkens. Her mouth sluices with saliva. She runs down the corridor to the women's toilets, and vomits.

THEN

September 1998

The baby, breech, kept being turned, then turning back; forty weeks and one day, then two, and still their life had not been transformed. Zoe couldn't stay away from the Complications chapter, *placenta accreta*, *perinatal asphyxia*. When it came to giving birth, Latin was never a good sign.

She'd convinced her Head of Department, a well-meaning if easily-disconcerted woman who always said 'Black', 'Jewish', 'Lesbian' in a lowered voice, to grant her a version of paternity leave.

'Only a fortnight?' said Penny, over red lamb curry at Thai Time. 'Seriously?'

'And I have to earn it. Make up the time, in advance.' She didn't tell Penny that a colleague had said: 'Do we have to call you Dad?' At least laying down the hours was a contribution, like storing food for the winter. By the time Penny's waters broke, Zoe was haggard, wired as a new father with a cigar. She'd had the bag packed since thirty-two weeks: yoga-ball pump; *Orchestral Film Medley vol.2*; nipple cream; Rescue Remedy; the list of names, Penny's (Isolde, Lysander),

Robin's (Sinclair, Roxanne), Zoe's (Hector, Lucy). Solemnly Zoe hailed a black cab although, by the time they reached the drop-off bay outside the maternity unit, they were hysterical about things they'd forgotten for the birthing pool: lily-pads, a backstroke-instructor. While Zoe stocked up on Twixes from the vending machine, Penny was amazingly brave and calm, leafing through scuffed lifestyle magazines.

Please let this be easy for her. We've been so lucky.

'Penelope Cartwright?'

'And my partner,' said Penny loudly, and Zoe, grabbing bags and books and wrappers, hurried after them.

They gave Penny a less good pool in the birthing centre than they'd seen on their tour, months before. She hadn't read the hand-outs and Zoe couldn't bear to explain what might happen if the baby wasn't born soon. The midwife wouldn't be drawn on underwater safety, maternal drowning.

'I'll never, ever, leave you, you poor frightened plonker,' Penny told her, taking both her hands, and the midwife went to fetch a colleague so they could marvel at the sight of these two women in love.

When they examined her cervix, Penny sobbed at the pain, and Zoe felt it too; not in her womb, that would be silly, but in her heart, which clenched in sympathy. 'It'll be fine,' she said, firmly stroking Penny's spine, kissing her damp hair, all the birth-supporter techniques. Nothing helped until the gas and air, which made Penny keep falling asleep. The friendlier midwives mostly left them to it: 'you're being well looked after'. Penny said women, matriarchy, were properly valued in a place like this.

Robin was being pushy; he'd claimed it was healthier for the baby if he was in the delivery room, but they kept dodging the issue: 'imagine his little Speedos'. And Penny's mother had been forbidden to fly over from Australia. It was just them, beginning their little family in this warm dim paddling pool, moaning, weeping, dozing, holding hands.

Hang on; Zoe rechecked her watch. Were the contractions slowing?

'What?'

'Nothing. Just . . . it's all fine,' and she hurried down the squeaky corridors to find a midwife; then, some time later, another, and then another, who eventually joined them, pressed and timed and said: 'ah, you might be right'.

So Penny's beautiful water-birth was denied her. Off she went in a wheelchair to dry land, and an epidural. While, far away, doctors gathered, prodded, forcepped, Zoe, teeth chattering, stood by the absolutely off-her-head Penny to reassure her, while gazing into the cold, shining sterile cavern of loss. Did she cut the umbilical? She couldn't remember; Rose was long and cross and Zoe was the first person, other than several medical professionals, to hold her. She was alive; so was Penny. When Zoe went to call the lift back down to the maternity ward, she dropped to her shaking knees in gratitude, feeling barely self-conscious. There on the chill linoleum, she pledged to guard and protect their daughter for ever.

It was love. Rose was her second true love. She would not, could not, ever lose her.

*

The fun began on the third day, when Robin and Justine brought several Balders and close friends to meet the baby. The nurses, who had given up attempting to limit Penny's visitors, protested, but Robin had brought them chocolates, so in he swanned. Penny had tottered weepily off to the toilet in her gaping gown and concertinaed support stockings. Was it Day Three Blues or the beginning of postnatal depression? How could one be sure?

Rose was propped on Zoe's lap, the better to be admired. There was no one mooing with pain or shouting into the corridor pay-phone; the heating clanked; the nurses murmured. Zoe, unable to stop grinning, was contemplating the back of Rose's head, the skin a little loose, the fluff, fair as Penny's and, in truth, Robin's, microscopically tangled. Was it salty? Sweet? Better not to shift her and start her crying; Penny was exhausted already. So Zoe stuck out her tongue as far as it would go and gently touched it to Rose's baggy suede scalp. Then she looked up.

The doorway was full of startled visitors. Justine lifted Rose out of Zoe's arms, and plopped her into Robin's. Even when Penny staggered back in, they didn't take their eyes off Rose. They exclaimed about how she resembled Robin, ignoring Penny's trauma.

When, a fortnight later, they had to register her, Penny said: 'We should forget to tell him. Or explain to them we're a special case.' But Robin and, frustratingly, the registrar knew their stuff. The registrar was just this side of polite; Zoe tried to steel herself to complain on Penny's behalf, but Robin flattered her until the woman began to unfurl.

Yes, they confirmed, Balder was going to be included.

'As a middle name, not a surname?'

'Definitely,' agreed Penny, as Robin said: 'No.'

'Which?'

'Is there a different box for each?' Zoe asked. 'On your . . . form?'

'No.'

The registrar's desk featured a school photograph of sons in forest-green V-necks, and beads – was that a crucifix? – around the base of her lamp. Standing up to Robin in his coiled yet charming public persona was impossible. He'd already changed his voicemail greeting to 'Robin and Justine and Rose', like the Athena poster, man cradling baby, mother(s) out of shot.

'It's fine,' said Penny. 'Just write it in. As long as we're clear that the surname is Stamper. Mad but fun. And less ugly than Cartwright.'

She smiled at Zoe, avoiding Robin's eye. Justine was waiting on a bench in the courtyard with a bottle of champagne and four crystal-effect fluted plastic goblets; leaving her out there had made Penny start crying, and she hadn't stopped yet.

'So, to confirm. The child will have neither the father's surname nor the mother's?'

'Zoe is the mother too,' Penny said, and Zoe, brimming, squeezed her hand. 'She needs an official connection, if she's denied it on the birth certificate. But, yes, that's correct.'

It was an extraordinary gift. Their future children would share a name: Zoe's. She and Penny could never split up, but that was fine, because now they were bound together, by Rose.

16

Now

In Zoe's brain, her mother is narrating: her incompetence, her disastrous choice of clothes. She's due at the mediation in Cumberland House, Garrold Street, Temple, in forty minutes but her battered brain keeps directing her towards Gerrard Place near Waterloo, where she once took herself around an exhibition of Trench Art: embroidered flour-bags, bullet-casing Virgin Marys, shrapnel engraved with children's names. Different part of London but, every time she tries to visualize the journey, hey-ho, like a wobbly divining-rod, off goes her mind again.

And now she can't even tell Penny, win her softness by confessing to another logistical mess.

Focus: Piccadilly Line to Leicester Square, then change. It's a short trot from Embankment; she printed the page at work because her *Compact A–Z* is stuffed with revealing reminders: *OLD LAPTOP cash***. Matt. insoles. RABBIT stuff y/no? check. Rose excema?? Cream + CHASE NEW BLADE.*

Rose's school is the only west London state secondary which offers fencing, mainly because there's no space for much else. Last week, in response to another urgent email about fundraising, Zoe had gone to the office to apologize for not joining in the Mums' Fun 5K 'n' Picnic and the school secretary had held up a hand. 'I'm not hearing that from you,' she announced, and Zoe stepped back, before realizing that Lorraine was sympathizing. 'I had . . . you know who. Your missus. In here the other day, bitching about you at full volume, into her phone.

'Oh God, who was she talking to?'

'You don't seriously think that someone was on the other end?' scoffed Lorraine.

So remember, Zoe tells herself now, reading posters about male pattern baldness and fertility fairs: there are people who believe you. But it doesn't help; she's childishly nervous, clutching her elbows like one of those perpetually cold thin women. The mediator was recommended by Nadia in Family Therapy: striped shirt, short grey hair, like a deputy manager. Accredited Mediation, his website explains, is the process of reaching amicable understanding and negotiating pathways going forward, via common ground and a fruitful and positive methodology. Which sounds great. She almost distracts herself with an advert for a nutritious milkshake, but panic is beating inside her chest, forcing the blood ever faster. What if the mediator is convinced by the others? Maybe this is the day that the children will yield.

There's the track again, rushing beneath her fast enough to ruin.

She walks up the escalator; even now, at this her time of gravest burden, it's important to work on buttock strength. Buttocular. Imagine if the mediator, like sun pouring through cloud, were to bring the truth. He might say: Zoe hasn't done anything bad. Why should she keep meeting you for coffee, only to be bullied? You can't force her to accept your mad plan, so stop saying she's malign. Let this be a normal sad divorce between the mothers, not a custody nightmare. It's time you got a grip.

Or: the kids have said what they want, so now you have to listen.

Or: that includes Rose.

She sees and discounts a sign to the Central Line – East: an anomaly best ignored. She must get Matty new shoes and chase the dentist, remember to thank her parents for tonight, find time before Tuesday to review a book about castration for *Classical Report*, hasn't even started writing her talk on Archaic fire imagery as a metaphor for sexual and/or narcotic rapture for the invitation-only Ancient Historians' Annual Meeting, buy tampons somewhere nearby: are there chemists at Waterloo? Even this doesn't help her register where she's going. It's only when she bursts into the clangorous sunlight of the South Bank does she realize that she's done exactly what her mother, and Penny, would expect of her: she's gone to the wrong place.

THEN

September 1998
This must be it, at last: happiness.

The absurdity of coming home with a new person. Even the postman was impressed by all the bouquets and presents, some from surprising people: Dawn's housebound father; Sara's greyhounds; colleagues in Physiological Metabolism and Islamic Art who had barely even said hello. Hilary Mint sent a hand-knitted miniature jumper, which Penny said was proprietorial.

'Of me? Of you? I don't—'

'I'm simply saying that it's no surprise that old Minty, with her lady-novelist bob, is suddenly clacking away at the cable-stitch. She's never bothered with me before.'

On day eight, Zoe's sister Claire turned up spontaneously, after a fight with her new boyfriend in Leicester Square. Zoe had always made her siblings feel rubbish, with her over-achieving and teacher-pleasing plus, their mother said, Claire was actually the maternal one. Half an hour into her visit, Claire, flinging out her arm to indicate penis size, smashed a glass of Shiraz all over Penny's new rosebud wallpaper. Zoe tried to hush her; Claire ended up stomping off in her Buffalo platform boots to catch the Oxford Tube, devastated. The next morning Zoe's father rang about how unwelcome poor Claire had felt. Life was so much harder for Zoe's siblings: no high-brow job like Zoe's, none of the same opportunities. And Penny said that Zoe staying up late to chat had kept her awake.

After Zoe's paternity leave, things became more delicate. Rose was not a sleeper. Robin wanted things 'the old-fashioned way', which meant ignoring parenting handbooks, while giving advice about timed feeds. He grew stubbled, as if he too bore the brunt. Luckily Rose was a notably merry infant, and Penny looked great for early motherhood, everyone said so. Even her breast-feeding excelled; the health visitor was delighted with her.

Although Zoe had read everything possible about bathing babies, burping babies, whatever she tried to do Penny managed better, faster. This must be how it felt to be a father. Why should Rose's nappy rash suffer because Zoe was checking about parabens? She tried to tend Penny too, but ruined things by being so clumsy, emotionally; embarrassingly yearning for them both.

There was never enough time to spend with Rose and, now that Robin was taking her off for an hour, then two, which was miserable for them both but naturally only really agony for Penny, how could Zoe monopolize what time was left? Penny said that the sight of her baby going off in the sling, proudly worn on Robin's chest like a preening male bird, made her desolate. Yes, they had agreed to this, but it was inhumane. Besides, he was endlessly trimming bits of time from theirs, 'like,' Zoe pointed out, 'a coin-clipper. Did you know Isaac Newt—'

'Christ,' said Penny.

He'd bring her back slightly late from his Movement-for-Dads class, or with only one mitten, and never apologize. Penny was so afraid that he could somehow get custody of Rose that even she would not challenge him. It all worked perfectly well, on the surface, and if they questioned one of his emails, he'd say threateningly, 'We'll have to meet up for a discussion'. Attrition, he seemed to believe, sheer force of personality, would make them yield.

But Penny, too, had force. She began to keep a record of

his affectations: winter shorts, interdental Waterpik, low-cal hot chocolate, disdain for email. He shunned dentists, refused to keep Calpol in the house, as if it were a maternal neurosis, not a normal tool of modern parenting, a chance of staving off disaster. Justine was expected to comply. However much he put her down, she deferred to him, only revealing an edge when they were apart: 'whatever the decision is,' she'd say, or 'I'll have to check with himself'. She'd sigh in irritation at Rose's modest dramas, and Zoe would want to pull her arms off, but never said a word.

'Where's her self-respect?' Penny would ask. 'How can she stand to let him think he's the clever one? It's weak,' and then Zoe would have to tread carefully. Penny didn't like her joining in the discussion of Justine's imperfections.

At least Justine was the aunt, biologically, indissolubly. Unfortunately, Zoe had fallen in love with Rose, the smell of her nape, her happy dribble, yet, for all the balanced snacks she made Penny and glasses of water left at her elbow, the bottles she warmed, jiggling Rose in her sling while she washed pans, what was she? A mother only because Penny had declared her so.

As Rose grew, there was more she could do for her, reading, tickling, freezing ice-cubes of mango and mashed lentils to reheat in tastebud-stimulating combinations. But, once she started baby-nursery, it was even more agonizing for Penny to wave her off with Robin, to give up a second of time with her child. For her sake, Penny's, Zoe forced herself to hang back.

Because their flat was so convenient, Penny's friends could

come by after work to discuss episiotomies, or hitting forty, and she'd tell Zoe: 'Go out! Enjoy yourself! Why don't you go clubbing, like a normal twenty-something?'

But it hurt to leave them. Penny was often upset when Zoe came home. Rose was too sweet and funny to stay away from for long. Zoe felt like an old child, although she knew that, compared to Penny's childless lesbian friends, and her own young lot, her life had such milky richness. Penny's standards of maternal devotion were exhilaratingly high; they'd spend hours, whole evenings, discussing the bad mothers they'd known, creepily cuddly with their adult sons or cold to their daughters. If ever they heard about a female colleague going to a really exciting conference, or writing a whole book, Penny would be disgusted. 'Her poor family. At least Rose will know how wanted she is.'

To please Penny, Zoe, sharing night-feeds, a zombie at work, forced herself to go to drinks in bars, parties in her old friends' shared houses, but it was hard to join in whole-heartedly. Penny's nicknames for them had started to stick: Aristotle; Bora; Hairiette. And what if Penny left one of her scented candles too close to the curtains? Or microwaved the bolognese in a carcinogenic plastic pot? Zoe said she wanted to make Rose's little meals out of love, but this reminded Penny of the thriftiness of her youth, which her wellbeing, her sanity, had depended upon escaping. She accused Zoe of penny-pinching. Nothing bad would happen to their baby with a bit of convenience food.

How could anybody truly be sure of that?

*

It didn't matter if none of Rose's baby-clothes were new, only that they had enough stores to keep her alive if, say, there were riots and they had to stay inside. In the night she'd approach the pit of fear, feel herself falling; she'd saved her whole life for emergencies, then spent it all on frozen margaritas in their first year, out with Penny's friends.

'You're joking. How was that a waste? What would you rather be doing,' asked Penny, tears already falling, 'living it up, or reading Turgenev back in Deadington?'

Someone had warned her that sleep would become their currency; she hadn't believed it, thought it only applied to straight couples. Until Penny had finished reviewing a book about Charlestonian influence on Australian modernist textiles, which she was hating, and should have been commissioned to write herself, Zoe had full responsibility for Rose's nursery-rhyme-themed nightmares and urgent calls for water, all the staggeringly early mornings, attempting to unblock her cursory nose so she didn't cough herself awake. Zoe was stretched beyond elasticity, enervated with caffeine and sugar, but that was how it was meant to feel.

Penny said she was square not to want wine, to unwind, yet she was scathing about how much her own friends drank, a bit sloshed far too often. They couldn't slip down that slope so soon into their lives together. Also, Zoe needed to keep her wits about her. Unanchored wardrobes, thin old glass, rusty nails in next door's garden: someone needed to stay alert.

17

Autumn 2000

Tuesdays were Zoe's: the best and most frightening part of the week. After nursery she'd wheel Rose's pushchair through Cadby Park towards the steamy Polish cafe. The staff never recognized her but greeted Rose and, even as she chased her very slowly around the bollards pretending to be a bear, and Rose cackled, Zoe would be rehearsing proofs of their relationship, in case she was questioned: Rose's words for socks and raspberries, the way she sawed at cheese like a little grasshopper with her miniature bottom incisors. She'd looked up step-parents in their parenting books, how to deal with this superfluity of love, but none of the authors seemed to think that made a difference. Adopting Rose would have been fantastic, but Zoe couldn't, so long as Robin was a Named Father. Legally, the best she could hope for was to apply for step-parent Parental Responsibility via the principal registry of the Family Division in Holborn, with a solicitor hiring a barrister to represent them before a judge.

Mad, the idea of hiring lawyers, like Californians.

'I will support you,' said Penny, and they went to fill out

the forms over pizza, although what if Penny died before the hearing?

Zoe was eating the penultimate olive, Rose sleeping like a marvel in the buggy, when Penny leaned towards her. 'Next table's trying to suss us out,' she whispered, and kissed Zoe on the mouth. Sometimes, a bit drunk after a party, or if they passed potential lesbians, Penny would stroke Zoe's cheek, her bum. It should have been sexy, but made her feel like an animal backed into a stall.

Penny sat down again, the kiss hardly begun. She reapplied her lipstick: Volte Face. 'Robin better not try to get PR for you-know-who,' she said. Lately, Justine had been calling Rose 'our child', which Penny hated. 'Who's he going to rope in next? His new girlfriend, the tall one? That's all we need. Poor little Rose. Let's not tell him we're applying.'

'Look, though, it does say we need his signature,' Zoe said, and Penny sighed dramatically, took a swig of wine. Zoe was trying to root out her tendency to fret, her dread of undue optimism, but the fear was growing.

'Well, we'll just have to wing it. I'm not letting that Plantagenet boss us around.'

Now Rose was enormous, almost two, climbing onto one of the outside cafe benches in her pirate T-shirt: such an unhushable, unstoppable little person. 'Careful,' said Zoe, holding Rose's sticky flipper, and they grinned at each other, and Zoe thought, this is good, the two of us, easier in a way . . .

Don't you dare. Even a selfish glimpse of how that would be was anathema, tempting disaster. Nevertheless, bystanders, smiling, asking Rose's age, couldn't possibly guess that she wasn't biologically Zoe's. People already sometimes said they looked alike. They appeared simply a woman and a child, even a mother and a daughter.

So when Rose fell off, catching her chin on the edge and howling, blood dropping fatly from her lip, Zoe lifted her in her arms, 'come on my baby, oh my sweetheart, yes my poor little girl, poor baby', and ran with her to the till, where strangers politely fussed and offered paper napkins, until Rose's cries calmed and the blood was blotted and she was found to be OK, a lucky escape, no skull bashed on the tiles, no tragedy this time.

'I baby,' she observed, and the old woman beside them refolded her polythene bag and smiled.

'All right now, your little boy?' she asked Zoe.

'She's a girl.'

'Oh.' The woman frowned, looked again at Rose's fair corn-cob fluff, at Zoe's dark heavy fall of hair: straight, Penny always said, as a plank. 'Does she look more like your husband?'

And Zoe smiled tightly, picked up Rose and, like screws being turned, the pain of love grew a little sharper.

But, even as she delighted at Rose's unusual toddler beauty, her evident genius, Penny was growing older. Every developmental landmark was another month of fertility lost. She kept commenting on how ancient she looked, spent hours inspecting herself in the mirror, pulling up bits of her face. Meanwhile, Zoe's fear, or gratitude, intensified. If Penny sank into delayed postnatal despair, how would Zoe rescue her? The idea of her taking to her bed, Robin coming to the door to claim his child, made her frantic. Penny's birthday came, followed by Rose's; they had a joint party with champagne and chocolate milk and a cake decorated in an approximation of Humphrey B. Bear, a yellow-bow-tied television character of Penny's youth, with six or seven of the cheaper dishes from the Moro cookbook, spinach and chickpeas, burnt aubergines, which Zoe under seasoned and over apologized for, and Penny's friends seemed barely to notice. Thom Pershore sent a Man Ray nude print, which turned out to be just a poster; Penny's stepbrother wrote a card which Penny read aloud; Justine brought roses the colour of blackcurrant yoghurt, a bunch big as a reasonably sized child, and earrings, which Penny whispered were naff but wore anyway. Even Zoe's father sent a postcard of Mayan glyphs from the Bodleian, signed 'Tricia' in his handwriting, and the Yves Saint Laurent lipstick for which she and Penny shared a passion. Lately, they had been exchanging messages via Zoe, but this was a major development: a huge leap forward.

Robin organized a cringey godparent-investiture in Holland Park; each parent, plus Justine, was allowed to nominate two. The dog-free wildflower nook was rammed. He had insisted on 'humble' canapés, which meant rolls of ham and cream cheese, and Justine's salami puffs. Over by the fallen log, Penny was having a heart-to-heart with several of her gang, her back turned. Was she ill? Falling for someone else? Why should there be a limit to disasters?

'Poor Pinny,' explained Nicky as they left, 'can't bear it. She misses being pregnant.'

'I don't have the option of dithering, you do realize,' Penny added. They'd had this conversation before but never in the presence of her friends, like chieftains agreeing a peace treaty while their henchmen sharpened knives. 'If you're going next, like I said you could, for balance, you have to hurry up. It wouldn't be fair to me.'

But they'd only just officially finalized the agreement with Robin. Certain topics – schools, specific timings of post-nursery drop-offs on alternate Fridays – had been sticky. They were too exhausted for his long reasonable-sounding late-night emails, signed 'with our love, Robin and Justine' but then, in real life, when he'd forced them to agree extra time so he could take Rose on a Hampshire nostalgia-trip ('the Black Prince promenades before his loyal subjects'), or returned her late after a victory-lap around the office, he would be maroon-faced, seething. Yet even Penny would save her rage for after he'd left. Then she'd barely sleep. He needed to accept that mothers were the most important, but it was impossible to tell him this directly, lest he unleash legal havoc. At least his attempts to dominate, his cold self-belief, united them.

What, asked Penny, was Justine thinking, letting him tyran-nize her?

For her second Easter, Rose had 'made' two egg-paintings, one with 'Mummy and Mama' printed on it in clear adult pen and the other with 'Daddy and Jesteen'; both households had them on their fridges. The nursery was in a community hall in Olympia, staffed by locals. Penny went in specially to warn them about newspaper interest; even now, in the twenty-first century, tabloids regularly outed gay people who had kids. But the staff were kind; accepting, even, as far as one could tell. They'd call out hellos, always remembered who was doing pick-up and which was Mummy and which Mama, agreed that Rose was lucky to have so many parents. They stuck her portrait of her enormous family, labelled in capitals, bang opposite the entrance doors. Then Penny turned up after drop-off at Zoe's work mid-tutorial, incoherent, in tears.

Zoe parked her in the hall by the microfiche until she could decently finish, then led her to the next-door greasy spoon, known to be BNP-y, but this was not the time. When Penny could speak, she revealed not death but something which seemed nearly as bad: Stanley's mum from nursery had been invited to Robin and Justine's for dinner ('bet he went all River Cafe'). And this morning she'd mentioned to Penny, over the sand-tray: 'I hadn't realized he has so much time.'

Penny had started explaining but Stanley's mum had cut in: 'Oh, but he told me "a generous third".'

They wanted to kill him, but at least they were united. Over emergency cheese toasties, they recalculated the current split of hours in the back of Penny's pocket diary, passing her little silver pencil to and fro. 'The good thing,' she said, calm at last, 'is that when you have one too, you'll be much safer with Rose. Even that sneaky old shit wouldn't dare to separate biological siblings.'

Zoe began a little speech: how astonishing it was that they had managed to produce one child. Twenty, even ten years ago, they wouldn't have dared; look at Penny's friends, some of whom would have loved motherhood, if they'd had the chance. They'd been so lucky, doing this in this era, in London, in academe; people were so glad for them, almost never said anything dodgy.

'Except your mum. I still haven't forg—'

'Well, yes.' But, she went bravely on, might not having another push their luck? Wouldn't it be better to have fewer ties to Robin, if they feared him so much already? And the expense, on their salaries, the worry, the delirium of sleep deprivation, the agony of being parted from Rose, even for Zoe, although obviously that wasn't anything like . . . They were still floundering in the brine of new motherhood, gasping for breath.

She managed not to mention the pain caused by loving while knowing that one was unnecessary; not to ask how, if something terrible happened, one would hide two children? Who would take them all in?

Penny shot out a hand to pick a feather from Zoe's collar. Zoe moved her lips comically, like a questing tapir, to kiss her fingers, but Penny moved away.

18

Now

Late again, reckless with self-disgust, she races down an escalator, along a passageway, more steps and then, like a benison from heaven, she sees that the Northern Line train in the other, correct, direction is standing at the platform. With a flash of satisfaction, she leaps on.

The doors don't close.

Arrogance, vainglory; it makes her want to puncture her skin, glance around for something sharp. The digital board says *B!3yxx####*; another layer of alertness glides into place for the famous warning-announcement about Inspector Sands, a whiff of smoke. She was driving Robin's scrupulously tidy car, collecting Matilda from Penny's Queensland friend's child's Bratz-themed birthday party, when the London tube bombings came on the radio. Afterwards she said, 'I hope Matty didn't understand what they . . . it was quite graphic.'

Robin answered: 'Good if she did. Sooner she starts learning about real life, the better.'

The incoming train, a voice screams, will leave momentarily. It isn't as if the mediator will be there to pass judgement; the website is categorical. But what if, in particularly desperate situations, he steps in? Could he be called upon as an expert adviser, if it did reach court; will Robin, faking calmness, mislead him?

Dawn said: 'You're going to have to tell the mediator what Penny did. And Robin will have to admit he's known all along.'

She wipes her temples, rechecks the time. There is dry pink skin all round her lips, like a clown. She picks Todly-hairs from her jumper, as if that will swing the mediator's decision. In a few hours she's meant to be starting a new life among Ozman's dining chairs on Goldhawk Road.

No way will Penny allow it.

There's a seat. She doesn't sit; she keeps having this sense of being hunted, among the strip-lights and echoes. Better standing, in the corner by the door. Then someone gets on: a neat shorn head. She can't properly look but what if it's Robin, bringing his solicitor with him, fresh from school? No, it's another thin angry man, arms folded, glaring at a different woman, with a baby in a buggy. Zoe tries to meet her gaze, but the woman glances away.

She's damp and frantic when she emerges at Temple tube, bolting out of the entrance like a puppy failing a sheepdog trial. There are lawyers everywhere: barristers in their white ties like lamb cutlets, clumsily suited young women and casual young men in rolled shirt-sleeves wheeling document files. All this lawyering-about is nothing to do with her, but it's easy to imagine being served papers; or is that America? Even if she could calculate the minutes left, while trying to orient herself, the phone makes it worse; which way does the moving arrow face? In their early days, before Zoe's flaws and faults had become more obvious, Penny found her perpetual lostness adorable, kept trying to help her learn London basics: 'See, you could turn left here and drive all the way to Headington. You definitely know that.' Every passer-by has earphones on; she is almost weeping by the time she finds herself, quite by chance, outside Cumberland House, standing in front of a vaguely familiar-looking woman by a bicycle.

19

Winter 2000

In October, Penny said that, every time she had a period, she wondered if their relationship was doomed.

In November, Zoe was asked to contribute to a *festschrift* for Professor Walter Šincek on Taboo in Athenian Tragedy, then invited to plug a gap in the Schools' Greek Confederation ('Love Sick: reconstructing Phaedra as hero'), on a Thursday evening, in Durham. How, Penny wanted to know, could she put her career before her family? Zoe ended up withdrawing from the *festschrift*, and everything else she could think of. The next morning, as Penny sat at the kitchen table in her porridge-crusted kimono and mothy Fair Isle hand-warmers, Zoe, rootling around underneath it for her work shoe, glanced up at Rose, boinging in a borrowed doorway-bouncer, beaming at her mothers, and accidentally started to cry.

'What? What?'

'I just . . .' but she was too sad to explain. How could she hold all this in her heart? Rose didn't truly need or want her, and Penny said Zoe's anxiety was probably damaging her, more so than the fumes from the flyover puffing through the sash windows, pollution-grime, black mould, seagulls shitting their psittacosis on the sill. Maybe, Zoe had begun to think, I'm not good for her.

Penny gave a deep, deep sigh.

'Sorry,' Zoe told her. 'I know it's not what you need. I'm tired, that's all. I mean, nothing like you must b—'

'What I need,' said Penny, pushing her plate aside, grabbing at a square of kitchen towel, 'is certainty. Commitment. This is devastating for me. If you can't guarantee we can try soon for the next one, I don't know what I'll do.'

Now

3.01 p.m.

Penny is mid-flow: 'coming back from the weekend, when several of my close friends were so deeply worried ab—'

It is a horrible office. They've tried to make it convincingly therapeutic, with a worried ficus, a grouping of mustard-yellow vases, artistic shots of railings, but it's still a room you'd be ushered into to hear grave news. The window is barred; the lighting flickers like a tic. Even though the mediator had been warned to expect four of them, there's been the usual seating problem, like at a school parents' evening; he's provided an assortment of cheap wood and stackable plastic chairs. Against the desk stands the only stranger: Tony Harcastle, Member of the Society of Mediators and Consultant in Couples Psychoanalytic Psychotherapy. His arms are crossed.

'Aha, Zoe presumably,' he says, with a smile like a packing-staple. Robin had insisted that they see a man. Penny, surprisingly, agreed. 'So you were able to make it.'

Penny is conspicuously averting her gaze, as if the mere sight of Zoe is harmful. Robin and Justine are sitting side by side: front-row witnesses to an execution.

'Hi,' she says.

And the room explodes: eye-rolling, exaggerated sighs. 'See,' demands Penny, 'how she behaves? Not even a basic understanding of the suffering we're . . . Imagine how this is for our children. My children. They're still so young, so unaware, and my little daughter is being snatched from me, in an atmosphere of—'

'So,' says the mediator. 'L—'

Penny nods at him mid-breath, like a marathon-runner; carries on. 'What you absolutely have to understand is that she lies. All the time. Nothing she says can be trusted, or e—'

'Thank you,' he says, 'ah, Penelope. There will be plenty of time for all to speak.'

Everybody is dressed for everyone else. Robin is wearing a burgundy shirt over a grey T-shirt, with neat dark jeans; the relaxed father, the humble man. His big sandy-grey head nods compassionately at everything the mediator says, but he's doing that thing with his jaw which shows he's angry; when he speaks his voice will go tremulously quiet, so one has to lean in. Justine sits very upright in a black jacket, as if under oath. Almost all Penny's visible garments are new, like a hermit crab displaying its valuables: high suede heels and bare tanned legs, a long swishy red-and-fuchsia dress like angry sangria, with a demure sky-blue angora cardigan over the top. She taps a new pen, Muji hexagonal, against a new flowered notebook.

The mediator has dragged his ergonomic chair to the near side of the desk, to show informality. The thought of a grown man solemnly learning unthreatening body-language from a textbook would have been funny, before. He explains the rules: no accusing, hands to be raised. They might work. Zoe and Penny know them already from the other mediator, with whom they had had only one session; Penny had suspected the mediator and Zoe of liaising beforehand, planning a stitch-up. She'd insisted it wasn't fair not to include Justine and Robin, and refused to return.

Penny opens her notebook, uncaps the pen. Robin, head inclined as if everything is very fair and reasonable and exactly as he'd intended, sits back; Justine leans forward. 'Who,' says the mediator, 'would like to begin?'

THEN

Winter 2000
However much Zoe pleaded with her not to raise their hopes, Penny wouldn't stop speculating: how they could get a boy this time around, how to protect poor Rose from the lifelong pain of being displaced by a younger sibling. Penny

insisted that Zoe had made promises, which Zoe herself could not remember, to transcend her youth and fearfulness and mad parents, and do what they all needed her to: hurry up.

Lately, Zoe had been panicking quite a lot in the women's toilets. Luckily the freezing high-ceilinged room was all the way over in Modern Languages, grimy metal windows flung wide but still scented with secret flesh. What if a passing sociolinguist recognized Zoe's smothered weeping, and told Penny? They weren't getting on; Zoe was too busy clawing herself up the ladder, trying to please Tricia, sucking up to Hilary Mint, even turning on the charm in the Spanish cafe, which had always been Penny's, and then not bothering to make the same effort at home. Worst of all were Zoe's fears. Why shouldn't Rose run free, as Penny had? What kind of mother would want their daughter to grow up scared of strangers, barely able to cross Hammersmith Broadway?

Zoe would, if it kept Rose safe. It seemed extraordinary that anyone made it through childhood, let alone someone so beloved, and therefore so marked for disaster. Was it so bad to keep a warning triangle in Robin's car? Whenever their defenceless girl wanted to totter along a wall or play hide and seek in the dark shrubbery of Marcus Garvey Park, they'd argue. Saying nothing felt like courting danger, and then how would Zoe face Penny, when she could have saved such pain simply by pointing out the risks from electrocution by leaky Rainbow Glo-n-Hug Bear batteries; leukaemia from night-lights; a persistent rash ignored; Robin, knowing best, feeding her an unhalved grape; one poor maniac on an Underground platform, imagining demons? Who'd be rash enough to assume that Fate wasn't already tempted, scissors out? Their lives could already be about to be devastated. Sometimes Zoe could barely touch Penny, for fear of something marble-sized in a breast, the first whisper of malignancy. However much it maddened Penny, vigilance was an act of love.

'Your mum had a point,' said Penny. Robin's car had been broken into for the fourth time; the police said it was The Addicts, being swept down from the redevelopments. Penny teased her, called them 'your lovely neighbours', but Zoe was growing anxious about needles in the playing fields. 'She says it's exhausting, keeping up with the neurosis, and she's right. My friends agree; they don't know how I stand it. Lying awake to keep watch in case Rose suffocates of snot.'

'That one time. She could hardly breathe. We both needed sleep, you specifically said.'

'It's like you don't trust me. When I'm the one keeping things running. You'd have no clue how to defrost a freezer, or insurance, or . . .' Rose rubbed mashed butternut squash into her own eye and started roaring. 'It's always been like this, me leading the way, and you benefitting. Even making Rose, yes Rose, yes Rosie, good girl, is because I drove it, I pushed . . . imagine if we didn't have her.'

'I'm not! I don't. I'll try to, not to . . . you know how incredibly gratef—'

'If you really were,' said Penny, 'you wouldn't be putting your career, this manic ambition, yet another paper on Eu-sodding-ripedes, before us having another child. It's *normal* to need more than one. Everyone else gets it. I see people around me pregnant again, or with two, or three kids, and – and my fertility is . . .'

'Shhh, shh. Don't cry.'

'You'd better. Robin won't wait for ever. I won't.'

Penny stood, began to brush her hair. The waves made a tearing sound, despite her new Mason Pearson hairbrush. Zoe's mind rushed to chemo; one day, she thought, I'll wish I'd kept a curl. 'We played in rivers,' Penny added. 'We ran wild round the quarries.'

Yes, thought Zoe, but you survived. Statistically, if you'd had more siblings, what were the chances?

It wasn't hard to imagine Penny standing on a sister's head to reach fresh air.

'Maybe I should do it myself, without you,' she said. 'Find someone who is ready. We'll see.'

20

Now

Tony Harcastle has given up completely. He doesn't ask for clarification every time Penny, or Robin, or Justine, refer, with fury and disgust, to 'her'. In fact, he no longer intervenes at all. Zoe had assumed that eventually he'll take control, but they go on accusing, and he swallows everything they claim.

'Her lack of communication,' Robin states, 'is pathological. My sister and I have been kindness itself, done everything to accommodate, to understand her. Why would anyone refuse to share a meal with perfectly reasonable people, to open up about their future plans?'

Justine nods vigorously. 'We've been astonishingly patient. But we have to get the children away from the disordered enveloping blackness in her, urgently. Of course they're broken by this split; she's made them be miserable, constantly expecting things to go wrong, exactly like her, and they'll stay that way to please her. Her darkness is so deep-rooted . . . it's generational, you see. The family is the same, this sort of morbid obsession with the past. Appalling mental health, and behavioural issues. I've learned that they go for months without speaking to each other.' Zoe opens her mouth. Her neck and chest burn with shame, or is it anger? She can't remember how that feels. 'Apparently, it's a thing for them, being proud of bearing grudges. Huge fallings-out. This dysfunction might work for, well, them, but we, we three, we've been bearing the brunt.'

On the floor beside Penny is a takeaway cup filled with strawberries. 'From your little garden,' she said at the start, 'for you.' Then, when Zoe did not reach out to take it, she commented to Tony Harcastle and the others: 'See? Even the kindest action?' and Justine winced with sympathy.

Robin holds up a hand, like a traffic policeman. 'We are all well-balanced adults. There is nothing wrong with us. I have invited her repeatedly into my home to discuss how to divide up the children's time fairly for all concerned, and she refuses. I have welcomed her to share her relocation plans. But, coming from a background where non-communication is normal, well . . .' and he shrugs theatrically. 'What can you do when someone simply won't engage?'

'Ever,' Penny confirms. 'Also, I'd like to state that Robin has been wonderful. Truly supportive; they all have, the Balders. Everyone, even my exes, has been so kind. They're terrified I'm going to hurt myself; I think she must want that. And none, none of us understand why she is doing this to me, to us. We've discussed it, and it doesn't make sense. She has deep psychological issues which she masks with pills, plus these very strong antihistamines for hayfever. Maybe that's why.'

'Medicalization,' observes Robin.

'As we all know to our cost,' Penny goes on, 'she has

completely brainwashed my children, our children.' She's practically howling; Tony Harcastle looks stunned. Robin, nimble as a sprite, passes her a cup of water. 'Feeding her parents' malign versions of the world straight into their brains. They're absolutely toxic, you should know that. Though of course it's them she's farmed the children out to tonight, so she can make her getaway.'

'It was for the mediation!'

'Nobody knows why . . . for some reason Matilda, my Tilda, is refusing to see me, and there is no possible reason except that she's told her not to. I am her mother. I am calm with her. I do *not* cry with her; not once. She has no idea about my – my grief. Oh God. This is killing me. Why else wouldn't she see me, when she knows I, I need . . . ohhh.'

Zoe imagines telling her: this is why. The dozens, hundreds of times, since the kids were little, they've heard you raging and blaming me: for not wanting more babies, saying I want to control you, or I'm trying to hold you back. You swear you can't help yourself, but you do manage to keep it together with certain people, just not with them; that's the worst bit of all.

But taboos build in increments, dead sea-creatures drifting, thickening, packing into limestone. What if Penny did have a breakdown, as she's been threatening all year? Imagine Rose having to cope with that alone. Or if she killed herself. She might; people do. And how could Zoe stand up alone to Robin, when even Penny has never dared challenge him, from the very first: his laying down the law, Justine's occasional bouts of boozy resentment and housework-refusal, the many, many subjects which enraged her.

Because, luckily, he was mostly a good father, Justine a loving aunt; they tell everyone this. Yes, he was extraordinarily tight, boring about solar power, cycling, 'tech'. He and Justine vetoed anything that made the kids' lives more enjoyable than theirs had been (Tangleteasers, iPods, ear-piercing). Zoe and Penny would discuss it secretly but never raise it with him: deserters from a just cause. It was easier to laugh about how much they hated it when a child came out with a Balderism, than to feel the pain when Rose said, aged ten, 'I wish their weekends could be abolished,' or on Friday mornings Matty begged: 'Please can you tell him not to take me to football. I really, really don't want to go.'

'It's difficult,' Zoe and Penny would say. What the kids must never know was how much they still feared a custody battle; he'd have the power, definitely. That was the reason for keeping quiet. Wasn't it?

Robin is explaining again. 'I was brought up to be very moral, and she has no morality. My daughters are in trouble, and it's her doing. She needs to take responsibility for that. It is certainly nothing we've done.'

Penny: 'I've given my life to mothering. It's her issues, you see. So much mental instability. You know she's forced Matty to visit a therapist, and encouraged Rose, too? As if there's something wrong in our, the, home-life, other than her? It's, it's disgusting, actually. She fetishizes pain. She's determined to deny me access to my child's living arrangements; this is a kidnapping. I've been advised to look after my own needs;

there's a real possibility of a collapse. I have a senior therapist on standby. He gave me his private number, begged me to ring day or night.'

When Zoe told Dawn this latest claim of Penny's, Dawn snorted her tea out of her nose, or pretended she had. This was on the phone. 'Load of cobblers. Wish she would, though,' she added. 'I'd kill to hear the conversation at three a.m.: "Go back to sleep, Diane, it's just another nutter".'

'When evidently,' Robin cuts across Penny, 'it's much more extensive Family Therapy we need, as a family, not individual work: no need for that. A long thorough course, together, to make her, help her, see that she can't act unilaterally. It's her doing, this disaster, because of her failure to communicate.'

Zoe takes an enormous breath, as if to blow out candles. 'You know that's not true. There've been endless meetings, coffees, one-to-ones, every combination. I've tried to work it out . . . no, let me. I've asked you to listen to what Matilda specifically wants, and Rose, instead of obsessing about schedules and "time arrangements". And all you'll say is that I must be a monster, because Matilda won't do what you want. She's old enough . . . she's been very clear. It was incredibly difficult for her, and w—' Justine starts to speak. Zoe ignores her. 'Her CAMHS person, who she had to see because she was struggling, no, you must know she was. She was truanting. Yes, she was. You can't just deny it, or say it was my fault. So,' she forces herself to keep at it, her eyes on the mediator alone, 'this man specifically said that all their miserable hostility towards me, which the kids keep witnessing, is making it worse. It's not me, alone . . . how could it be?

And this is unnecessarily . . . it should be about me and Penny splitting up, not some kind of Gothic four-way divorce.' Penny gasps, but Zoe will, must, be clear. 'Their problem, their main issue, is that I still haven't forced the kids to do what they're insisting on.' She wills Tony Harcastle to help. *Say it.* 'And, well. I won't.'

Tony Harcastle glances at Robin, as if he has the last word, but Robin will speak when he's ready. 'All we ever wanted,' notes Justine sadly, as if giving a eulogy, 'was a better relationship with her. We are united on that. But she's incapable of it, because of her familial issues. History repeating itsel—'

'Sorry, what?' says Zoe.

'See?' says Penny. 'The constant interrupting; I've told her and told her.'

'She's always been like this, apparently,' Justine goes on. 'Certainly since I've known her. Entirely selfish, not caring what it's doing to Robin, to all of us. Penny is distraught. She can't speak to Tilda without sobbing her heart out.'

Penny, stuffing tissues back into her handbag, scowls. Justine looks stricken; sorry, she mouths, but Penny pointedly turns away.

'And, for the record,' Justine adds, 'Robin hasn't bullied her once, he's an extremely thoughtful man.'

Robin finally steps in. 'We know ourselves. My sister and I hold family values to be . . . paramount.' He gives a quick modest smile. 'Yet she rides roughshod. I'm sure you see that, Timmy.'

'Tony,' murmurs his sister.

Penny leans closer, jabs a finger in Zoe's face. 'How can

you live with yourself? So much damage. Rose wastes her time with drawing and fencing, not interested in relationships; if she fails her exams, it's your fault. Because you're abandoning her, the child you swore you would raise with me. How can you live with yourself? Don't think for a second you're taking her with you.'

'If it comes to it,' Robin comments, 'I have friends in the Met.'

'He has,' Justine says. 'Eminent.'

'Sorry,' says Zoe. 'I . . . wait, you're threateni—'

'Not a threat,' says Robin with a look at his sister.

'It bloody is a threat,' says Penny.

'And Matilda's issues at school, what do you expect with your mothering? Yours, and Tricia's? I know you've met the Head. Absolutely classic, going behind our backs. I've arranged my own appointment to see him, and I'm bringing expert support.'

Even mentioning that Matilda rang earlier from St Clement's will add grist to their mill. But saying it will let her down, yet again. Zoe can't do it.

She does it. 'You brought a lawyer into her school,' she says to Robin, by looking at the top of his ear. 'Why would you do that?'

'See?' Penny says to Tony Harcastle. 'She n—'

'I,' spits Robin, 'have rights.'

'So do I!' Penny says.

'Yes! Yes, you do, but she has to want to . . . you can't drag her about like a, a spaniel.'

'She's my spaniel!'

Last week Zoe happened upon a mention of the damage done, by even the best-intentioned adults, to children raised in communes, expected to suppress their instinctive attachment to one specific parent, for collective harmony. Apparently, this fact was too widely known to need explanation, except for Zoe.

And Zoe let it happen, twice: not only across the two households, but also with Penny. For Penny.

'Sadly,' says Tony Harcastle, 'we are nearing the end of our allotted time.'

Penny and Zoe accidentally exchange glances, like a lion and a tiger passing. Penny looks victorious; Zoe has stuck to her promise, has not used her last and most desperate weapon, as she had faithfully promised Penny, and now it's too late to change her mind.

Then Penny says: 'Tell them about the psychiatrist.'

'Me?'

'Obviously. When you were pregnant.'

And Zoe understands that all the years of concealing things from Robin, unity against him, are over. A different game has begun.

21

Then

Winter 2000

All she'd said was how brief their pre-motherhood idyll had been. But Penny was outraged. They'd had over a year before babies: more than enough. How could she not understand that?

It had already been a bad few weeks: Penny's grant application to study at the Plath archives at Smith was due, and she'd not made the deadline for inclusion in a Patrick White conference in Connecticut. Rose developed croup on a Robin weekend, as they realized from her startling seal-bark, and he had failed to tell them.

He was a bully about Christmas, too. After almost seven hours in his flat, pork rillettes and unswallowably dry venison and a tense Monopoly tournament with his mother, Zoe had a sinful thought: might this turn Penny off having another baby with him? Then, when Penny went upstairs and they could all hear the occasional sob as she ran a bath, a new idea came: or put him off us?

Rose, who had self-sleep-trained, started climbing, weeping, into their bed. Zoe was asked to take over the third years' BARBARISM(S) seminar from Dusty Fowler, who was moving to Chalkidiki to research the Cappadocian origins of the double-bouncing *tromakton* dance; not, she wished everyone to understand, the *atsiapat*, which was similar but much less interesting. Then Dr Rainfold, Penny's exciting new boss, with whom she'd had a very successful lunch, wrote her a lacklustre reference for Smith.

Penny was inconsolable. Luckily it was a Wednesday, so Rose was at Robin's. They ended up in A & E, Zoe rubbing Penny's back, wondering: what if Robin found out about this?

So much for the improved Zoe she'd willed her nasty self to become: unselfish, loving without conditionality. Not even devotion to Rose could help her become a good person; in fact, the stronger her love, the harder it was to imagine their world expanding to include another baby, let alone one that she herself had produced, and that would start soon. It was like running downhill, not knowing how to stop unless you fell.

Then they went to stay with Nicky at her ex's ex's pet-friendly guesthouse in Poole, where there were arguments, inadequately hushed, and unsuccessful sex, and telling Zoe off in front of 'the girls' for interrupting, and Zoe walked alone in the freezing garden when Penny drove with the others to the pub in a rage, and wasn't back for hours. On Sunday night, after they had dropped off the hired car and tubed home with a urinous Rose and too many bags, Penny came in when Zoe was sitting on the loo and told her: 'You might as well know, everyone's appalled at your behaviour.'

Much later, off went Zoe, trotting down to Robin's flat,

225

the stairs wet with moonlight, only a car alarm to be heard, to put a note under his door, taking care to avoid the doormat. It said: 'We want to make a start on baby no. 2 w/you. This Thurs?'

Now

3.58 p.m.
Among the promises Zoe and Penny made, as well as to love each other for ever, and to be true always, was this: never to give Robin or Justine any information which, if it came to court, could be used against them.

'Poor, poor Tilda,' Justine murmurs, shaking her head compassionately. Penny's hiding her victory smile; actually, Zoe can't bear to look. 'It explains so much about how she sees the world: the need to rebel. There's a serious consent issue, to impose psychiatry on a child, a foetus, against the will of the other parents.'

Robin ignores her. 'I will have to speak to my lawyer.'

'It wasn't even Matilda,' Zoe points out. 'This was before that pregnancy.'

Penny leans forward, hands on thighs. Her wedding ring shines. 'Now you can see why she's always trying to get doctors to prescribe crap for the poor kids. They're perfectly fine, or would be if they weren't infected by her unstable, damaging inf—'

'I should have been informed,' says Robin.

'I know,' Penny tells him, which is a lie. 'I wanted to.'

Zoe has a pure clear image of puking at their feet. She keeps her lips clamped shut, but her mind is saying: this is unbearable. Then: it's not even them at their maddest. Christ, what the kids must have heard. Although, before things disintegrated, and Robin weighed in, were things any better? The kids weren't allowed even to ask if they could stay with their mums for an extra hour, if they were ill or for a birthday. Zoe and Penny never said, 'I will talk to Dad for you.' They all upheld the myth that neither child had any closer bond, any preference.

As if she were on a mountain, scaldingly bright cold light, her eyes sting. She understands now that it wasn't only with Robin that the taboo applied. It happened constantly, every night. I was the worst. I put Penny before them, without question. Oh God. What have we done?

THEN

July 2001

'Whatever you are, you're definitely not depressed,' said Penny.

They were just home from Portugal: not a success. Zoe had hoped for spume-dashed crags, salty maritime sex, but their gypsy-caravan-style plastic cabin trembled whenever Rose stirred in her *cama de crainça*, and on their last night

Zoe dragged them on a quest for *autêntico caldo verde*, which turned out to be at a roadside trailer where groups of sullen truckers waited for waffles. The argument caught fire right there, while the truckers watched. They spent a fortune on Lilt and Haribo Brixx and tokens for the nearby *PARQU'INFANTIL!!*, then trudged back through the sand dunes to continue into the night.

'You're going to have to sort yourself out,' Penny said on the ferry home. 'It's ridiculous, how much you fret, how little pleasure you take from things. No, not bloody lupin beans, I'm talking real things. Why aren't you happy? I would be. You should be.'

So she went to be fixed, for Penny's sake. The GP, whom Penny knew from before, handed her a depression questionnaire but agreed that there was no need for concern about her surprisingly high score, 'given the strain you're both under, now that you're expecting. Quick, wasn't it? You must be delighted.'

'Yes,' said Zoe.

'Pop back anyway next week, to catch up,' the doctor told her, and Zoe did, although Penny worried that the Black Prince might hear rumours. 'He'll think Rose isn't being kept happy, or safe, even. We mustn't give him ammo.'

Thrilled as Penny said she was, Zoe's pregnancy wasn't exactly unalloyed, even for her. She couldn't stop comparing: 'Bet you won't have to be stitched up. How do you not have stretch marks? Are you moisturizing? You said you weren't. And look at that jawline, how's that fair, when I'm the one doing facial exercises? Bet you've noticed mine is softening. Did you notice how I put the Black Prince in his place when he said about pregnancy being hard work? He's never once acknowledged the toll it took on my body. He has no empathy, none. How can Justine stand it? At least he's pleased about this. Can't you be? You'd better not pass your negativity through the placenta. Last thing we want is another little pessimist.' She said their friends had noticed Zoe's gloom, and wondered how Penny endured it. This settled like a stain; which friends, exactly? How long had Penny been discussing her?

A fortnight later, Zoe was offered a psychiatry assessment. What had she said, Penny wanted to know, to earn such preferential treatment? It wasn't as if Zoe was sitting about staring sadly into the twilight, or failing to get out of bed. And wasn't it normal, not looking forward to much; inevitable in grown-up life? Their evenings and weekends were filled with broken sash window-cords and nit-lotion and other nursery parents to meet at the adventure playground. They all looked like grandparents but at least, unlike Zoe, they weren't ruining their own children.

Someone somebody else knew had lost their five-year-old to measles. A chunk of cornicing crashed onto the pavement below; what if another squished Rose, or fell on a passing pensioner, someone else's baby? Also, pregnancy meant feeling constantly nauseous, gnawing sugar off crystallized ginger and drinking nasty teas, going to the loo expecting blood.

She sang to the foetus in the bath to help it feel safe, but who was she kidding, when she was passing on doom and sorrow, and all her flaws were sloshing about in the amniotic fluid, the shyness, irritability, which made her so difficult to endure. Not epigenetic trauma, though; Penny said that was basically made up.

She told Zoe she was too on edge, unliveable-with, and Zoe knew she was right. At least she would be sharing the parenting with the others. Her potential to damage would be lessened, as a team.

'I'll cancel the appointment,' she decided. 'Shouldn't I? There must be loads of actual lunatics, people who think they're sausages, or Napoleon. I'm fine. Although . . .' And again she was gripped by the feeling of what Penny had said: her unliveablewithness. 'Do you think I need to go?'

Penny deserved better than all this harping on danger; the angsting made her, Penny, feel constrained. Everyone agreed that Zoe was controlling, that the amount of time she spent with Rose was unhealthy.

'She's perfectly fine without you,' Penny would say. 'Stop hovering.'

'But she was right next to the socket! I know you hate those special child-locks, but shouldn't w—'

'No way. I'm not changing my life for babies. They can adapt.'

'But so many things can go wrong.'

'Why would they for us?'

'Why would they not?'

'Christ. Look, when you moved to London, you'd hardly been anywhere. Admit it; I'd sent myself to the other side of the planet, by myself, set up a home, a job, and you were still in the bottom bunk in Tredgar Avenue, terrified by ghost stories, footsteps on beaches and faces at the window.'

'That's not the . . .'

'Don't try to get out of it. You told me. Forcing yourself to stay awake past midnight every night in case of robbers.'

'That was when I was little. And you swore you wouldn't tease me.'

'I'm not teasing! It's a simple fact. I was the one making an adult life, whereas you've had it handed on a plate. Admit it. Well, that's not what I want for my babies. No way are my children being brought up in a state of fear. Now you're pregnant, let's be honest. You owe it to the baby to deal with your problems.'

Penny had heard all about psychiatrists from Chrissie, who'd advised her not to believe a word they said and tell Zoe to resist Western medication. But this was a smiling, interested woman, not the uncertain trainee Zoe had expected: an adult. At least, older than she was.

'Obviously you got someone senior,' said Penny, later. 'The minute they spotted "lesbian mothers" on the referral form, they'd be over it like a rash.'

The psychiatrist wore small green earrings; there was an apple-green throw on her generic NHS office two-person foam sofa. It was a relief to hear someone else say sex mattered, tenderness and kindness mattered, that arguments didn't always need to be won. She explained that marriage was a vessel which required filling, particularly after stressful times, and that 'family circumstances have clearly taken their toll'.

Zoe didn't mention that even if the specific person floating inside her, whoever she or he would turn out to be, wasn't ruined by the awful luck of getting her as its petri-dish, she would probably damage it in some horrific yet inevitable way. She definitely loved it already, her fruit-sized faceless diagram-child, but could easily visualize crushing it accidentally, chucking it off a building: not because she wanted to, but because she couldn't be trusted not to. And if, say, she were to fall onto a tube track, then the foetus might die and she survive, which was the opposite of what was needed. Although dying in childbirth, blood on the sheets, wouldn't be so bad, if it meant the baby would have a happier life, and at least Rose would be free.

'Do you have children?' Zoe asked, to be polite.

'No,' said the psychiatrist. Then, more firmly: 'No.'

'You are joking?' said Penny when Zoe reported every detail: clothes, hairstyle, how she ended with another referral, for psychotherapy. 'Another? God, and I was the one who begged you to do it, when I've been on that waiting list for over a year. I'm the one with screwy relations and a miserable child-hood. Out there in whoop-whoop, let alone the bush . . . you have no idea how tough it gets. I'm not even joking. So what exactly did you say to her? Not the obsession with dying in childbirth? When, if anyone was going to, it would have been me.'

'We'll swap,' offered Zoe, 'if my psychotherapist's better. Or I'll ask them to let you go first. I'm really fine. Basically. The poor people in the waiting room; I'm nothing like that bad.'

'Presumably you told them about your own family stuff?'

'Only in the gathering of facts, when she asked about background.'

'Well, that's it, did you not realize? It does give a sort of . . . gravitas.'

What if the therapist couldn't or wouldn't help her? Or the wait was months? Or she was allocated the last good one, and Penny was given an idiot and slithered into unreachability, while Zoe naively thought their world was becoming happier? She never found out. They were meant to be going to the seaside with Rose when Zoe caught a particularly bad bug, or food poisoning. She was sitting on the loo with jagged stomach cramps when Penny, convinced that they would miss the train, rang the emergency doctor for advice about rehydration granules. 'He wants to know,' she shouted through the door, 'does the tip of your shoulder hurt?'

'What?'

'Your shoulder.'

'Yes. Why?'

Three hours later, Zoe, heavily anaesthetized, dreamt of nothing, while the surgeon lifted her scalpel.

Now

3.59 p.m.

Penny is pretending to be gazing out of the window, her chin raised as tears trickle down her cheeks. Robin is explaining something to Tony Harcastle. Justine, closed as a nun, looks at her lap. Then Penny says, prettily, resignedly, like one facing the guillotine, 'I know I'll be punished for having mentioned her mental health. But why conceal it? Isn't honesty best? And there's more.'

Zoe's body is rioting. Her skin heats, her lip cracks: she can taste blood. This should be a moment for buried courage: her mettle tested. There is a thick and sickly silence, in which her heart seems to cling to her chest wall. She gazes at the back of her once-love's hand, the vein beneath the ring finger, the nails she has kissed.

Tony Harcastle looks like he's dredging his mind for official mediating guidance. He glances from one combatant to the next: a pigeon at Wimbledon. He seems disappointed. 'So, to clarify. There were difficult feelings when you were pregnant, with your,' he gestures, to encompass the others, 'your daughter, Matilda?'

'Not Matilda,' says Zoe. Claiming her, stating she was the one who bore her, still feels anarchic, as if Zoe is meant to pretend Matty was raised in a hydroponic pod on mineral wool, tended by all. She straightens her back. 'That first pregnancy, it was . . . was ectopic.'

'I see.'

'We lost him,' says Penny, with a wobble. 'Or her, possibly.'

Hang on, thinks Zoe. After what you did, you're not having that. She can't look at her, or Justine, or Robin, or Tony fucking Harcastle. She fixes her eyes on the window bars, filthy paint oozing down spear-heads. She needs to rupture the membrane, let in the cold air of truth. In another existence, as protagonist of her story, mortally wounded but still brave, still right, she would shut up, like a hero: for the sake of present and future peace. Everyone, including Family Therapy Nadia, her parents, their exhausted friends and colleagues and probably now Tony Harcastle, knows what's best: that she keep quiet. Even her kids would want her to stand down.

But there are no children here, no innocents to endanger. She's done that already. It's time to vent the fury.

There must be fury. It's in there somewhere, if only she had the energy to find it, dig it out. Think back, she tells herself.

And, as if in one of Robin's unsettling school wall-charts, *THE HUMAN EYE*, down the funnel of the past a blur of indeterminate shapes merge, to a point of clarity. She remembers a fortieth birthday weekend, maybe ten years ago, Matty toddling, Rose uncontained, when they went to stay with Penny's friends. Her life had changed, and she had barely noticed. She can still see the bags of sliced white bread beside an industrial toaster; beer bottles on a deep slate windowsill; their bed, drooping with other people's skin-cells and sadness; the cold rain. What she maybe saw, and has tried to believe she didn't ever since: not repressed, nor forgotten, but pushed aside, to make life liveable.

She hears Tony Harcastle saying: 'Actually, we really are at the end of our time.'

'Were you thinking of further sessions?' asks Robin, smooth and pleasant, as if they've been on a short introduction to water-colouring. Penny comments mournfully: 'Well, I don't know what my life will be then, whether I'll have access to my children. The thing is . . .' But Zoe doesn't care. She's looking at Justine, sitting there as if none of this has been her doing, merely the help-meet to the Black Prince, and is remembering.

22

July 2001

A hospital bed.

Yet there was no evidence that time had passed, as if a slice of consciousness had been cut from her life and the gap invisibly stitched. Even when the pain began, and Zoe kept pressing the alarm in her hand although there was a nurse sitting right beside her, checking, or was that some sort of test, she didn't understand what had happened, or that she didn't understand, so kept circling in and out of confusion like a beetle failing to right itself. The next time she woke, and saw Clive, her father, smartly dressed, for him, in a shirt with all its buttons.

'Oho,' he said, peering from his great height. His gentle eyes were delighted. 'She stirs.'

Where was the baby? She couldn't move her hands up to her stomach; was she asleep? Someone should . . .

He held a straw to her bleached lips. There were tubes, emerging from the sheets around her legs, through which cold water might be piped as in a factory. When her mother, weeping, left the room, he would want to follow. Zoe slept: release.

When she woke again, there was Penny.

She needed comforting, but Zoe couldn't remember what she had done to upset her. It wasn't the first time. There should be people keeping notes. Before she could moisten her lips, Penny said, in a voice full of joyful relief: 'Hello, you.'

This time, Zoe stayed awake.

Penny was rosy with happiness that she was alive, every foggy question and gesture rapturously received. She guessed that Zoe had no idea what had happened, and didn't mind. If anything, it made her kinder.

'My poor darling,' she said, luxuriantly stroking the back of Zoe's hand. Zoe tried to keep her eyes open, to explain, but their clean pure chamber, this marital fug, felt fragile, easily torn. Penny was describing something horrible that had happened to someone they knew, but it didn't much matter because Rose was – Zoe kept asking – perfectly safe at nursery, Penny promised, she absolutely swore it was the truth. Zoe tried to believe her, but something was not right.

'I'm sorry,' she whispered. And although Penny was crying herself now, she was kindness incarnadine, no, incarnate. She explained, as if describing a play, how Zoe's blood pressure had dropped and her pulse risen, or was it the other way round? At any rate, her haemoglobin had fallen, and then the ultrasoundologist had . . .

'Yes.'

'Oh good, great. You do remember?' and Zoe convincingly agreed.

'But tell me again,' she asked, as if clarification was the only issue. Penny couldn't. 'Shhh, shhh.' Zoe was stroking her hand now, like a reflection. 'But how quickly did they . . . it. Did it.'

'They took you straight to theatre,' Penny said. 'It was awful. They wouldn't even let me stay. That old bitch Dr Jessop, Marilyn, she told me . . . oh, I never thought it would be you who'd get ill.'

'It's OK,' said Zoe. 'We'll be OK.' She knew she should ask about the baby, was it alive, had Robin been told, was Rose all right and did she know not to expect a sibling just yet, but Penny was too upset. When Robin's sister, Penny's ex-girlfriend, Justine, walked with exaggerated care to the doorway, but did not come in, and Penny turned her head in her direction, Zoe, a small wheel in a machine merely playing her part, closed her eyes.

'I don't understand.'

Rose was pressing her bed-control, *zzzzzu* up then *uzzzzz* down; she and Penny had only been visiting for twenty minutes but already Zoe was drowsy. Sounds were enormous, bouncing off the life-saving devices; she could smell disinfectant and mushroom soup and cling-film from lunch many hours ago. Ordinarily she'd be wanting to lift Rose's little vest and kiss her silken tummy, breathe in her plumptious cheeks, but even the slightest joggle of the bed was intolerable. Please go.

Looking down at Rose's golden hair, the infinitesimal bunches held with glittery ice-cream-cone hairbands, kept bringing her back to what had happened, like a stirred puddle. 'Can you re-explain?'

But even Penny was confused about the quantity of blood:

the number of pints transfused, how much had been sloshing around in her abdomen.

'Babado . . . what?' said Rose.

Penny's eyes met Zoe's. 'It, the incision, looks massive, I made them show me under the dressing, but Marilyn Jessop said you'll only feel grotty, her word, for a few weeks, and then you can totally get back to normal. Including . . . you know. Trying,' she smiled, with a glance at Rose, '*encore*. Whenever we like. The great thing is that you've still got one fallopian tube. You do look knackered, though.'

Zoe was keeping it together; they both made their voices bright. Through its layers of dressings and gauze and gown and sheet and blanket, she touched her wound. 'They couldn't do a . . . ?'

'Keyhole? No way. Too much . . . you know. Emergency laparotomy.' Penny winced sympathetically. 'Poor you. Poor girl. You'll miss your surprising stomach muscles. Now you'll be wobbly like me.'

'Come on. Yours is practically invisible. And at least,' Zoe said, nodding significantly at Rose, 'you did get a . . . consequence.'

Penny had brought her love-tokens: lilies, a net of oranges, bed-socks, sweet smoothies and oily pasta salad; Zoe didn't want to hurt her feelings, gulped it down. A mania for order had gripped her, so that a bottle-lid left on the faux-wood sliding table or a sweet-wrapper missing the bin was too much. 'You're hard work,' said Penny, although she scratched Zoe's head, which she refused to believe she didn't like, and the raking sound was enormous. 'Time to take this beast back to nursery. Then maybe,' she sighed, 'I'll drop by again later, although it's difficult. I'll see if Robin can . . .'

'Honestly, don't. I'll be fine,' Zoe said, although Penny's odd casualness lingered. She knew she was unbearably demanding but this didn't stop her wishing Penny would stay. She sensed it again on the phone the next day, when Penny had arranged for Zoe's parents to visit. Zoe asked them to bring high-waisted knickers; they brought Tricia's size, not hers, plus Ben, Zoe's brother, who had recently returned from backpacking in Columbia. Zoe could hear them at the nurses' station, then approaching her room for what seemed like hours. Ben smelt strongly of roll-ups; he put his dirty boot on the edge of Zoe's bed, coughed dramatically upon her. Tricia started crying about his lungs. When Zoe asked, she thought politely, whether they might be able to exchange the knickers, her mother was extremely upset and went to sit in the car while Clive told Zoe off. By the time Zoe herself came home that evening, her parents were back in Headington.

All weekend, Penny seemed distracted; had Zoe upset her? She kept saying how exacting she was being, how oversensitive about every smell and gesture. Zoe was, indeed, appallingly needy, in amazing pain from morphine-induced gastric disarray, frightened of infection. By Tuesday, her paranoia and clinginess were giving Penny cabin-fever. The nurses had instructed Zoe to take tottery little walks outside but Penny couldn't bear the slowness, would say she needed more speed, fresher air. She began to go for long walks herself; seeing various friends, to let off steam.

'Stop grilling me,' she'd say. 'You're driving me out, that's what's happening. If you weren't so suspicious and vigilant, I wouldn't need to spend time away from my home. And no, of course it's not Justine. You're the one who's fixated, not me.'

'I don't think I am,' said Zoe, but maybe she was lying. Penny had uncovered the old shameful fear, as if Justine were back in the spare room, a scent of shampoo in the air, and Zoe was missing something. What was the evidence that Penny still wanted her?

Zoe found a small pigeon feather on the pillow and cried because she was too feeble to change the sheets. Penny's mother sent a gift-basket of brownies, raucous with cellophane. Zoe's parents would ring, ask to chat to Rose, but Rose, aged almost three, was terrible at small-talk, and Tricia's irritated sighs were audible across the bedroom. When her own friends came over, they held her hand as she explained about drains and stitches, but not the atmosphere, Penny's absent impatience. Telling them, asking for advice, did not cross her mind. It would be unfair to prejudice them against Penny. She'd notice; she noticed everything about Zoe's friends.

Once Zoe was back at work, when she wasn't hobbling to follow-ups at the clinic, or pretending to care about her students' revolutionary theories ('Was Homer a woman? In this essay I'll inspect if he . . .'), she'd lie on the mums' big bed helping Rose colour in princesses while Penny went to the cinema, or somewhere, for a break. The flat felt empty;

when Penny came home, they gave her inexpert head-massages, tried to make up for the cooking and constant laundry, Zoe's incapacity, as if there wasn't a chasm of fear at her feet, something frightening glinting through the mists.

In November, they had an appointment to see if Zoe, at least physically, was ready to start again. Two separate doctors asked which hospital had done the first insemination; Penny was jubilant. Then a nurse, who'd already made Zoe cry by saying 'good girl' when she wiped the gel from her stomach, passingly mentioned Pelvic Inflammatory Disease.

Penny gasped. 'Are you saying that, wait, all along she's had a sexually transmitted . . . I could have got it?'

'It's very common,' the nurse explained. 'Symptomless. I could have it. You c—'

That afternoon, Penny, still teary but calmer, held Rose to her breast. 'Darling,' she said, 'imagine if I'd never been able to conceive you, if I'd caught the clap, whatever it is, from one of Mama's tragic exes. God, the irony; as if she'd been the one fighting them off.'

'Not for want of wanting,' said Zoe, but already Penny was talking about getting herself scanned, for future babies.

'To think I could have lost you,' she said to Rose, who was picking her nose.

Penny intended to get going much, much more quickly than Zoe could face. She was trying to be understanding, but presumably even Zoe couldn't deny that this was a big setback, a delay which Penny's fertility could not afford. Was Zoe sure she didn't want to leave the next, second, one to Penny, too? If not, they'd have to crack on, so that the third child, which Penny definitely and unquestionably had to have in the nearish future, would be possible.

So why wasn't Zoe ready? They had a particularly loud row in the popcorn-scented foyer of the Prince Charles after a special edition screening of *The Hunger*. Penny had pressed Zoe on whether she thought Catherine Deneuve was attractive. Zoe, trying to be rakish, said: I'd have both her and Susan Sarandon. A brace.

Penny said it was thoughtless; she knew Susan Sarandon was one of Penny's own favourites, and wasn't that exactly like her, trying to copy and take over everything, leaving nothing for Penny? It was difficult to follow but, eventually, Zoe understood how insensitive she'd been. The row didn't stop; Penny still wanted Mongolian Crispy Lamb in New China round the corner, gossip on the tube-ride home, while accusing Zoe of worse and worse crimes and, when Zoe was too sad to start cheering up, Penny was enraged. She became so upset that Zoe agreed to start sperming again the next month.

But, before they could, they had to re-persuade Robin.

Despite his noisy sensitivity, all his single women friends, he and Justine had been rubbish since the ectopic: no extra help with Rose, no nourishing casseroles. Penny was exhausted by the skivvying, but thought Robin was avoiding them, spooked by Female Troubles. Even the houseplant he'd brought round was regifted; she'd seen it first in their bathroom.

'When? Weird, I thought we haven't been downstairs for ages.'

'Oh, I don't know,' Penny said. 'I could be wrong.'

She hated that they'd have to convince him all over again. 'We should force his hand. As it were.'

'Maybe he needs a bit of time.'

Penny wasn't having that. 'It was only to balance things that I decided you should go next.' She was often crying when they reached this stage; she couldn't understand why Zoe was being so stubborn. Neither could Zoe. 'You were meant to have this one quickly, so there was still time for me to try again. I said you could, because you adored Rose so much. But maybe it should have been me. My body requires another child.'

Zoe was still too young to know that hormonal clutch of urgency; that was why she hadn't yet given in. But he had to agree. He must, if he understood how much their marriage needed it, how unhappy it was making them.

'I'll round him up,' Penny said. 'Like a gnu on the veldt,' and she stroked Zoe's cheek. And Zoe, so grateful, as sure as she had ever been that she was loved and safe, said: 'OK. I trust you. Yes.'

23

Now

4.22 p.m.

Here comes Zoe, ejected into the corridor like a bit of gristle.

It wasn't even a grand gesture; the session was virtually over when she stood up. She saw Robin's chin lift; Justine groped for her bag-strap, as if Zoe was planning an assault. Penny placed a hand on the forearm of each: restraining her fighters. And Zoe walked out.

'Hey!' A chair scrapes behind her. Don't look back. Her teeth are clattering. This is why she can't play chess: if they can predict her probable next move, say left down the corridor, won't they suspect she'll try to be clever and head right instead? Keep moving; no time even to check her pulse, find out if she is still breathing. All that matters is not being caught. They'll hear her frantic footsteps, rattling this security grille; easy to guess which way she's chosen. The sound of their voices will turn her to dust: all that triumph and loathing. Whacking her hip into a door frame, squeezing past a thicket of stanchions and mops and warning cones, she finds another way down: a stairwell, dusty, bare, as if, during renovation, the intestines of the building were forgotten.

She needs to see out, spot them hurrying away, but she

can't shift the window frame. Does it even face the right way? Are those voices? Every door she tries, out to the second floor or the first, requires a card-key or a key-code; she can't go back upstairs, can't shout, bang on the glass like an escaping patient, dangerous, paranoid. A section of ornamental iron-work banister, leading to a host of fire extinguishers, then through a door and down one more windowless flight of stairs, grey-matted, anti-skid-edged: built for a stampede. There should almost be blood.

She arrives at the bottom, in the basement.

The only way outside ends in the area for bins; above it, the gate back up to the street is elaborately padlocked.

As the years passed, and her love for Zoe receded, Penny has come to anticipate, then despise, her fear of danger. She's said it's pathological, narcissistic, to expect the worst to happen to those she cares about, when no Stamper has ever died from a midnight walk or a beach swim between red flags. The children don't need her hysterical bubble-wrapping; they know that Penny is the one to listen to, that Zoe should be ignored.

But sometimes Zoe might want a little danger, too.

A wheelchair-lift waits at elbow-height beside the railings, its platform guarded by a CCTV camera, railings, signs in black and yellow threatening trespassers with swift and expensive retribution. Young Zoe would give up, go back, apologize, but that Zoe is dead. If she could reach the platform, summon the agility to climb it, she could probably step over the railings.

She does have muscles, and a lack of concern for pain. It

is easy, relatively, to heave her elbows, a foot, onto the textured metal, haul up her weight, then struggle over the low gate to the pavement. She's at the rear of the building; her knees feel grated. To her, yes, left there's a tiered church spire, grubbily gilded by the sun behind it. Embankment tube, then Northern Line up to Leicester Square for the Piccadilly, would be less logical so probably safer; she needs to dash back for the movers, but what if Robin and Justine are racing to Stag Street this minute? Which, realistically, Zoe has no hope of doing simultaneously; she's already confused by which way's east. Isn't the Strand meant to be in Covent Garden? It would possibly be better to go right, towards what might be the river, as if she were going on a date.

She rounds the corner and, bang: there is Penny and Robin.

Then

September 2001

No one could understand why Zoe was being so difficult. Was she depressed, after the ectopic? All that anaesthetic set people back, everybody knew that. But enough was enough.

They agreed to see a therapist, specifically the marriage counsellor recommended by Leonara's new Swiss husband, Davide. Penny had brought Zoe to a party at their 'apartment', full of pink marble and golden coasters, where they drank brandy with Leonara's latest youthful friends and talked about

Leonara. 'There is no "Leonara obsession",' Penny kept saying. 'You and Davide looked very friendly. I bet you discussed her. Don't you want us to be happier?'

So off they went. The psychologist, too, was Swiss, her plastic surgery recent. Penny wanted to go into the last few years, the strain on them both, but the psychologist, who had been on television, asked few questions, talked instead about previous celebrity clients, patients, 'friends'. But the issue which put Penny off was that her sister-in-law was the Associate Dean of a famous English Faculty; what if she said something negative? 'I can't trust you not to bad-mouth me.'

Afterwards, Penny made a special effort, brought home tulips for Zoe, sent peonies to Zoe's mum and, to her dad, an interesting ('to him') *National Geographic* article about Linear B developments. And, when she finally managed to tempt her new famous colleague to dinner, a radio personality who'd written a scurrilous biography of John Betjeman, she even said that Sara, a huge fan, could be invited too, provided Dave, and the greyhounds, stayed at home in Norfolk.

Among the other guests was Justine; Penny said this was absolutely normal, that it was vital to integrate her into their lives, as an ally against Robin. The next weekend Justine invited them downstairs for her birthday dinner: Rose too, in her tiny pyjamas. She sat on their laps, playing with Zoe's hair, Penny's necklace, writhing when anyone mentioned bed. Eventually, Zoe tucked her up in her bedroom at Robin's: no Blu-tak allowed, a pile of musty clothes. She fell asleep almost instantly. Zoe waited beside her for a little while longer, in case.

Eventually, she went back through to the living room and found more wine, relative warmth, as if a loving haze had been thrown over them while Zoe was absent.

This time, they used one of Robin's jam-jars.

24

THEN

Autumn 2001

'We've been told to make our ladies do them,' said the health visitor, holding the post-natal depression questionnaire at arm's length, as if considering Zoe's answers through her nostrils. 'You're not obliged but we do ask.'

'It's fine. I'm really fine.' Zoe smiled. It was easy to please the clinic. Penny had warned her to be careful; the last thing they needed was for Robin to be tipped off. Zoe had ticked mainly 'most or all the time' but she made so many jokes that they didn't seem concerned.

The health visitor's quite enormous under-chin, almost a whole new lower face, bulged as she looked at the form. With her cold stare, her pink-flowered blouse looked ironic, or post-ironic, like a uniform. 'Thirteen out of fifteen? Isn't that a lot?' she asked Jan beside her, who was tucking into her cheese-and-pickle although it was, Zoe noted hungrily, only ten thirty-four.

It had helped, distraction-wise, that Penny had come for the first two weighings. She'd dazzled everyone, even Jan, the steeliest midwife, with her lactation knowhow; shown Zoe how to fold Matilda's naked frog-legs into the weighing-pan, and where to borrow a biro to update the red wipe-clean record book with her small achievements: rolls over; sits up.

'They'd better not try to make you wean her early, no way. But God, it's fun, isn't it, all the fuss? I couldn't get enough of these health-centre visits.'

Zoe pretended to feel the same and so, although she cried on the slow walk home each time, they let her leave. Matilda still barely reached the thirty-sixth centile, wasn't putting on much weight. Zoe's breastfeeding was disastrous, her milk-production feeble, and Matilda screamed with colic for three hours every evening, her hard stomach against Zoe's palm, no heavier than a modest textbook. Nothing, not even holding her in the tiger-in-the-tree position, or those pointless homeo-pathic granules, could soothe her.

Zoe ought to be delighted; it was such great good luck that her second pregnancy had implanted in absolutely the right place, gone perfectly. Focus on the milestones, she read; be proud of yourself and of Baby.

But poor Matilda took after Zoe in all the wrong ways. Tricia relished describing what a greedy baby Zoe had been, 'gnashing at me with her gums', which became one of Penny's favourite phrases. When they introduced Matilda to Zoe's parents she had cradle-cap, and Zoe was so focused on removing it before it could put Tricia off her that she picked all the way to Headington, until Matilda's reddish hair was full of the stuff, like infantile nits. Robin claimed the auburn came from his side of the family, that those long fingers were Balder too. But, emotionally, Penny said, since Matilda's first day on dry land she had been the spit of Zoe: easily startled, hard to soothe, quickly trapped in arguments of her own devising.

Penny had wanted to time the inseminations to give the male sperm a chance, but she had also kept saying 'bet you're the one who gets the boy'. Zoe had glimpsed others' babies' whelky penises, their mighty wrinkled balls; it was almost a disappointment, not needing to adjust to that strangeness, but mainly she was relieved. Penny would have minded so much if it was Zoe who'd had their son.

Maybe it was because she hadn't believed she could produce a real live baby herself, right up until Matilda was lying, gooey and blooded in her arms, that she'd overdone the closeness with Rose. It was hardly fair on Penny. Rose's enthusiasms, her weird hobbies, were all Zoe's: bean-growing, pebble-collecting, learning silly poems. 'Who's going to play with her if she's wittering about ammonites?' Penny wanted to know. Unlike Zoe, she'd been a success at primary school, so did have a point.

Going back to work after the ectopic had been gruelling, her organs wincing under lecture-hall lights; it was worse after Matty, her genitals scalpled open, trembling and squeamish and exposed, like a sample on a microscope slide. But Penny was tender with her, succouring, counselling; perhaps the awfulness of the ectopic had healed them, and arguments were a phase they'd grown out of. She called Zoe 'little one'; could imagine how terrible she must feel. In fact, she should look after herself better; go properly part-time.

'Are you totally sure you can't wait till next year to write your Greek thing? My poor swot, always putting herself under so much pressure. Let me look after you.' All that grief and loss, for both of them, were still making Zoe irrationally paranoid, on top of the tiredness. Whenever Penny came home even slightly late, or simply wanted to chat on the phone from the bath, letting out the tepid and topping up with scalding water, laughter audible behind the closed door, the sick, crushed sensation under Zoe's ribs swelled, like scrunched-up paper re-expanding. She couldn't not ask, not worry, however much Penny explained the insecurity was all in her head. It was no wonder Penny needed space.

When Matty was nearly one, it began to seem that the tension was lifting. Penny still mentioned having several babies, but thought Matilda was hilarious, and Zoe allowed herself to imagine that Penny might let herself be satisfied with their existing children, not yearn for even more. One Sunday morning they were sitting on the sofa, watching Rose on the rug bending upside-down like a paperclip to make her little sister giggle, and Zoe said: 'Oh my God. Do you realize we are The Parents? Ours used to look fondly at us, being fools, and now we . . . we are the ones looking. We're the grown-ups.'

'My dear mad wife,' said Penny, leaning over to kiss her. 'So now will you stop being so insecure?' and Rose shouted 'Yuk! Snoggers!' and Zoe thought: I'm happy. It's happened. I really am.

Also, her Euripidean women book was almost finished. Penny hated the Big E, suspected Zoe and Philly Rush, her co-author, of plotting to start another project right away.

'You could never resist an older woman. Admit that you've got a little crush.' And Zoe did wonder what would happen if she did, although not on Philly, whom she could never fancy, with her clogs and chlorinated hair and her husband. Besides, the sensation of Penny being a bit insecure, even jealous, felt all wrong. How could Zoe want her to suffer? The goal was being an academic power-couple, still flirty with each other, desired but unavailable to others, pushing each other towards new heights. For the first time since pre-Matilda, she felt a lightening.

Then they went to see the new lesbian film, starring that woman from the other lesbian film, and something broke.

Perhaps it was the Christmas scene which set things off. In real life, December was already looming, the first Robin would have with both kids. He'd mentioned driving them all the way down to Hampshire. Zoe lived in silent dread of it; Penny cried at the very idea. She'd never got over Rose being taken from them for her second Christmas, although Rose seemed irritatingly to have loved every bit of it, still reciting the momentous events of Christmas morn, the miracle of her old-school stocking ('an a *wal*nut, an a liquor-ice').

Or maybe it was Zoe's unthinking reference to the protag-onist's ever-present ex. Or her revived sex-life ('Ugh,' said Penny), or her new girlfriend's publication of a critically acclaimed volume of poems (Penny's 'Hah!' reverberated right around the BFI auditorium). Also, they were meant to be celebrating: Zoe had somehow managed to have her latest short-term contract extended. She'd be staying in London for another three years. Penny couldn't believe that Hilary Mint wasn't involved, hated how low-key Zoe was being, but everything was still just about cheerful. They'd gone to Thai Time, were paying the bill, Penny snaffling up the orange Matchmakers, when a pregnant woman squeezed past their table. She was quite young, in a sleeveless mauve top Penny would definitely not approve of, and Zoe thought phew, we're getting away with it, when Penny pushed away her cheque-book.

'You OK?'

For another moment, two, Penny said nothing. Then she looked up. Her face was hard. 'If you stop me having another baby,' she said, 'we are over.'

Now the pressure doubled, tripled. Every nappy-advert fuelled her; even Matilda's babyhood, the smell of Oilatum, the milky apple sweetness of her cereal.

'Can't we try to enjoy her? It's sad if we miss all the good bits because we're so focused on having the next.'

'You're only saying that because you don't want another,' Penny shot back, already flushed with anger and dislike. 'It's nothing to do with her. Anyway, she is not an easy baby.'

'So how does it make sense, having more?'

But Penny refused to accept that their fights about early mornings, research-time, television-time, were a problem, or the continual troubles with Robin, who behaved as though their agreement was something temporary, pending his unanimous decision. His emails, superficially pleasant, were slithery, like corporate statements; at every drop-off he'd add a few minutes, say he was planning to take Rose and, soon, Matilda, off for 'time to run free' in his parents' Hampshire garden. Rushing out of work to gather the children from today's combination of nursery and Robin/Justine/Penny was fraught, but so, often, was home. In among the telly and made-up songs and incredibly boring but comical games, there were arguments, like sand on a sheet. Penny's friends felt that Zoe was thoughtless to take Rose spontaneously to a film about a cartoon fish. Whatever Zoe claimed, everyone else agreed that the terrible sleeping-bags of felt-tip-coloured cotton-wool she'd made for Rose's shell-family was a deliberate snub to the 1890s doll's-house patchwork quilt Penny had bought years before, for her future babies. Also, everyone, yes, including Justine, was mystified about why Zoe was so sure that a third child with Robin would be the end of them. Zoe was full of doubt in all other spheres; people found it significant that on this, Penny's dream, she was adamant. And Penny had asked around the other parents at nursery; three children was no more stressful.

'And don't tell me again they're all rich. We could have had a gorgeous flat in Fulham, too, if you'd come with a place of your own.' If Zoe genuinely wanted to stay together, Penny reminded her, again and again, she'd have to accept that her behaviour was terrifically controlling. There was a risk that Penny wouldn't be able to conceive. Zoe's emotional cruelty, her oversensitivity about Justine, was taking its toll. 'You might as well admit it, that you're trying to go back on your promise. I'll never recover from that, which presumably is what you want. And then you can keep Tilda to yourself, make her even more obsessed with Mama, shut everyone else out of bonding. Yesterday she wouldn't let me do her farm puzzle: total rejection. How do you think that makes me feel?'

The ice was creaking, perilously thin. Every time a row broke out, Penny would move swiftly to accusing Zoe of snapping at her heels, trying to eclipse her professionally: invitations to give papers, somehow getting herself recommended for a new, better three-year post in Newcastle, as if that could work. What, she'd commute? Stay in a Tyneside Travelodge? Good luck with that. It made Penny want to chuck in her own job, go off to train as a therapist, a midwife, even. Given her own mother's breakdown, to which she'd only recently admitted, it was urgent that she had some light-heartedness, with people who wanted the best for her. Justine had said that she was spending a few days with Jayne, who was currently living somewhere like Henley, subletting a grand flat from a closeted opera singer, and Penny could join them; maybe she should.

Zoe booked her train tickets, packed her a lunch. She felt like meat-fibres being pulled apart, but she'd been gathering articles on how to avoid divorce, asked her two married friends very theoretical questions about their husbands and fidelity. Penny had made her swear not to discuss their private life. Zoe's friends were all puritanical, indoor children, too square to have worthwhile relationships, so how could Zoe trust their opinion? If Penny thought everything was fine, apart from the obvious issues, why was Zoe still complaining?

'Have a great time,' she said. 'Give them my – my love.'

Rose had a puking bug, Matilda a black eye from a swing, and there was almost no time to fret, except at night. When Penny returned, in a fantastic mood, Zoe managed to wait until she came to bed before broaching her formal request; that they agree to wait a little longer for another child. Why make things even more difficult, given the cost of children's coats and nourishing snacks, the endless negotiations about whose turn it was to go to the library? It was bad enough dealing with Robin, let alone being two mothers in academe.

The row lasted for weeks. What right had Zoe to put her fears before Penny's perfectly reasonable needs? If she were less ambitious, the precarity of her job wouldn't be relevant; normal lecturers drift from one post to the next, or go part-time. Aiming for a permanent lectureship of her own, this young, was asking for trouble. Why should what Zoe wanted come first? And round they went again.

Then Penny took Robin out for dinner, one to one. Zoe, overcooking Basque prawn stew for friends of her youth, couldn't relax, for fear of a return in tears, or worse. If she didn't get better at navigating her way between the rocks and whirlpools of how she ought to be, she'd lose Penny.

When Penny did come home, the friends were still there; 'Sorry,' she said. 'It's important.' So they went. Zoe could see that the news was bad. She started washing the pan.

'Hello?' said Penny.

Robin was having reservations about having a third child.

It was like a cellar door slamming shut, with them beneath it. Zoe would have impregnated Penny herself that evening, if it could have soothed her. But Penny was beyond consolation.

On two successive Thursdays, Penny's day, Zoe came home from work sure she had lost all three of them. At the sight of Matilda spreading rice pudding on her high-chair tray and Rose practising her Phonics, not packing up to move back to Australia as Penny sometimes threatened, she was trembly with relief.

Friday morning: Zoe, due in early to send a fax for Hilary Mint but not daring to admit it, made Penny tea. Penny was brushing her hair in the bathroom, her cheek still creased with pillow-seam. The row of heart-shaped beach stones petered out halfway along the window frame; they could never remember who'd given which to whom. When the kids leave home, Zoe reminded herself, we can go abroad and rekindle our ageing romance, get brown, start smoking, frighten the chambermaids. The letterbox rattled. Rose had lost her chief hairslide; when Zoe went to look again in the hall, Penny, holding an open envelope, unexpectedly smiled at her.

'You OK?' asked Zoe, for the thousandth time.

'Guess what,' said Penny. 'We have something to look forward to, at last.'

25

Now

4.31 p.m.

Until a few seconds ago, stepping onto the escalator, Zoe thought she had made it. If Penny and Robin had noticed her, double-backing, racing away down a side street, they did not pursue. No need for a rooftop helicopter air-lift; her luck seemed to be holding. She pushed through the gates at Embankment tube, headed for the Northern Line, willing the Underground network to be free flowing, no passenger incidents; if others are suffering, let it not be today. There might, after all, be time to stuff a few single gloves and adapters, her *Atlas of the Ancient World*, into boxes before Des and co. load the van.

The escalators are like a computer game: in her path, beginning to descend, tourists in the middle of the steps propping up desk-sized suitcases wrapped in polythene, laughing. Bastards. There are the Londoners too, being borne up towards her in the opposite direction, a girl in army trousers with bare golden arms, a beautiful tall person holding a canvas: emanating sparks of interest, potential, like a dream, distantly reverberating. No time for curiosity: she slaloms around the tourists, sweating, in need of a pee, water, nutrition, sleep. Or, no: first packing, then escape. Around this suitcase and . . .

Too late, she realizes that the woman she's about to pass is Justine.

'Oh, Christ,' she hears her say.

Justine has a fleck of mascara on her cheek, and probably a revolver or a hammer in her handbag. As Zoe tries to slip past her, Justine the virgin warrior, *venatrix vincit*, shoots out an arm to grip Zoe's sleeve, hauls until she's jammed in close beneath her, on the next step down. She puts her mouth beside Zoe's ear. Her breath fluffs her hair.

'If you dare try to keep my brother's children away from him, reduce his time with them even by an hour, you will regret it. I'm warning you. He is a good, brave man, has spent his life building a family, getting to this poi—'

'I'm not,' Zoe says, 'trying to stop anyone from seeing them. Jesus. I can't keep s—'

'If necessary, you won't have access at all. Jayne knows the top family lawyers. If we need to call in favours . . .' They're nearing the bottom of the escalator. To the left, the tube-train is squealing into the station: a great, sleek, curling muscle. Zoe lumbers behind Justine, caught in a flock of heedless travellers. Together they wheel around the corner, hurry along the sharp curve of concrete, towards the opening doors. As she waits to climb into the train, she sees Justine, a little ahead, glance behind her, turning, not quite concentrating on where she's putting her feet. Below her lours the famous gap, like a mouth. Inside Zoe, something seems to surge: it has been so bad, and isn't Justine the reason?

All it would take is a push.

Then

September 2003

'No way. It sounds like a sex party.'

'It definitely isn't. Honestly. I guarantee.'

Since the invitation had arrived, Penny's mood had improved. She wouldn't stop talking about it: Beth's big party for her fortieth, in a house somewhere near Canterbury, everyone from the past there. Then it emerged that Beth was borrowing the house from someone called Donald, to whom they were expected to pay £79 each (£59 for children) per night.

'So it's a hote—'

'Not exactly. Less official. Tax reasons, or inspectors . . . there are all these ridiculous rules. No one can afford to install fire doors, and it's an enormous house. Ancient, apparently: an oast house, or is it a mill? Quite important; maybe even listed.'

'But it's . . . safe?'

'Course,' said Penny. 'Donald wouldn't live in a dump. The Balders have known him for years.'

And maybe she was right: a weekend in the country was what they needed. It wasn't as if they could afford lovely hotels, on two lecturers' salaries, and Zoe's constant scrabbling for teaching made proper family holidays impossible. Even their child-free time was ruined by her worrying about research. Penny still had not forgiven her for booking them a crappy long weekend in the justly undiscovered town of San Cesare on the Puglian coast, then trying to fit in a trip to the Museum of Folklore and Musical Culture, claiming she hadn't known that the whole area was inhabited by ethnic Greeks with their own peculiarly fascinating dialect.

It was a chance for Zoe to try harder with Penny's beloveds, Beth and Bill and Jen, Nicky, Nikki; they were so much more entertaining than Zoe's friends. Which was where the sex party they'd all once been to came in.

'I'd really hate it,' Zoe had said, when Penny suggested they join Bill and Jen at another one. 'Sorry. I know I'm unadventurous. But I'm happy with you. I don't want to share.'

'OK,' said Penny, maybe 70 per cent reassuring. 'But all we'd do is watch. That's the only reason they went, to see what it was like. Just to spectate.'

'I swear you told me,' Zoe reminded her, 'in our early days, about a dinner you'd been at where dodginess had happened in front of everyone, one of them doing something to the other. In their bed.'

'OK,' Penny agreed. 'Yep, once.'

'At Bill's and Jen's, wasn't it? Are you positive you didn't join in?'

'I was with Justine, babe. She's much too uptight.'

'But if sh—'

'Oh, can you leave it,' sighed Penny. 'So what if I'm up for something fun, for once. At least, funny. We wouldn't have to do anything. Although –' she checked her smile in the window: her mirror-face – 'if we ever did go to a party like that, think how gorgeous we'd look together. How turned-on people would be.'

It might be a good sign, Penny thinking of sex. But Zoe needed to check once more: 'So, to be sure, that definitely isn't the plan, is it? For this weekend?'

'No. OK? Enough.'

'And, hang on, so Robin and Justine are coming after all?'

'Daddeeee,' said Rose. 'Yay!'

'Yes, but we'll ignore him,' said Penny over her head. 'It is our weekend, not his. He can take them off our hands when it suits us, but we're calling the shots. Now he's let us down about you-know, or trying to, he'd better back off.'

Zoe would have booked the wrong trains, so Penny sweetly organized the whole thing. She sat with an arm around Zoe despite the fascinated couple opposite, Rose organizing her fruit pastilles, Matilda lolling heavily against Zoe's chest. When the train shot into a tunnel, she could visualize the rock-fall, the shrieking metal twist, so vividly she started sweating, until her best jumper, unwisely worn to make a good impression on arrival, began to smell of fear.

'Did you bring work?' asked Penny.

'No.' And they smiled at each other.

But the cab to the house took for ever. Penny, pre-period and sore, kept being kicked by teething Matty, wriggled into by Rose, who was nursing yet another cold. Rose started whinging about a toy St Bernard she'd seen at the station shop with *I WUV YOU* on its plush neck-barrel. 'Oh no,' mouthed Zoe over their little heads. 'Did we remember Humpy?'

At the closed-up train station, Penny had said Zoe was ridiculous to worry about locals reacting badly. 'They don't care,' she'd said whenever Zoe looked behind them. 'They're too busy thinking about slurry to gay-bash us in the underpass.' They had argued a little about Robin already, how to make an opportunity to speak to him. Penny was incredulous: 'You promised. Don't start lying about it now.'

The night seems unnecessarily black; swollen trees on one side, edgeless as fog. Zoe and Rose peered out hopefully for deer, owls, wild boar, but there were only moths and insects hurling themselves like idiots against the windscreen. The back seats smelt of cheese. As the meter went up and up, Radio Kent began a phone-in about civil partnership: shouldn't straight couples be eligible? The cab-driver made demurring sounds. What if Colin from Gillingham said something terrible about buggery? Or Penny decided to weigh in?

'Don't, please don't,' Zoe whispered.

'Mama's a scaredy-cat,' Penny told Rose, whose soup-plate eyes glistened. There were no lights or whiffs of wood smoke through the branches, no sounds of a Gatsbyish welcome. The cab nosed down the track.

'At home,' Penny commented, 'Ozzy summer, a rural place like this, you could be completely snowed in. Sometimes you couldn't get to school.'

'What, actual . . . drifts?' asked Zoe. She was imagining pub-goers flouting speed limits, hidden bends concealing oncoming headlights; perhaps she could make a rigid cage for Matilda with her forearms, brace them against the seat in front. 'Seriously?'

'Course. Not Mudgee, but out by Thredbo, or the Brindibellas, everyone'd have snow-tyres, four by fours, proper ones. Landies; kids piled in together. God it would be great. You townies.'

And Zoe, who had never not managed to reach school, stared out over the fields, ardently praying. Anything could happen, while a parent looked elsewhere.

It was only September, but Penny was already miserable that the English winter was closing in. The road was glossy; a dull mist of drizzle clinging to every leaf. There were no streetlights or reflectors, only a red flood from a passing car. Zoe held a hand up to the glass, squinting into the blur which seemed to press, soft and dangerous, against the bones of her face. Water dripped on the car roof; above it, creepers looped every trunk and twig together, centuries of dead timber, waiting to fall. The headlights blazed against handfuls of lichen, moss thick as turf. The car slipped, bumped painfully across a pot-hole, righted itself. Penny always joked about Zoe's avoidance of dark side streets, parks at night; she said Zoe saw villainy, danger everywhere, was far too easily spooked.

Zoe had not yet confessed that she feared the dark itself.

She must have made a little sound; Rose, always alert, looked up. Zoe squeezed her soft plum kneecap, stroked her forehead. 'Are you freezing?' There was something eerie about how much colder it was here than on the dual carriageway, where streetlights and petrol stations promised help in an emergency. Penny had told her to pack the hot water bottle, but it was still at home, upended in the sink like an atrophied muscle. What could they do if Rose wet the bed? Rose and

Matilda were the youngest kids staying, but Penny hadn't asked about the exact arrangements, found Zoe's passion for knowing where their next meals were coming from oppressive. Donald was a great cook, legendary, so couldn't she just have faith?

Zoe feared that meant showing-off food: grouse, a fuss about truffle oil. And their friends were all childless, or had proper full-sized adolescents, so there would be big kids running around with the babies struggling to follow, and ungated stairs and unguarded fires and unfenced ponds.

This was not a good idea.

They edged round the back, into a yard, its cobbles divided diagonally by shallow gullies: the sort of place you'd gut a pig. Stacked tyres and piled-up planks and bottle-crates crowded around them like bonfires waiting to be torched. None of the windows on this side of the house were illumin-ated; deep trees blocked their view beyond.

It was almost eleven. 'Are they all in their bed?' whispered Rose loudly, and Penny laughed.

'Well,' she said. 'That's the question.'

Fetching their bags and hold-alls, Rose's favoured pillowcase and Matilda's frog; nappies; waterproof sheet; jars of rustic chicken and sweetcorn baby-food; individual long-life juices; four bottles of Goranga Ridge Cab Sauv for Donald; necklace and dramatic flowers and more champagne for Beth; fully movable plastic pony, one leg Elastoplasted, plus reins, bridle and stable-girl; plush wombat wearing one of Matilda's Babygros; Penny's Cokes; tampons; light-up sparkly keyboard preprogrammed to play the opening of Beethoven's Fifth;

vanilla Chupa Chup; three storybooks written by an old boyfriend of Penny's; antiseptic cream, eyewash, tweezers and a bandage sling; only one slipper; stained bibs; bag of apples; thermometer; dresses; absurdly small swimming costume; infant ibuprofen, one sachet leaking; Zoe's *Greek Poetic Fragments* vol. II, in case of a quiet moment, took a while. Zoe, still so tired and mysteriously sore, couldn't face saying hello and then having to come back outside so, like a comedy waiter, she tried to carry everything at once, dropping tights into puddles, a battery-operated ambulance flashing its blue lights.

Penny clicked her tongue. Matilda was grumbling. 'God, she's going to kick off yet again. Did you bring my scarf? Christ, where's Humpy?'

'Humpy!' said Rose.

'She's definitely here. Somewhere.'

'Come on, everyone in,' but Zoe, adjusting her grip, looked up at the overhanging roof, higgledy-piggledy casement windows, pipes spurting rainwater, bleeding rust. According to Donald, it had been an illegal pub; the country house of a well-known BBC philosopher; then a squalid hippy strong-hold, notorious for goats and drumming workshops, squatted by those of his students, lovers, children, who had taken their experiments with hallucinogenics a little too far. When Donald, their host, had moved into what had most recently been an old people's home, vermin, some of it unusual, infested the crumbling wattle-and-daub, the lacy roof. After generations of dodgy expansion, partial demolition, boardings-up and falling ceilings, the house had many crooked guest rooms but heating only in the kitchen, and the bedroom Donald shared with Terrence, his boyfriend.

'Is this . . . are we sure it's s—?'

'Well, hello,' said a voice.

They squeezed down the corridor, between an old white pram, rolled rugs, a woven wicker bed-head and an umbrella stand in the shape of a . . .

'Why that a elephant leg?'

'It's just pretend, sweetheart,' said Zoe.

Penny was already making Donald guffaw about Zoe getting lost at Charing Cross station. There was an enormous hall with an unlit fireplace and a piano being used as a table. The living room looked like a lounge in a rehab unit: bony sofas, wooden church chairs round the walls. Torn seat-cushions leaked orange dust, or green-and-yellow vomity chunks, and the room smelt sweet; not right.

'Come in, my pretties,' said Donald, as if they'd been unnecessarily dawdling, had already disappointed. He was tall, beaky, with longish grey hair swept back from his widow's peak and tucked behind his ears, and a silver man-brooch pinned to his lapel. Penny was sure he was distantly related to a Sitwell. He watched them unloading: 'Whose is this extraordinary raincoat?' and 'oh, merino, very nice,' and 'mmm, baby rice-cakes, you shouldn't have'. Penny said he had always been camp, even when he was straight.

He smiled, pale of lip, looking at the wine label, shutting it in a cupboard. 'Lovely glass of something,' he said. It wasn't a question.

Robin was on his way, bringing Justine, 'probably' Jayne Shaunessy, and his own new girlfriend, who was still married to a boat-engine-parts millionaire. Usually, Penny found this latest twist in his love-life enraging. Tonight, luckily, she was distracted by telling Donald all about Jayne: her too-formal weekend-wear; her commitment to hair-spray; the previousness in her tone, as if presuming shared knowledge.

Penny jumped up whenever she thought she heard the car. On the train she had given Zoe extra details about Donald's straightish past; apparently, he'd gone out with both Justine and Penny ('fleetingly').

'Does he still see Justine much?'

'I think she's over him. Well, I know.'

The flagstones were icy under the thin soles of Zoe's awful brogues; Penny said she looked like a police cadet. It was such a confusing house, wonky black floorboards and dim partial staircases, identical white doors revealing unmade beds or chalky scoured baths, starkly strip-lit: no loo paper, no shower-curtain, just a patch of turquoise soap beside the basin and a fierce tang of disinfectant. Despite the thickness of the walls it was stunningly cold, as if damp were pushing up from underground. Rose's miniature teeth were chattering.

'I'll put her to bed,' Zoe said.

'Smell not nice,' observed Rose, standing very close to Zoe's leg, and Zoe thought: that's my girl.

They'd had hummus sandwiches on the way, to Penny's disgust. At the station she'd bought a chicken tikka lattice, a jumbo pack of spicy tortilla chips and two bars of coconut ice, had crunched away at them, 'mmm, de*lic*ious,' until Rose was begging for a taste. 'And don't embarrass me by saying you're hungry when we get in. We'll eat whatever we're given. Don't start being weird.'

Their room was largely bed, sagging, chenille-covered, with one chest of drawers on top of another, barricading a second door; a plug-less oil-heater; uncovered pillows and one stained duvet; pale mottled carpet in art-deco ridged waves. Up here, the sweet smell mixed with a shelf of mildewed science fiction, centuries of inadequate heating and sad food and the wrong kinds of quiet. There was barely space to de-concertina the travel-cot. The long window's many panes rattled urgently as Zoe lowered Matilda inside. They'd agreed that Penny was mostly excused maternal chores this weekend, because it was her gang, her world; however, she'd be waiting downstairs, would be hurt if Zoe seemed not to want to join in.

Zoe had better hurry. She made a chrysalis of stinky quilts for sleepy Rose, pressed her nose to the smudged glass, the mineral cold, and saw not a dash of stars but utter blackness, as if the world outside were cut from felt, and the only life was at her back.

Saturday breakfast, after Rose and Matilda and Zoe had been playing for dozens of hours, was scant: Special K and border-line milk on the living-room table. By lunchtime, a reheated baked potato each, ham OR tuna mayonnaise, with chopped-up iceberg lettuce from a catering tub, seconds frowned upon, Zoe was starting to despair. There were no new-laid eggs or windfall pears but also no immense air-conditioned super-market nearby, in which to buy emergency animal comics, distract Matilda with pipe-cleaners. They found a second living room, containing a set of damp-spotted annuals from forgotten television shows, a video machine, and a large collection of erotic figurines arranged around the fireplace, like nursery-children waiting for a story: ballet-girls, naïads beneath waterfalls, shepherdesses in, only, hats. Rose was very interested.

'Actually,' said Zoe, 'it's someone else's room. We have to . . . I think he'd be angry. No, no, don't cry.'

The rain sheeted down; Rose could not be persuaded into the jungly garden, rioted when they went out anyway. Zoe tried to seem carefree but her green Converse All-Stars, which she had brought despite Penny calling them her boy-shoes, were sodden, slippery, and her grey coat had seemed too Londony for the country so she was wearing layers, under which she copiously sweated while her face and hands froze.

Donald was alternately intimate and scornful, teasing Zoe then ignoring her, or making comments about her 'physique'. When he said, 'I'm not even planning to make a profit,' Zoe expected Penny to nudge her, but she'd left the room.

Jayne hung around the hall, smiling tightly, fiddling with the piano. Rose, flat-dweller, still unable to ride a bike or swim, had fallen under the banisters' spell, trying to weave herself between them like a human slinky. Naturally Matilda had managed to wee out of the side of her leak-proof pull-up. Penny went for a walk with Justine and Robin. 'I'd better. For us. Try one more time to make him stick to his promise.'

More hours to fill; Zoe was rubbish at inventing games, pretending to be a generic insect, a lamb in a stable, asleep, but Penny must not know this. She hated anything negative about motherhood. Guests were loudly arriving downstairs; there were bursts of laughter, like the first glistening lobe of water seeping under a door. Zoe told herself that her true love was close by, the other mother of her children, the woman whom, were it legal, she'd have married within a month, or, let's face it, earlier, if she had been pressed. Penny will surely protect her from smug poshingtons, malicious Donald-friends. It was her job.

Zoe and Rose wrapped themselves in blankets, ate digestives and warm Babybels, waited like sailors' wives for the walkers to return. When at last they appeared, pink-cheeked, Penny tetchy, Rose was unimpressed with her fried egg and Matilda had developed nappy rash. More and more guests were arriving. Marnie, Bill's stepdaughter, went in search of magic mushrooms with a pink wind-up torch. Bill himself had brought something, unspecified, in twenty small manila wage-packets.

Zoe settled Rose in her byre, Matilda into her travel-cot. She tried to think of reasons to stay with them, holding a socked foot, patting Matilda's small haunch, heavy against the netting, but they fell asleep quickly. Downstairs, there was no sign of dinner. It seemed gauche to ask for toast. Penny was eating little packets of pub-peanuts brought by Bill, still attached to a cardboard topless woman. 'Use my lipstick if you've forgotten yours,' she told her but, when Zoe did, and went to find her to check how it looked, she was whispering in the corner with Nikki and Chrissie and Nicky. At the sight of Zoe, she winced. 'Oh no. God. Much too much.'

Zoe scrubbed at her mouth in the loo, wondered about late trains to London.

Beth made a speech about being furious to be forty. Penny, beside her, said 'unlike some,' and pointed at Zoe. Zoe tried chatting to an obviously lesbian old neighbour, in a sort of jerkin; Penny would have been amused by her outdoor ruddiness, her signet ring. Where was Penny, anyway? Feigning interest in the books on the mantelpiece, a Tarot guide, novelizations from a seventies soap set on a ferry, Zoe thought hungrily of the remaining banana. Donald, lord of misrule, held a beer-glass of something towards her, as if rewarding a dog. 'Little drink?'

Self-assured country people were milling around by the front door in muted rainwear, or hunched over lighter-flames sharing cigarettes. She could hear Justine's laugh, and Robin's; glass broke, and they laughed harder. She dawdled upstairs again; which was their door? How could they have forgotten Humpy? When Rose woke without him, the night would be long. If only Zoe would spot him lying casually on the disgusting carpet. Please, please, she prayed to him, as to a capricious god. We need you. It'll all be all right, with you.

But there was no Humpy. Hesitating in the corridor, blood banging in her ears like a frightened pervert, she tried to block out the bass thumping from the speakers downstairs and realized that she could hear a child, bellowing. When she found the right room and grabbed the handle, the wailing stopped, but she couldn't turn it properly; it slipped in her palm. Maybe a bit unnecessarily, she rammed the door with her shoulder, burst in.

Rose was standing, wet-legged, on the rug, holding up her arms: a reeking Victorian beggar-child in too-small *102 Dalmatians* pyjamas. In her little alcove, prone in her travel cot, Matilda, the world's lightest sleeper, lay silent. It seemed too much to hope for that she too could be alive.

Some minutes, several hours' worth, later, Rose, re-dressed in leggings and a knee-length jumper, was soothed. Penny would be furious at her absence. Zoe closed the door softly, piled the ammonia-drenched bedding into a bath like a fat-armed laundress and went down to consult her about pillows. But Penny, in the highest of heels, a cowl-necked stretch-velvet top, was being playful with a boomy tall clearly straight man, lifting his wrist to admire his big watch. Zoe approached, realizing, too late, that the man, Bruce, was hoping to keep Penny to himself.

'Why were you so bloody long?' Penny hissed when Bruce announced he was going outside for a slash. 'I was abandoned.'

Zoe, piss-scented, found what was probably her glass and took a swig. Before she could explain adequately, Bruce and his big watch had reappeared, his Full Head of Hair, of which he looked so proud, refreshed. His inward-slanting teeth were stained with wine. 'The question,' he said, smiling satanically, 'is whether babies can tell the difference.'

'Oh God. What've you been telling him?' asked Zoe, as lightly as possible.

'Now, now, girls,' said Bruce. 'You've got to admit it's an important point. Scientifically.'

As if sensing discord, Beth approached. Apparently, she still intended to foster, when she had time. Zoe tried to like Beth; everyone else adored her. 'Don't you think she's attractive?' Penny often asked. 'You can't not. I don't believe you.' It was true: who would not gaze at those big cow eyes, air of womanly strength and general up-for-it-ness, and not want to be enfolded, to sink into that bosom? But it wasn't fancying, let alone desire. Not once, in Zoe's dreams, during sex, even when alone, had she ever imagined wanting anyone but Penny.

'Been suckling each other's young?' asked Beth. 'Like a little babushka?'

Zoe, forcing herself to smile, started explaining, but Beth wouldn't leave it. 'When Rose was newborn, you must have attempted it? Or is that somehow . . . illegal?'

'We did try,' said Penny, and everyone oo-ed. 'Greedy old Rose was completely up for it. Not that Zoe actually produced anything.'

Terrence opened the whisky. Someone turned up the music. Bill lurked in the corner; he beckoned Zoe over but she pretended not to see. Earlier, changing quickly in their damp room, Penny had said: 'At least I know you'll never leave me for one of this lot. Why doesn't Jen deal with those eyebrows? And Siobhan's up-do; even Beth's little formerly straight protégée, Ali, Alice. So bony. Did you notice her collarbones? Like a coat-hanger. Those closety types are always a mistake. Classic Beth. Poor Beth, she deserves love, not a hetty. Oh, but you probably fancy her though, don't you, in that awful fisherman's jumper, like a lighthouse keeper?'

'I hadn't noticed her,' said Zoe, although Alice was much closer to Zoe's age than any of the others. She had short neat hair and the kind of discreet hygienic jewellery a nurse might wear, or a vet. Zoe should be used to this by now, but the idea that someone so wholesome and girly could be interested in women, like having sex with women, at least one of them, was still extraordinarily interesting.

'You'd better not have,' Penny said, and she tapped out their secret code: for ever, on Zoe's wrist-bone, then her bottom lip.

Zoe held her breath, for more, for a kiss.

'Come on,' said Penny. 'Let's see who's up to no good.'

26

Now

Justine, unaware of her lucky escape, is letting loose a new bolt of venom. As she returns, once again, to Zoe's crimes, Zoe recognizes that the reason she didn't push her into the gap wasn't kindness, or decency, but simply the fear of being caught.

'You can't stop me informing the police,' she's saying loudly. 'If I should so choose.' Zoe averts her eyes from the women sitting inches away, seven Tasty-Fresh Southfields carrier bags on the floor between them, looking up with interest. 'What you're doing is illeg—'

The merciful screech of metal racing through a low dark tunnel drowns her out, for now. Zoe is gripping the overhead bar; Justine has wedged herself in the corner. A fatherly-looking builder stands between them, his burly rucksack and spirit level like staves on a barricade. Let him be travelling to the end of the line. What if Matty has a strop in a Headington all-day brasserie and Tricia has to take charge? Or Penny unleashes her mercenaries, an army of private social workers and psychiatrists? The urge to destroy is growing stronger, again: to bring havoc, if only upon herself. She gazes at the vein and muscle on her forearm as it flexes, her knuckles bulging yellow like the ends of chicken drumsticks. She wants to bite it, hang off the bar with her whole weight until her bones snap.

And, as Justine starts up again about custody arrangements, she remembers Hilary Mint saying: 'Those threats are all they've got.'

Zoe had been weeping discreetly on the phone; the only time she cried within earshot, shameful as flashing her bum.

It's true, Hilary told her, pretending not to hear. Whether or not the adults think it's fair, *any* judge would ask children, including those of Matilda's age, what it is they want. 'No one, I guarantee, will force them to go somewhere they'd prefer not to be, spend time with any parent who's demonstrably unstable, now they're of the age of reason. So, if Matilda is happier being with you, as you say, you're whom she will choose. And Rose: well, let's see. She might alternate for a bit, but you're still very close. She's in a quandary. Let it evolve. Look, Penny's grief and rage are immaterial. If you, and they, can endure, stand firm, it will work out.'

At long last, Justine submits to the impossible noise in the carriage. The hectoring stops; out comes her phone. Zoe pretends to look away. But, still, she watches her, typing angrily. Every hair is haloed by light, the dry skin between her eyebrows, the nostril-spot. On either side of her mouth the flesh droops. She shines, but not with warmth, or hope; she is the worm and her dark secret love has ruined everything.

No, thinks Zoe. That's not it. How can I keep forgetting? The destroyer was Penny.

Then

September 2003

Each time Zoe tried to go to bed, midnight, then one-ish, Penny took it badly. They were back in the old muddle, Zoe not being fun at Penny's friends' parties, or trying too hard. Penny was laughing with, surprise, Justine. Zoe touched her hand to her chest. It felt as if a pastry-cutter had removed a section of rib-cage, twisting it to reveal her throbbing heart. All she needed was to lie in the seething cold while Rose exhaled, Matilda snuffled, the music thumped. No, that wasn't right; she'd worry about what was going on downstairs.

She started trying to explain but Penny was gripping her hand.

'Come with us,' she whispered moistly in Zoe's ear.

'Why?'

'Why not? Be spontaneous, for Christ's sake. Oh, I don't care, do what you like.'

It was as if sodden sand was filling her chest; she felt extraordinarily heavy, cast down. 'No, it's OK. I'll come. What's up?'

'Forget it.'

But Justine was grabbing an unopened bottle, gesturing towards the door. Anything could happen if Zoe didn't come too, keep an eye.

'Where are we going?'

'Apparently something's happening in one of the bedrooms. We're going to have a look.'

*

The front hall was so dark. Cigarette-dots blazed in the open doorway, a torch-lantern, a glint of blue from outside; she could make out children on the window seat, failing to conceal bottles: beer and what looked like Amaretto. Nicky, of Nicky-and-Steph, and Beth were hooting with laughter. Marnie was smoking a spliff near the cars, beneath the children's window. It made Zoe feel ferocious, to imagine a prong of this permissiveness touching Rose's pink brain. But Penny nudged her, grinned. Shaking back her freshly rebrushed hair, she kicked her heels into the corner.

'Won't you lose them? I'd b—'

'No way. And shh. Take yours off too.' An echo of getting undressed for bed, together; Zoe complied.

One boy, barely a teenager, had his eyes closed, leaning his head against the navy glass. 'Shouldn't we check if he's OK?'

'Nope. One day that'll be our kid.'

'That's what I w—'

'You can't go around stopping everyone from having fun,' Penny said loudly, with that scoffing sound which always felt conclusive: the definitive statement about just how square and boring Zoe was.

But what if he died? Still frowning behind her, Zoe almost tripped, put out a hand and touched soft flesh.

'Ow, you . . . my lip! God, that was your ring. Is there blood? Christ, that . . . I'd better not be scarred.'

The impact, Zoe was sure, had been so slight. Knowledge of her wrongness settled and congealed; Penny would insist on a brightly lit mirror, a minutely critical inspection of her face. Even if there was no sign of injury, she and Zoe would be out of joint.

Yet Penny, unusually, barely stopped. 'Not now. Jesus. You have no sense of . . . hurry up.'

All the wine, or the sweat and cold air, had made her light-headed. The blackness pressing upon them, the infinite night outside, pushed terror in.

'Shouldn't we go back?'

'Why? Not now.' Penny had taken Beth's hip flask.

'I . . .' This wasn't right; the house was too huge, muffling itself. Was something moving behind them? She heard a creak, a clatter, then silence. Her scalp was alive with fear. 'It might not be safe,' she said. 'For, for the kids, if we're far off,' but Penny wasn't taken in.

'It's fine. Christ's sake.'

At least they were out of everyone's earshot now. Her heart was filling her chest; waves rushed through her ears, into her lungs. This corridor seemed entirely new. They passed a crucifix propped in a wall-hollow, turned down another corridor of powdery whitewashed stone. 'Hang on—'

But here were Steph, Nikki, French Lucie, huddled in the murk; even Chrissie, standing apart like a famous person, laser-dot of cigarette glowing by her mouth.

'Are y—'

'Shhh!'

'Isn't this Donald's room?'

The door was ajar. Dance music swelled, receded; in the room's depths, low-lit, she could see movement. 'One at a time, still?' called Nikki, and Penny laughed.

'Are they . . . taking drugs?' asked Zoe.

'Oh Christ,' Penny said.

Nikki stretched out an arm, patted Zoe's head.

Zoe forced herself to stand there a little longer, praying for Penny to decide to leave.

That long-ago night in Stag Street for Penny's birthday, before they lived together or had babies, the evening before she properly met Robin, this same ferrous edge, the whisper of fire, was in the air.

Where was Justine?

Terrence was dancing very close to possibly Inge, or Beth, his dark arms crossed across her pale back. Which was visible because . . . where were their tops? Bill was in there too, his white belly glowing like a beach-ball in the shadows; he wasn't dancing, because there was somebody in the way.

Zoe licked her chapped lips. So cold; even her nipples stung. 'What's happening?'

'Shh. Isn't it obvious?'

Oh no. Zoe had never seen anyone have sex, never even heard it. But here it was: on the cusp. 'Are . . . is th—'

'We'll just watch,' murmured Penny, like love in her ear. 'Be instructive.'

'But . . .'

'Spotted Jen yet?' Penny asked.

Earlier, Zoe had heard her tell Jen she looked sexy, and Jen had put a kiss-mark on her jaw. 'I promised her dear husband,' Penny added, as if they were popping into a charity raffle, 'we'd at least look in.'

When Zoe first noticed what Penny presumably had seen

already, Jen in someone's arms, kissing, or being kissed, she had felt a pang for big soft lacklustre Bill. They had this in common: the pain of knowing one's attractive partner couldn't be entirely tamed. Could that be Nicky? Steph had her back against the corridor wall, looking miserable. Zoe narrowed her eyes; the person with Jen was definitely female. Bill was standing extremely close by. An uncomfortable feeling, a crackle, crept over her neck. Where had Penny gone earlier? She turned to ask, but she'd disappeared. Bill and Jen and the woman were cheering as someone else joined them; Jen's hand against the dark of her collar, her mouth on hers. Under Bill's pale belly, his sagging pants, someone's arm was moving, and it wasn't his.

That was when she left.

She'd tried to lower her lids, blur the view with her lashes. Prude, she imagined Penny saying, like a long slim blade slipping between the ribs, separating flesh from skin. A thought slid in, when she wasn't guarding against it: I am being hollowed out.

No, no, she was lucky. There were so few lesbians, as Penny always said, let alone single ones, and those were all crazed; the miracle was that she'd been chosen by the only good one. Who, if sometimes she tipped into unkindness, was only saying what it was healthy for Zoe to hear. If Penny could be a bit preoccupied with her gang, who weren't particularly friendly, and Zoe was wishing this weekend could have been in a centrally heated house with her own friends, cooking together in a clean kitchen, that was a mark of her drabness, her avoidance of anything like fun. If only she could break her own leg and be air-lifted home; or, better, walk bravely through picturesque snow with the babies to Elhambridge station, where a kindly guard would stop the London train and bundle them on, jam tarts and beautiful iced cakes in a cardboard box, travel cases safely stowed in a rack above.

Even here she could hear shouts of laughter, layers of conversation passing at a distance, like clouds beneath a plane. The next corridor seemed even colder, as if it stuck out from the rest of the house; chill pouring up like a smell into her toe bones.

'Stop overthinking,' Penny said, in her mind.

She was beginning to feel sick. A black window rattled to her left; if she looked, she would be seized by the fear of what might be outside, although she needed the fresher air, needed to calm down. The only door in the passageway was closed; had she been here before? What if a couple was behind it, having sex; there was a sense in the house tonight that everyone, almost, might be, as if decreed by Donald: nothing out of bounds.

I like bounds, thought Zoe, and felt hot self-pity gathering in her sinuses, ready to make her sneeze. When Penny realized she had sneaked off to bed, there'd be a fierce whispered quarrel in that horrible room, being told she'd ruined their weekend. Could she claim an ailment: a sore throat, an ache? Penny would see through it, but returning to Donald's room, even bumping into any of the others, was beyond endurance.

Then she had an idea: she could pretend she'd gone up to

check on the babies, because Rose was still upset about Humpy, and then accidentally had fallen asleep herself.

It might work. It was plausible. The corridor was too hushed, the air denser than usual, as if the strange heat of her body were making it ripple, as above a flame. She thought of Greek mountain pines, the susurration, the fear before the god appeared. There was a shuffling sound, like a bag on the floor or an elbow against plaster. Mid-step, she waited; infinitely slowly she lowered her foot. There was something terrible around the corner.

She heard a murmur; a woman's voice, a sound as if someone were trying to hide pain. She opened her mouth; better that they know she was here, she thought. This broke her spell of fear. She put on a social smile, tried to slow her breathing, on down to the end and there in an alcove, in a confusion of whispering and faces suddenly turned, stood Justine and Penny, of course.

Part Three

Destruction

Now

Everyone thinks they'd be good in a crisis. But some of us are so battered and bludgeoned that, when the storm hits, we can think only of lying on the forest floor, in a mulch of leaves and robin-feathers, hibernating for a year or two until the trouble has passed.

'Why haven't you been answering,' Zoe's father is asking. 'It's important. I've tried your home phone, and your office, spoke to your boss. Very odd man. Where are you?' He has rung her mobile already, repeatedly; while she was running away from the mediation, then deep underground in the tube.

'Sorry. What's up, are you OK? Are the kids? I'm in a rush so—'

'Well. Mum has a terrible headache.' He waits; she waits. 'So, sadly, she isn't up to tonight.'

When Zoe's children were small, and her parents still pained her as sharply as in her childhood, and teens, and twenties, Penny would say: 'Clive's a dear man. But you do realize that Tricia always, always comes first? Which is pretty appalling, if you think about it. I mean, if we were in a disaster . . . no, I know that idea freaks you out, but you can't control my thoughts. Anyway, it's good for you to deal with it. So, if there was a flood or something, bushfire, a cyclone, no, listen, Clive would definitely rescue old Trish, thoroughly lipsticked, above you both. He'd watch you sink under the flotsam, or is it jetsam. But I wouldn't do that. I'd save the kids. It's what parenthood should be.'

She's only now, pausing beside the dirty walls of the station exit, wondering if that was weird. She'd often imagined scenarios, the last lifeboat, the siege of Leningrad, where there wasn't enough room or food for them all, when, if Penny was not put first, she'd know, even while she continued to exist beside them, at least for a while. If Zoe were in charge, she would never find the strength to make Penny suffer. Which means she has no right to consider herself a mother, the good kind.

'Hello? I don't have time t—'

'I'm here. Christ, Dad. OK.' Only a fool could imagine that her own personal nadir has been reached. 'You realize they're about to arrive, don't you? You both were meant to be . . . are you honestly saying that you can't?'

Penny would say: remind him we've never asked for a thing, that Tricia promised and promised to help us, three mornings a week she said, when Rose was born, and she came, what, once? Those dozens, hundreds of times she's offered things, spectacular trips to Whipsnade safari park, Alton Towers, and then was mysteriously tied up on the day. Don't tell me,' she'd say, 'that you've forgotten when you were in hospital and afterwards, unable to do a thing, and I begged them for help. The kids and the emotional propping-up, your sadness, I couldn't do it alone. And again, what, one visit? You said she didn't even ask how you felt, remember that? So don't you defend her, after all those hours of crying. It's only thanks to me that you can see her selfishness.'

As if there's any point arguing with a devoted man, Zoe begins: 'Dad. I know she has . . . But it's a bit of a crisis. And,' she adds, lobbing the wolf a last desperate bit of gazelle, 'the kids were really looking forward to seeing her. You know they've b—'

'I'm very sorry, but you'll just have to accept it. Mum is exhausted.' He sounds shattered himself, worn out by kindness. 'Don't be difficult, please.'

'For f—'

'So what would you like me to do with them? They'll be here any minute. Why don't I say we'll go out for a special treat, cake at the Copper Kettle perhaps, they think the world of Mum there, and then they can go back to yours tonight. Or . . . well, I'm sure that Penelope won't mind; I'll ask her.'

'Oh God. No, you really, really mustn't ring her. Please. Honestly. I did explain to you, how she's behaving. Even the postman commented.' She can hear the unattractive note of desperation, piling one fact on top of another as the one beneath it slips away. 'I told Mum, in fact,' although what actually happened was that Tricia mentioned having sent Penny a card, Zoe objected, and they haven't spoken since.

'I don't think she . . . maybe I've forgotten.' Tricia must

never be slandered, even when it's true. 'And that's just silly. They're always upset, aren't they, teenagers?' He sounds like Zoe's mother reading out something absurd about Political Correctness from the papers. He has done everything any daughter could hope for, to help her through this disaster, but Tricia's indifference to the existence, let alone the content, of anyone else's feelings has rubbed off. 'I'm sure Penelope can contain herself. I'll have a word.'

'Please!' She closes her eyes, tries to master herself. 'OK. Listen. Do you remember, I'm moving out my, our stuff today? From the shared – the family – from the flat? Tonight. And they're a bit old for . . . thing is, the only possible way the complicated timing of it all can work is if they stay at yours, tonight.'

'Then, tell you what: how about if I phone up that new Premier Inn near the roundabout, and ask them for a last-minute deal? Matty's wild about an all-you-can-eat breakfast, I still think of her little face in the New Forest, by those muffins. And it would be an adventure, wouldn't it, staying there by themselves.'

Drop me to the depths like a stone, thinks Zoe. Let me be confined to hospital: calmness, peace, not even mountains and a sanatorium bath-chair but a white room and a pale green curtain, a metal bed-frame. 'Um. You realize they're fifteen and twe— it's probably illegal. And if it isn't, they've had a horrible . . . it's really bad, what they've been dealing with, the mad screaming and fury. Even if they wanted to, which I don't think they would . . . it's kind of you, Dad, but. It's not a good idea. It wouldn't work. Please believe me.

Look, let me think.' She's too tired to do this. It was hanging in the balance, that she could get away with any of it, her, their, escape, and now there is no chance. She will tell Penny she is sorry.

But the keys. Ozman runs a very small chain of pretend-Italian gelato shops throughout the Uxbridge and Hammersmith area, open late for the young. He is leaving the keys in something called a keep-box padlocked to the railings in an alley beside the Goldhawk Road flat, to which Zoe has been given the combination: 8883.

8883. A beautiful number.

Her father is persisting. 'Why not jump on a coach and meet the kids there? You're only an hour away. Simply tell the removal firm you'll leave your key to the new place under a flowerpot and they can drop it back tomorrow. You must have flowerpots. Charm them; think of your mother,' he suggests cheerily, then adds, more quietly: 'are you worrying about the extra cost?'

How would Penny handle this?

There would be drama, and noise, all hands on deck; Nicky and Steph, Beth, Robin, Justine.

'No,' says Zoe, prodding at her sore left shoulder. Pain should help, sharpen her focus. Dawn always says that Penny's kindest to Zoe when her shoulder's bad: 'Makes you small. Not a threat.' Maybe when Zoe is settled in Goldhawk Road, she'll start exercising. Imagine being strong, having muscle, and not even thinking about Penny's teasing, her suspicion. Imagine putting the key in the door of a flat inaccessible to any of the others, closing it behind her, knowing that they could turn up at the kids' schools, let loose as many emails as they want, but they could not come in.

'Dad,' she says, as if she's another woman entirely. 'OK. Here's what I need you to do.'

THEN

September 2003

The morning after the party; Penny was awake already, her beautiful eyes bright. When Zoe turned her head and saw her, she smiled. 'Hello, you silly.' She sounded so loving. 'Why do you get all insecure? There's nothing to fret about.'

The relief, after such a horrible night: dread and grief, scrappy dreams of panic. Penny needed comforting, too; unbeknownst to Zoe, she'd spent ages downstairs at the party trying to persuade Robin one last time about another baby, had ended up enlisting Justine's help. 'That was the whole point, you see. Chatting, getting her to convince him when they were both a bit pissed and relaxed. All I wanted, darling, was to come up to bed with you.'

Zoe ended up apologizing, for creeping around the corridors, for assuming the worst. They'd been arguing more often, not only about babies: carnage was piling up by the roadside, so many fires never fully extinguished. For the sake of peace, she'd say sorry for anything.

Then Penny said Justine was feeling hurt, too. It was terrible to be so suspicious of old friends, to accuse the two of them of having been up to something. If anything was going on, which it definitely wasn't, why would they choose the corridor of a cold weird-smelling house? You're right, Zoe said. I see that now.

In the cab on the way to the station, her throat full of bottled-up misery, she looked over the soggy fields as Penny, more in sorrow et cetera, reminded her Zoe's own mother couldn't stand it when she became really vexatiously tense. Even the constant asking 'are you OK?' made Penny feel invaded. She explained that she was only trying to help Zoe not sabotage the best relationship that she'd ever had.

'I know I'm sometimes a bit stern,' she said, as Rose shrilly accompanied Kylie's 'Can't Get You Out of My Head' on the taxi-driver's radio. 'It's fear, you see, that anything could jeopardize us,' and Zoe's heart melted.

'Sometimes,' Penny explained that evening, over beans on toast, 'You don't realize how much like Tiny Tricia you are. Don't sulk, Jesus. I'm trying to help. You know,' she added, tilting her head towards the children, 'how much I'm struggling, since the Black Prince . . . you know. Betrayed us. I don't know how I'll bear it,' and Zoe felt it again, the fear.

There was no alternative. They clearly had to find another man for Penny. So why wasn't Zoe helping to think of one? On every single other subject she caved but, so far, when it came to launching an entirely separate family extension, a whole new circle on their perilous Venn diagram, months passed, and still she managed not to give in.

'Are you even asking around, like you promised? Let's face it, I know what you think.'

'What do I think?'

'All the usual stuff, we'd need a new car, we'd need to move house, we're tense all the time because of bloody Robin. That it's already hard. And starting again with someone else wouldn't be fair on our existing kids.'

'Or on the third one. Completely different dad, separated from Rose and Matty every other we—'

'Well, what about on me? Anyway, maybe the third one would be better off without Robin.'

'But the other man, the other dad, might be wo—'

'I'd sort it,' Penny said. Which meant that she'd find someone else to do it, whether or not Zoe agreed.

She looked into informal donation through a charity, but decided that the risk of unscreened semen was too high. Also, presumably the donor wouldn't want to co-parent? She was pretty sure she could persuade Robin and Justine to have the new offspring a third of the time, but what if that gave Robin the idea of having another, with some other woman; even a couple? She cornered Zoe into watching a documentary about estuaries, because of the gay architect friend-of-a-friend in the second half, although he was even older than Robin, and had sideburns like a badger and a ponytail. When Zoe was eventually steamrollered into a meeting, Penny had gone off him. What about Huw the conservationist; would Zoe ask him again? Was the reason she was dragging her feet that she'd set her sights on yet another job?

At last, completely flattened, Zoe agreed to meet another potential father in his neat rose-carpeted flat in a mansion-block near Kew: soft opera, naval biographies, an office-style coffee percolator and a rotisserie-microwave. The man, Simon, had expressed many doubts, but Penny could tell that he'd yield, if pushed. He specialized in ecclesiastical misericords, which he was happy to explain, was only thirty-one but wore a beige V-neck under a grey flannel jacket and preferred not to discuss his sexual affiliations with a stranger.

Back at home, she tried to sound positive about him, his thoughtful provision of elderflower cordial, the view of blossom outside his gleaming bathroom window. Penny hesitated for weeks, then said she was going to turn him down. What was the point in trying? The damage was done. Their arguments began to incorporate Zoe's parenting: her thoughtlessnesses, spoiling Rose by taking her out for cake, reassuring Matty for hours about meteorites, without the least understanding of how damaging it was to Penny's bonding with them. She needed more time, not less, if her wounds were ever to heal, making up for the ghost child Zoe had stopped her having.

More of both of them, not only Rose. There could not be any question of treating Matilda differently. If the delicate structures they'd built around their elder daughter – no more time with any parent, least of all Zoe; no preference ever expressed – weren't imposed on her little sister too, it would be utterly unfair on Rose, and on Penny, who'd had to bear it herself the first time round. It would be favouritism. How could Zoe, who claimed to care about Penny, be so unable, or unwilling, to anticipate her feelings? 'You might as well admit it,' Penny said. 'You're trying to edge me out.'

So this was where Zoe's crime deepened. For Rose, who hated even a night away, she drew weekly timetables for both fridges. She hushed Matty if she ever asked for Zoe, Mama, when it was Mummy's night to put her to bed, because Penny insisted on alternating, an iron rule, and Matty quickly learned, her clever girl. Zoe let her baby go from parent to parent and never know who her primary person should be, or even that she might have had one. When Zoe promised to take Rose to see an interesting fallen tree, and Penny was outraged ('you specifically said let's go for a coffee later. Don't I matter at all?'), or agreed to watch another episode of nonsense with Matty, she always hurried, evaded, moved a little away from her child on the sofa, lied, to them and to Penny, so that Penny wouldn't feel left out. It was unforgivable, but she caved, every single fucking time she caved, like the pathetic runt she was.

27

Now

5.20 p.m.

Des's lads are waiting in Stag Street, drinking Lucozade and lobbing an orange at each other.

'Get yer gay vitamins off of me,' says one.

'Oi-oi,' Des tells them. 'None of that.'

He's younger than Zoe expected, with a neat Assyrian beard and collar-length dreadlocks; his forearms are dappled with muscle. Despite his ragged T-shirt and faded jeans, he smells very clean. She can't think how to talk to him; Penny would say she was trying too hard. Or being stand-offish. She doesn't have a single instinct left.

And look at the place. Biros all over the floor, knickers, scarves wrapped around side-plates; she was deluded, to imagine making a successful getaway. She smiles extra hard at the lad who said 'gay', in case one day he sees someone being beaten up and could step in.

They're meant to be on the road at half five; it's not much of a road, more like two corners, but she'll be allowed to sit in the front of the lorry like a mascot. And they'll carry everything upstairs. There's still too much to pack: Matty's special soap and science folder, the other Pyrex jug, her father's terrible ancient shirt, which one day she will be grateful for. Yet, as Des and his lads scout the rooms, they do not comment on the overfilled bags for life, whistle only a little at the wobbly columns of books. They don't ask about her husband. Des must have warned them.

'It'll be fine,' he says; he's obviously done this before, moved the pathetic goods of divorcing wives. She imagines him and the lads sitting around her future kitchen table, the girls', no, Matty's life improved by knowing this younger, decent, straight man. She makes coffee, introduces them to the desolate bathroom, apologizes for the loose duvet and inadequately packed box-files, the blue IKEA bag in which Matty's private world – tracksuit bottoms and old soft toys and balled-up school letters – lies bared. But they don't mock or smirk, not even at the sign on the bedroom door made by Rose in pottery:

> *Mummy + Mama*
> *'s Room*

They're local lads, she discovers; afterwards they'll be at the Old Crown. Penny won't like that.

Gradually, their calm confidence steals over her. It begins to seem possible that, even with less time to unpack than she'd expected, and God knows what she'll find in Goldhawk Road, and the kids rocking up starving and unsettled after their brief trip to Headington, plus however her father excused her mother's failings, and will they have to get a takeaway, which would be a treat for Matty, eventually this might be

OK. She takes a spare toothbrush for Rose, some pants, a couple of tops which won't be missed, in case, and forces herself not to think about it. Instead, she tries to visualize herself as a true Amazon, galloping strong and tall; as Artemis, Athene, or a hero, although she can't think of any female ones. She'd need spear and helmet; yes, obviously it's two and a half millennia later, and her tits wouldn't fit in any breastplate. That must be why the image doesn't take.

She won't let it be a bad omen. When the front door jiggles, then scrapes open over the mat, Zoe almost calls out again, 'Remember the rabbit,' thinking it's one of the lads coming through, with spare cardboard boxes or a carton of juice. If only she could chisel off a section of the girls' pencilled height-marks in the hall: proof, slid into an artefact bag. She'd meant to buy the lads biscuits, not the healthyish kind she insists on getting for the kids, to Penny's repugnance, but something more straightforwardly enjoyable. Do they usually go for chocolate? she wonders, picking tape from her hair, or custard cr—?

THEN

2006

Zoe's new job, which she'd hoped would help, did not. Penny detected the hand of Hilary Mint who, any idiot could see, was trying to sabotage them, turn Zoe into her daughter.

'Did you even think about how the hell this would work? Roehampton, of all places; really? You'll be relaxing in a window seat while I'm, what, meekly skivvying away in the background? Can't you set up private tutoring, external exam marking or something, for experience? Or wait for somewhere nearer? Or better paid? I can't believe you are doing this to me, again.'

But jobs in Classics were thin on the ground, even if they involved long commutes on trains too elbow-packed for marking. Why wouldn't Zoe simply admit to being wildly ambitious, when it was ruining their lives? Penny grew angrier each time Zoe came home late, kept saying that one of them had to give up their job and it wasn't going to be her. 'I can't stand it, the way you're always snapping at my heels.'

Once, as they crossed Oxford Street, she compared Zoe to a rescue dog: her neediness, the way she was always wanting a friendly pat, or a foot against her leg in the night. She still referred sort-of-affectionately to Zoe's tail, or her withers, and then accuse her of taking things ridiculously personally. She'd say: 'I need to be free to speak my mind, not be answerable about every least thing.'

'But I'm your partner, wife, whatever, and I can't ping back from all the criticizing. I want to but I can't.'

Penny wouldn't buy it. 'That's your problem, not mine.' Besides, Zoe *was* a dog: the worst kind of stray, with a life-long fear of umbrellas, motorbikes, strangers; gnawing at her tail. Was that, or Lesbian Bed-Death, which all Penny's friends said was unavoidable, the reason Penny seemed not to fancy her? She'd think, 'I don't want my sex-life to be over,' but Penny said the worrying was in itself a huge turn-off.

What was normal? She knew no one to ask. There were no lesbian bars or clubs left, except a few Penny scoffed at. Now that Zoe mostly wore skirts, had hair almost as long as Penny's, how could any passing lesbian guess that she was one of them? There should be a system of flags to signal affiliation. Penny said her hands-in-pockets walk gave her away, as if passing as straight were simply a question of effort. Say she were single, and needed to meet a lesbian, what kind would she even fancy? No one who'd fancy her back, obviously, let alone tolerate her, longer term. Whenever things went wrong with Penny, she'd remember how narrowly she'd escaped from spinsterhood.

There would never be another lover. She was thirty-four.

They'd had a difficult year; then began another. Penny was struggling with completely unreasonable work expectations which were leaving her no time at all for research; not only a bovine second-year seminar group and a doctoral student protégée-turned-challenger, but an uncomfortable spell as co-leader for the Research Assessment Exercise: stressful fortnightly meetings, scrabbling to extract the work from recalcitrant colleagues, then sitting up at night choosing which of their tedious articles and chapters to submit in order to guarantee any departmental funding, while absolutely no allowance was made for the fact that she had to produce her own.

'Lucky we've had Robin, in a way,' said Penny, 'or we couldn't both have been academics. Not that we can ever tell him. He'd use it against us in court, you know he would. Although if you weren't always working, we wouldn't need him, would we?'

Then her chief English department rival, Ginny Buffery, was asked to a Bloomsbury Group conference in Tokyo: Ginny, with her special walk, her waist-length red-gold hair and the long linseed-coloured scarf she always wore, to give an impression of even greater volume. Why would anyone choose her over Penny?

Every evening, as Zoe pushed open the street door, her spirits would sink at the thought of the hours ahead. What state might Penny be in? Would today have been ruined when Penny bumped into a pregnant colleague, or started her period, or found one of Rose's old bibs shoved behind the bath-towels?

There was an envelope on the kitchen table; A4, firmly addressed by Hilary Mint in her usual green Pentel R50 Rollerball. 'Here we go,' said Penny. 'What's she sent you now?'

Now

5.47 p.m.
It's Penny, who is meant to be in Battersea.

She doesn't bother to look for Zoe. She stands in the hallway and starts shouting, at whichever lad happens to be there: 'Why are you doing this to me? Don't listen to her, she's dangerous. Whatever she's claimed, it's a lie. I've seen you before, you with the earring. When did she pay you? Do the neighbours know you're here? Tell me the address you're taking my property to. You do know she's illegally denying me access to my young child? You absolutely cannot remove any goods without my consent.'

Des, refilling his water bottle in the kitchen, lifts his eyebrows at Zoe. His entire scalp, she notices absently, moves in sympathy. He's balancing against his hip a carton containing Zoe's bank statements; the lasagne dish Sara gave her for her twenty-first; a home-made book-end; the black-and-gold Las Vegas mug to which Matty's attachment is, she hopes, fleeting.

'Sorry,' she mouths. 'Sorry.' He'll leave, of course he will. The tap squeaks off. He lifts the carton higher.

And Penny rushes in. 'What are you taking? Put that down. You realize that she's mentally ill? You are exploding my life, crushing our daughters. My doctor says you're at risk of endangering m—'

'Please, stop,' says Zoe. 'You knew this was happening.'

'You're lying! I didn't know anything about you helping yourself to my possessions, our basic family assets. You can change your mind, make them put everything back. You have to, for my sake.'

The sleepiness is rising again, threatening to pull her down to the splintery floorboards. She should let this, her pitiful last stand, reach its natural end. None of the adults' solutions works and, even if she did give in and tell the kids to comply, again, and somehow managed to live with a third of Matty and less of Rose, she would be no mother.

Penny always says mother-love is the strongest, the truest: the best.

This is the moment when another woman would rise. Adrenaline should rush through her arteries like flood-water through a sewer, so she can grab the bus-bumper, hoist it high above her baby's pram. So where is it, the righteous rage?

And then, like a whisper, she realizes something worse. Say she did escape to the new place and wait for the kids, even met them at Marylebone station, they won't come back with her. She has been delusional. Penny and Robin and Justine are much more powerful than she is, their poison purified by hatred. The children have been brought up to let their will be pulverized; she allowed that to happen. Isn't it more realistic to accept that Rose, if not Matty too, will stay with Robin and Penny in Stag Street, maybe visit Zoe a few times in her sad little attic, and eventually that too will peter out? So, if she goes now, she's abandoning her children, exactly like those mothers Penny used to tell her about, before mother-hood.

Penny, inexhaustible, follows Zoe across the kitchen, the hallway, herds her upstairs into the bathroom, then down again into what was their bedroom. The woman Zoe cherished is in pain and she feels . . . nothing. No pity, no mercy, no rage. It's like passing a shouting zealot on the street; she can only think of getting away. Apparently unruffled, neither smirking nor showing distaste, Des and his lads continue, shouldering boxes, hoisting bags. Penny follows them into every room and Des merely offers his back, nodding slowly, not responding except to say, 'I'll leave that to Zoe,' and then Zoe, as if his calmness is catching, says, 'We'll discuss it tomorrow,' as though that could possibly be that.

They could load up the van and drive off, but Penny's too sharp; she won't be distracted. There's no way to make this stop. Now she's trying to block the front door.

'I don't know what to do,' Zoe whispers to one of the lads, burly and grizzled, older than the rest, who's manoeuvring a washing-basket of textbooks.

'Tell you what,' he says. He'll say he's had enough of these mad dykes, summon Des and head off to the pub. But he lowers his head, whispers: 'Pretend you're going to fetch my phone out of the van. Hop up in the cab and we'll be right behind you. Four mins, max.'

Whatever sacred irreplaceable rubbish she's forgotten, the items she'd decided mattered above all others, she'll have to do without. Cut the ballast, let the balloon take flight. 'Really? But then you'll be stuck with her.'

'Not bothered,' he says. 'Better us than you.'

Out in the hallway, Penny's raging about estrangement. But maybe this is possible. Zoe's father might already have put the kids on a return train. As long as she ignores the part she can't think about, where Rose has to decide where to stay tonight, all Zoe has to do is reach the flat door un-noticed. In ten minutes, she could be sitting up front, swigging Irn-Bru, about to pull up outside Goldhawk Road Tesco. 8883. Realistically, what could go wrong?

The removal man turns back, side-eyes the door, bends closer. 'Know what? This isn't OK.'

'You see, the thing is, she's . . . in what sense?'

'How she is. Your missus.'

'She's not . . . Actually, you're right. But I can't just leave, wi—'

'What are you meant to do, ask her about every spoon?'

'Yes. No. But she says I have to. Although someone I know,' she ventures, thinking of Hilary Mint, 'did tell me: "You're hoping she'll give you permission to leave her. But she never will." Do, do you think maybe she has a point?'

The removal man's cheek flickers, as if he's biting it. Penny is screaming at Des to put down the bike pump. 'Well. That,' he says, 'is what I tell my girl. Stand up for yourself. Do it, *then* ask if it's allowed.'

'You're right. I know. That's . . . you're a good dad. Is she, what, about my age?'

'She's three,' he says.

THEN

2006

Hilary Mint, probably meaning to be helpful, had posted her the *Guardian* Education supplement, with the perfect permanent lectureship neatly circled. Cambridge, with its eager supervisees and dark-panelled rooms, oars, stained-glass, at a college whose principal was a famously welcoming lesbian composer. Yes, Roehampton would be annoyed, but imagine how much easier their lives would be if Zoe had job security, let alone the chance of Cambridge schools, Cambridge houses: a whole house of their own. Didn't Penny hate her competitive colleagues, charmless Dr Martin Rainfold and his drab Medievalist wife, her literal-minded undergrads? She'd be a jewel in any college's crown. Wasn't it worth Zoe applying and, if the completely impossible happened, shouldn't they, whisper it, move?

Penny paused. Her eyes were wet. Was it pride, or excitement, or . . . then her mouth pinched, and Zoe understood it was not going to go well. 'Do you even care about how I feel?'

'You know I do.'

'Ha!' said Penny.

Zoe's insensitivity: that was the first thing. But also her sucking-up, scrabbling all the way to the top: grotesque. 'What will people think about me? That I'm – what? Less clever? Less successful? You'd be, what, barely thirty-five and a Cambridge sodding don? How do you think that makes me look?' It was noticeably manipulative, given how unstrategic Zoe was generally, to have forced her (Penny) into a position where she (Penny) would look bad dissuading her (Zoe).

'Are you denying that you'd have applied like a shot, if I hadn't objected? Be honest, of course you knew she was sending that advert. You thought you could go for it anyway.'

'But I thought . . . you said you wanted us to be star academics! Isn't that, isn't this the same?'

'Nothing,' said Penny brokenly, 'matters anyway. I know I can't stop you.'

However much Zoe explained that it couldn't possibly reflect on Penny, and that she was trying to support, not humiliate, her, and also that it might have boosted Penny's career, about which Penny herself was always so worried, Penny wasn't having it. She knew, as did everyone else she discussed it with, that malign intentions were involved. Besides, she was much more experienced about academe than Zoe. 'Why don't you just admit,' she asked, 'that you'll have schmoozed someone, or Hilary will have pushed for you? Isn't Solveig whatsit there, who you reviewed so glowingly?'

'I don't know if—'

'Yes, you do. What a coincidence. And everyone wants to hire women in their thirties. Lucky you. It's probably a done deal.'

'You know it bothers me when you say that. Like when you were sure I'd get that stupid scholarship; it makes not getting it so much worse. Please, love. I keep asking y—'

'Anyway, if nothing in crappy grey Cambridge comes up for me, what then?'

'Then you keep your job here. Where they value you, and it's one of the best places, and commuting isn't so bad.'

'And spend my life on a train? No way.'

'I would. You know I would, for you.'

The atmosphere over dinner was horrible. What excuse could she invent for Hilary? It might please Penny if she used the supplement symbolically to line the hutch of Ginger and Tarzan, their current rabbits; maybe she could sneak one last furtive look. But everything would enrage Penny. She crumpled up the paper, shoved it into the kitchen bin's depths, then fished it out and left it conspicuously near the top, littered with the children's ketchup and fish-finger crumbs. They'd never speak of it again, she thought; their marriage would be the better for it.

But, hard as she tried to be understanding, uncontrolling, she couldn't quite. A bad summer holiday; then another; some time in the winter that followed, she was at the doctor's for Rose's tonsils when she spotted a Royal College of Psychiatry leaflet entitled: *Marriage Trouble? Home Shouldn't Be A Place of Suffering*, with a sad purple woman beside some wilting flowers.

Under the number for the Manic Depressives Fellowship came Pimlico Couples Crisis (PiCoC).

'Yet another therapist; how extremely lesbian of us,' said Penny. 'Maybe you'll believe this one.'

'What about?'

'That rows are normal,' said Penny. 'That you're going to destroy us, if you keep picking and neuroting. Everyone can see this except you. It's only because you have no experience of normal families that you can't; Trish 'n' Clive still together, no good aunts, not even godparents. None of your friends have had marriage stresses, have they? Exactly. Too young. Everyone fights.'

This therapist was going to save them. They were allocated a calm man whom Penny took against, because he refused to let her read her list of accusations, fresh from their home printer, out loud. Zoe had wanted to discuss sex, or at least be allowed to mention it, because it seemed to have stopped completely; Penny had recently said that, in their early days, whenever Zoe touched her in the bath, with desire but also simple admiration, it had felt like sexual abuse.

She'd also hoped to raise the subject of Justine. But, at the end of their second session, the counsellor said he couldn't continue. Penny had cried so loudly that colleagues elsewhere in the building had complained. Penny threatened to report him. She looked like an exploding bun, shiny-eyed. She stamped through the fire-door and down to the ground floor. 'Can you hurry,' she shouted.

But Zoe lingered. It felt like the last day of term; there was still a chance of being invited home for Christmas by her favourite teacher, charades, tartan nightshirts, all the children opening stockings.

'It's bad, isn't it?' she whispered, hoping for hope.

'I don't like to . . . but yes.' Were his eyes kind, or simply knackered? 'Crazy. Sorry. Good luck.'

More time passed, more damage. Then Penny herself, as she often reminded Zoe, subsequently, found a forgotten copy of the *TES* on the tube and brought it home, and next thing she knew Zoe had left Roehampton and was installed in Penny's very own Humanities Department, only a couple of roads away, befriending her friends, colonizing her libraries and cafes. 'Don't you realize,' she'd say, 'how hard I had to work for this, and you've just swanned in?'

Zoe didn't even seem that thrilled about being permanent, at long last. 'You're essentially a miserable person. It's not my fault,' Penny observed. 'You never want to go anywhere with me, do anything. Think of how you were when you were a teenager, alone in your bedroom while Tricia sulked. No wonder you never take pleasure in things; you don't know how.'

Then came Utrecht.

28

THEN

Winter 2010

At last, everyone was saying: a proper grown-up lesbian Hollywood film.

Penny wanted to go with Nicky and Steph, all the Ozzie gang but, in the end, she agreed to be taken as a date by Zoe, to a cinema on the King's Road where staff brought mixed nuts and cocktails to your very seat. They needed something cheering; Robin's Christmas with the kids was hanging over them. Penny was determined to spend it in Vienna, which was as far into Eastern Europe as she was willing to go. Zoe knew she should agree. There had been so much difficulty lately, weekends always darkened.

Maybe we'll snog in the back row, she thought. Maybe it will help.

For the first few minutes, the film seemed perfect: a glamorous married female couple, one of whom was Julianne Moore, albeit in cargo shorts, who'd both had a child by the same donor. It didn't bother to go into details about their pasts; they were simply, unapologetically, attractive adult lesbians, as if putting them on a big screen wasn't a radical act. Even the bit when their desultory sex while watching cowboy-porn was interrupted by their almost-adult daughter was OK; that, at least, hadn't happened to Zoe and Penny. But Zoe began to have a crumpling feeling, as when she heard or read or watched anything touching on the subject she always had avoided, even in theory: adultery.

She'd concealed from Penny how much it scared her. Fleetwood Mac and Abba; they'd horribly split up. A new novel by a writer she'd always liked who'd famously divorced, a box-set about unfaithful lawyers: the vulnerability of relationships, even if straighter and more fragile than hers, was too unsettling to think about. She'd always hidden the contaminants away.

Now, beside her, Penny breathed. Zoe's awareness tightened; something corrosive was heating in her chest, too close to her heart. She watched Annette Bening registering the presence of Julianne's red hair in the kids' father's shower. As if on a merry-go-round Annette's world slowed, quieted, stopped, but she still had to sit through dinner, comprehending the truth.

'What?' whispered Penny loudly. 'Where are you going?'

'Nothing. Loo.'

'Jesus,' Penny said, and stood. 'Not this again. Don't start now.'

Zoe tried to make her sit, but Penny followed her through the wall-carpeted corridors, other films booming like nearby spacecraft, through to the confusingly signed Laddies. She wanted to hide in a booth with the door shut and deal with the anguish in private, but Penny would not let her. She said that it was for her own good.

They repaired things, eventually. Penny said she was sorry for the pain she'd inadvertently caused, not that she'd done anything wrong; Zoe was sorry too. It was she who, disloyally, had doubted them. Only later did she wonder if any of the other lesbian couples she'd seen in the cinema had ended up in the corridors too, having the same horrible argument. Her skin and hair-roots hurt, as if she were Velcro, being torn apart hook by hook.

So, for the sake of marital harmony, when she was instructed to do her bit for her new department and apply to the Utrecht symposium on Classical Families the following February, she begged for Penny to be invited too.

It wasn't the first time she had tried. Penny hated not being asked to conferences. Besides, re-bonding was urgent; it felt as if they were unmoored, as if Penny was on the verge of announcing that she was taking a sabbatical in Costa Rica, returning indefinitely to Australia, leaving Zoe for a first year with a special interest in Katherine Mansfield.

The symposium was being held at half-term, already bagsied by Robin for a week with the children in the Isle of Wight: no television, plenty of fresh air. Perfect timing: Penny could lecture about Christina Stead and Step-families, Christina Stead and Father-Love, any of the usual permutations. Zoe would willingly pay a supplement for her meals, but could Renaat send the invoice to her work email, if he wouldn't issue the invitation, formally, to them both?

Penny guessed. When Zoe swore that Renaat would have asked her if he'd dared, she only became more enraged.

'I don't want,' she spat, 'a pity invite. The damage you've

done to my career, merely by suggesting it, and don't tell me that was accidental. How did you wangle your own invitation? Isn't he the man you met at LSE? I knew you'd been all over him, I said it at the time. Fine. Go, if you're really desperate. It's only Utrecht, in winter.'

She said she'd stay with Nicky and Steph, who were holidaying in Poole. Wasn't that near the Isle of Wight, where Justine was bound to be with Robin, and the kids? Was she planning to meet Justine, away from the others, or spend time all together, wind-tossed on the ferry with Rose and Matty? Zoe came up with tempting alternatives: how about going for a city break with Inge? Or visiting German Karolina for a weekend, a week? Penny rejected them all, accused Zoe of trying to block her closest friendship. She was appalled that Zoe still had it in for Justine. When would she get over that bloody birthday weekend, stop trying to establish what exactly Penny and Justine had been doing in the alcove? Had she forgotten, yet again, that they'd been talking about Robin? Penny had gone through who had been standing where so many times, what each of them had said, and she had demonstrated there was absolutely nothing to justify Zoe's accusations. Her paranoia was unbearable. Honestly, was it any wonder that Penny needed a break? If she chose to see Justine, that would be down to Zoe.

'I'm truly not accusing,' Zoe said, but it wasn't true. There was the familiar ache in her knuckles, as if she were being slowly poisoned, but Penny would say that was her jealousy. There was no one to confide in. Penny was probably right; the problem, again, was Zoe.

But, on the surface, she was blithe and carefree, or tried

to be. When Penny and Justine went out for dinner on Justine and Jayne's eleventh anniversary ('steel: no one counts that'), then chatted on the phone in the bath for over an hour, Zoe almost completely managed not to probe, although it felt like a tooth-nerve pressed. But, of course, Penny knew. It made her feel claustrophobic, to be mistrusted all the time. Seven terrible years of pleading, begging Zoe to change her mind about having another baby, had broken her spirit. Her friends were concerned. 'There's nothing left in me. People did say I should do it without you, behind your back. But no, like an idiot, I put our marriage first, and what I most desperately longed for fell by the wayside. You know what? I should have gone ahead.'

Zoe pressed her knuckles to her chest, realized it might look melodramatic, put her hand down. Don't cry, you stupid fuck. 'Seriously? Even though it would have smashed up our re—'

'It's what I needed.'

'But . . . but that would have been terrible. Like an affair.'

'Well, I wish I had.'

'Think, though! I don't see how we could have recovered from that. Please, my l—'

'You are the one who stopped me. You did the damage, you must realize that. Everyone else can see it, they all agree. Why can't you?'

Yet, when Utrecht approached, Penny was surprisingly cheerful about Zoe going. She even tucked a postcard in her suitcase: 'Have fun, my little weirdo, in the charnel-house of

Agamemnon, and don't get frostbite. Or be taken captive by strapping Dutch Sapphists.'

By the time Zoe read it, the damage was done.

She couldn't keep asking what Penny's plans were. She seemed amazingly, encouragingly, cavalier. Still, Zoe was trying to learn from experience. So often, before, she'd blithely assumed things were OK; it was better to double, triple check. 'Are you absolutely sure you don't want me to pull out? That time I went to Nottingham, the kids were tricky, and it was only one night. What if they come home early with Robin?'

'It's really not a big deal,' Penny said. 'I'll see my friends, have fun. Or I can abseil in, ravish you in your dorm.'

'I wish,' said Zoe. 'You know it's a single. In the attic.'

But, secretly, she was excited. Since booking the flights, she'd been researching interesting food in her *Let's Go* guide. So many painful Christmas city-breaks, chosen to distract them when Robin and Justine were back in Hampshire with the kids, had been ruined when Zoe tried to track down deep-fried artichokes or pintxo or skordalia, and Penny wanted pizza. This was her chance, alone.

Because she went away so rarely, she over-organized her schedule. Lunch on Saturday was to be with Dr H. P. (Henriëtte) van Bouwmeester, formerly Senior Lecturer in Classics at University College, London, before her return to the Netherlands. Henriëtte van Bouwmeester was chiefly Latin but Zoe barely knew anybody going to the symposium, and this woman might have advice.

'She'll probably be one of those towering Puritan lady-priests with a ruffly collar. Or traffic you to the tulip-farms,' said Penny, who was highly amused by the whole thing. 'I can't believe you made her book a vegetarian restaurant. You can borrow my rain hat but be very careful not to lose it. Is that her photo? Oh dear.'

They talked twice on Friday; Penny'd had an awful day at work before leaving for Poole, and Matty had rung from the Maritime Museum, in a state about having had a nosebleed all over her dolphins project, and Rose's new hoodie had been nicked and, as usual, they seemed to be mainly sitting in the Wighte Crowne Inne playing the slot machines, while Justine drank spritzers and Robin reminisced. And, meanwhile, lucky Zoe was gorging on rye honey-cake, chocolate sprinkles, fruit salad and three types of herring, smoked, green-salted and raw, at the breakfast buffet of her otherwise very low-budget hotel, not a care in the world.

She met a Professor of Twentieth Century Commonwealth Literature, based at Kings, who had never heard of Penny and this felt dangerous. She was congratulated excessively for her most recent publication, her co-editing of the allegedly unedit-able fourth volume of the *Cambridge Companion to Greek Tragedy* and, although her heart rose, inflated to bursting with joy, discomfort speedily set in. She kept wanting to check behind her, in case Penny was passing. It seemed rash, worse than immoral, not to be changing the subject, instantly preparing excuses and justifications: possibly calamitous. When someone said she was making a name for herself, she felt sordid, ashamed as if she had courted it, then, again, elated. Penny would not overhear.

What if Penny really were simply having a holiday, and then Nicky's unendurable positivity, Steph's angry drinking, made it miserable, so she came home early? If so, oughtn't Zoe do the same? But she had a grant to be in Utrecht, and a paper to give. That, she told herself, was the reason she stayed.

When she walked into Eethuis Broccoli, and saw the back of the woman she was meeting, straight grey bob, white shirt clinging awkwardly round her bra strap and her narrow shoulders, Zoe decided, despite extreme hunger and a promising online menu, to forego a starter. At two-thirty a famous Libyan scholar was lecturing on Metabasis, Pollution and the Greek Concept of Linear Fate: a perfect excuse to get away.

Now

6.04 p.m.
Zoe almost does it, climbs into the van and is freed. But it's not so easy. Penny is still shouting. Someone needs to calm her; imagine if the children have to visit her on some kind of hospital ward, where weeping and rocking will be par for the course? Or suicide: if Zoe, as Penny often prophesies, makes her do that, the girls will be ruined. Isn't it Zoe's job to stop her?

She is, she realizes, wildly thirsty. Penny seems to have

pulled most of the DVDs into a pile on the carpet; she's standing protectively beside the chipped-gilt chair one of Justine's ancestors is said to have bought from a descendant of Bismarck. When she sees Zoe, she starts accusing her of trespass, violation. 'Don't you dare think about stealing this,' she shouts. 'There are laws.'

Zoe wants to tell her to keep it. But wouldn't it be cleverer to pretend she cares, a sort of negotiating tactic in the middle of battle's tumult? She's about to say something when, although the front door must be still open, she hears the bell ring. Then Robin's voice, wobbly with rage, fills the stairwell: a man used to giving instructions.

'What on earth,' he says, 'is going on here?'

29

Now

So that's the end.

Zoe, at least the wreck of her, stands before Penny's fridge. She pulls open the door, takes a packed-lunch sausage roll, begins to chew. But the cold puff pastry sets against the roof of her mouth in a fatty lump; like an owl ejecting a pellet, she spits it into the toilet. Her grandmother would never throw out bread, as a matter of principle, and here she is, profligate, discarding vital calories. Turns out that everything is inheritable, except heroism.

She'd thought that what she wanted was the kids. Really, what she wants is to give up.

She can't go into the living room, where Penny weeps in Robin's spindly arms, spent. In the kitchen Justine is checking which implements Zoe has taken; moving condiments aside with one finger, like a detective; flicking through the remaining cookery books. Robin calls through to Zoe, confident that she will hear him: 'No one could think this an acceptable solution to our, our catastrophe. To recap, yet again, we need an urgent family meeting to discuss next steps. It goes without saying,' and he pauses before saying it anyway, 'that we won't consent to you leaving until we have confirmed the children's timetable.'

'You all right?' says Des, from the corridor.

Zoe jumps, wipes her mouth. His gaze encompasses all the lunacy he has ever witnessed, the other blasted houses of unhappiness. 'I know,' she says. 'It's, it must seem . . . sorry.' She wants to ask: Is this the maddest you've ever dealt with? Is Penny deranged? Have I overreacted? Tell me what you've heard her say, and what you thought. Was I right to want to leave?

But Des, on whom she has relied, is looking edgy; Penny has rattled even him. Who wouldn't want to cut their losses, after this mess? And maybe they're right. It is a violence against their family, to be kidnapping, or at least cutting off, Matty from her absolutely equal mother. Possibly it is a crime. Zoe has been naive, minimum, for assuming she could manage it all, take possession of Ozman's conveniently cheap attic and begin a new life of autonomy. Even the most optimistic narrator couldn't believe that she would pull this off, given the combined wrath of the others: her own father and mother and the children's father too, and her wife, her wife's lover.

Yes, lover, of course. Why not admit it now?

Then Des speaks. 'That's her fella?'

'Sorry?'

'The kiddies' dad?'

'Oh. Right. Did, did Dawn not tell you, about us?'

He only looks. He's surely seen the trainers and textbooks which clearly belong to children, jumbled up with hers; he must have heard Penny. But all Des says is: 'We did want to spring you. But it's probably better if, well. Under your own steam.' He wipes his palms on his hips, takes out his phone. 'Did you say you've got the key? To the new place. It's only round the corner, right?'

'He gave me a code. I don't think, though . . . I might not . . . I mean, I won't be allowed t—'

'It'll be fine. We can definitely press a few buttons,' he says and his calm assurance, the lack of dithering anxious self-undermining doubt, are a dose of courage, straight into the vein.

THEN

February 2011
From the front, Henriëtte van Bouwmeester was rather different. Her excellent skin, her dashing striped watch-strap, her energetic hand gestures and laugh, were so much younger than that silvery hair. Zoe began to suspect that not dyeing it was an expression of coolness, at least of not caring. Was she even forty?

Zoe had forgotten to put on mascara before leaving the hotel. Henriëtte van Bouwmeester's dark eyes were thickly lashed as a child's. Her glasses-frames were bright red, her English unbelievable. She said she played the hummel and Zoe kept thinking she'd worked out what this was, butting in, like a Labrador retrieving the wrong tennis ball; a mandolin, was it? A lute?

Henriëtte laughed every time she interrupted. When Zoe apologized she said: 'But enthusiasm is wonderful.'

Usually, at this point, Zoe would say that Penny, whom she lived with, hated it when she butted in: easier to get it over with. But what if Henriëtte van Thing, who seemed so friendly, was embarrassed for her, or appalled?

'I like your socks,' Zoe said a few minutes later. They were cobalt with silver waves and, as they both considered her ankle, Henriëtte said: 'Ah, yes. My girlfriend bought them.'

'Oh!'

Penny always said her uncoolness was extraordinary. But who could not be astonished at the sight of a woman, with boldly asymmetrical earrings and sharply cut silver hair, who could fall in love with, fancy, other women? Even the fact that women could live together was still astounding; Penny said she should grow out of it, but wasn't the transgression part of the thrill?

'Girlfriend?' she asked. 'Or . . . girlfriend girlfriend?'

'Girlfriend girlfriend' said Henriëtte, smiling into her eyes.

She drank more apple juice; it felt as if she could never be quenched.

They laughed more than one might have expected, for strangers. There was only one awkward moment, and it was entirely Zoe's fault. 'Where are you staying?'

'It's somewhere near.' Zoe had already imagined describing the drab disappointment of her hotel to Penny, or even her mother; hitting that perfect note. 'You can spot the other niche academics a mile off. Sorry, a kilometre. They've corralled us all together. The mad hair, those carrier bags. Did you notice the waist-length plait? I think he's Belgian. And the poncho-lady? And the man with all the ham?'

But Henriëtte didn't smile. 'That is not kind,' she said, and Zoe, chastened, ate more bread, trying to think of a justification, but then Henriëtte went to the loo and when she came back it was forgotten.

A little later, Zoe shyly mentioned her idea for a book, opening out from her recent daring article ('Women Beware Women: Bacchic idealization, Dionysian idolization and the maligning of Pentheus').

Henriëtte smiled. 'I would like to read that.'

'Honestly? Wow. It's not even your speciali—'

'Of course.'

'But why?'

'I'm interested. You have,' Henriëtte said simply, as if it were demonstrable fact, 'an intriguing mind,' and Zoe had to look away.

Penny claimed that Zoe flirted with everyone. She said Zoe's question-asking was calculated to make people feel important. What if Henriëtte assumed the same? Or if, completely wrongly, she thought that Zoe, who hadn't fancied a single person since Penny, was signalling interest? The mere idea made Zoe lower her eyes; she could barely look up again, for the shame.

Henriëtte, who definitely wasn't flirting either, who of course loved her volunteer-lifeguard girlfriend, very lightly touched Zoe's sleeve to make a point about the democratization of theatre. She laughed at Zoe's analysis of the subtle status-gradations in the available puddings at the official conference restaurant. They'd already covered the size of horses' cheeks, the Fibonacci sequence in broccoli, the layout of medieval cities with reference to ghettos and abattoirs, and the sexual orientation of various ultra-macho classical heroes; still there was far too much to talk about. When was the last time she'd been able to discuss fate, for example, Oedipus, Pentheus, Orestes, without feeling inhibited, instantly boring? If she tried at home, Penny made comic snoring noises, but Henriëtte was wholeheartedly, unmockingly, as interested as Zoe. If, Zoe ventured to think, she lived in the Netherlands, they could possibly be friends, hang out at the Plas Laagraven while the girlfriend hauled drowning swimmers out of the reeds, have peaceful daytime parties in those bell-fronted houses built of small dark bricks, their lives exposed to anyone who passed the windows.

With the window behind her, Henriëtte's hair seemed brightly lit as a painting. When one of the staff, swabbing tables, the mop thumping up against the counter, lost patience and approached their corner with a spray, they stood, and she discovered that Henriëtte was no taller than she was. Eye to eye, they grinned at each other like comrades, embraced swiftly goodbye, and even that was not quite a standard hug between new friends, but a joining of breast and groin and thigh, like the opposite of peeling.

And that, for the next six hours, was that, almost, until an email arrived: *come for a drink and meet my friends after dinner*, said Dr H. P. (Henriëtte) van Bouwmeester.

*

The email said: *we will be there from nine.*

Zoe, Dr Z. H. Stamper (London)'s paper was scheduled for five past five. The weeks of worrying about her peers' reaction had been replaced by a fizzing in her stomach, as if the *Uitsmijter* at breakfast had misaligned with her gastric needs. The postcard from Penny, which she had perhaps expected Zoe to prop on the windowsill, remained in her case. It was the twenty-first of February; she had been thirty-nine for a month. She thought about the ectopic baby only a few times a day; she had two tops which she liked, was wearing one of them, and her favourite brown boots, much resoled. There was a *drogisterij* near Janskerkhof 2; she wandered in, gazed blankly at the shelves, bought, because of the breakfast herrings, the cheapest tube of toothpaste and rubbed it over her teeth with a finger, considering life before plastic toothbrushes, the reek of the past. Say she did go out for a drink, what should she do about dinner beforehand? She ought to find a place for a simple sandwich and do some reading, although she'd have to remember not to mention the luxury of time to Penny.

At one minute to five, during the first Tragedy Panel discussion of poor Malcolm North's inaudible analysis of the Dramaturgical Significance and Ethical Ramifications of the 'Carpet Scene' in the *Oresteia*, Zoe prepared to climb onto the stage. She noted the step not to fall off, the microphone not to crash into. Then she turned her head and noticed that Henriëtte had arrived at the back of the auditorium.

30

Then

Ten past eight, Dutch time. In an Indonesian restaurant on Alendorpstraat, beginning the ninth tiny dish of her solitary *rijstafel*, spicy prawns very like the previous prawns but slightly drier, Zoe decided not to ring Penny.

Henriëtte's friends were confusing. Despite faultless English, they joked together in Dutch. It felt like having no sense of humour; Penny sometimes accused her of this.

She wondered if they all worked together, were they, crucially, gay; two of the women had similar wedding rings but that wasn't necessarily proof. Turning up at their dinner table, scrumpled paper napkins and mussel-shells everywhere, had been awkward. It hadn't crossed her mind to drink alone in the Indonesian restaurant; now she decided not to mention where she'd eaten, in case it seemed she'd only gone there because Henriëtte had said her girlfriend was from Suriname, although Zoe wasn't quite sure where that was. When they moved on to a bar with a famous beer menu she thought, fine, I'll manage another half-pint and then go.

But they were squashed into a dark wood corral edged with brass rails; the group grew bigger and friendlier, stylish academics from Thrace and Stanford joining the throng. They were Zoe's age or younger, seemed unashamed of their passionate enthusiasm for Longinus's *On Sublimity*, or cannibalism or Ovid's women or Minoan crop rotation; you couldn't have guessed, by looking, that they were Classicists.

They kept buying rounds of neat Dutch gin, showing her how to exhale the fire after each sip. There was singing. The air grew hot; the windows steamed. Zoe, about to down her latest *jenever*, found that her gaze was trapped by Henriëtte gesturing as she talked with a colleague from Madrid, one strand of silver hair sticking to her neck, and that she was smiling.

Much, much later, well after midnight, most of the others had dispersed. They were in a little frosty park near the bar; a pale cat, electric in the moonlight, flounced over the grass. They talked about nothing; the cold was hilarious. Zoe's tights-toes felt damp. Someone limboed under a barrier to Spanish pop from a block of flats. In the playground Zoe watched, or was watched, as Henriëtte and her friend Sanne, also her boss – the hierarchy here seemed completely flat, none of the scrabbling flattery and deference Carla Thackarray engendered, at least in Zoe – passed a hip-flask between them, until Zoe realized that there was nothing she wanted more than to feel the freezing metal against her lips. She held out a hand to take it.

Their eyes caught.

Then Sanne remembered she had to collect the sound system from the Universitaire Eetzaal for tomorrow's closing reception. Henriëtte offered to do it for her.

'It is really fine,' said Sanne, laboriously climbing off the see-saw. 'I mean, I am too drunken to drive much, but.'

'I'm able.'

And Sanne said something in Dutch, and Henriëtte waved it away, and Zoe found herself saying: 'I'll come with you.'

Henriëtte had a small car, black or navy, parked down an alleyway in a modest gap in a thicket of plants, succulents and mahonia and others Zoe didn't recognize. For once she didn't beg for time to examine them; she didn't think of it. Under the street lamps the herringbone cobbles shone, although it hadn't rained; it was strangely difficult to explain this.

Henriëtte drove fast. Something had happened; it was there again when they lifted the huge speakers into her back seat, an amp into the boot, moving aside blankets, a book about Chicago, an inner tube and a framed old-fashioned poster about Italian wheat which she said was a present from someone who knew her love of bread.

Back they drove to the main auditorium, left the equipment in a locked store to which Henriëtte, efficient yet unboastful, had a bunch of keys. 'Where exactly is your hotel?'

Zoe read out the address, carefully written on her conference folder.

'Your accent is atrocious,' said Henriëtte.

'Atrocious?'

'Yes.'

After that, they were quiet. Henriëtte drove them over another canal, then alongside what seemed like the first one, across a familiar bridge. The night slowed; time caught in a notch. The drive, dark, swift, confident, was complicated by Henriëtte taking her hand.

Lanterns swung on metal brackets along the half-frozen canal. Students were laughing, holding each other's handlebars while cycling, despite the impressive cold. Zoe swallowed, but her throat was dry. Every front door they passed gleamed with care; no rubbish in the gutters, no graffitied metal grilles or hungry men with sleeping-bag stoles. Very, very lightly, Henriëtte began to stroke Zoe's palm with her fingertips. The near side of her face flushed blue, then orange, as they paused near a falafel restaurant. She was so close that Zoe could see the tight downy curl of her jawline, the minute puckering of lobe around the sparkling ear-stud, like scalloped scone-dough. Henriëtte touched Zoe's fingers, top, sides, underneath, all the inner surfaces, so newly erogenous that she could barely see. Each breath felt like something to be negotiated. She turned her head minutely, then a little more, but Henriëtte kept her eyes on the road.

At a turning, past a corner Zoe recognized from her speed-walk to the conference this morning, Henriëtte kissed Zoe's hand-back, and a wave broke over her. Then Henriëtte let her go. The car slowed; she flicked on the indicator, parked smartly between bicycles. Although only this morning everyone Zoe had seen seemed to be heading for the conference, eager throngs of Hellenists bearing tote-bags stuffed with promotional bookmarks and stolen breakfast rusks, no one passed. The street was dark, as if the lamps had switched themselves off at their approach, but a bulb had been left hanging from scaffolding, illuminating building-work, so that the steering-wheel, Henriëtte's hand-bones, Zoe's nylon-tighted knee, were touched with licks of light.

31

Then

The inevitable was upon them, in this little car, under this flickering bulb. Henriëtte, holding Zoe's hand above her head, was kissing along her inner arm-skin, moving towards her elbow-crease and, even in this moment of the most extreme chaotic pleasure, so anxiously turned on that her atoms threatened to break their molecular bonds and shatter, Zoe thought: I feel like a corn-cob.

Which she told Henriëtte, who laughed.

And then they were kissing, the first of four long incandescent kisses. Throughout the first, Zoe's hand rested on Henriëtte's movingly bony shoulder. During the second kiss, Henriëtte put her hand in Zoe's hair and lightly pulled it, and such heat poured over Zoe's skin that she thought she would faint. Because of the cold they kept having to turn on the hot air, then roll down a window to let fresh air in, but this would dispel the condensation on the windows and make them visible again, so back on with the heating. They became thirstier, drier, amused by the sounds of their mouths unsticking. At some point during the next kiss, Zoe's hand of its own accord moved down to Henriëtte's woollen trouser-hip, one finger casually tucking inside the waistband, upon her living skin. Henriëtte moved the back of her hand down Zoe's breast; it brushed against Zoe's nipple.

'Do you like that? Oh yes, yes you do.'

By this stage they had left the tops of the car windows open: conscientious zoo-keepers airing a burrow. During their final, knock-out, kiss, they each turned to slurp in some night air, then back, their lips cooled.

'Oh your mouth,' said Henriëtte. 'We must go to the hotel.'

'Because . . . ?'

'If I don't have water soon, I will become desiccated,' said Henriëtte. 'Of course.'

It was past two in the morning. They peered through the passenger-side window; still no sign of conference delegates, returning late from extra-mural sessions in beer bars, plenary lectures in the red-light district. Twenty, maybe thirty metres to the front of the hotel, and what were the chances that they'd bump into anyone who knew them?

Potentially, high.

'Help me,' said Henriëtte. 'Wa . . . a . . . ater. Hurry.'

So off they went. Arm in arm like students, faces frozen, bodies hot, they ran towards the entrance. 'Are we still drunk?'

'Absolutely. Not.' Henriëtte greeted the night-porter politely in Dutch, had almost reached the stairs when a snort of laughter escaped her, which set Zoe off again. Up they went, hauling on each other's arms, trying to keep quiet. There were CCTV cameras, possibly working, on every landing. 'If,' Henriëtte half whispered, not at all quietly, 'we were heterosexual, we could kiss right here and no one would blink. But . . .'

'But,' Zoe agreed. Then she held Henriëtte back. 'Look. Listen. I'm . . . well, you know. I told you. I can't, really, I don't think, I mustn—'

'I very badly need a drink of water,' said Henriëtte. 'That is what I absolutely want.'

They reached the second floor. Zoe, emboldened by lust and booze and wildness, said, 'I would kill to let you in. But. I am not going to. I am not.'

She filled a toothbrush-cup of water in the shower room, took it out to Henriëtte in the strip-lit hallway. Henriëtte drank as Zoe watched, her legs weak with desire.

'You're absolutely not coming in. I can't let you.'

'Please,' said Henriëtte. 'I too mustn't. Your bosoms are oh my God. Impossible. We can only cuddle. It is four o'clock in the morning, we must sleep.'

'Nope,' said Zoe, before they kissed again, up against the door frame, and this time it was her hand in Henriëtte's hair.

32

Now

6.35 p.m.

'Hello,' somebody calls from out in the hall, sounding nervous. 'Are you still here?'

At the sound of Matilda's voice, Penny stands; Robin rubs his face, clears his throat. They move to the open flat door and freeze, as if *in flagrante*, because there, there on the stair, right there, stands Clive, and Tricia, and Rose, who is carrying her grandmother's handbag.

'Oh, God. It's everyone,' says Zoe. 'Hello.'

They assume their positions: Justine stand-offish; Penny broken. Matilda grimaces up at them, shrugs. Rose is gnawing her thumbnail; Zoe's father, frowning hard, focuses on recapping a biro.

'Hi, Dad.'

Robin, who believes that he has a way with old ladies, rushes towards Tricia, kisses her, offers her his arm. He doesn't know that Tricia has always enjoyed hating him. Nevertheless, whenever they meet, she and Robin and Justine behave like old pals. Now she permits him her cheek, murmuring in surprised delight as if he's happened upon her mid-*passegiata*, and not in a dingily corniced stairwell in a former bookbinders just north of Hammersmith flyover. She looks up at Zoe, dusty-kneed, speckled with dead fern-fronds, loose threads of tinsel and pompom-wool and garlic-skin from the kitchen floor, God knows what else in her hair. 'What a journey,' she says.

Penny pushes past Zoe. She stands, vestally sombre, looking down from the top step, clearly waiting for Zoe's father to embrace her. Then she turns to Rose: 'Oh, thank God, my baby. I didn't know if I'd see you. I was sure I'd be st—'

'Let's go on inside, shall we?' says pleasant, responsible Robin and he leads them all into the mothers' flat.

Then

March 2011

Oh, the mess one can make of a confession.

Zoe lasted less than a month after her Utrecht trip, her fall, before telling Penny. So much for doing anything to avoid upsetting people. The guilt was grinding at her; also, she was fraying under the stress of remembering it was a secret, trying to keep so many strands of awareness constantly alive. She'd been so used to confiding every speck of shame and grubbiness; hadn't they promised to tell each other everything, right at the start?

So she admitted it, almost all of it. The kiss was abbreviated, boiled away, like a leaf-skeleton. She couldn't earn credit for controlling herself – only just – at the moment of possible full adultery, but that was a tiny price to pay, to spare Penny's humiliation, or, be honest, to feel less ashamed. She made everything seem nothing; it was brutal and necessary, emergency surgery, so that they could live.

The odd thing was how hot and brief the flare of Penny's anger felt: several matches struck together, then burning out. Zoe kept wondering why she hadn't wrung more capital from it, cross-examined her as thoroughly as she always interrogated every motive, achievement, preference, and Zoe's one incomprehensible refusal. Instead, she kept joking about Henriëtte's homely white shirt, her wholesome girlfriend, her excessive skiing.

Zoe never contacted Henriëtte again. It was worth it, for Penny's sake.

Now

6.38 p.m.
And suddenly Zoe understands why Penny didn't whip out this convenient hand-grenade in front of the others, during Mediation, and silence her. It wasn't decency, or honour, which kept her from mentioning Henriëtte. It was because Justine was in the room.

And she always has been. Was that why Robin became involved, at the very beginning; why he and Justine are now so militantly on Penny's side? Despite the years of indignant denial, she was there long before Utrecht, probably ever since.

All along, Zoe knew, and she knew that Penny was lying. When she was in her hospital bed, and Penny lovingly and solemnly swore there was nothing going on: all lies.

It feels like they're lip-syncing. Robin's charm is thin as a chocolate Santa. She wants to punch it into smithereens. Tricia is asking him about his work. Zoe's father, in one of his favourite unfortunate V-necks, nibbles his glasses-cord and is quiet ('Clive, stop that,' says Tricia. 'You look like you're at a special school'). Tricia reaches into her microwave-sized handbag, finds a wet-wipe and swipes ketchup from the corner of Matilda's mouth.

Matty is wearing baggy tracksuit bottoms, fluorescent plastic soldier-earrings and a purple hoodie so cheap it has a sheen; Rose, floral denim dungaree-shorts and a self-knitted bulbous lemon-yellow cardigan. Penny has always hated Zoe's attempts to tidy up the kids before visiting the grandparents, but it's necessary; Tricia would be put off them if they were grubby, or had chosen terrible outfits themselves. Now Zoe looks from her offspring to her mother and thinks: don't you dare.

But Tricia, for now, is behaving. It's Penny who starts weeping, then removes herself to the toilet, from which the cries come ever louder. The kids' attention slips to the side, then back to their grandparents; Tricia is telling them about her recent highlights. 'Clive,' she says after a couple of minutes more, 'I need a coffee. Hello?' and Clive heads towards the kitchen. The kids pander to Tricia, Rose showing her raccoon videos on her phone, Matilda offering to fetch biscuits: 'not one of your mother's knitted-muesli ones,' Tricia calls after her. 'No oats.'

Clive bobs into the living room. 'Anyone else want coffee?'

It's amazing, the power of social smoothing. It could almost be a normal family gathering. Robin and Justine are making their little requests: 'just hot water for me, thanks,' says Robin.

Penny comes in, sits down. Zoe watches her. She's thinking: I've tried to make this the story of an ordinary happy marriage. But she had a different version, running next to mine. I felt so guilty about Henriëtte, all of it, that I missed the obvious. Every bit of Penny's loving generosity, her kindnesses and love-notes, was distracting me from the truth.

The waters are up to her throat. She takes a last breath. 'If,' she says, and all but Penny turn to look, 'we could . . . can we go to our, outside? Pen. I need to talk to you.'

Penny purses her lips; there's the whiff of a smirk. She hates her; Penny, that is, hates Zoe. Is that the right way around?

'Go on,' says Penny, crossing her hands in her lap, angling her pretty head almost placidly, a maiden summoned to the block. Her lieutenants, Nicky and Steph, Justine and now Robin, even Zoe's turncoat mother, keep insisting that she is unable to contain her grief and shock. So how come she's managing now? 'Whatever you've got to say, I'm, I'm ready.'

Their children are right here. Can she honestly believe they should be witnesses? 'No,' Zoe says. 'Not in the flat. You can say whatever you want, to me, but you are not in charge.'

And boom, the room collapses in on itself.

Justine gasps operatically, as if her basest fears about human nature have been realized. Penny buries her face in her hands and begins to moan. Robin, now on his feet, wipes his palms on his trousers as if preparing to wrestle. Zoe's mother, herself no stranger to the ring, makes a sound as if in pain; Clive rushes to her side. Now she and Penny are crying, contrapuntally.

Why, Tricia begs her husband, is she being ignored? It's the theme-tune of Zoe's childhood: the first clatter of rain against the windows, a sharp wind starting up. Her own children look fraught; Rose, standing comfortingly beside her grandmother, swallows, takes a step towards Penny. Zoe gives her and her sister an encouraging smile, but her face feels stiff.

'Where, where are you going?' asks Penny.

Zoe's heading up the stairs, fetching Todly's wire carrier from where she'd hidden it behind Matilda's shelving unit. She brings it down. 'Matty, could you fetch me his blan— actually, I'll do it. Treats, Todly. Treats!'

Penny sounds close to hyperventilating. The grandparents' summit is in disarray.

'I'm waiting,' her mother says falteringly, in the direction of her father. He clears his throat.

'Right. Yes. Mum and I feel that this has gone on long enough. For the sake of th—'

'If I may,' interrupts Robin. 'We're all very grateful for your support, Clive and Patricia. I know Justine and myself are, and the children. But—'

'I don't . . . understand,' says Zoe's mother, blindly holding out her hand for one of Clive's tissues. Todly is nosing near her handbag. 'Why does no one take into account how painful it is for me to see this, this failure. My grandchildren . . .'

Penny is saying, 'I c-c-cannot endure this, this is killing me, you have to agree right now to my lawyer's financial outline or . . .'

Rose, too, is crying, but as adults do, quietly. Zoe, still rattling the treats jar, hurries into the kitchen, grabs the Todly-catching double-ended oven glove. How, she's wondering, can she signal loyalty to Rose, but covertly, to spare Penny's feelings?

Then she catches herself. She goes to stand beside Rose, her daughter. She puts an arm firmly around her. 'Yes,' she says. 'Yes, it's horrible for everyone. I am sorry.'

' "Horrible",' scoffs Penny, and a flicker of confusion crosses Matilda's face, as if this might be another word she's misunderstood.

'The cruellest aspect,' says Justine, 'is the years we've put into building our family.'

'We were taught to cope,' Tricia announces. 'Someone keep that rodent away from me. Taught to put others first at all costs. This selfishness, not understanding how hard it is to be a wife . . .'

Zoe's father takes it. He even nods.

'How could you do this to me?'

'Zo,' her father says. 'Sweetheart, this is so upsetting for your poor – for everyone. Can you reconsider? I cannot believe that there isn't some kind of civilized arr—'

'At least we're all clear about her priorities,' Penny repeats, projecting clearly as if wearing a wire. 'To wit, escaping me, not giving a toss about the kids' welfare. That particular pose has been given up completely, don't you dare interrupt. I'd like –' she raises her voice – 'you to please confirm that if I only get a third of Tilda's time, if I'm denied the chance to rear her, Rose will spend very little time with you. Agreed? Yes.'

Zoe's trying to think. Can Penny be right? What if two separate things are going on here: whether the kids should conform exactly to the parents' schedules, and whether Zoe should leave. Are they even connected? If the true and honest reason for ending the marriage is to escape Penny, which might save Matty – possibly Rose, too, if she wants somewhere else to go – but, mainly, Zoe herself, Zoe is as selfish as them all.

But Penny is carrying on, revving up again for greater drama. She plumps herself back on the sofa, squeezed far closer to Tricia than can be wise: Blitz spirit. Needs must. 'Come here, my babies,' she says, holding out her arms.

Rose checks something on her phone; Matilda puts one hoodie-toggle in her mouth. Todly, the traitor, hops closer to Penny's shins. Penny is explaining: 'It has to be fair. Though why would Rosie even want to stay in that, that place? We all know poor brainwashed Matty will feel she has no choice, at least in the short term, but surely anyone can understand the basics of equality. Robin?'

'Exactly.'

Justine is nodding too. Loyal to the end, she stands next to her brother: a tableau of family happiness. Nadia, Gerard,

Tony Harcastle would be delighted with them. 'Fairness is enshrined in ou—'

'We're all aware, thank you, Justine,' says Robin.

And then Matilda grabs Todly. She passes him over to Zoe. Zoe can't see Penny's face, or listen to the outrage, because Todly has spotted the carrier and is wriggling to be free. Claws, a warning-grunt; blood beads along her arm. This is good. She stuffs him through the door, accepts his blanket from Rose's arms, closes the wire catch, straightens up.

At the sight of the rabbit, confined, Penny reaches a crescendo. Zoe, irritated now, not feeling saintly at all, thinks: not again. It has to end. I have to choose to be the dog who wins.

Also, it's boring. If Penny sinks, then let her sink, because otherwise she will drag the rest of us down with her to the deepest water, and leave us there, entangled in her malevolent stormy dramas, while she steps on our heads and pushes herself up for air.

Zoe is not going to let that happen. This is a love story, but not Penny's.

THEN

2012

Zoe, in another surge of desperation, was having a secret comfort-read of her list of therapists when she thought: what if I saved us? Isn't it worth another try?

So, she persuaded Penny, and off they went to meet Melanie Cardozo: the death-knell.

Melanie Cardozo saw couples expensively in her garden office, a perfect plywood-lined chamber like an intellectual sauna. 'Don't go believing everything she says,' Penny warned after their first session. 'You're always longing for an expert adviser, aren't you. Did you notice all those Freuds? No way has she read them. I wonder where she bought those weird slip-ons, like a little elf. Anyway, she's bound to favour you.'

Penny was sure they were her favourite patients, but they had four sessions with, somehow, no progress. Every week it was the same: Penny would head to the upper deck of the 295 to Latimer Road and Zoe was expected to follow, then sit beside Penny and tell her in advance about whatever she was planning to raise. 'You'd better not make me look bad.' Once they'd arrived and were let inside the sauna, when Penny wasn't crying, she'd try to extract details about Melanie Cardozo's personal life. Then, afterwards, they'd walk to the bus stop home, and the recriminations would begin.

'See? Even your beloved Melanie thinks we're fine. She told you that marriage is about compromise, so you'd better start. Also, it's beginning to look creepy, how little responsibility you're taking for our unhappiness. You've been refusing to go out for dinner with me for months, or to let me near you, so no wonder things are bad. You know you are driving me away. Is that what you want? And what were you thinking, telling her about those work-drinks? I wasn't jealous. Stop trying to put me in a bad light. She's far too soft on you already. Don't deny it. She was so into your grandparents, why Clive and Tricia are such weirdos. All that intergeneration stuff, diagnostic criteria . . . I can't believe you trotted out that story about Granny Stamper, on her knees scrubbing English parquet at double speed, not knowing if her family had been killed. You always told me it was private. And what about my lot? The Cartwrights have suffered, too.'

A few minutes into their fifth session, as golden leaves swung and drifted down onto the wet front lawn, Melanie Cardozo commented: 'You have had so much therapy together, previously. Would one of you like to tell me: was it helpful?'

'No,' said Penny.

'Um,' said Zoe.

Melanie Cardozo clasped her fingers. 'Zoe. Please, look at me. Could you explain?'

Zoe, not even realizing she'd glanced at Penny, returned to meet her gaze. Her neck muscles crackled. Melanie Cardozo's eyebrows were tilted with concern; her irises, dark as chocolate buttons, seemed unnaturally still. Zoe thought: if I could talk to her privately, I'd tell her that water can turn into ice, then back to a liquid, over and over again, but an egg is irrevocably . . . boiled.

'Penelope,' Melanie Cardozo said. 'Is there something you wish to add?'

Penny shook her head, although she'd made an impatient sound.

'It's fine if there is,' Zoe told her, reaching between the chairs to touch her arm. 'We promised we'd always talk.'

'Penelope?' said Melanie Cardozo. 'It can be better to raise difficult issues, even if we think distress will be caused.'

'Hang on,' Zoe said, 'as in what? What does she . . . what do you mean?' Like a dim bird, missing the migration, she registered Penny's odd half-smile as it vanished.

Penny would not look up. She kept her gaze on her lap; as the quiet grew, sections of hair freed themselves from where she'd tucked them behind her ears, slipped forward.

Then, as if, after the shaking of hands, she had pulled a dagger from her boot, Penny told Melanie Cardozo what she had done, a decade before.

It had absolutely not been an affair; it was vindictive of Zoe to say so. And the timing, on which Zoe still kept being hung up, didn't matter. The point was how unhappy Penny had been.

So why did it matter whether it had begun when Zoe was first pregnant with poor whoever-it-was, or when she lay in hospital afterwards, death cut away, her spatchcocked entrails tacked together, fresh bright O- sloshing towards what remained? It was, Penny insisted, typical of Zoe to obsess. They'd been going through intense stress, a demanding and lonely time, for Penny. Picking over the timetable, as Zoe persisted in doing, stirred up the pain for them both. Penny, said Penny, felt bad enough.

'Zoe,' said Melanie Cardozo after a time, 'I notice that you haven't spoken. You knew all this already?'

Zoe had to force saliva into her mouth before she could speak; a squelching sound in the thickening quiet. She tried to explain that yes, she did sort-of know; Penny had admitted it, what, four years ago, five? The issue was that Zoe hadn't had time, then, to slot the facts neatly together. She'd simply thumped them in place with her fist: that would have to do. There had been so much blood under the bridge since then.

And no, she hadn't been nursing resentment all this time, exactly; she'd tried to put her fears behind her. But she'd failed. And Penny had been so certain, so vehement, about what Zoe was allowed to feel.

Penny spluttered.

'Wait,' said Melanie Cardozo. 'Please.'

Also, recently, Zoe went on, she had begun to look at the timings more carefully, and had realized what she . . . what it meant. She'd been told so often that she was paranoid, actually mad, when really it was she, Penny, who was lying. 'I wasn't mad at all.'

'Oh Christ, not this again. Here we go.'

'So,' Melanie Cardozo said carefully, ignoring Penny, 'you didn't realize until recently, how much it had affected you. But you told your previous therapist?'

'No. No. I didn't.' Zoe swallowed: again with the spit. Penny had sworn that what had happened with Justine was a brief rekindling. As if picking up where they'd left off, cleaving unto a familiar body, wasn't betrayal. Yet surely that only applied if it had been, as Penny claimed, a one-off, or two or a few? If it did apply. Did it?

Trying to untangle this under Melanie Cardozo's calm scrutiny was making her more confused; she needed paper and a pen, a desk-calendar, receipts. At the time, and ever since, she had wanted to ask someone: Is this OK? But she never could, because Penny had said people would misunderstand, take sides unjustly. Exposing her, endangering their mutual friends' opinion of her, would have been another kind of betrayal.

'Mm,' said Melanie Cardozo. 'Penny?'

Penny explained everything. Justine had taken advantage of her weakened state, and/or Penny had needed an external source of strength to deal with what Zoe was going through. And, after her surgery, Zoe had been really impossible, and the emotional labour – Zoe could see her watching Melanie Cardozo, who gave a tiny nod – of coping with her had been more than anyone could have borne. Zoe's own mother, Penny pointed out, had offered help, then failed to provide it. She, too, had found Zoe's sadness unbearable, her negativity.

'So,' observed Melanie Cardozo, looking at Zoe. 'You were quite alone?' And Zoe, nodding, heard Penny vigorously agree.

They had almost run out of time; they needed months. The first vast block of granite had begun to shift. Penny started to explain how the intervening years had compounded their troubles. 'The other baby,' she began, 'had n—'

Melanie Cardozo looked puzzled. 'Sorry, so in the end you did have a third child?'

'No,' exclaimed Penny, bright with outrage. 'That's exactly the problem. She refused, she blocked me from having the child I needed, my body needed, even though I beg—'

'This was going to be with another man, who we hadn't

even found,' Zoe added quickly. 'It was insane; as if the situation with Robin, the existing dad, wasn't tricky, and painful, enough. From before I got pregnant, to . . . well, it still goes on, actually, Matilda's entire life later. Her raging and trying to pressure me to agree, screaming at me so often in public because she couldn't believe that I was standing up t—'

'Well, of course! She stonewalled. Ironically. Wouldn't even discuss it. After all we've fought for, to have my own wife banning me from what I wanted more than anyth—'

And, at this, Melanie Cardozo intervened.

'So. To be clear. As well as all the other complexities of your own relationship and your family arrangements, Zoe had a traumatic surgery, a difficult time of loss for you both, during which time you, Penny, re-engaged with your previous lover, coupled, ah, with years of turmoil about having a third child in another family unit, plus, as I understand it, a professional and social imbalance due to your age-gap, which gradually shifted, creating tension which, it seems to me, has been pathologized. So, Penny, can you see why Zoe might feel there are aspects to your relationship which make her very unhappy?'

The room stilled.

Oh my God, thought Zoe. Finally, Penny will understand. Also, it's true. She's right. I am unhappy.

She willed Melanie Cardozo to meet her eye, but she kept her gaze steadily on Penny. The pause lengthened. At last, Melanie Cardozo said: 'Penelope. Has any of all the therapy you've had together generated any insight into wh—'

'No,' said Penny. 'Not one person I've spoken to understands why she's doing this, how dragging us all down into the misery, which is her nature, if we're honest, can achieve a thing. I do suspect she's being dictated to by Hilary Mint, that's her supervisor, who she listens to more than me. Or it's an affair, it must be. Because I can guarantee there's no logical reason why she'd want to give up all that we have.'

Zoe turned back to Melanie Cardozo, whose expression was as focused and serious as ever. Yet something had changed, as if a cartoon light bulb had switched on above her head; revelation. Penny, Zoe could see her thinking, absolutely does not get it.

Melanie Cardozo's gaze shifted to Zoe. Knowledge passed between them, like a kiss of life, or a cyanide pill. Do you understand, she seemed to be asking, and Zoe thought: I do.

Now

7.06 p.m.
'No. No.' Penny is screaming at her, her face wet and flushed. 'What the fuck are you st—'

Zoe pretends that her ears are stopped up with wax, sealed over; she is oilcloth, and the chaos and crisis slide off her, onto the floor. 'Where's your bag?' she asks Matty. 'Trainers on. Run up and find your headphones. Grab some more biscuits or something, for now. There'll be food. Don't worry.' She does not speak to Rose, not yet, but her eyes signal clearly: You too.

Isn't that enough?

Not quite. Rose is merely fifteen; in an ideal world she might stand up to them all and announce, clear and true, that she's going with Zoe, for tonight at least, for some peace. Poor child, though: who would envy her having to do that? So Zoe says: 'Rose. Your jacket. And, unless you'd rather not, your sports kit and books for tomorrow,' and Rose nods. Then Zoe notices that her fencing-case and school-bag are already at her feet.

'What the hell is going on?'

It's like magic, this refusing to hear the others. 'Take those bags,' she tells the girls. 'It's fine. And your skateboard. We'll bus it so you won't have to drag y—'

'Can I bring Basil?' says Matty, holding up her papier-mâché funeral urn.

Zoe glances at Penny, whose mouth is open in a terrible, silent wail. 'Of course you can,' she says.

On the pavement, hurrying them along Stag Street, she tries her childhood Greek trick again, which she's only ever done alone. That's the point. But, above London, the sky is Ionian blue; a tree on Rayney Mews, an aspen or poplar, susurrates. If she squints, imagines the roar of buses and tourists as mere mountain noise, feels her body within her clothes and her heart inside her chest, her would-be-brave unsatisfactory selfish little soul, she can almost imagine herself, not as a Greek girl this time, young, unmarried, but a woman, a tired worried mother of almost-grown children, no cleverer or stronger or bolder than any other but definitely Greek, with a chance of a future. And so she walks forward.

Acknowledgements

Thank you:

To Elaine, Jane, Jean, Kate, Alex, Lottie, Maggie, Martha, Shauneen, Rachel, without whom.

To Claire Baldwin, Jane Bridges and Prof. Louise Sylvester, for their professional expertise.

To my father, for making me interested in almost everything.

To Holly Harris, for inspiration.

To Matilda Hinson, for Todly-permission.

To Camilla Elworthy, friend and unparalleled publicist.

To Peter Straus and all at RCW, and Maria Rejt, Becky Lushey, Lucy Scholes, Laura Carr, Lucy Hale and all at Mantle, Picador and Pan Mac, for their faith, vision and hard work; I'm a lucky author.

To Mag Leahy, every day.

To my children.

Charlotte Mendelson's previous novel, *The Exhibitionist*, was longlisted for the Women's Prize for Fiction and was Novel of the Year 2022 in *The Times* as well as a book of the year in *The Guardian* and *Good Housekeeping*. Her other novels include *Almost English*, which was longlisted for both the Man Booker and the Women's Prize for Fiction; *When We Were Bad*, which was shortlisted for the Orange Prize for Fiction and was a book of the year in *The Observer*, *The Guardian*, *The Sunday Times*, *The New Statesman* and *The Spectator*; and *Daughters of Jerusalem*, which won both the Somerset Maugham Award and the John Llewellyn Rhys Prize. *Wife* is her sixth novel.